Echoes
of KASSEL

Deborah J. Kelly

Echoes of KASSEL

Deborah J. Kelly

TATE PUBLISHING
AND ENTERPRISES, LLC

Published by Tate Publishing & Enterprises, LLC
127 E. Trade Center Terrace | Mustang, Oklahoma 73064 USA
1.888.361.9473 | www.tatepublishing.com

Tate Publishing is committed to excellence in the publishing industry. The company reflects the philosophy established by the founders, based on Psalm 68:11,
"The Lord gave the word and great was the company of those who published it."

Book design copyright © 2015 by Tate Publishing, LLC. All rights reserved.
Cover design by Niño Carlo Suico
Interior design by Gram Telen

Published in the United States of America

ISBN: 978-1-68028-361-7
1. Fiction / War & Military
2. Fiction / Romance / Military
15.02.20

Dedicated to the memory of my mother, Edith Joy Innes, whose selfless acts of love and kindness were a priceless gift to all who knew her. She liked this story.

Contents

Characters 9

Prologue 11

November 1943 17

December 1943 43

January 1944 85

February 1944 99

March 1944 143

April 1944 165

May 1944 171

June 1944 181

July 1944 207

August 1944 239

September 1944 247

October 1944   267

November 1944   313

December 1944   323

January 1945   341

February 1945   351

March 1945   357

April 1945   373

May 1945   379

June 1945   385

August 1945   387

October 1945   393

December 1945   401

February 1946   403

April 1946   409

September 1946   429

October 1946   433

January 1947   435

March 1947   437

Epilogue   439

Characters

Oswin Amsel – schoolmaster

Fräulein Bosch – school maintenance lead

Helma Brandt – mother-in-law of Major Rager

Lieutenant Manfred Braun – assistant to Major Rager

Annamarie Mauer Dietrich – wife of Hermann Dietrich

Hermann Dietrich – vice chancellor and minister of finance under Heinrich Bruening (October 1931–May 1932), died July 2, 1934, in a raid during the Night of the Long Knives

Klaus Dietrich – brother of Klara Mauer

Lenz Dietrich – brother of Klara Mauer

Liese Dietrich – sister of Klara Mauer

Reiner Dietrich – brother of Klara Mauer, dispatched to Russia in the German Army

Erwin Durr – friend of Ida Rager

Frau Waltraud Eichel – school mistress and Sepp Rager's teacher

Bram Eldering – renown violin instructor

General Major Johannes Erxleben – *Wehrmacht*-commandant of Kassel August 1, 1944–April 4, 1945

Fräulein Farber – niece of *Gauleiter*, Karl Gerland

Heiner Freeh – driver

Karl Gerland – *Gauleiter* of Kurhessen beginning November 1943

Trude Hoffmann – Major Rager's housekeeper

Inge – housekeeper for the Meissels

Gitte Kleefeld – school maintenance supervisor and personal friend of Franz Meissel

Willi Knappe – Kassel Gestapo agent

Hans Leitner – Kassel mortician

Bernhardt Löning – Kassel Gestapo agent

Fräulein Magda – Major Rager's former nanny

Franz Meissel – cousin of Klara's Uncle Lothar Winzig

Maria Noll – sister of *Frau* Hoffmann

Annette Rager – daughter of Major Rager

Kurt Rager – *Wehrmacht* major and war production minister of Hessen

Ida Brandt Rager – deceased wife of Major Rager

Sepp Rager – son of Major Rager

Herr Schaefer – defense attorney

Rosine Staude – *Frau* Hoffmann's neighbor

Herr Vogler – superintendent of the Henschel tank factory

Karl Weinrich – former *Gauleiter* of Kurhessen

Lothar Winzig – great-uncle of Klara Mauer

Frieda Mauer Winzig – great-aunt of Klara Mauer

Prologue

Three weeks after my grandmother passed away, I flew from Los Angeles up to Seattle to help my father sort out my grandparents' belongings and prepare their house to be put on the market. His older brother and sister, who both live in California, were not physically up to the trip or the task. My father's other three siblings live in the Seattle area and came to help as their busy schedules enabled them.

It was a much more daunting and time consuming task than I had anticipated. About halfway through the second day while my father was still working on the garage, I started sorting through my grandmother's bedroom. I was throwing out the useless things and boxing up the valuable items to be sorted through later by all of her children.

Although my grandmother was quite a bit younger than my grandfather, she had lasted only six months following his death. I paused every now and then to look at the photograph of my grandparents that sat in an old oval frame on her bedside table.

Every time I would look at the picture, it always struck me how young they both looked when the picture was taken. Grandfather was tall and handsome, and even in the photograph, you could see his remarkable eyes. Grandmother was shorter than him, barely coming up to his shoulder. She had long wavy hair that fell well past her shoulders. Her enchanting smile lit up her beautiful face. There were snowcapped mountains in the background. I wondered where the picture was taken and under what circumstances.

I really knew little about my grandparents' history. When I was young, we would visit them regularly, but I was always eager for my father to give me permission to go outside to play. I didn't enjoy sitting for hours at a time listening to the adults talk.

I remember my grandfather as a kind man. He always had candy in his pocket, and he was liberal in giving it out to us. He had a warm smile and a wonderful sense of humor. I found great comfort in hearing at my grandfather's funeral that he had made a decision to trust Christ as his Savior at their church in Seattle through the efforts of his brother and a traveling evangelist. He taught Sunday school for over twenty years and served as a deacon in the church. I knew him as someone who was always encouraging others to live a life of purpose for the Lord.

I learned at my grandmother's funeral that she had received the Lord before she came to the States. She also taught Sunday school, and she sang in the choir until three months before she passed away. After her children were grown, my grandmother had played with the Seattle symphony. Many of her friends who came to her funeral were associated with the symphony.

I remember that she was deathly allergic to seafood. My grandfather would always tease her about not being able to eat the delicacies when they lived right by the sea. She didn't talk a lot, but she was the kind of person who loved children and was very good with them. A lot of pleasant memories came flooding through my mind as I was sorting.

I missed them already, but what a comfort it was for me to know I would meet them again in eternity. What a comfort to my whole family who, for the most part, are following the good examples they had set.

In the bottom drawer of grandmother's bedside stand, I found an old watch that had long ago stopped ticking and a leather case on top of a rather worn out book. I opened the leather case, fully anticipating that it might hold an old pocket watch or a coin, but it held neither. Set carefully on a piece of red velvet was an emblem of some kind. My heart skipped a beat as I recognized the swastika symbol in the middle of a circle set with an eagle on the top bar of the badge. I ran my hand along the edges of the insignia. There was something dark about it.

I knew that my grandparents were German, but I wondered why my grandmother would have this badge and why she would have kept it all of these years with the other seemingly important things she had stashed in her nightstand. I decided to take a break. I took the leather case down to the garage and opened it as I showed it to my father. I asked him if he knew what it was.

"Where did you find this?" he asked abruptly in response to my question.

I shrugged. "In grandmother's night stand."

"What else is in there?" he asked, putting down the plastic bag that was in his hand and taking the leather case out of my hand.

"Just some old books and some papers," I responded, not sure why he seemed so touchy at seeing the item.

My father closed the leather case quickly, slid it into his pocket, picked up the plastic bag, and resumed what he was doing without saying another word or answering my question.

It seemed like a long time before I realized he wasn't going to answer me. I decided to forget about it and went back upstairs to finish the drawer I had started. I settled back down on the floor and took up the worn-out book that was underneath the leather case. The book was covered in decorative brown leather, and there was a long, thin leather string that wrapped around it. I unwound the string carefully as it was so well worn-out that it was almost to a breaking point and opened the book to the first page. I recognized my grandmother's tiny, neat handwriting, but

I did not recognize the words. The book must have been a diary of some sort. I flipped through the pages. It was written entirely in German.

I set the book on top of her night stand and moved on to the other items in the drawer. There was a pile of loose papers, official-looking papers, but once again, they were in German. I was thinking that my aunt Annie might want to have the diary. She and Uncle Joe are the only ones that I know who know any German. My uncle Joe lives two blocks from her, and when they are together, they sometimes speak German. In fact, Aunt Annie has spent most of her life teaching German in a Christian school. Maybe I would take her the papers on the bottom of the top drawer too.

A week later when I arrived home, I called Aunt Annie and told her I was going to bring her grandmother's diary. She was surprised to hear that I had found such a thing.

Not long after Aunt Annie received the diary, she called me. She sounded like she was crying. "I just wanted to thank you for bringing this to me," she said.

"Aunt Annie? Are you all right?" I asked.

"Yes, dear," she responded. Then I heard her blowing her nose away from the phone. "You really need to read this," she said when she came back to the phone.

I laughed into the phone. "I can't read German, Auntie."

"I know you can't," she responded. "Your father should have made you take German when you were in school." She sighed. "I'm going to translate it for you—word for word. It may take me a long time, but I'm determined to do it."

I laughed again. "I don't think it's necessary for you to go to all of that trouble," I said. "I just thought you would like to have it."

"*Doch!*" she responded. "I'm going to translate it, Kristin. You need to read it. It's our story," she said with determination in her voice.

"What story?"

"Mother's story," responded my aunt faintly.

A whole year passed without me even giving the conversation one thought. Then it arrived. The week before Thanksgiving, I received a big yellow envelope containing the thick, type-written manuscript of my grandmother's journal. I could hardly believe Aunt Annie had gone to all of that trouble for a journal. I laughed out loud at the dozens of fifteen-cent stamps she had used on the envelope.

The evening before Thanksgiving Day, after I put the children to bed and after I put a log on the fireplace, I curled up by the fire with a large cup of tea and pulled the manuscript from the yellow envelope. This was my first and would be my only opportunity to read something of this length for quite some time.

November 1943

Dear Journal,

Aunt Frieda gave you to me this morning. You are to be my only companion from now on.

Early this morning, I said good-bye to Klaus, Lenz, and Liese at the railway station in Sinsheim. Liese was clinging to me and weeping. I do not think I will soon forget the sad look and the tears on their faces as they were standing there on the platform—Liese's especially. It felt like my heart was being ripped out of my chest as I watched them fade away. We have never been apart. I know Aunt Frieda will take care of them; however, I am left feeling like I have abandoned them. But what choice do I have? Uncle Lothar has been so insistent that I go to Kassel and find work.

For the last three weeks, I have heard them arguing at night when we are all in bed. Good Aunt Frieda. She is so worried about me going to a city that has just been so horribly bombed and all on my own. I don't know what to think of Uncle Lothar. He doesn't seem to be worried about me dying there. He is just concerned that I send them money to care for my brothers and sister, just as Reiner is doing. Sometimes, I think he was born without a heart.

I shouldn't say such bad things about him. He has made arrangements with a distant cousin to help me find work in Kassel. I heard him tell Aunt Frieda there are plenty of jobs there now.

The train was quite crowded on the way to Kassel. I found a seat facing an old couple who greeted me when I first sat down. They had plenty of trouble getting up out of their seats every time they needed to get something out of their suitcases, and this they did several times during our long journey. I finally offered to help them, and then I almost wished that I hadn't, because they wanted something different from their suitcases every fifteen minutes or so, and I was stuck helping them.

About an hour before we arrived in Kassel, the old man wanted a cup of coffee, and then his wife decided she wanted one too. They were so unsteady on their feet that I just rolled my eyes. I could picture them making their way from the dining car, trying to stay on their feet with the cars jostling back and forth and their coffee spilling freely from their cups. I offered to get them the coffee if they would watch my bag. The old woman seemed quite relieved.

When I got up out of my seat to go to the dining car, one of the military officers across the isle who had stared at me every time I took one of the suitcases back down for them smiled at me. I would have been flattered if it weren't for the fact of who he is. *Why are the handsome men always for the wrong cause, and why do they look so smart in their uniforms?*

I made it back to my seat with the two cups without spilling much coffee at all. The old man paid me back. On accident, I looked over to the other side of the car, but the officer who had smiled at me was busy reading some papers. He wasn't wearing a wedding band, but he probably has five girlfriends.

Every time the train came to a stop, I would check and double check to make sure I didn't miss my stop. Finally, we started pulling into Kassel. Even though it was gray and foggy, I could see some of the bombing damage as we crept closer to the city. It is hard to describe how devastating it looks. I have never seen anything like it.

The old man and his wife made efforts plenty in advance to get their things together to get ready to get off of the train at the main station in Kassel. I tried to help them. They told me that this was their first time returning home since the bombing. After seeing how bad the train station looked, I wondered if they even had a home to go back to at all.

The officer who was sitting across the aisle had already left his seat by the time I helped the old couple get their luggage down and had mine in hand, but he was right in front of me getting off of the train. I was surprised when he turned around and gave me his hand to help me down. I don't even think I thanked him. I headed down the platform as fast as I could, but something made me look back. The officer was still standing there helping the old couple get off.

Uncle Lothar had told me to go to the ticketing counter when I got to Kassel. I was supposed to meet *Herr* Meissel's housekeeper there. I followed some other passengers down the platform, but I stared at the twisted metal and rubble in front of us. The station and the platforms to the left were all badly damaged. I followed the couple in front of me into the building on the right.

Herr Meissel's housekeeper knew that I would be carrying my violin, but I didn't know what she would look like. When I finally found the table that had been set up as the ticketing counter, I saw a girl about my age, with reddish hair, standing nearby, looking like she was looking for someone.

When she saw me, she extended her hand. "I'm Inge. Are you Klara Mauer?" That name still sounds funny to me.

I followed her out of the train station and through the streets of Kassel. I have never seen such an awful sight as I saw today—

buildings bombed-out, glass, brick, and rubble everywhere. In places, you can't even find the street to walk on. There are dirt paths being carved through burned out buildings where people walk through to get to the other blocks. Inge said they were still pulling dead bodies out of basements in the inner part of town. I suppose that the fog made it look even more eerie.

Inge seemed friendly enough, but she hardly made much conversation the whole way to *Herr* Meissel's house other than to ask me why on earth I had come to Kassel. I told her that I had to find employment. She laughed at me and then said, "Well, there are plenty of jobs here because so many people are dead, and everyone else has left."

I wondered to myself why she was still in Kassel, if it was such a dangerous place, but I said nothing. It took us fifteen minutes of walking through the rubble until we finally came to a block where most of the buildings were still standing.

In contrast to the city center, *Herr* Meissel lives at number eight Heinemannstrasse in a most attractive house across from a very lovely park behind the *Stadthalle*, about a forty-five-minute walk from the train station. Inge led me into the house through a side door. There she showed me the room in the basement where Uncle Lothar's cousin is going to let me stay.

I put my suitcase and my violin down next to the bed. The bed is covered with a thin, white comforter, one of those old kinds like I saw at Uncle Lothar's mother's house once. It looks like it has seen better days. There is a small table and a lamp beside the bed. Up above the table is an oblong window near the top of the ceiling, but you can't see anything outside. It is covered with blackout cloth. I tried to smile at Inge when she showed me the room. I did not want to seem ungrateful.

Next, Inge took me upstairs to introduce me to *Herr* Meissel and his wife. We found them both in the parlor. *Herr* Meissel has a mustache just like Uncle Lothar's, and he was warm in his greeting to me. His wife was not. I don't think she is happy that I am here at all.

There is a lot of fancy woodwork in their parlor and dining room, and they have very fine furniture and curtains. We had a nice dinner; after which, *Herr* Meissel said that he was sure I was tired from the journey and would want to rest.

When I tried to thank them for the supper and their hospitality, he interrupted me to say that we would go over to the school first thing in the morning. He has a friend who is going to try to get me in there. When I happened to look *Frau* Meissel's way, I saw her sigh heavily. So, I excused myself for the evening and came directly to my room.

It is cold and a little damp, but I am underneath the old, white comforter right now, trying to faithfully write in my new companion all that has happened today.

I miss Klaus, Lenz, and Liese terribly. I wonder if they are already asleep for the night. I wonder if they remembered to say their prayers. It is my prayer that they will never have to leave home like I did today. Maybe tomorrow, I will have something to write to Reiner about. I don't feel very comfortable here at all, but I am going to try to make the best of it. I don't want to let Uncle Lothar down.

....

November 12, 1943

Dear Journal,

I was up very early this morning. Neither *Herr* Meissel, nor his wife ate much this morning. After a light breakfast of toast, *Herr* Meissel and I set off for the school in the dark.

As we walked down Kirchweg, past the imposing *Stadthalle* and multi-storied apartment buildings, he was quite talkative, asking me if I had ever heard of the brothers Grimm. Of course, I have heard of the brothers Grimm and their fairytales, but

Herr Meissel was aghast to hear that I have never read them. He promised to loan me his copy so that I could read their writings.

Herr Meissel was bemoaning that the old part of Kassel that had many grand, gabled houses built in the seventeenth century was now destroyed by the firestorm caused by the bombing. He was clearly proud that Kassel's fine *Landesmuseum* has so far survived the war, but he told me that after the bombing three weeks ago, the collection of manuscripts and clocks, including the Egg of Nürnberg, had been removed to another location for safekeeping. He went on and on about some Rembrandt and Van Dyck paintings, but I have no idea why.

Herr Meissel told me that when I had a chance to see the parts of the city that were not bombed, I would be taken by all of the Roman architecture. He explained to me that the twin towers of St. Martin's that I had seen in the fog among the ruins yesterday was the place that housed the burial vaults of the Hessian princes.

I suppose that I should have appreciated everything that he said. While he was talking, I tried to seem interested. By the time we reached the school, my head was swimming with all of the facts he had just given me. I hoped that I wasn't going to be tested on them.

The school is a good ten-minute walk from the Meissel's house, straight down Kirchweg. The primary school is a three-storied, red brick building that sits long on Herkulesstrasse. The name, *Bürgerschule* 13, is prominently displayed above the front doors, and there is intricate brickwork in the pattern of multiple Xs below each one of the windows. The boy's classrooms are on the ground and first floors. The girl's classrooms are on the top floor.

Just before we went into the building, *Herr* Meissel turned to me rather abruptly. "The women who work here and most of the teachers are party members. You must be very careful not to cross anyone. Do you understand me?"

I swallowed hard. "Yes, sir."

I followed *Herr* Meissel in the front entrance, and then we took a narrow staircase to the basement. At the bottom of the stairs, two older women were sitting around a square table drinking their morning coffee. They stared at us as we went by.

Herr Meissel stopped in the doorway of a small office down the wide hallway. He fiddled nervously with his hat for a moment. I was still pondering the consequences of crossing a party member. A kind looking, shorter woman who walked with a slight limp came around the corner and almost ran into the back of *Herr* Meissel.

"Franz!" she said in greeting when she saw that it was him.

Herr Meissel greeted her with a "*Heil* Hitler" and a kiss on the cheek. "Gitte, how are you this morning?"

"I am the same as always," she said back to him in a teasing tone.

"Gitte, I have brought Klara with me. I wanted you to meet her," he said, gesturing in my direction with his hat.

I swallowed hard and tried to look respectful.

"*Frau* Kleefeld, this is *Fräulein* Mauer," said *Herr* Meissel, formally introducing us.

Frau Kleefeld extended her hand to me, and I shook it, giving her a slight bow. She invited us into her office, where she sat down at her desk, and then she looked at me from head to toe.

"Our enrollment has almost doubled in the past three weeks since they consolidated schools following the bombing. It is so much harder to keep this place clean than it used to be. I have a uniform that I think will fit you, *Fräulein* Mauer," she said. "I am going to try you out today, and at the end of the day, we can discuss your employment further."

I tried to have a pleasant look on my face, but oh, how I was afraid inside. I didn't remember *Herr* Meissel saying anything to me about what I was going to be doing at the school. Maybe it was my fault for not asking. I looked at *Frau* Kleefeld, wondering when she was going to ask to see my papers. I was sure that would be the next question.

Herr Meissel thanked *Frau* Kleefeld, and then he left. *Frau* Kleefeld asked me to follow her. She took me down the hall to a closet, where she removed a gray, knee-length, pinstriped dress from a hanger and handed it to me.

"You may change in this room here," she said, pointing to her right, "and then I will introduce you to *Fräulein* Bosch, who will give you your first assignment."

Before I could ask her any questions, she left me. I watched her return to her office, and then I went inside the room to change. The dress was a little large on me, and I felt awkward in it. I swallowed hard, gathered up my own dress, and made my way back to *Frau* Kleefeld's office. She did not look me in the eyes. She got up and led me to the two women at the square table. They were still sitting around drinking coffee.

Fräulein Bosch must have been the oldest woman at the table although the other one was not much younger. They were both at least twice my age. She didn't seem at all happy when *Frau* Kleefeld told her I was the new help and she should see to it that I have work responsibilities for the day.

"Well, come on, *Fräulein* Mauer," she half shouted to me. "I'll get you started cleaning the toilets." The other woman just laughed.

It has been a long time since I felt as down as I did in that first hour. I waited until after she handed me a bucket with brushes, soaps, and rags and left me alone in the toilet rooms upstairs before I began crying.

To my shame, I think that I was only feeling sorry for myself. At first, all I wanted to do was sit on the floor and cry. But when I heard a noise outside the door, as if someone were going to come in, I got busy in a hurry. I found that I could cry and work at a good pace. All the time I was telling myself that I must not cry, but that I must make this work. Klaus, Lenz, and Liese are counting on me.

I don't know how much time went by, but soon, the other woman came into the room. She was wearing her pinstriped dress and carrying a mop. I was on my hands and knees just finishing scrubbing up the better part of the floor.

The woman leaned her chin on the mop handle and watched me for a minute. "You're an eager beaver, aren't you?" she snarled. Then she turned and left, taking her mop with her.

A few minutes later, *Fräulein* Bosch came in, in a huff. "If you're done with the toilets, then come and tell me. I have a long list of other things for you to do. Emma is to do the floors. And I'm warning you; don't try no heroics here neither. We're all doing our best for the *Führer*."

Before I could apologize, she turned to leave. I gathered up my cleaning supplies in a hurry and tried to follow her. By this time, I could hear the unmistakable sound of children. Out in the hall, *Fräulein* Bosch stopped in front of me and turned her back to the wall to let the children pass. I quickly followed her example. One of the boys who marched past us looked like Lenz. He was even holding a little cap in his hand, like the one Lenz wears.

After the children had gone by, I followed *Fräulein* Bosch back to the basement, where she handed me some more rags and a can of polish. For the next three hours, I worked at polishing all of the lights, door handles, and rails in the hallways and staircases. *Fräulein* Bosch would come to get me when a classroom was on recess, and I would work in the classroom until the teacher returned with the class.

In the afternoon, I went up to the girl's classrooms on the third floor and started polishing. At the end of the day, around four o'clock, *Frau* Kleefeld found me in the far stairwell.

"It's past time to stop for the day, *Fräulein* Mauer," she said. She seemed to be surprised that I was still working. She took a hard look at all of the light fixtures and at the railings I had just polished, and then a little smile seemed to creep up her lips. "You have done a nice job. I will tell the schoolmaster that I would like to keep you. Providing all of your paperwork is in order, on Monday, he can put you on the work roster and payroll."

"Thank you, ma'am," I responded politely. Only after she left, while I gathered up the polish can and dirty rags, did my heart start trembling. I am going to have to talk to *Herr* Meissel about my paperwork.

I didn't have anything to eat all day, and so I was very happy to have a good supper. I am underneath the old, white comforter, trying to get warm. It was raining when I left the school house, and I did not have my umbrella. I have hung my pinstriped dress up on the door frame to dry. Now, I am going to lay you aside and go to sleep. I am glad that I will be able to sleep late in the morning as I am very tired. I will try to write to Reiner tomorrow, and maybe I will get a chance to talk to *Herr* Meissel.

....

November 13, 1943

Today is my first Saturday in Kassel. I did try to get some extra sleep this morning, but the dogs next door began to bark a lot, and so I was awake. For a moment, I almost forgot where I was. I missed Liese coming and jumping in bed with me.

After breakfast, I put on my coat and decided to go across the street to walk in the park. On my way out the front door, *Frau* Meissel stopped me. She wanted to know if the school master had discussed my wages with me and when I was going to be able to pay them something for the room.

I was a little surprised at her questions and the forwardness. I told her honestly that no one has discussed wages with me but that I would be sure to let them know when that happened. I was glad to see that she seemed satisfied with my answer as she seems to be a person who is never satisfied with anything.

It was refreshing to leave the Meissel's house and to take a stroll around the park. It is on a piece of land in the shape of a long oval behind the *Stadthalle*, surrounded by trees. There are plenty of flower beds, which will probably be very beautiful in the spring, and on the west end, there is a small fountain. From the benches on the east end, you can see the shadow of a castle on the top of the hill, far to the west. I think that I will spend a lot of my free time there.

After lunch, I sat down and wrote to Reiner. He will have four long pages to read, if he ever gets my letter. It is a long way to Leningrad. I try not to think of the danger he is in every day. I am sure that he must battle the weather there as well as the enemy and those thoughts make me afraid for him. I hope that he will write me back soon, so that I will know that he is well.

I managed to catch *Herr* Meissel alone in the parlor this afternoon, but before I could bring up the subject of my paperwork, he told me we needed to go down to the police station.

"We must get you registered," began *Herr* Meissel with a twitch of his mustache, "and the sooner, the better. They don't like it if you take all of the four days they give you."

I breathed in deeply. Uncle Lothar told me before I left home that I would have to register, and I knew I would need proof of registration to show to the superintendent at school. "About my identification," I began after swallowing hard. "I don't think—"

"Hurry on down and get your papers, child. We should take care of this straight away, now that I have secured employment for you."

I looked up at him. "But—"

"Quickly," he said, interrupting me again. *Herr* Meissel rose from his chair. "I'll just get my coat from the closet and meet you at the front door."

He left the room before I could catch his attention again, and I went slowly down the stairs to the basement to get my papers— fear rising in my heart with each step I took. I had to tell him;

otherwise, we might be walking into a dangerous situation. Uncle Lothar had been so confident on this point, but I remember Aunt Frieda's hesitation and her doubt.

I put on my coat and, with papers clutched in hand, I climbed the stairs. "I really think you ought to look at my papers first, *Herr* Meissel," I managed to say as I approached the front door.

"There is no need for that, *Fräulein* Mauer. Lothar assured me your papers are all in order, or I would not have ventured to gain you employment."

Herr Meissel gave me a hard look. After seeing the look in his eyes, the look of trust, I lost my tongue. *If Uncle Lothar was so confident, why was I so afraid?*

In five minutes, we were at the station. The officer that was on duty at the main desk said that he would do my registration as the registering officer was not in on Saturdays. *Herr* Meissel introduced me as *Fräulein* Mauer, told him I was a niece of his distant cousin and made small talk with the officer as the officer was looking over my papers. I took in a breath and held it, waiting for him to see the inconsistencies in my paperwork and thinking of the exact lie I would tell to try to smooth it over.

Herr Meissel continued the small talk, and it wasn't long before the officer handed me back my papers and stamped my registration form.

"Oh, I forgot to write in your name," said the older officer as he pulled back the stamped registration form from my hand.

"Klara Mauer," I said quickly and spelled it for him.

"There. You will need to report to the civil service office if you do not have an exemption, but you're all set here, *Fräulein* Mauer," he said as he extended his hand with the form without looking at me. He must not have looked at my papers either. What a stroke of luck!

I now have my registration papers and no one, not even *Herr* Meissel, is the wiser. I am tired from this escapade and from writing to Reiner, so I will not write so much tonight. Tomorrow, I am to go to morning mass with the Meissels.

....

November 14, 1943

This morning, I went to mass at St. Marien Rosenkranzkirche with the Meissels, but I did not take communion. I thought I saw *Fräulein* Bosch there, but it was for only a moment, and I wasn't sure. This afternoon, I fell asleep on my bed while I was supposed to be reading the writings of the brothers Grimm that *Herr* Meissel loaned to me.

I am not in much of a mood to read fairytales. I wonder what everyone at home is doing. I wonder how they are getting on without me.

....

November 17, 1943

Today is Wednesday. I have been so tired in the evenings that I haven't had strength to write. I will see how far I get tonight before I tire out.

Monday was quite a stressful day. I started the day by arriving just at the end of the coffee time. I really don't want to have coffee with those women every morning. I'm not sure they would want me to join them anyway. It seems that they spend an inordinate amount of time talking about their neighbors and who they will next turn into the police for breaking some law or unwritten rule.

Fräulein Bosch, who makes no small show of the fact that she is a party member, told me to go clean the toilets on the boy's floors and then to do the ones on the girl's floor. She let me know that that should be my first task every morning. While the others were sweeping and mopping the hallways, I cleaned the toilets, the sinks, and the floors in each toilet room. I guess the newest person always gets the most unsavory job.

Every Monday in addition to the other tasks, *Fräulein* Bosch said, is window cleaning day. She sent me to the top floor to clean the windows—inside and out. I spent the whole afternoon cleaning the soot out of the furnaces in the basement and restocking the coal bins. I never did speak with the school master, and I didn't even see the supervisor, *Frau* Kleefeld, not even once. By the time I left the school, my arms were really aching, and it was raining again. I think I left my umbrella back in Sinsheim.

Frau Meissel asked me about my wages again at the supper table. *Herr* Meissel choked a little on his drink. "We'll get that all straightened out, my darling," he said nervously. Then he winked at me.

On Tuesday, *Frau* Kleefeld came wobbling down the hallway as I was hanging my coat in the closet and told me I had to go upstairs with her to the school master's office. He wanted to see me. I hoped that I had not already done something wrong. She took me directly to *Herr* Amsel's office on the ground floor while she explained to me that after the bombing, he was appointed the head master for both the boys' and the girls' school.

Herr Amsel is very short and stocky. With the hair missing on the very top of his head, he looks like our next-door neighbor in Sinsheim. *Frau* Kleefeld introduced me to him. He gave me a weak hand shake, but he did not ask me to sit down.

"*Fräulein* Mauer, is it?"

"Yes," I responded, putting my hands down to my side.

"*Frau* Kleefeld wants me to add you to the work roster, so that is what I will do," he said, taking a seat in his squeaky chair mid-sentence. "Provided your identification is in order," he added, looking at *Frau* Kleefeld with a sharp eye.

Frau Kleefeld gave him a weak nod. *Herr* Amsel continued, "Payroll will be handed out on Friday. Do you have any questions?"

I just shook my head, relieved that he wasn't going to ask for my identification. I knew *Frau* Meissel would want to know what my wages would be, but I didn't even care to ask. I would pay the Meissels whatever they wanted for room and board and send the rest of the money home. That is what Uncle Lothar told me to do.

"If you have no questions, *Fräulein* Mauer, you are dismissed. *Heil* Hitler!"

I walked back down to the basement with *Frau* Kleefeld. When we reached the bottom stair she turned to me. "I'll need to take a look at your identification."

I swallowed hard while I pulled my registration form from my pocket and unfolded it for her to see. "This is what they gave me on Saturday when I went to register," I said, hoping she would be satisfied with the one paper.

Frau Kleefeld's lips turned on her face as she nodded. "I'm supposed to see your identity card, but I guess this will do." Then she handed the registration paper back to me. "We will be making another contribution to the Winter Relief Fund with this paycheck. I assume that you will be participating as well?"

I nodded half-heartedly even though I did not know what the Winter Relief Fund was.

"And I will need your party number. You are a member of the National Socialist Worker's Party?"

I looked down at my shoes. "I am not yet twenty, *Frau* Kleefeld," I said.

"I see," she said, raising an eyebrow. "Well, never mind. You'll have your chance soon." *Frau* Kleefeld headed for her office without saying another word.

When I turned around, *Fräulein* Bosch was waiting for me at the table. She had been listening to our conversation. "Tuesday is floor polishing day," she said with a sneer in her voice. "You should do the toilets and then start on the floors."

So, all day long, I polished the floors. I learned pretty quickly that I had to time which sections of the floors I did, depending on the classes and the children's exercise times.

You will never guess what the Wednesday task is, so I will tell you. Rain or shine, Wednesday is white washing day. Today, *Fräulein* Bosch had me start on the walls in the far stairwell. She gave me a rickety old ladder to climb on. I had to scrounge around in the basement for a while before I found some crates on which to prop the ladder on the steps.

Despite trying to be very careful, my pinstriped dress is a little splattered with paint. I washed it in the laundry sink next to my room, and now, it is hanging on the door frame. It is quite damp down here in my room. I hope that the dress will be dry by morning.

....

November 19, 1943

Somehow, I have made it through a full week at the school. I hardly recognize my hands. Thursday was a long day, starting with cleaning the bathrooms, working on removing more soot from the furnaces, and then continuing with the white-washing in the stairwell.

Frau Kleefeld came around and inspected my work, and then the trouble began. She wanted to know why the floors in the girl's classrooms had not been polished.

I stumbled on my answer to her. "Emma was to do those floors, and I was to do the boy's classrooms. Those were my instructions from *Fräulein* Bosch."

Immediately, I could see that *Frau* Kleefeld was displeased. "Did I misunderstand?" I asked.

Frau Kleefeld shook her head. "And why has not the painting in the other stairwell been started? It should have been done by the end of today."

My mouth hung open and my chest froze up. "I—*Fräulein* Bosch only asked me to work on this stairwell."

"If Emma has been cleaning the bathrooms, polishing the floors in the boy's classrooms, and cleaning out the furnaces, you should have had the painting done by now."

"But I have been doing all of those things and the painting," I said quickly.

Frau Kleefeld's eyebrows dropped in confusion.

"What am I to be doing?"

"Never mind," said *Frau* Kleefeld before I could finish my question. "Perhaps *Fräulein* Bosch has made a mistake."

And this is exactly the "mistake" that *Fräulein* Bosch has made. From something that *Frau* Kleefeld said to me this afternoon, it is clear to me that *Fräulein* Bosch has been giving me instructions to do things, but is telling *Frau* Kleefeld that I am doing something else. Somewhere along the line, the work is not being done. I don't know about Emma or *Fräulein* Bosch, but I have been working so hard that I can hardly hold my head up at suppertime.

And yes, you guessed it—Friday is polishing day. My hands are getting really dry from all of the soaps, water, and cleaning agents. Also, at the end of the day, the schoolmaster paid us, minus the money he deducted for the Winter Relief Fund. Once I give *Herr* Meissel the money for the room, I will only have half left to send home. I also need to buy an umbrella and a light brooch like Inge has so that I can be seen in the dark on the way to school.

It is hard to believe I have been gone from home for over a week. I hope that they don't forget about me. I think about them all of the time.

November 26, 1943

Dear Journal,

I am sorry to have neglected you for so long. I have something extraordinary to write today. When I got home from school, there was a letter waiting for me from Reiner, which he had sent to Sinsheim and a letter from Liese. I am so happy to hear from them. I read both letters twice.

Reiner reports that he was sick for a little while but is feeling better now. He was not able to say where his unit is, but from the things he did say, it is cold and dreary. He talked about the men in his unit and what they do when they are not fighting. In closing, he said that he thinks a lot about happier times and hopes we will all be together again soon.

Liese says that she misses me, and she wants to know when I will come back home. She said Aunt Frieda has been looking after them. From something Liese said, I can tell that Uncle Lothar was disappointed with the money that I sent. We got paid today. This time, I will be able to send most of it home. I hope he will be more satisfied.

The confusion about the work assignments continued into this week. Several times each day, *Frau* Kleefeld tracked me down, and if I was alone, she would grill me about my work assignment and ask me why I hadn't done this or that. Each time, she was asking me why I hadn't done something that Emma or *Fräulein* Bosch were supposed to do. I don't know where this is all heading.

But the extraordinary thing I have to tell you is this. Today, being Friday, was polishing day. I was in one of the classrooms on the first floor, finishing up the light fixtures, when the class came in from outside a little early. Maybe I was a little slow.

The boys were all riled up from having been outside. The teacher, *Frau* Waltraud Eichel, is a middle-aged woman that I have seen in the halls before. She has quite a stern expression and a commanding voice. She came into the classroom with the boys, told the children to take their seats, and to be quiet. Then she turned around and left the room for a moment.

I quickly finished up the last light and was climbing off of the chair, hoping to get out of the room before she returned, when I saw a boy in the back row on the far right, dump the chalk bucket over the head of the boy in front of the boy in the row to the left. The children were all laughing, except for the one with the chalk all over his head. He stood to his feet and began to whimper, his eyes and his red lips being the only discernable feature on his now white head. I was standing there stunned at what I had just seen, when *Frau* Eichel came storming back into the room.

"Sepp Rager," she bellowed out as she headed straight for the boy behind the boy with the chalk on his head. *Frau* Eichel grabbed the boy in the last row by the ear and dragged him out from behind his desk.

She had the wrong boy! I must have had an astonished look on my face. At that moment, *Frau* Eichel realized that I was still in her classroom.

"Did you see what happened?" she asked me directly.

All I could do was nod. Then I pointed at the boy who had done the dirty deed. "He did it."

Frau Eichel's face twisted up as she frowned. "You're mistaken," she said as she dragged the wrong boy to the front of the classroom by the ear. She turned back to me for a moment. "Don't just stand there. Get a mop to clean up that mess, *Fräulein!*"

I was so confused at what I was seeing that I didn't know what to do next. *Had she not heard what I said?* I grabbed the can of polish and my rags and headed for the door as I heard her punishing the wrong boy in front of the whole class.

I felt badly for that boy all day long. After we all got our pay for the week, I put on my coat and was headed out the front entrance, when I saw a boy and a girl sitting on the curb in front of the school. I took a second look, because all of the children were gone for the day, and because I recognized the boy from the classroom. I walked back to them, and as I got closer, I could see that the girl was crying.

"What's the matter?" I asked the girl as I stooped down.

"Our nanny hasn't come for us," replied the boy with his hand on the girl's shoulder. "And she is afraid to walk home without her, because father will be angry with us."

"You're Sepp, right?"

"Yes," he said, a little surprised that I knew his name.

"Is this your sister?"

"Yes," he replied again.

"What is your name?" I asked the dark-haired girl.

"Annette," she said, blubbering a little.

"Well, Sepp and Annette, I don't think you should wait out here in the cold for much longer," I said, looking up at the sky. "And it will be dark soon. How far is your house from here?"

Neither one of the children knew quite how to answer me.

"Do you usually walk home?" I asked.

Both of the children nodded.

"Why doesn't your father want you walking home alone?"

"Because we have to go through bombed buildings," the little girl blurted out.

"He doesn't want us to take the street car, because we are supposed to get our exercise," Sepp added.

"All right then," I said, straightening my shoulders. "Why don't you both take a hand. I'll walk you home."

I reached down to dry the little girl's tears, and then I offered them my dry and worn-out hands. I asked the little boy if he knew the way home. He said emphatically that he did, and so we started down Herkulesstrasse in the direction that he said we should go.

On the way to their house, we did pass by a couple of bombed-out buildings, and I imagined that their father would not want them climbing or playing on the unstable piles of rubble. We also had to cross a couple of very busy intersections, including the wide and impressive Wilhelmshöher Allee with its trolley tracks.

Somewhere along the way, I told the little boy that I was sorry that he had been punished today for something that he didn't do. He looked up at me with his big brown eyes, and then he looked down at the ground with a forlorn look.

"Why such a sad look?" I asked him.

The boy stopped in his tracks, lifted up his jacket, and pulled a folded-up piece of paper from his pocket.

"I have to give this to father when he gets home," he said, looking down at his shoes. I opened the piece of paper and read the message silently. Then I shook my head and sighed.

"I told her you didn't do it," I said out loud as I patted him on the back. I folded the paper back up and put it in my coat pocket. Then I took his hand back in mine, and we resumed our journey.

"Don't worry about the note, Sepp. I'm going to write one of my own," I said, finally coming to a conclusion.

Sepp led us toward the center of town, then we crossed Wilhelmshöher Allee, passed a bombed-out park, and started up Amalienstrasse. We had already walked thirty minutes, in the opposite direction of *Herr* Meissel's house when I began to wonder how much farther we had to go.

An elegant, light brown, three-story villa which sat on the edge of the hill at the end of the street came into view. It stood out in sharp contrast to the houses around it, because so many of them were bombed-out, while it was unscathed. I paused, looking at the house for a moment, wondering who could possibly live in such a place, when the children tugged on my arms moving me forward. We crossed Terrassestrasse and headed toward the front door of the villa.

An older woman opened the door before we got there. The children both ran inside, skirting past her. I stared at the sight behind the woman. The polished, marble floors in the grand hallway beckoned to a large room at the back of the house where the remaining light in the sky poured in three picture windows displaying a magnificent view to the south.

I brought my eyes back to the housekeeper and stumbled over my next words. The woman in front of me was wearing a crisp, white apron over a rather plain dress. There were gentle streaks of gray running through the top of her curly, dark hair. Her bright eyes were slightly magnified by the thick glasses she was wearing.

"I, um. Pardon me, ma'am, do you have a pencil or a pen I could borrow? I would like to leave a note for their father," I said, looking up to her, not even introducing myself.

The housekeeper's brow fell in perplexity, and then she turned away from the door for a moment.

"Certainly," she responded. "Oh, please. Come on in."

I looked around the front hall while I was waiting. I don't ever remember being in a home as palatial as that. There was a crystal chandelier hanging in the middle of the two-storied hall and a grand staircase rose up the right side of the hall to the first floor. I pulled the paper from my pocket and unfolded it before the housekeeper returned with a pencil.

"Please disregard this note," I wrote. "Sepp was punished in error." I signed my name neatly, folded the note back up, and handed it to the housekeeper. Then, I wished her good day and let myself out the door.

It was dark by the time I got back to the Meissel's house, but I am glad that I helped the children. I wonder what has happened to their nanny.

....

November 27, 1943

I took a long walk in the park across the street today. When I came home, I wrote to Reiner, Liese, Lenz, and Klaus. The Meissels left the house around noon, and so, in the early afternoon, I got out my violin and played it a little. Inge came down when she heard the music and tapped on my door. She sat on my bed listening to me play for a while, and then she asked me if I knew the song *Wir sind jung, die Welt steht offen*. I told her I was sorry, but I did not. Then I told her that if she had the music, I could play it.

She shook her head. "I can sing it for you," she said. "Didn't you ever sing this in the *Bund Deutscher Mädel?*"

I listened to her sing the song. I had never heard it. She does have a nice voice.

We had a cup of tea together before the Meissels got home. Inge told me that *Frau* Meissel is very cold to her also. *Frau* Meissel is tall and slender with bushy, light hair. If she would smile more, she would probably be considered by some to be pretty. I begin to wonder, though, from things that Inge said, whether she is ever happy.

Tomorrow, I will go with the Meissels to mass.

....

November 29, 1943

It was bitter cold when I got up this morning, and my nose was frozen solid by the time I got to school. The day did not improve as the sun never came out. My hands nearly froze off of my arms while I was washing the windows.

Frau Kleefeld found me cleaning out the furnace in the basement and wanted to know why the light fixtures in the hall on the ground floor were not polished on Friday. I didn't know how to answer her since that was Emma's job. I don't understand why she thinks it is my responsibility to do everything, and I don't understand what the other two women do all day if the work is not getting done.

The only sunshine for the whole day came when I was leaving the school at the end of work. Sepp and Annette were sitting there on the curb at the entrance again.

"What has happened to your nanny?" I asked them out of curiosity.

Sepp shrugged.

"She didn't come," said Annette sadly.

Without wasting any time, I offered them each a hand, and we started off toward their house again.

"Did your father punish you for what happened on Friday?" I asked Sepp right away.

"No," he replied. Clearly, he had already forgotten all about it.

"Good," I responded smiling. *Maybe my note did help.* "How old are you, Sepp?"

"Five."

"How old are you, Annette?"

Annette reached up with her mitten and wiped her nose. "Five."

"I am six minutes older than her," piped up Sepp.

"You're twins," I said. "That's good. Then you have each other for company."

Halfway through the bombed-out building section, we passed by the remains of a small park. A woman sat hunched over on one of the benches that still stood in the park. She was talking to herself and swaying back and forth on the bench. I tried to steer the children around the bench, but as we passed by, the children turned their heads and stared at the woman.

"There's *Fräulein* Magda," they both said at the same time. I tried to hurry the children away from the woman, because I could see that she was drunk. When we were safely out of earshot, I asked the children who "*Fräulein* Magda" was.

"Our nanny," said Annette matter-of-factly.

I looked back over my shoulder at the woman and shook my head. It was no wonder to me that she did not show up to take the children home. The rest of the way to their house, I wondered if I should say anything to the housekeeper, but when we reached the end of Amalienstrasse, the children took off across the street and headed for the front door. I decided that they would probably tell her they had seen *Fräulein* Magda in the park.

I was so cold when I got home that I sat for over an hour in the front room with the Meissels before I came down to my room. I am under the thin white comforter now, but I am still cold.

December 1943

December 2, 1943

Every day this week, I have taken Sepp and Annette home from school. Every day, we have seen *Fräulein* Magda drunk in the park. I decided yesterday to take a little detour around the park, so the children wouldn't have to see her, but I saw her figure sitting there on the same old bench.

Annette told me proudly that her father is in the military. I decided, after she told me that, not to interfere in any way. So, I have been leaving after I watch the children safely cross the street to their house. I don't know how much longer I should take them home. It is so far out of the way, but I cannot just leave them at the school all alone. I asked them today where their mother was. They told me that they don't have a mother. She's dead. I wished that I hadn't asked them.

Tomorrow is Friday—polishing day.

December 3, 1943

Dear Journal,

This evening, I find myself in a warm room under a heavy white comforter. I can hardly believe what has happened today. My head is still spinning.

Today started out like a normal Friday. I got to school a little early, because the dogs were barking earlier than normal. *Frau* Kleefeld came out of her office when she heard that I was there. She had a horrible look on her face. She told me that I was to go see the schoolmaster, immediately. I set down my bucket and went upstairs to *Herr* Amsel's office, where I waited for fifteen minutes before he invited me into his office.

He didn't ask me to sit down, so I remained standing. He fumbled with some papers on his desk in a nervous manner, and then he folded his hands and looked down at them. He told me that he was going to release me from work today, and that I should leave immediately.

"Why?" I asked, before I could bite my tongue. "What have I done?" I had the sinking feeling that I had crossed someone, just as *Herr* Meissel had so sternly forbidden me to do on my first day, and now I was suffering the consequences.

Herr Amsel never lifted his eyes. "You have been insubordinate, *Fräulein* Mauer, and your work is not up to standard. I'm sorry," he said lamely, reaching for an envelope. "Here is the pay for your work this week."

Herr Amsel stood to his feet, rested his hands on the desk, and then looked up at me for the first time since the conversation had begun. "Good-bye, *Fräulein* Mauer."

I must have stood there for at least a minute before what he had just said sunk in. I took the envelope from his desk, turned around, and left his office in a daze. The secretary gave me a frightened glance as I passed by her desk. She must have heard the whole terrible scene.

When I got out into the hall, I looked up at the light fixtures. *Who was going to polish them today? What had just happened? How was I insubordinate? What was wrong with my work?* I guess that I was in too much of a daze to cry. I certainly did not want to face the women around the coffee table downstairs, but I had to get my coat. The women. *Where they responsible for this?*

I took my time walking back to the Meissel's house. All the while, I was feeling sick at the thought that I had just lost my employment. The first person who would find out would probably be *Frau* Meissel. I wondered how angry *Herr* Meissel would be with me. I didn't know how much trouble he had gone through to get me the job, but I thought he would be plenty angry. Then there was Uncle Lothar; he would probably be angriest of all.

I managed to slip in the lower door undetected, but Inge heard me in the basement and came to see who was down there. She saw me crying. I told her what had happened, and she tried to console me a little. When I had dried my tears, I told her I was going to go over to the park so I could think, but I asked her to promise me that she wouldn't tell the Meissels. She promised.

I put my coat back on and crossed the street to the park. I had been sitting by the fountain for about fifteen minutes, staring at the dark castle on the hill and brooding, when I heard a man's deep voice asking the woman who was sitting two benches down from me if she was *Fräulein* Mauer.

I glanced over at the voice, and to my horror, I saw that the man was a *Wehrmacht* officer. I shut my eyes for a moment and then rose slowly off of the bench and turned away from him. I was hoping that he wouldn't notice me or come after me.

But before I had taken ten steps, I heard his hurried footsteps on the gravel behind me. My heart stopped beating for a minute. *What could the officer want with me?* I was already in enough trouble.

"*Fräulein* Mauer?" I heard his voice from behind. I froze in place and swallowed hard. The officer made his way around me and stopped directly in front of me. I couldn't look him in the eyes.

"Are you *Fräulein* Mauer?" he asked. Something in his voice drew my eyes to his. I tried to look calm. Standing in front of me was the officer from the train! It had been three weeks, but I recognized him immediately.

He pressed his lips together, and then he turned his head to the side a little. "Have I met you before?" he asked, a little puzzled look in his nice eyes.

I shrugged coolly and stared at his insignia. He was a major. I wondered if he would remember that he had seen me on the train.

"I, uh," the major stumbled over his next words. "I am Kurt Rager—Sepp and Annette's father," he said, extending his leather gloved hand for me to shake. My eyes grew a little bigger when I realized who he was.

"You are acquainted with them?" he asked, trying to get something out of me.

"Yes," I said, finally finding words to say. "They are wonderful children, sir."

The major seemed pleased to hear my compliment, and he almost smiled. I looked up into the major's eyes. He was even more handsome and intimidating than I remembered, but I was determined not to let that affect my judgment.

"I have been out of town and didn't get your note until yesterday afternoon, *Fräulein* Mauer," the major continued after a brief pause.

"My note?"

"The note about the punishment," he said, reminding me.

"Oh, yes," I responded, still not sure why we were having this conversation or where it was headed.

The major shifted on his feet and drew his right arm behind his back. "Yes, about the punishment," he began. "As I said, I didn't get the note until yesterday afternoon, when my housekeeper also informed me that my nanny hasn't been picking the children up from school. Then I heard from the children that you have been bringing them home.

"I went immediately to the school to speak with Sepp's teacher, but she insisted that there was no error in his punishment. I asked to speak with you, but *Frau* Eichel said that you were gone for the day. When I went to the school this morning to find you, to get the story on the punishment, and to thank you for bringing them home"—the major paused for a breath—"I found out that you had been dismissed."

At those words my stomach began to turn again, and I looked away from the major, embarrassed.

"*Fräulein* Mauer," said the major to get my attention again. "*Herr* Amsel informed me that he dismissed you himself, this morning, for...for insubordination and for poor workmanship. I asked to speak with the one who had leveled the insubordination charge against you, figuring I already knew who it was. Then he started to sweat."

I saw the major smile mischievously, and then he continued. "He left me in his office with the promise that he would be right back with the person who had charged you, but when he returned ten minutes later, he was alone. He made apology and said that the one who had charged you was in class and could not be disturbed right then, but that I was welcome to make an appointment with the secretary on my way out."

The major stopped for a moment and crossed his arms on his broad chest. I kept looking him in the eye, still unsure where he was heading with the conversation.

"Then I asked *Herr* Amsel if I could speak with the one who supervised your work." The major let out a short laugh. "He called out to his secretary and asked her to go get a *Frau*—"

"*Frau* Kleefeld," I said, helping him with the name.

"*Frau* Kleefeld," he repeated. "I waited for quite a while, and then *Frau* Kleefeld appeared, looking as nervous as a kitten in a yard full of dogs."

When the major finished his sentence, I bit my tongue. It seemed to me that the major was amused at the situation that was causing me great distress.

"*Herr* Amsel asked *Frau* Kleefeld if you had been dismissed today, and she responded yes. Then he asked her if you had been dismissed because of your poor workmanship. After she hesitated a moment, she said yes again. Then he sent her back to work. I thanked the schoolmaster and left his office. But on the way out, I asked the secretary if she knew where you lived. She told me that she did not.

"I thought I was out of luck, until I ran into *Frau* Kleefeld in the hall by the front entrance. She was waiting there for me."

The major paused for a moment and took a more serious tone. "She asked me if you were in any kind of trouble. Then she lowered her voice and told me that you were her best worker, that she could always count on you doing a good job in half the time of the others, and the truth was that you had been doing more than your fair share of work."

The major looked carefully at me to see how I was taking what he was saying. "She told me that she thought I ought to know that you were really dismissed because *Frau* Eichel was furious when she found out that you had left me a note about the incident in the classroom. And apparently, um, there is something going on between her and the schoolmaster."

The major lifted his hat and then replaced it on his head. "*Frau* Kleefeld was kind enough to tell me your address, and the housekeeper told me you were here."

After hearing the truth about why I was dismissed, I turned away from the major, afraid that the tears would start down my cheeks again. I didn't want him to see them.

The major continued in a softer tone of voice. "*Fräulein* Mauer, please forgive me. I have not come all of this way to cause you any pain, but it appears that I will not be able to sort out any of this without hearing from you. I have heard the story from Sepp, but

I want to know from you what happened in the classroom and why you have been troubling yourself to bring my children home. I can see that you have gone a great deal out of your way to do so."

At his mention of the children, I turned back to him. I figured I had little to hide from him, now that I knew why he had pursued me.

"Would you like to sit down, *Fräulein?*" he asked, gesturing toward the bench I had been sitting on earlier. I nodded, and he followed me over to the bench. When I sat down, I stared out at the fountain. His inquisitive blue eyes were making me nervous.

I told him what I saw in the classroom. He seemed to be listening carefully to what I was saying. Then I continued. "As for your nanny, I found Sepp and Annette in front of the school the day that incident happened. Annette was crying. She was afraid you would be angry if they were to go home alone. I-I couldn't just leave them there. So, I walked them home. That is when Sepp told me about the note from *Frau* Eichel. He was afraid he would be in trouble with you. I thought that you should know that it was not necessary to punish him again for a crime he did not commit in the first place."

I stopped to breathe in a big gulp of cold air and looked at the major. "On Monday, we found *Fräulein* Magda," I said softly.

The major turned his eyes from the fountain to me. "Where did you find her?"

"On a bench in the bombed-out park. She was drunk," I said slowly.

"Drunk?" he asked, quite surprised.

"Yes, drunk. Every day we passed by there, and she was sitting on the same bench."

The major shook his head and sighed. "She lost someone in the bombing," he said, looking away.

"Then she is probably still grieving for them," I replied sympathetically.

The major turned his eyes back to me. "She lost a cat," he said dryly and without emotion. "At any rate, she has left and taken all of her belongings, without so much as a resignation or a word," the major said as he breathed in deeply. "I am without a nanny, and you are without employment, because you were brave enough to stand up for my son."

I was surprised to hear these words coming from the major. I was surprised, because I had supposed all along that he would blame me for what had happened.

The major rose to his feet and took a couple of steps away from the bench. Then he turned back to me. His tone of voice took a sudden turn toward determination. Because I could see on his face that he felt some responsibility for the whole situation, the fear that had been in my heart when he had first spoken my name was all but gone.

"*Fräulein* Mauer, as I see it, we can proceed in one of two ways. Either I can go back and speak to the head master on your behalf to see if he will come to reason and reinstate you in your former position, or, I don't know what experience you have with children—"

When he said that, quite unintentionally, I let out a short laugh interrupting him.

"What?" he asked.

"Forgive me, *Herr* Major. I am the oldest of five children, sir, and have done nothing since they were born but look after them."

The major nodded. He seemed to have made up his mind as to the desired course of action. "You can see that I am in need of a nanny, and I know that you are in need of employment. This may seem a little sudden, but I can think of no one better to offer the position than to the one who has already demonstrated care and concern for my children, when it wasn't even your responsibility to do so. Would you consider this a proposal, *Fräulein?*"

All during our conversation, I had thought that I was going to end up being in some sort of trouble for something I had done. But this turn of events and his offer took me totally by surprise. When I thought of his thoroughness in interrogating the schoolmaster over my dismissal, the effort to which he had gone to track me down, and the faith he was bestowing on me by his proposal, I almost couldn't breathe.

Right then and there, I tried to remind myself who he was—an officer of the Third *Reich*. *Why in the world was I even contemplating his proposal when I should have walked away with a firm but polite no?* I looked in the direction of the Meissel's house and tried to think fast.

I have never been in such a dilemma before. I already knew it would be unbearable for me to return to the school or to face *Herr* Meissel, but how could I work for such a man?

I breathed in deeply and looked the major straight in the eyes. "Yes," I said. "I accept your position." At that moment, my heart was beating so hard that I thought I might faint.

A look of sudden relief came over the major's face. "Very good," he said with a smile. "I am late getting to work this morning," he continued a little nervously. "Would you walk with me back to the house where I left my car?"

I nodded, and we started back to the Meissel's house. As the consequences of my decision were slowly sinking in, my head began to hurt.

"Would it be possible for you to pick the children up at noon and take them home for their dinner? I have just found out today that *Fräulein* Magda has only been taking them to school in the morning. Normally, they come home to eat, and then they are returned for the afternoon classes."

"Certainly," I responded.

The major stopped for a moment and put his hand on his brow. "If you could return them by two o'clock and then collect them again when school is out? Oh, and I can send Heiner here to pick you and your luggage up in about an hour, if you would like."

"My luggage?"

The major sighed. "Yes. You will be staying with us?" he said, half as a statement, half as a question.

"Of course," I said, although I had not understood that. "It won't be necessary to send someone for me," I added. "I only have one suitcase."

"Very well," he said. "But it would be no trouble at all. I apologize that I do not have the time now to speak with you about any of the details of our arrangement. I beg your pardon and promise that we will have that discussion this evening." He looked at me to make sure that I had heard him.

"I understand," I responded with a forced smile.

By this time, we were back at the Meissel's house. The major extended his hand to me and thanked me. As he left the sidewalk to get into his car, I turned around and saw *Frau* Meissel peering out of the front window at me while trying to conceal herself behind the curtain.

I breathed in deeply and climbed the steps to the front door. There were so many thoughts going through my head at once. Inge opened the front door for me and stepped to the side as *Frau* Meissel came quickly out of the front room demanding an explanation.

I looked at Inge, but she just looked away. Then it occurred to me that Inge hadn't kept her promise. She had told *Frau* Meissel that I had been dismissed. I didn't know what to say to *Frau* Meissel.

"I will be packing my bag and leaving this morning," I said quickly. "I will give you the money that I owe you with my thanks for your kindness to me."

As soon as the words were out of my mouth, I turned and went as quickly as I could to my room in the basement. I shut the door behind me and leaned against it. *Had I done the right thing? Had I made the wrong decision in the park?*

I heard the dogs barking next door. Then I looked down at my hands and thought about cleaning the toilets and polishing the light fixtures. I breathed in deeply and pulled my bag out from underneath the bed. If I had made the wrong decision, I would soon know it.

It took me ten minutes to pack; after which, I sat down and wrote a quick note to *Herr* Meissel. I folded up the note with the money I owed him for the room. I picked up my bag, my violin, and the ugly pinstriped dress and headed back up the stairs.

I didn't see Inge in the hall, but I found *Frau* Meissel in the front room staring out of the picture window. She came to me immediately when she saw me in the doorway.

"What is going on, and where do you think you are going, *Fräulein* Mauer? Do you know who that man is?" she asked almost hysterically.

"I have taken employment with Major Rager, ma'am," I replied calmly. "If any letters come for me here, please be kind enough to forward them to his residence."

I handed her the letter for *Herr* Meissel, picked up my violin, and said good-bye. I left her speechless. I was sorry that I did not have a chance to see Inge one last time, but maybe I'm not really sorry. I am sure that she betrayed my confidence.

I headed toward the school house at a more contemplative pace than when I usually traveled in that direction. I was determined to return the pinstriped dress and to have the whole experience put behind me. I imagined that Sepp and Annette might be glad to see that I was the one who would accompany them home today for dinner.

And they were. *Frau* Kleefeld was surprised to see me standing in her office door. I handed her the dress and simply thanked her. Then I went upstairs and waited for the children to be released at noon. Annette came out first, but Sepp was not far behind her.

We did not see *Fräulein* Magda in the park as we passed by. Sepp carried my violin case for me the whole way to their house. All the while, Annette was asking me what was in my suitcase.

The housekeeper opened the front door for us almost immediately. She gave me a cool welcome, but she did greet me by name. The children ran toward the back of the house.

"I am Trude Hoffmann," she said. "Major Rager phoned to tell me to expect you. I have prepared your room upstairs. If you would follow me."

I followed her up the wide staircase on the right. She mentioned that the major's room and the guest rooms were on the first floor. Then we headed up another staircase to the top floor, passing Sepp's room, Annette's room, and then a nursery. My room is at the very end of the hall around a corner. I set my violin case down just inside the door.

"I know you would like to get settled, but you should join the children for dinner immediately. They must be back to school promptly at two o'clock."

"Certainly," I responded with a smile as I put my bag down next to the violin. The room is small, but it is not damp. I followed the housekeeper back downstairs, through the living area and into the dining room. I couldn't help but stare at everything. The house is so beautifully decorated, and there is a grand piano in the living room.

When I entered the dining room, I asked the children, with a smile on my face, where I was to sit. They were already seated in their places, and out of the ten seats, there was only one more place set.

"You sit here," Annette said with a giggle, pointing to the chair with the empty place setting. "And then you give us instruction on how we are supposed to eat our food." The first thing I noticed was that their manners at the table were very good. Someone has taken the time to teach them how to hold their knives and forks properly.

As we were finishing our dinner, the housekeeper came in to remind me that it was time to get the children back to school and to tell me that the major's mother-in-law would be arriving this evening in time for dinner.

On the way back to the school house, I wondered why the housekeeper had told me about the mother-in-law. I think she meant to warn me. When I arrived home with the children this afternoon, the mother-in-law was waiting for us in the hall.

Major Rager's mother-in-law is not at all as I expected her to be. She looks too young to be a mother-in-law. She is tall and slender, has stylish brown hair, and was immaculately dressed. From her appearance and the angle of her chin, she leaves you in no doubt that she is an important member of high society.

The children lined up stiffly to greet her when they came in the door, their eyes bright with eager anticipation of the presents that they were hoping she had brought them. After she introduced herself to me as Helma Brandt, she smiled at them proudly, patted them on the head, and went with them into the living area.

I looked at the housekeeper, who was still standing politely by the front door. She motioned with her head that I should follow them, and so I did. I sat awkwardly in the living area with the mother-in-law while she questioned the children on how their father was caring for them and how they liked school.

I was surprised at the relief I felt when the major came strolling into the living room. I stood to my feet immediately. He looked over at me for a moment, and then he went and gave his mother-in-law a kiss on the cheek.

"Kurt, you are home so late. I expected that you would be here when I arrived," she said in a whiny tone while she was holding both of his arms in her hands.

"Well, Helma," he responded. "You know how much work this war is. Hello, children."

Sepp and Annette were busy playing with the presents their grandmother had brought them, but they did stop for a moment to greet him.

"Have you had time to get acquainted with *Fräulein* Mauer?" he asked, looking from me to *Frau* Brandt.

"Not at all," she confessed. "What has happened to *Fräulein* Magda? She was such a delightful girl."

"I, for one, am ready for supper," he said, changing the subject immediately. "Has Trude come to call us yet?"

"Kurt! I haven't had a chance to change into my evening attire yet. I hope you don't expect me to eat in my traveling clothes," the mother-in-law scolded him as she headed for the stairs.

Major Rager let out a sigh after she left and sat down in an arm chair looking tired. A moment later, *Frau* Hoffmann came in and announced that supper was ready.

The major turned his head around. "I'm sorry, Trude. Helma's just gone up to change. We'll probably be another half hour."

"Very well, sir," the housekeeper replied.

"And this might be a good opportunity for us to conduct some business, *Fräulein* Mauer," he said, looking up at me at last. "Why don't we go into the study?"

I followed the major through the double doors off of the living room into a large square room at the front of the house. A burgundy, blue, and brown carpet covered almost the entire floor in the room and there was a fireplace on the inner wall. Another set of doors next to the fireplace led to the hallway.

"You're the one I saw on the train the other day with your grandparents," he said as he closed both sets of double doors securely behind us.

"My grandparents are not living, sir. Actually, I had just met those people that day on the train," I responded.

"You were so kind and patient with them, I just assumed. Please have a seat," he offered me as he sat down behind a large, hand-carved walnut desk. He reached over to the corner of the desk, picked up the two ledgers sitting there, and put them into one of the desk drawers, while I took a seat in a dark leather chair on the other side of the desk. *So, he remembered me after all.*

The major leaned back in his chair and rested his head to one side. "I don't think I had time to tell you about my mother-in-law."

I shook my head.

"Helma will be here for the better part of a week. She comes down every now and then to spend some time with the children and to cheer me up," he said with a little sarcasm in his voice. "If at all possible, it would be best for her not to find out that you have just started today. She will have enough criticism to dole out without being armed with that fact."

"Yes, sir," I responded.

"I think you will find this to be a rather unusual week in our household. I hope you will be able to see your way through. I suspect that everything will return to normal when she is gone. Now then," he said as he sat forward in his chair. "I would like to go over your expected duties."

I tried to sit up straight.

"My children are the most precious thing in the world to me, *Fräulein* Mauer," he said, after a long pause. "It is important to me that they have the best care and the best instruction. I know that this is not your profession, so I hope that you will allow me to insert myself when I feel it is necessary."

"Certainly."

"Contrary to what you will probably witness this week, I do not subscribe to these new ideas of how to rear children, but instead, believe that they should be given old-fashioned discipline and instruction."

Before the major could say anything further, his mother-in-law knocked on the study door that led to the hallway and entered, thoroughly interrupting our conversation. She was wearing a stunning green evening gown that shimmered in the light when she moved.

Mealtime with the mother-in-law was an interesting occasion. I have never experienced anything like it. I said as little as possible. She peppered the major with questions about what the latest gossip was from the general command headquarters where I gathered he is working. Every time she would ask him another question, he seemed to give me an uncomfortable look although I still don't even know what his position is.

He might have been uncomfortable, but I felt just as awkward sitting at an unfamiliar table, eating with strangers. I was uneasy listening to their conversation, but there was an entertaining side, watching the two of them dance around one another. I noticed that the major got some detailed information out of her, and that he did so seemingly without her even noticing. She interrupted their discussion several times to give correction to the children, but the children just ignored her.

After supper, while the mother-in-law was reading to the children, the major asked me to step back into his study.

"There is one thing that I must do immediately. I need to fill out these security clearance papers," he said as he pulled some papers from a drawer. "It is just a routine clearance form that I have to submit for approval for anyone in my employ that has access to sensitive information, as you will, living in this house."

I was looking into the major's eyes as he spoke to me, but I had to look away for a moment to compose my thoughts. I had not anticipated this. I put my hands together and looked up, hoping that he wasn't going to ask to see my papers.

He took a pen in hand, and then he asked me to spell out my name.

"K-l-a-r-a M-a-u-e-r."

"Where were you born?"

"Berlin," I answered.

The major looked up in surprise. "What is your date of birth?" he asked next.

"The twelfth of May, 1924."

The major looked up at me again as if he was going to say something, and then he wrote it down. "And the name of your father and mother?"

I hesitated long enough for the major to lift his eyes to mine, impatiently. Then I swallowed hard. "Hermann and Annamarie."

"And your National Socialist German Workers' Party identification number?"

"Pardon me?" I said.

"Your party identification number?"

"I am not yet twenty, sir."

The major blinked. "You're not a party member?"

"No, sir," I said softly, looking down at my hands.

He cleared his throat and scratched the back of his head. "We'll need to rectify that before too long. But for tonight, I think we are all set. I hope you will be able to find your way around the children's rooms to help them to bed this evening and to assist them with their drinks of water," he added with a telling smile.

"Yes, sir," I responded politely. I left his study as quickly as possible so that I could catch my breath. I am worried about the security clearance, but what can I do about it except hope that they cannot find me?

I did manage to get the children successfully to bed. The major mentioned to me that they would be going to a military ceremony tomorrow with the children. I don't know if that means I am to go along or not. I don't think I could stomach it.

It is almost midnight now. I am all tired out from such a tumultuous day, and I must get some sleep.

....

December 4, 1943

All day long, I have wanted to crawl into this comfortable bed and disappear. This morning, I got the children dressed and downstairs in time for their breakfast. *Frau* Brandt was just as chipper this morning as she was last night. Breakfast conversation consisted of her comparing the breakfasts of Berlin with the meager one she was having this morning. As for me, this is the best breakfast I have had since I came to Kassel. I do not know if the major is usually so quiet every morning as he was this morning. Perhaps he just had a lot on his mind.

We had no sooner finished our breakfast than the major asked me to see that the children were dressed up warmly and in more formal clothes. He made it clear that we were all leaving as soon as Heiner could bring the car around to the front door.

I saw more of Kassel today as we were on our way to the general headquarters. Major Rager was telling his mother-in-law about the anticipated ceremony as we rolled down Wilhelmshöher Allee. I did not understand what we were about to attend, but I did understand that the major was getting a new boss, and that today was to be the new *Gauleiter* (governor) of Kurhessen's installation. It was all I could do to keep from gasping when the major said that the Minister of Armaments and War Production for all of Germany, *Herr* Albert Speer, was going to be there.

I held tightly to Sepp's and Annette's hands and followed the major and *Frau* Brandt up the stairs and into the headquarters. There was quite a crowd outside the general assembly chambers. I tucked my head under and passed by the SS officers and Gestapo. I began to feel ill just passing by them. The whole room was already full, but the major found us three empty seats on the front row on the left hand side. I picked Sepp up and sat him on my lap.

I was proud of the children. They sat very well through a rather long ceremony. I got to see the new *Gauleiter*, Karl Gerland, up close as he passed right in front of us to meet *Herr* Speer at the front podium. I clapped along with the rest of everyone in the hall, but I was wondering secretly what had happened to the former *Gauleiter*.

The newly installed *Gauleiter* calmed the crowd, and then he introduced the *General der Infanterie*, Otto Shellert, who took a case from his pocket and set it on the podium. In a rousing speech, the General thanked *Herr* Hitler, *Herr* Speer, and the people of Kassel for their indomitable spirits in the aftermath of the British bombing in October.

I was shocked to hear him call Major Rager to the podium. *Frau* Brandt reached over and squeezed my arm. I looked up at her. She was almost in tears from pride. I held onto Sepp with all of my might.

If I could have, I would have left. It really was more than I could bear. I watched *Herr* Speer pin a decoration of valor onto Major Rager's uniform, and then I closed my eyes. The *Gauleiter* added that he had performed admirably during and after the bombing crisis and was to be highly commended for keeping the German war machine going.

My head was pounding. *Why did I agree to take this position?* I was startled out of my thoughts when Sepp broke free of my grasp and went to hug his father as he was returning to his seat.

I looked up in time to see the major look down at me. He must have seen the pain on my face, because when it was all over, when he had shaken almost every hand in the room, when *Herr* Speer was gone with his SS men and motor escort, he asked me if I was feeling ill.

I lied and told him no. Then I looked at his decoration. *Why is it so hard for me to separate this man from the ones in Berlin and the ones in black?*

I had to step aside, because there were more people waiting to congratulate him. I tried to concentrate on taking care of the children. They were quite restless after sitting still for so long. I watched the women as they came through to speak with him. I saw how proud his mother-in-law was of him, but there was something else in the eyes of the women who were there.

They were gathering around him like flies attracted to a cake cooling on the window sill. He is very handsome, he is single, and he has just been decorated. I almost felt sorry for him, the way they were dripping all over him. For a moment, I wondered if he would be the kind of man who soaked up that type of attention or if he would shun it.

On the way home from the ceremony, I rode in the front seat with Heiner, but I tried to look back at the major when he wouldn't notice. I imagine that he did not like all of the attention. He was sitting there with Annette on his lap staring out the window with a thousand things on his mind, just as when we had been on the way to the ceremony that morning.

Heiner leaned over and asked me softly, "How do you like working for the most important man in Kassel?"

I tried to smile in reply, but what he said hit me like a blow to the stomach. I almost had to gasp for air. *What have I gotten myself into?*

Tomorrow, I am to go to mass with *Frau* Brandt and the children, and we will light a candle on the Advent wreath.

....

December 8, 1943

Last night, just as I was about to go upstairs for the evening, the air raid siren went off and made a terrible piercing sound. *Frau* Brandt was in the living room reading, and Major Rager was in his study. They both came out into the hall at the same time. The major asked me to get the children dressed and bring them to the basement immediately.

I ran upstairs and did as he said. The children were groggy, and it was hard to get them dressed. I had never been in the basement before, but as we were going down the stairs, it suddenly got very cold. I followed the children to a room underneath the dining room and found *Frau* Brandt sitting on a chair reading her magazine and the major sitting on the floor pouring through some papers.

The air raid siren had stopped by the time the children sat down beside me on the floor. The major got up and quickly turned the light out. The only remaining light was an old lantern that was sitting in the middle of the floor. Annette put her head in my lap bumping into Sepp's head on the way. *Frau* Brandt looked up at me with a displeased look on her face when the fussing commenced.

I looked over at the major. Both of them seemed quite calm, but all I could do was wonder what was going to happen next. I swallowed hard and tried not to move my legs or disturb the children.

With nothing but silence, dreaded anticipation, and a chill in the air, my mind wandered to the questions Annette had asked me after mass on Sunday. She always has questions. What holds the clouds up in the sky? Where do raindrops go when they disappear into the ground? Why is there blood on the feet and hands of Jesus, hanging there on the cross? Where does God go when the air raid siren goes off?

I don't know how I am supposed to answer all of her questions. The first two weren't so difficult, but I find it very hard to answer her questions about God. I have my own questions.

In less than an hour, the siren wailed steadily again, and the major and *Frau* Brandt got up to leave. I woke the children and put them back to bed.

The major told *Frau* Brandt this morning that he expected many more false alarms like last night as the radar alerts the air raid head when there are bombers in the area, but their target is not always Kassel.

Since Heiner is the driver for the major and several other dignitaries in Kassel, he seems to know a lot about what is going on. I asked Heiner this afternoon when he thought the British bombers would come back to Kassel. He told me that they did hardly any damage to the assembly plants and factories in October. He thinks that they will be back any day.

December 9, 1943

I have had an unbearable headache the whole week long beginning on Saturday, but the good news is that I am sure it will go away tomorrow morning. All day Sunday, I listened to her ramblings. Sometimes, the comments about how I handled the children were said to my face, and sometimes, they were said to the major when she thought that I was not listening.

I have been a nervous wreck all week long, thinking that at any moment the major will dismiss me. Maybe I would be better off humbling myself and going back to *Herr* Meissel's.

I think the children are confused by the see-saw of her spoiling, followed most assuredly by her criticism. Of course, the children each got lavish presents for Nikolaustag from her. The major has been absent at every evening meal this week. I do not know if that is his regular habit or not. He seems to handle her quite smoothly, though. I don't think I have ever known someone as diplomatic as the major.

At any rate, *Frau* Brandt is leaving with all of her ten suitcases in the morning. I wonder if Major Rager will be home for supper tomorrow evening.

Dear journal, I am going to put you in your hiding place now under the bed and go to sleep, because I think that if anyone ever finds you and reads you, I will be in big trouble.

....

December 10, 1943

Dear Journal,

I have made a big mistake, and now, I don't know what I'm going to do or where I will go. I took the children with me to the shops on Hohenzollernstrasse this afternoon. I am down to only one pair of socks, and I was hoping to purchase another pair or two. Annette didn't want to leave the house because she was playing with her dolls, and Sepp didn't want to have to walk anywhere. I couldn't leave them at home, and I am so tired of having to go without socks while they are drying.

The children complained all the way to the shops, but then I had trouble tearing them away from the displays in some of the windows. The first two stores were entirely out of socks. We were on our way to a third store when I ran directly into *Herr* Meissel. He was the last person I really wanted to see. I haven't seen him since the morning I was dismissed from the school.

After we exchanged greetings, he began to lecture me about how embarrassing it was for him that I was dismissed from the school. He told me that I should have conducted myself differently, and that I should have heeded his warnings. He hoped I had learned my lesson not to cross important people.

He said that *Frau* Meissel was very concerned for me because I left so abruptly. Then he told me that she was certain I would not be in the employment of Major Rager very long, because he was a very important man and deserved the most skilled and responsible of employees.

I was trying to keep my eyes on the children while *Herr* Meissel was lecturing me, but I was feeling ill inside. Although I didn't want to hear it, I felt that everything he was saying was true. All I wanted to do was leave the sidewalk. He was speaking to me so intensely that people were staring as they passed by.

At last, *Herr* Meissel, unaware of the damage his hurtful words had done, wished me a good day, and I resumed my search for socks in a catatonic state.

It never occurred to me that there was any reason to hurry home until we were walking up the street to the house. My heart sank to my feet as I saw the major waiting impatiently in the front hall for us to return. Heiner was standing at attention just inside the front door.

He had told me at breakfast that he had a five o'clock dinner engagement to which he was going to bring the children, and he had even told me what clothes he wished for me to dress them in for the occasion.

"Where have you been, *Fräulein?*"

"I'm sorry, *Herr* Major," I began weakly. "I thought you're engagement was at five o'clock."

The major let out a baffled sigh as he glanced at his watch. "It is already five fifteen."

I opened my mouth, astonished. My conversation with *Herr* Meissel had eaten up forty-five minutes of my time, and I didn't even notice. "I-I will get the children dressed immediately," I said as I tried to shuffle them up the stairs.

Major Rager shook his head. "There is no time for that. They will have to go as they are dressed. Outside and into the car, children."

I watched in bewilderment as the children scrambled into the car after the major. Heiner shut the door with a thud and hurried around to the driver's seat. They took off in a cloud of exhaust and I was still standing there—baffled, shamed, embarrassed, sorry.

I thought I had been doing so well; not one word of rebuke from the major. But now, I had kept him waiting, and that is the one thing that I know I must never do. The belittling lecture from *Herr* Meissel now seemed to be nothing to me in comparison with my sin of causing the major to be late for his engagement.

As if this all wasn't bad enough as soon as they had left, *Frau* Hoffmann informed me that a police inspector had stopped by the house this afternoon and had inquired as to the reason I had not yet registered that I was now living at the major's residence. *Frau* Hoffmann also informed me that the major had assured him that he would personally vouch for the authentication of my identification and asked the inspector to register me based on the major's word.

All of this happened before I made the grave mistake of being late in bringing the children home. Now I am sure that the major will dismiss me and all the things that *Herr* Meissel said about me being incompetent are true. It seems there is nothing I can do to fix this mess I have caused, and there is no one to blame but myself.

I was too sick to eat anything for dinner, and I couldn't sleep, so I was wide awake when they returned from their dinner party. I put the children to bed, but the major didn't say one word to me. I wish he had, at least, said something.

I have now been in Kassel a whole month. It seems more like a year. I wish I had never come to Kassel.

....

December 16, 1943

Dear Journal,

I cannot begin to explain how awful I have felt, all week long, every time I am around the major. I cannot look him in the eye. He hasn't said anything directly to me about my mistake, but between his mother-in-law's opinion of me and my own foolish actions, he has plenty of reasons to dismiss me.

Despite my fears, I can't help but feel as if I owe the major a great deal for giving me this position, and I am determined to do everything I can to keep it.

For that reason, I was happy to tell *Frau* Hoffmann, with no uncertainty, that I would help her with the major's party tomorrow. She told me that the major always hosts an event for staff of the general headquarters at this time of year. I want the major to see that I am grateful.

....

December 17, 1943

After I took the children to school this morning, I helped Heiner bring up some extra tables and chairs from the basement and the special decorations for the party. In between my trips to school,

I spent as much time as I could helping *Frau* Hoffmann in the kitchen. Once the children were home, one of my biggest jobs was to keep Sepp from eating all the food we had prepared. I finally sent the children up to the nursery to play.

A half hour later, I brought the children down and fed them. At seven o'clock, I hurried them upstairs as the guests began to arrive. Sepp and Annette were so slow to get into their pajamas, and they kept telling me they wanted to go downstairs. Finally, I got them into bed and gave them a hurried kiss good night. I knew *Frau* Hoffmann was counting on my help, so I did not stay for a bedtime story.

When I came down the stairs, I suddenly realized why *Frau* Hoffmann had asked me if I was going to change my clothes. I looked down at the dress I was wearing under the apron. I didn't have anything better to change into anyway. All day long I had looked forward to the party, but there was so much to do that I didn't even have time to run a brush through my hair.

On my first trip out of the kitchen with plates in my hands, I met the major. He was dressed handsomely in a uniform I had not previously seen, and he was wearing his Knight's Cross. He asked me if I knew where *Frau* Hoffmann was. I leaned in the direction of the kitchen.

After I had put the plates on the buffet table, I saw the major greeting some of his guests. On the next trip, when I was bringing the food to the table, I saw a tall, slender, blonde woman come in the font door. She was wearing lipstick and a fur cape. Her dress was slim and fashionable. The major greeted her warmly. I turned around quickly, because I didn't want to see it.

On the very next trip out to the food table, before I had set the food down, I saw two Gestapo officers come in. My hands shook immediately. I found a place to put the food down quickly. *They must be guests of the major, or why else would they have come?* I thought I could feel the whole mood in the room change when they came in. I went back to the kitchen as quickly as my feet would take me.

I must have looked shaken, because *Frau* Hoffmann asked me if I was ill. I stayed in the kitchen until she asked me to take out more food. Although the major told *Frau* Hoffmann to expect fifty people, it was so crowded that it seemed like there were more than a hundred.

I was trying to make my way through to the food table when I heard the major say to someone, "Stay away from my nanny, Lieutenant."

I stopped and looked back at the major. A tall, brown haired young man with a charming smile turned around to greet me. "Don't let Major Rager scare you away. I just wanted to meet you, *Fräulein?*"

"Mauer," I said. I couldn't shake his hand because I was still holding two plates of food, so I continued on to the table. Then I returned to shake his hand.

"This is Lieutenant Manfred Braun," the major said, "and he is not to be trusted, *Fräulein*," he added. The others in the circle, including the blonde woman who was leaning close to the major, laughed at the major's comment. But I think he was serious. The lieutenant took me by the arm and stepped away from his circle of friends.

"Major Rager has told me a little about you, and I am delighted to finally meet you."

"Has he?" was all that I could think to say.

The lieutenant leaned in close to me. "I am his assistant, you know."

"Are you?"

"Yes. He is a very intriguing man to work for as I am sure you already know. But did you know that he holds the distinction of being the youngest major in the army of the Third *Reich?* You don't have to know him very long to find a good reason for that."

I was trying to listen politely to the lieutenant, but all the while in the back of my mind, I was thinking that I should be getting back to the kitchen. I wanted to get back to the kitchen. The longer I stayed in the hall, the more chance I had of running into the Gestapo.

"But enough about Major Rager. Now, tell me something about you, *Fräulein* Mauer. Where are you from?"

"Sinsheim," I responded immediately.

"Sinsheim?" he said, sounding a little disappointed. "I don't know where that is."

"It is in the area of Heidelberg."

The lieutenant's nose twitched. "Tell me a secret about you, *Fräulein*," he said next. "Everybody has a secret."

I looked into his eyes while I was trying to think of something unimportant to tell him.

"*Fräulein* Mauer?" I heard Heiner's voice behind me. "*Frau* Hoffmann is looking for you," he said with a serious look on his face. I turned back to the lieutenant.

"It was a pleasure to meet you. If you will excuse me," I said with a polite smile. On the way back to the kitchen, I saw the blonde woman hanging on the major. She even leaned over and gave him a kiss on the cheek. So, he does have a girlfriend, and she is quite beautiful.

Frau Hoffmann scolded me for taking so long, so I apologized to her. The lieutenant tried occasionally through the evening to distract me from doing my job, but for the most part, I was able to successfully avoid him not because I didn't want to talk to him but because I didn't want to get in trouble with *Frau* Hoffmann. I was not, however, able to avoid the Gestapo.

About halfway through the evening, they moved in on me as I was replenishing the punch bowl.

"*Fräulein* Mauer, is it?" asked the short one with the glasses. I looked up. *How did they know my name?*

"We would like to have a word with you, privately," the taller one said, raising his eyebrows and extending his hand toward the front door. I swallowed hard. This could only mean one thing. All I could remember thinking was that I hoped the major wasn't going to be in any trouble for employing me.

Once we were outside, the taller one turned on his flash light and moved to the side of the driveway by the wall. He walked the perimeter of the front of the house until he seemed satisfied that no one was listening. The shorter one with the glasses stood by me with his hands crossed in front of him. I clasped and unclasped my hands, trying to look calm and trying to stay warm.

He cleared his throat and then introduced himself as Bernhardt Löning and his partner as Willi Knappe. "*Fräulein* Mauer, we must speak with you confidentially," he said. "You should tell no one of our conversation."

I nodded. Then the short man continued. "As Major Rager's nanny, you are in a most delicate situation, which will expose you to information that will be very valuable to us. It is your duty to keep your eyes and ears open to all of the dealings Major Rager has."

I looked from *Herr* Löning over to the tall man, confused. This wasn't what I was expecting to hear at all.

"We would ask you to look for anything that is suspicious in any way, be it a telegram he might receive, a meeting with someone, papers you might happen to see, conversations you might overhear—anything that might cause you to think that he is not conducting business in the best interest of the Third *Reich*, or anything out of the ordinary."

"I don't understand. Is he under suspicion?" I blurted out before I gave my question any thought.

Herr Knappe tugged at his collar and twisted his head. "We cannot be too careful with men who have such a high position. Everything that is done must be in the best interest of the *Führer* and of the Fatherland. The only way to keep everyone honest is to be looking out for one another. Do you not agree, *Fräulein?*"

I nodded even though I wasn't sure that I did agree.

"So, we will be in contact with you in the future," the shorter man said as he stepped aside. "If the major should inquire after our conversation, please be kind enough to tell him that we were just socializing. You must not say a word of this to anyone. Do you understand?"

I nodded as he gestured that I was free to return to the house. My lungs felt like they would explode from need of oxygen as I headed for the front door, and my mind was spinning.

As I stepped into the crowded and noisy hall, I saw Lieutenant Braun standing directly across from me at the bottom of the staircase. And he saw me. He watched me come in the front door, and then he watched the two Gestapo agents come in behind me. My heart fell. He would surely report this to the major even though it was not what it seemed.

A movement at the top of the staircase caught the corner of my eye, and when I looked up, I could see two starry-eyed children peering out between the banister legs at the crowd below. I set aside the conversation that had just taken place outside and concentrated on moving through the crowd toward the stairs. I needed to get the children back to bed before the major saw that they were up.

"Friends of yours?" asked Lieutenant Braun as I passed by him to climb the stairs.

"No," I replied, turning around slightly to look him directly in the eyes.

"Back to bed. Come on," I said to the pajama-clad children as I shuffled them up the stairs to their bedrooms. "Tomorrow will be a big day, and you must get your sleep," I told them, because that is what my mother always said to me. After some moans and grumbling, I was able to get them back into their beds.

I closed Sepp's door and leaned back against it. Those Gestapo men were asking me to spy on the major. *Why would they ask me to do that?*

On my way down the stairs, I sighed. I didn't see the two Gestapo men in the hall, but Lieutenant Braun was still standing in the place I had left him at the bottom of the stairs.

"What did they want?" he asked dutifully as soon as I reached the bottom step.

I glanced around the room, and then turned my head toward him quickly. "They wanted to be on my dance card," I said cryptically. I watched his expression closely.

He narrowed his eyes. "And what did you tell them?"

I swallowed hard. "I-I told them I won't be dancing this evening."

Lieutenant Braun smiled expectantly, missing the meaning I was trying to convey to him. "But you will dance with me?"

As he shifted on his feet, waiting for my answer, I saw the major behind him, across the room. The blonde woman was still attached to his arm. *Did she never leave his side?*

"I'm sorry, but I cannot even though I would like to. If you will excuse me, I must get back to the kitchen." Lieutenant Braun stepped aside and bowed politely as I passed by.

When I got back to the kitchen, *Frau* Hoffmann did not scold me. She was bending over the sink, her arms covered in suds.

"Let me clean up, *Frau* Hoffmann," I offered. The relief on her face was worth the effort I knew I would expend in the next two hours.

Throughout the day, I was struck by the hard work that *Frau* Hoffmann put into the party. She is probably in her late fifties, but I did not see her age until that moment. She did a remarkable job preparing the food for this occasion, and I could see then the toll it had taken on her. I pulled out a chair and told her she should sit for a moment.

"I haven't sat all day," she said wearily.

I grabbed the rag from her hand and took my place at the kitchen sink. From the kitchen, we could hear the Victrola, the laughter, and the chattering. Over the course of the next hour, the laughter died down and then the chattering, until all we could hear was the music. I looked over at the pile of dishes still to be washed and at the stack *Frau* Hoffmann was drying.

"Why don't you go home, *Frau* Hoffmann," I suggested at last. "I'll finish washing and put the rest of these dishes away in the morning."

"Bless you, Klara," she said, calling me by my first name for the first time. "Major Rager has given me tomorrow off, so I will see you on Sunday," she said as she hobbled toward the door to get her coat. "Thank you for helping me today."

I wished her good night and kept washing. When she was gone, I sneaked over to the door and peeked out. All I could see was Major Rager, with the blonde woman still attached to his arm and several others talking in the living room. I returned to the stack of dirty dishes at the sink.

My mind was in a whirlwind, my emotions bobbing like a leaf riding on a fast moving stream. Meeting the charming and persistent Lieutenant Braun had to be the only pleasant moment of the evening.

The encounter with the Gestapo was frightening and unsettling. They have imposed themselves on me by asking me to do a most dishonorable thing. If anything, their demand of me has caused me to want to hide any information I might have concerning the major. But I am afraid of them, and I know very well that I must fully cooperate or face the consequences.

I rolled my shoulders back and kept washing the dishes. All of these things were enough to cause me distress, but there was something else that seemed to be bothering me, even more than that—the beautiful, blonde woman.

I looked down and saw the major's smile in the soap suds. When I looked up at the blackout cloth on the window in front of me, I saw it there too. I closed my eyes, and the smile he gave me on the train came back to me.

What was this strange feeling coming from my heart? I took in a deep breath as I slowly realized that I was jealous of the blonde woman. I closed my eyes tight. *What a fool I am.*

I have really started to fall for the major. I have allowed myself to think that the major's kindness toward me is something more. This must be why the blonde woman bothers me so.

I kept washing the dishes, but all the while I was talking to myself. No matter the feelings I have inside, no matter how kindly he has treated me or how handsome I think he is, I know that these feelings must cease. He has hired me to care for his children—that is all, and I must not be presumptuous and stray beyond that responsibility.

A tear slid down my cheek and into the dishwater. I heard the door to the kitchen turning on its hinges. I brushed the next tear away as I turned to see who had come into the kitchen.

"Do you know where I can find *Frau* Hoffmann?" asked the major with a pleasant smile when he saw just me in the kitchen. "I wanted to thank her for all of her hard work."

I tried to still my heart. His smile always did that to me, but I knew that this must end.

"She-she's gone home for the evening," I said as I turned back to the dirty dishes. "I told her I would finish cleaning up."

"Yes," he said. "You have been a big help to her. Well, never mind. I'll let her know later."

The major paused for a moment, and I turned back around to see why.

"I'm going to turn in for the evening. Good night, *Fräulein,* and thank you for your contribution tonight. You were not obligated to help, but I see that you did so willingly and capably, and I think everyone enjoyed it."

I smiled weakly at his compliment. I wondered for a moment if I should say anything to him about the Gestapo, but

I could see that he looked tired and that he was happy from the successful party.

I told him good night and turned back to the dishes. The kitchen door went *swish* as the major left. I dropped the dishcloth and stared at the blackout cloth in front of me. I decided that I had to tell the major about the Gestapo. How could I work for a man on whom I was supposed to be spying and not somehow get caught in the middle? Either I had to trust him enough to tell him, or I should just leave. And I am in too deep now to leave.

....

December 18, 1943

I forgot that *Frau* Hoffmann had the day off today. When I woke up, it was pretty late. The children were amusing themselves in the nursery. I hurried to get them dressed. The major was waiting on breakfast in the study. I apologized for being late, put the oatmeal on to cook, and started toasting the bread right away. I know he likes it light brown, so I was careful not to let it go too long.

As we were finishing breakfast, the major told me that he was going to take Sepp with him this morning to some event. He said he would leave Annette with me. Annette began to cry and blubber that she wanted to go along too, but the major did not give in to her.

As usual, I had said close to nothing at the table. I was thinking about and planning what I would tell the major about the Gestapo when I had the opportunity. I wanted to get the words just right. When I looked up from my plate, I saw the major look away. He excused the children and pulled his napkin from his lap to place it on the table. I stood to my feet when he got up. My heart was pounding.

"Sir," I said quickly as he was turning to leave.

"Yes, *Fräulein* Mauer?" he said, turning back to me.

I had his full attention now, but nothing came out of my open mouth. I cleared my throat. He raised his eyebrows as if to say, *what is it?*

"The two Gestapo men who were here last night," I finally said in a burst.

"Yes?"

"They, they took me aside and asked me to watch you," I said with a tremble in my voice. The major's face narrowed in confusion. "They wanted me to report back to them if I saw you doing anything, or knew of any dealings you had that were-were not proper," I continued.

I watched the major's face turn from confusion to graveness. "And, shall you spy on me, *Fräulein* Mauer?" he asked in a sarcastic tone.

I hesitated a moment, and then answered him. "I have always understood that personal assistants, including nannies, were obligated to keep and to guard the secrets of their employers, not report on them. And that is what I shall do, unless you direct me otherwise."

Although the major is not one to display his thoughts openly on his face, I thought I detected a sign of relief and approval at my carefully crafted answer. Then he shook his head. "That is a noble sentiment, but you will never make a good party member unless you change your thinking on the matter, *Fräulein*."

I was staring at the table, but my eyes went straight to his. His tone of voice was such that I could not tell whether he was warning me that I must convert to that way of thinking, or whether he was teasing me.

"We will be back late this afternoon, *Fräulein*," he said as he left the room.

I thought it was a rather odd response to my revelation to him, but I don't know what response I expected. I just hope he understands that I have given him my loyalty.

After the major and Sepp left, I cleaned up the breakfast dishes and put away the rest of the dishes from the party. Then I searched the house for Annette. It was very cold outside, and I felt certain she had not gone out without her coat. While I was looking a second time in Sepp's room, I heard a noise above my head in the attic.

The stairs to the attic are hidden behind an unassuming door outside of my room. I found the door ajar and mounted the narrow, bare, wooden stairs to the attic. There are three small windows that illuminate the attic, one on each side of the house and one at the back, but it was dark under the eaves.

"Annette?" I called to her for the fiftieth time. "Are you up here?"

Suddenly, my eye caught a slight movement under the eaves to my left. It was there that I saw her hiding behind a rather large, old trunk. She giggled when I finally found her.

"What are you doing up here?"

Annette said nothing. She was dressed in a swanky woman's dress, had a string of beads dangling from her neck, and was struggling to keep a pair of large shoes on her tiny feet. I laughed at the sight of her. "All you are missing is a nice hat," I said.

She giggled again.

"Where did you get these clothes?" I asked her.

"From the trunk," she responded. "They're mommy's."

I lifted the lid of the trunk beside us. It was packed full of clothes, shoes, hats, scarves, and even some jewelry. Annette struggled to get on her feet, and then she reached in for a hat.

"I don't think we should get anything else out of here," I said, feeling a little funny about it. As Annette pulled the hat out of the trunk and raised it to her head, a small envelope fell to the floor at her feet. Annette adjusted the hat on her head and staggered around me and across the floor. She didn't seem to notice the envelope.

"Look how beautiful I am, *Fräulein* Mauer," she said.

I picked the envelope up off of the floor and brushed away the dust. Then I looked up at Annette.

"You are all ready for a summer picnic," I said.

My eyes moved back to the letter. The envelope was addressed to *Frau* Ida Rager in Kassel and was postmarked December 1938, almost a year after the children would have been born. While Annette was prancing around the attic in her outfit, I took the letter out of the envelope. The letter had been read often. It was quite worn.

As soon as I began reading it, I felt that I should not have opened it up. It was a love letter to Ida. I have never read such sappy, unrestrained, and lustful writing in all of my life. The most shocking part came at the signature line. It was signed, "Passionately, Erwin."

I looked at the postmark again, and then I looked up at Annette, who was staring at the reflection of her image in the window on the south end of the house.

I shoved the letter back into the envelope and called to Annette.

"I think we should put these clothes back now and go downstairs. I have a very special project for us to work on." I took the hat off of her head and slipped the letter back in the lining on the inside from where it had come.

It was really none of my business who wanted to kiss and hold and love whom. I helped Annette get the dress off, and we folded it carefully back into the trunk. When we got to the bottom of the stairs, I closed the attic door securely behind us. There were secrets up there, dark secrets that I didn't want to disturb.

It was late afternoon when the major and Sepp returned from their outing. The smell of gingerbread cookies must have drawn them into the kitchen. *Frau* Hoffmann had done me a big favor by cashing in a few of her food stamps on some sugar. Annette and I had been working on baking and making a gingerbread house all afternoon long. Mother and I always did this before Christmas.

"What is going on in here?" asked the major as he came into the kitchen followed by Sepp.

"We're making a gingerbread house, Father!" said Annette with excitement.

"So you are," said the major.

"I want to make one," piped up Sepp with a pouty face.

I had anticipated this. "I have extra pieces of gingerbread for you, Sepp," I said with a smile, "but you must wash your hands first."

The major took a careful look at Annette's gingerbread house, and then he swiped a cookie from the counter.

"We used to make gingerbread houses when I was a child, but I don't believe the children have ever done one," the major said with a little sadness in his voice. "I am sorry that I kept Sepp away so long."

"Don't worry," I responded. "I'm sure he'll catch up quickly."

In the end, Sepp's gingerbread house was very well constructed, and he required very little of my assistance. I think he may have a talent for building. He also ate half of the gingerbread cookies while he was working.

Tonight, I will go to sleep with this one happy memory and try to forget that I am far from home.

....

December 19, 1943

Today, I went with the children to mass. The major told me a week ago that his late wife's last request was that he would take them to church every Sunday. Although I know that he tries to take them, this is the second week that it has fallen on me. He is always in his study, talking on the phone or doing his paperwork. I do wonder sometimes what keeps him so busy. At least he has kept his word to me and always takes time for the children on

Sunday afternoon. That is when I have time to do some writing in you, dear journal.

This afternoon, we lit the last Advent candle. Christmas will be next Saturday. I wonder what it will be like to spend Christmas in Kassel. With the war and the city center in ruin, the grand Christmas market at Friedricksplatz is but a memory to *Frau* Hoffmann, and anyway, there is no extra money to spend.

I sat down and wrote a letter to Aunt Frieda and Uncle Lothar to send with the money the major has given to me for my salary. I know Uncle Lothar will be happy to get almost double what I was sending them when I was working at the school.

I haven't heard from Klaus, Lenz, or Liese lately. I hope that Aunt Frieda will help them make their gingerbread houses, because that has been one of our only traditions for Christmas. How I wish I could see them all and be with them for Christmas, but I know that is not possible.

I wonder if Reiner feels the same as I do. I haven't received a letter from him in over a month. When I think about last Christmas, it only makes me cry. How much has changed since last Christmas and not for the better. Dear journal, I do wish that I had never come to Kassel.

....

December 26, 1943

Dear Journal,

Christmas has come. The major locked the children out of the living room after noon, and I helped him with the Christmas tree and setting the presents out. I even made two small plates full of nuts and goodies and put them under the tree, just before the major rang the doorbell to let the children know they could come downstairs.

The most enjoyable part of it was to see the happy faces of the children. The excitement and the feelings that I had as a child came back to me last night. Something in the way Annette sat gazing at the candles on the tree made me remember our last Christmas together in Berlin. For a few brief minutes, I was a child again, lost in the memories of the past.

When I returned from my pleasant journey, I found myself back in bombed-out Kassel. And all of the circumstances of the war do make me wonder, at this time of year, what is the significance of the Christ child. At mass, they said that the Christ child came to bring peace on earth, but I do not see peace. All I see is the blood that is running down the face, hands, and feet of Jesus and the candles I am supposed to light to pray for the souls of my parents and the souls of all of those who died in the bombing raid.

I can only wonder what kind of world we will all have when this is all over. So, I suppose any happiness we can bring to the children at this time of year should be welcomed. The major was very kind to include me in the private time that he had with the children, but it was awkward for me. I miss my own family terribly. And how I wish we were all in different circumstances.

Today, I went to mass with the children, and then I spent the afternoon with them. *Frau* Hoffmann told me yesterday that the major had a dinner engagement at *Fräulein* Farber's house. I think that is the blonde from the party. He went out of the house all dressed up, having never said a word to me about his engagement.

It was too cold to play outside, and so we played in the nursery until they were bored. I do not understand how they get bored so quickly. There are so many toys in the nursery that I would think any child could play for a whole month straight and not get tired. There are two wooden rocking horses with fluffy tails. Annette has a kitchen set with play dishes and food items. Sepp has a very smart play wood working bench with tools and equipment. And there are many other fancy toys I have only seen in store windows that Annette has told me are from their grandmother.

After supper, we played hide and seek until almost time for bed. I read them two stories of their choosing, and I let them crawl into bed with me for the reading.

Sepp is quieter and more reserved than his sister and has a very mechanical mind. I think that he will do well in life with anything that he can put his hands on. I do not see a whole lot of his father in him. He is very ticklish. Annette, on the other hand, is talkative and outgoing and less ticklish. She likes all of the frilly things. I imagine that she is probably like her mother.

I shouldn't have, but I let the children stay up a little later than usual. They have another week before they have to return to school. I hope that we are able to get out of the house this week. I think they need some fresh air.

January 1944

January 1, 1944

It is now almost midnight on the first day of the New Year. Major Rager took the children to New Year's mass. He invited me to go along, but I politely declined. The house was very quiet when they left. *Frau* Hoffmann was off for the day. I enjoyed the silence.

I sat down and wrote a letter to Klaus, Lenz, and Liese and also a letter to Reiner. Then I got out my violin. It has been a long time since I played it. I went down to the living room and sat at the piano to tune up the strings. Then I got up and set my music on the piano. I played my violin for twenty minutes straight. I can still hear *Herr* Eldering's instructions in my mind. He was always very patient with me.

After I played through a couple of songs, I went over to the Victrola. There were a number of works by Bach in the record box. I found one for which I had the music and placed the record on the turntable.

I was in the middle of playing Bach's *Wachet Auf*, along with the record, when I was startled to see that the major and the children had returned from mass and were standing in the doorway listening to me. I stopped immediately and must have turned red as the record played on. The major motioned for me to continue. I hesitated for a moment. I had no desire to play in front of them. I put the violin and the bow down on the piano and went straight for the record player.

"That was absolutely beautiful, *Fräulein*," said the major, clearly stunned by what he heard. "You should not have let us interrupt you. Where did you learn to play so impressively?"

"Berlin," I responded shyly. "I had the privilege of studying under *Herr* Bram Eldering."

The major made his way to the piano, picked up my music, and skimmed through the titles. "I forgot that you were from Berlin. I have always thought that it would be a good thing for the children to have music lessons."

"It would be, sir," I responded quickly. I didn't say it, but music has always been a wonderful escape for me.

Major Rager looked over at the children and then back at me. "Would you be willing to teach them?"

I thought for a moment. "Yes," I replied. "But are you willing to listen to them practice?"

The major let out a short laugh. "Perhaps you could give them lessons before I am home in the evenings?"

"Perhaps," I responded in a daring attempt at teasing. Then I thought a moment. I think that Sepp may be well suited to the violin, but I think Annette may do better on the piano. I didn't say this to the major.

After I put the children to bed, I went down to the piano to gather my music. I don't know what time it was, but it was quite late. As I closed the lid on the Victrola, I heard a loud knock on the front door. The major came out of the study and glanced at me before he headed to the door to answer it. I did not see Lieutenant Braun, but I know it was him, because the major greeted him. I heard the lieutenant ask for me. He said that he wanted to dance with the most beautiful girl in all of Germany.

I saw the major look over his shoulder toward me. "Lieutenant Braun, it is very late, and you are very drunk," the major said. "Go home."

Since I could not go upstairs without being seen, I retreated back into the living area. I was embarrassed that the lieutenant was calling for me.

"I am certain she will want to see me, sir," I heard the lieutenant say very loudly.

"I am certain that you should go home, Lieutenant. And that is my final word to you," said the major firmly.

I heard the door close. When I peeked around the corner, the major beckoned me out to the hall. "I hope that you have not done anything to encourage him, *Fräulein*," he said, trying to hide his amusement.

"Certainly not, sir," I responded, trying to keep my embarrassment hidden. I think he saw that I was mortified, because he went back into his study without saying another word.

....

January 13, 1944

My headache has returned. The major's mother-in-law is back in town. She came by train from Berlin yesterday. *Frau* Hoffmann told me that next Thursday is Sepp and Annette's birthday. Apparently, *Frau* Brandt always comes for the occasion.

This afternoon when we got home from school, *Frau* Brandt was upstairs in her room. The major asked me to go to the pharmacy to get something to soothe *Frau* Brandt's stomach. He said she wasn't feeling well, and he would look after the children while I went.

More than an hour later, I returned home with some powder for *Frau* Brandt. The door to the major's study was closed. I hung up my coat and went straight upstairs, where I heard the children giggling. I was afraid they would disturb *Frau* Brandt.

I found Sepp and Annette in the bathroom. They had discovered a pair of scissors in *Frau* Brandt's overnight case and were taking turns cutting each others hair. I gasped when I saw the damage that they had done to one another, and then a pit began to grow in my stomach.

I knew that they were going to have their portraits taken the next day. And I figured *Frau* Brandt would be furious when she saw the state of the children. The hair on the left side of Sepp's head was mostly chopped off and a big chunk of hair from the top of Annette's head lay on the floor in front of her.

As winter follows fall, I knew that this incident was going to end up being charged to my account as my mistake even though they were in the major's care while I was gone. I didn't want him to get in trouble with *Frau* Brandt either. There was only one thing to do. I grabbed the scissors out of Sepp's hand, closed the door to the bathroom and gave them both a good scolding. Then I set to work.

Sepp, Annette, and I were the first to report to the dinner table for supper. I heard the door open to the study, and a moment later, Major Rager appeared in the doorway to the dining room. He stared at the children while he headed toward his seat.

His hands curled around the back of his chair as he looked directly at me. "I don't recall asking you to take the children to the barber to have their hair cut," he said as an opening salvo.

Sepp was standing patiently behind his chair as was Annette. I kept my eyes on the major. "I didn't take them to the barber," I said.

The major sighed. "Then who cut their hair?"

For a moment, it felt as though I had lived through this scenario before. All of my life I have defaulted to this same position. Every time Uncle Lothar would launch an attack against my siblings, I was there to try to shield them and to take the blame.

I closed my eyes for a second. "I cut their hair."

The major crossed his arms and blinked. "Why did you take it upon yourself to cut their hair today, the day before they are to have their pictures taken?"

I thought briefly about all of the times *Frau* Brandt had complained about me, about the mistakes I have made since I came to work for the major, of the demand the Gestapo have made on me to spy on him, and about the uncomfortable position I was in at that moment. Then I made up my mind to try to protect them.

"It was the only way to fix, to fix the problem."

"To fix what?" he asked impatiently.

"The damage done with *Frau* Brandt's scissors during child's play," I finally blurted out.

Sepp and Annette were standing quite still and their eyes were cast down. I was pleased to see that my scolding had left the proper impression on them. The major seemed to notice this too.

He hesitated a moment as we heard *Frau* Brandt coming down the stairs. "And where were you when this child's play was taking place?"

"At the pharmacy."

I thought I saw in his expression that he was connecting the fact that this happened on his watch, but he didn't have much time to process my answer because *Frau* Brandt came into the dining room with her usual flare. We waited for the major to seat her, and then we set about eating in silence. Nothing else was said on the matter until halfway through the meal when *Frau* Brandt finally noticed that there was something different about the children. A look of dissatisfaction came over her countenance.

"You always take such risks, Kurt," she began. "What a gamble for you to have the children's hair done the day before their pictures. Perhaps you thought I wouldn't notice because I am not feeling well."

"They have a new barber, Helma," said the major cheerfully as he worked on cutting the vegetables on his plate. "And this is the latest style. I do hope you approve."

The major shoved another bite of potatoes into his mouth. I stared at my plate, but I thought I could feel her cold eyes on me.

Frau Brandt sighed as she rested her fork upside down on her plate. "I do not approve, but as there is no reversing the process, I see that you have left me no choice in the matter."

"Do you really dislike their new looks that much, Helma?" asked the major as he took a sip of his drink.

Frau Brandt took a good look at the children before she shrugged. "There is nothing that can be done with Sepp, but your nanny should roll Annette's hair tonight, if she is to have any chance of looking half decent tomorrow."

"I'm sure *Fräulein* Mauer will do everything she can to make sure the children look their very best for the pictures," said the major as he gave me a look of satisfaction. And that, dear journal, was the conclusion of a matter that could have ended very badly for both me and the major.

....

January 14, 1944

Frau Brandt insisted that I accompany her today with the children to get their birthday portraits taken. First, we could not find clothes in their wardrobe that suited her. The children are growing fast, and it seems that there are fewer items that fit them every day. She complained loudly that she sends the major plenty of money and that he ought to be able to buy them some decent clothes.

She fussed with Annette's curls until they were beyond repair, and Sepp was all out of sorts. We finally made it to the photographer's shop on the other side of the Fulda. The photographer began with a lot of patience but ended an hour or so later with little left. I hope for his sake that he has taken at least one photograph that will please *Frau* Brandt. He must have been glad to see us go.

I did my best not to do anything to annoy her, but the whole afternoon was quite a disaster. At least there was no mention of the haircuts today. I am glad to finally be in bed for the evening.

....

January 20, 1944

Today is Thursday, and it is Sepp and Annette's sixth birthday. *Frau* Brandt planned an elaborate party for them after school, and they were both allowed to invite two friends.

Even before the party began, I could tell that *Frau* Hoffmann was losing patience with *Frau* Brandt. Nothing *Frau* Hoffmann did seemed to be good enough for *Frau* Brandt. Although she tried not to show it, *Frau* Hoffmann did not see the necessity for spoiling the children so. She told me that herself. I tried to stay clear of the kitchen and kept to my room until I absolutely had to go downstairs.

For his part, Major Rager mostly stood off to the side and stayed clear of his mother-in-law. I thought I detected a tinge of sadness in between the smiles of amusement. I suppose he must be missing his wife on such an occasion, but it is hard to read his expressions.

After the party was over and *Frau* Hoffmann and the other children had gone, *Frau* Brandt tried to complain to the major about the pictures the photographer had taken. Major Rager picked Annette up into his arms and kissed her on the cheek.

"I'm sure he's done the best he can with the photographs, Helma," he returned after she had gone on for a while.

Frau Brandt slumped back on the couch and sighed loudly. "Am I not to get any sympathy from you, Kurt? What a disappointment this is to me. You know I always make a point to come here for their birthday, because you never see to getting their pictures taken."

The major reached down and brushed what was left of Sepp's hair aside. "It's time for the children to go to bed. Would you like to tuck them in, Helma?"

Frau Brandt let out another big sigh. "Your nanny can see to that, Kurt. It is all I can do to drag myself to bed, after all I have done today."

That was my cue. I got up from my chair quickly, told the children to give their grandmother a good night hug, and then took them upstairs. I think she is going back to Berlin tomorrow morning. It will be nice when everything can return to normal.

<hr />

January 22, 1944

I have had the worst of news today. I can hardly see to write. It has happened as I feared. This morning began as a happy day, after we said good-bye to *Frau* Brandt. The children seemed untouched by her departure, and there seemed to be a lighter spirit in the house.

Everything was white with a light dusting of snow when I got up this morning. Later in the morning, after *Frau* Brandt had gone, the sun came out, and the children wanted to go outside to play in what was left of the snow. I was sitting in a wooden chair on the back porch watching them make all sorts of shapes with their snowballs when the major came out with a letter in his hand.

He had been in his study all morning long, and I guess I figured the letter was his, but then he handed it to me and told me that it had just come for me. I looked at the writing. I recognized my uncle's scribbling. It was addressed to *Herr* Meissel's house but did not have the new postal code "16." Inge must have brought it over, and she didn't even ask to see me.

I put the letter down in my lap for a moment, but when the major stepped down into the yard toward the children, I tore the envelope open. In my heart, I felt that something was wrong. There was really no reason for him to write to me.

Oh, how can I write this? I will just copy word-for-word what he wrote.

> We have heard from our neighbor, Franz, who is also outside of Leningrad, that Reiner is dead. He and another soldier were killed in an explosion during a skirmish. They have buried what few pieces of the bodies were left. Whatever money you are able to send us from your employment is that much more important to us now.

I suppose, at that moment, that I was just in shock to read that my brother was dead, but I was also angered by the heartlessness with which my uncle coupled the news with a reminder that I was to send them money.

I looked up to see the major bringing the children toward the porch.

"It's time for dinner, *Fräulein* Mauer," he said.

I don't remember getting up or going inside. All I remember is sitting down to the table and thinking that Reiner was gone now, that I would never sit and eat another meal with him, that I would never hear his wickedly happy laughter ever again, and that I would never see him grow old.

I tossed my napkin down on the chair and got out of the dining room as quickly as I could. I didn't want anyone to see my tears or my pain.

I don't know how long I lay on my bed, curled up in a ball. I couldn't stop crying. *Frau* Hoffmann knocked on my door, but I didn't respond. She came in anyway and stood there, holding her hands at her waistline.

"The major has sent me to see if you are all right," she said softly, after clearing her throat.

I looked at her for a moment and tried to fight back another wave of tears. She looked at the letter that was lying on the floor beside me, and then she came slowly over and picked it up.

After she read it, she sat down on the edge of the bed. "Who is Reiner, *Fräulein* Mauer?" she asked softly.

I didn't feel like responding.

"Is he your father?" she asked, seeing that I wasn't going to say.

I shook my head.

"Your boyfriend?"

I shook my head more vigorously.

"Your brother?"

I nodded and curled up tighter. *Frau* Hoffmann waited a moment, and then she set the letter down beside me and left the room.

In maybe ten minutes or so, I sat up on the bed and stared out at the bare branches of the tree outside of my window. It felt as if my heart were breaking again. I know this feeling well, but this time, I am alone.

As I was fighting back some more tears, the major knocked on my door. *Frau* Hoffmann must have said something. I was quite surprised to see him. I stood to my feet and wiped the tears from my cheeks.

"I'm sorry, sir," I said. "I didn't mean to interrupt your dinner."

"Please sit down, *Fräulein* Mauer," he said. "You haven't interrupted anything. Will you tell me what has happened?"

I took in a big breath of air, trying to keep the tears from flowing. It was too awful to say out loud.

"My uncle has written me that my brother, Reiner, who was outside of Leningrad is…is dead," I managed to say. "He was just seventeen."

The major stood there very still. I looked out the window. "We were always very close."

"I am very sorry to hear this news, *Fräulein*."

I looked up at him. "He has been buried in Leningrad. I won't even get to say good-bye," I said in a fresh wave of emotion. "I am trying to dry my tears, sir," I finally said. "I don't want to upset the children."

"*Fräulein* Mauer," he said. "You needn't worry about the children, under the circumstances. I will see to them for the remainder of the day. You-you should take some time to rest."

I looked up at him, and then I found the words to thank him. I have been sitting up here in my room ever since. I have nowhere to go, and there is no one to comfort me. How much more will Klaus, Lenz, and Liese be grieving? And I am not there to comfort them. The thought of that is almost worse than the pain I feel.

I remember when I first got to Kassel. It seemed that everyone was in mourning. There weren't many people who had not lost family members, neighbors, or friends in the October bombing. Now the sorrow of loss has fallen over me like a cold blanket of snow.

January 25, 1944

The sting of the news about Reiner has given way to a dull disbelief on my part. There seems to be no remedy but to carry on, to live with what is left of your heart once the one you love is gone. As you will see, life does go on.

Since *Frau* Brandt's latest visit and Reiner's death, *Frau* Hoffmann has been unusually friendly to me. I found out that she lives with her sister on the east side of town in the village of Oberkaufungen, and she confided in me that her sister is very ill. I can see that her sister's illness is weighing heavy on her mind. She also mentioned to me in conversation that she has worked for the major as his housekeeper for over ten years now.

As for the children, I have been giving them music lessons after school for almost three weeks, not counting the week *Frau* Brandt was here. They were both excited to learn something new, at first. Now they are both giving me a hard time when I ask them to practice. Sepp actually has a really nice touch on the violin. Annette just plays with the keys on the piano. I am determined to keep them practicing, if only to give them something constructive to do with their time.

My first surprise of the day came while I was running an errand for *Frau* Hoffmann this afternoon. I happened to come upon Lieutenant Braun as he was waiting for a friend outside the café on Kaiserstrasse. He spoke to me first and asked me if I had done something different to my hair because he said it looked very pretty in the sunlight. We talked for a few minutes, and then he asked if he could buy me a cup of coffee as his friend had not shown up.

Lieutenant Braun seated me at a table inside and then proceeded to order us both a cup of coffee and a pastry. This time, he did not ask me to tell him any secrets. We just sat there and talked back and forth for over half an hour. He was pleasant and polite. All too soon, he said he had to go, but not before I thanked him.

Uncle Lothar never allowed me to go out with anyone. I did not say anything to Lieutenant Braun, but I was wondering the whole time if this counted as a first date. It sure did feel like I always imagined a date would be.

The second surprise of the day came after supper this evening. The major told me that his mother-in-law had invited us all up to Berlin for some occasion of hers the third week of February. I tried not to let the displeasure I felt show on my face. The last thing I feel that I can endure is to see the major's mother-in-law again so soon.

To my relief, the major seemed to have no intention of taking her up on her offer. He told me that he had decided instead to take the children to Garmish that week. Then he asked me if I would be willing to accompany him and the children on their trip. He explained that he would like to take Sepp skiing but would not be able to do so unless I was along to see to Annette.

So, it seems that everything is settled. This is a very generous offer for the major to make, and I am very excited at the prospect of going to Garmish. I can only imagine how fun it will be for the children. For me, it will be a chance to get away from Kassel and a respite from having to go to the cellar so often when the air raid siren goes off. I wish we were going tomorrow.

February 1944

February 1, 1944

This whole, horrible day was cold from the very beginning. I got the children up, fed them, bundled them up, and then took them off to school. When I got back to the house, *Frau* Hoffmann asked me if I would run a couple of errands for her. She said that the major had given her the morning off to go with her sister to the doctor's office.

Frau Hoffmann gave me a list of groceries and a handful of food stamps. Then she gave me detailed instructions on where to go. I told her I was glad to help and set off on the errands. It took me over two hours to get most of the items on the list. The shops were crowded. By the time I got to the front of some of the long lines, the storekeepers were out of the items we needed for the day. I think that is why *Frau* Hoffmann is always in such a hurry in the morning.

When I came in the kitchen door, I nearly dropped the bag of groceries on the floor. I was busy thinking about how upset *Frau* Hoffmann would be with me that I was too late getting to the market to get her any flour. After I put the groceries away, I went upstairs to gather up the dirty linen from the bedrooms.

It was almost eleven o'clock when I dropped the final load of linen onto the pile by the laundry sink. I hadn't quite shut the door to the basement because I didn't have a free hand on the way down, but at that moment, I was certain I heard a faint knocking sound upstairs.

I climbed the stairs as quickly as I could, but by the time I got to the top of the stairs, I heard the major greeting someone at the front door.

What was the major doing home at this hour? The formal manner in which he addressed the person at the front door caught my attention. Every part of my body froze in place.

For the next fifteen minutes, I was stuck there on the stairs to the basement, like a statue. For the next fifteen minutes, I listened to a conversation that I was certain I was not meant to hear.

The major invited his guests in, and through the crack in the basement door, I could see two men. The one with the dark hair and wearing the most distinguished uniform made it clear to the major that he could only stay a minute. I could not see his face as he stood with his back to the basement door. The man with the dark hair then dismissed his companion and sent him back out to the car. After the front door closed with a thud, the major invited the remaining guest into the living room.

"Really, I cannot stay but a moment," the man said nervously.

"Then I'll be brief, *Herr* Colonel," began the major, drawing his right arm behind his back. I stepped down a stair and away from the basement door. It seemed like the major was looking directly at me. Despite my distance from them, their words were as clear as if I were standing right next to them.

"The answer to your confidential inquiry is yes. I believe it is possible for us, with some modifications to the Fieseler assembly plant, to set up a facility to manufacture the jet engines for the Messerschmitt 262 here in Kassel; although I do not understand why you would choose Kassel for such an important project as this."

The major's guest paused before he spoke. "Do you have any hesitation to take on such a project, *Herr* Major?"

"None, *Herr* Colonel. With the proper equipment and supplies, we could have the factory up and running in, perhaps, three weeks or less. However, as I am sure Lieutenant General Galland is already aware, Kassel may not be the most advantageous place for such a plant. We are already an Allied high priority target with our *Schnellbomber* and tank factories. I can think of half a dozen other locations with a much lower profile to place such a project."

"Yes, for certain," replied the major's guest. "There are better locations. But the preference of the high command is to have you in charge of the production. You have been highly recommended to us. Your reputation for efficiency and results are unmatched by your counterparts."

There was a slight pause and then the major spoke. "If it is determined that Kassel is the best location for the project, *Herr* Colonel, we will proceed without delay. I understand that the engine on the ME 262 may well win us the war, and I will do whatever I can to make it happen."

While the major was speaking, I breathed in slowly and tried to shift on my feet without making any noise. I wanted to go back to the kitchen. I wanted to go up to my room. I wanted to be anywhere other than on the basement stairs listening to that conversation, but I was stuck fast. At last, I sat slowly and quietly on the third step down and buried my head in my arms.

The mysterious guest laughed heartily. "You are as accommodating as your good reputation, *Herr* Major. And I am glad that you understand the importance of this project."

The man paused a moment, and I leaned back toward the door. Then I heard the man again, almost in a whisper. "Major Rager, this must remain between you and me, but the Lieutenant General has ordered this project forward without the specific knowledge of the *Führer*. My task is simply to find a suitable location for the manufacture of the engines. I hear what you are saying and will report back to them your analysis of the situation. Perhaps, after all, they will decide that it would be best to headquarter this project in Neuberg."

I heard a heavy sigh, and then the guest continued. "I have heard that you are a good man. If they should decide to transfer the project to Kassel, you must take extreme care with your reports. It is becoming increasingly difficult to accomplish what we must in order to give the *Führer* what he demands. Sometimes, it is necessary to do so in this manner. We do no disservice to the *Führer,* and I would not leave you thinking so, but we are counting on your discretion. Do I have your word, sir?"

"I will keep your confidence, *Herr* Colonel," the major replied. "And I will follow the orders I am given, but you should know that I will give a full and honest report to the *Führer* or his staff, if I am called upon to do so. You and your committee must plan accordingly, but you may always count on me to do what is best for the Fatherland. *Heil* Hitler."

"*Heil* Hitler!" returned the mysterious man. "I will let you know the final decision."

I heard some measured steps in the hallway, and then I heard the front door open and shut. I rose to my feet and turned to climb the two remaining steps to go out to the hall just as the major pushed open the door to the basement, startling me.

He looked down on me with disappointment. "What are you doing here?"

I turned a bit on the stairs. "I-I just took the bedding down to the laundry room for *Frau* Hoffmann."

He clenched his jaw. "You were eavesdropping on me."

My eyes grew big, and I lost my voice for a moment. "I-no sir."

"I hope not, *Fräulein*, because that is exactly the kind of thing that can only get you into trouble."

On the way out of the house to pick up the children, my mind was replaying the major's words to me, over and over again.

I was swinging. I swung from thinking that I had caught him doing something wrong, to wondering if his warning to me was kindly meant.

With these fretful thoughts in tow, I crossed the street and started down the second block. A black Mercedes pulled up alongside me and slowed to my pace. When I finally looked over, I saw one of the Gestapo men from the party in the front passenger seat. My heart, which was already low, sunk to an even lower state.

The driver pulled the car over, and the short Gestapo man got out. He tipped his hat to me in greeting, opened the back door, and told me to get in.

When I hesitated, he forced a smile. "We'll give you a ride over to the school."

I really had no choice. They had warned me that they would be in touch, and now, I was going to be questioned. The dread rose into my throat, and I let out a slight cough as I climbed into the back seat.

"Good afternoon, *Fräulein* Mauer," said *Herr* Knappe, the tall one with the deep voice, as he pulled away from the curb. I met his eyes in the rear view mirror. "How are you getting along at the Rager residence?" he inquired.

"Very well, sir," I replied with an unsteady voice.

"Have you anything to report?" asked *Herr* Löning as he turned toward me and threw his left arm on the top of his seat.

I took in a quick breath and narrowed my eyes. "Only that the major speaks with *Fräulein* Farber nearly every evening. Well, she does do most of the talking," I said nervously.

The two men looked at each other. They were clearly not interested in hearing the gossip.

"We would like you to tell us anything you can about the visit that was paid to Major Rager this morning," said the tall one, without any formality and without a smile.

I shifted my gaze to *Herr* Löning. I was having a hard time processing the thought that they knew he had received a guest this morning and were now asking me about it. *Had they been watching the house?* I was prepared to tell them all about *Fräulein* Farber's calls, but I didn't expect this.

I didn't expect it, and I needed to make up my mind quickly. Was I going to keep my word and keep his confidence, or was I going to tell them everything I heard just to keep myself out of trouble with the Gestapo?

"I-I...what?" I stammered, looking back to the tall man.

"The major had a visitor this morning in his home?" asked *Herr* Knappe.

"Yes," I said.

"What can you tell us about it? Who was present and what was said?"

I looked out the window as we turned onto the street where the schoolhouse was. I didn't really want to say anything to the Gestapo men. I shrugged. "All I know is that he had a guest this morning. I don't know who he was."

"Did you overhear any of their conversation?" asked *Herr* Löning, leaning toward me.

"I was in the basement, seeing to some of the household chores," I replied, trying to hold my voice steady. I didn't want them to see how frightened I was, or how angry I felt that they were prying into the major's affairs.

"You must have heard some of their conversation."

"I can't remember anything specific," I replied curtly. "I am a nanny. I look after his children. I am not meant to hear his conversations."

The driver pulled the car over to the curb and parked across the street from the schoolhouse. He set the parking break, and then he turned to face me. For five or six more minutes, *Herr* Knappe threatened and tried to get me to tell him more. The shorter one with the wire rimmed glasses never said a word. He just stared at me with his piercing eyes.

"We are wasting our time, Willi," spoke *Herr* Löning at last with a twitch of his nose. "It is clear that the major does not conduct his affairs carelessly. He has obviously taken steps to ensure that she does not hear or see anything that is inappropriate for someone in her position. Am I correct in this, *Fräulein* Mauer?"

"Yes," I replied with relief.

"Which means that you are going to have to go out of your way to gain the information that we are seeking," stated *Herr* Löning craftily.

My countenance fell. The tall man cocked his head at an angle. "It is your duty, *Fräulein*. If you don't want to get into any trouble, you need to think about that the next time you turn a blind eye to his business. We must all keep our eyes and ears open."

I pressed my tongue onto the roof of my mouth, hoping desperately that they would see no resistance in my eyes. At that moment, children began to exit the school, and I prayed that they would soon release me.

"I must not keep the children waiting in the cold," I said as I searched for any sign of Sepp or Annette.

"Yes, of course," *Herr* Löning said. He scrambled out of the car and opened the back door for me. "Until next time?" he said after he rolled his thin lips in toward his mouth.

For a moment, I was afraid that *Herr* Löning could see straight into my heart, but then he stepped aside and I was free to go. Without another word, I crossed the street and went as fast as I could toward the children. I drew in a couple of gulps of cold air, and the sick feeling in my stomach slowly subsided.

I got away with telling the Gestapo nothing this time. I hope it will be a very long time before I meet them again, and that next time, I will have even less to say, because I am not going to overhear any more conversations. I wonder if this whole thing was a test from the major, to see if I can keep a secret.

February 3, 1944

If I am going to tell you everything that has happened today, dear journal, I am going to have to find a better hiding place for you where no one can ever find you.

I have been in this house for two months now. I have had to endure the criticism of the major's mother-in-law, demands from the Gestapo for information about the major's affairs, and expectations from the major that I have not always fulfilled. Despite the discomfort that all of this has caused me, I am beginning to see why he so naturally commands the respect and loyalty of everyone who knows him.

I waited in dread all day yesterday and then this morning, for the major to speak to me, but he didn't say a word. It was quite unnerving to me to find him outside his study door, waiting for me to come home with the children this afternoon. He isn't usually home at that hour. If it were possible, I think that the harsh look that he gave me was worse than the look he gave me on Tuesday. He asked the children to go directly to the nursery, and he demanded that I follow him into his study. I knew right away that this was it. He was going to dismiss me.

After I took a seat, he came directly in front of me and sat down on the edge of his desk facing me. He was frightfully close to me. Then he took in a deep breath.

"*Fräulein* Mauer," he began. "Or whoever you are," he said under his breath. "I am in a very precarious position at the moment. Your security clearance papers got lost somewhere, but finally made it to Berlin last week. Now Berlin has a slight problem with your identification. It seems that you do not exist in their copious records."

At hearing his words, my heart dropped to the floor, and I found it a little hard to breathe. The major had vouched for my identification, and they had failed to find me at all in their system. At first, I had thought that this would not matter, but, in that moment, I saw what a problem it was. My head started to spin as I looked up into his face. I could see that he was trying not to lose his temper.

"Before I have to turn you over to the SS," he continued crossing his arms, "I would like for you to tell me who you really are."

I let out a little gasp and looked away from his piercing eyes.

"*Fräulein?*" he said, leaning forward in an attempt to regain eye contact. I looked up at him, but my mind was jammed with so many thoughts at once that I could not speak. *Could I possibly run from the room and out of the house without him catching me?*

"*Fräulein,*" he said again. "You have put me in a most uncomfortable position. It does not sit well with the top ranking officials of the Third *Reich* to have an unknown entity with such free access to their war production minister's personal and corporate affairs. And it does not sit well with me. You have betrayed my trust and my confidence."

I looked up quickly. "I have not betrayed your trust or your confidence."

The major's voice rose gradually as he spoke. "How can you say that you have not betrayed my trust when I have been supposing all along that you are who you said you were, when you are not?"

When I read the disappointment on his face and thought of the trouble I had put him in, my eyes began to tear. I bit my tongue to try to keep from crying. All I could think was that this was not the time for me to lose my composure. I don't know why, but I tried to get up out of my seat.

"Sit down!" commanded the major. The force of his voice frightened me, and I complied immediately. "You're not going anywhere until you tell me your real name."

He began again, this time a little gentler. "Are you an informant? Have you been eavesdropping on all of my conversations?"

I looked him straight in the eyes, having no idea what to say. The accusations that he was throwing at me were completely false, but there was no way for me to prove that to him. He began to pace the floor in front of me. "Who do you answer to? Who are you working for?"

"I don't understand," I said in a small voice. "You are my employer. I did not apply for this job; you offered it to me."

"Yes, that is true," he said, calming himself. "If you were an informant, your name would have checked with no issue." Major Rager narrowed his eyes. "Let's start with your papers." He extended his arm toward me.

I looked up into his critical eyes. They were no match for me, and I had to look away quickly. He had chosen the one point on which I was truly guilty. It was no use wondering how it had gotten to this point. I walked straight into this, hoping I could hide right under the nose of the authorities. Now I was going to have to face the consequences of my foolishness and so would my family.

"Klara Dietrich," I said, my voice shaking. "I am Klara Dietrich."

He was unmoved by my revelation. "Your papers. Hand them over."

"They're in my coat pocket," I half whispered. He waved his hand toward the study door, giving me permission to go get them. I stumbled out into the hall and retrieved the identification papers from my coat.

"My uncle made me promise that I would use my mother's maiden name instead of my own when I left Sinsheim," I said lamely as I handed him my papers. He took them from my hand without looking at me. I sat back down in the chair and looked up at the major to see if his expression had softened at all. It had not. I closed my eyes for a moment. The truth is painful.

"I suppose next you are going to tell me that you are related in some way to Vice-Chancellor Dietrich of Berlin," said the major with sarcasm in his voice.

My eyes flew to his. He must have seen the surprise in my face. I was almost counting on the fact that he wouldn't know who my father was. I nodded slowly. "I am."

The major was visibly surprised. "He is your uncle?"

"He is my father," I said, correcting him. "Hermann Dietrich was my father."

"Hermann Dietrich," the major said as he took a second look at my papers. "Did I remember his position correctly?"

"He was the vice-chancellor and minister of finance," I said numbly.

"Hermann Dietrich of Brüning's cabinet? Then your father was, at one time, second in line to president. I'm trying to remember," he said, scratching the back of his head. "That was almost ten years ago. Vice-Chancellor Dietrich ran in conservative circles and was an outspoken critic of the *Führer*, as was Edgar Jung. They were both implicated in the anti-National Socialist coup, and your father was...."

The major's voice trailed off as a ghostly look painted his expression. "What do you know about what happened to your father, *Fräulein* Dietrich?" he asked in a way that led me to believe he already knew.

I looked up at his blue eyes before I responded. He didn't know how hard it was for me to answer his question. For almost ten years, I have tried to forget what happened. Sometimes, I go for days without thinking about it. Lately, I have gone for weeks. But from that awful day on, I have had the responsibility of my siblings, and that in and of itself is a terrible reminder. I have thought about it less often since I came to Kassel, but all of the old feelings, deep inside, came back when I saw the SS men at the ceremony.

I cleared my throat, and then looked out the window at the trees in the garden. I have never spoken of this to anyone. It has always been a forbidden topic, and one which would spell doom to my family should anyone ever find out. I looked back at the major in agony, but he was waiting for my explanation.

"The SS came for him in the night. Someone telephoned my parents to warn them they were coming. My father sent us out the back to the neighbor's house with our nanny. They took my mother too, and I am sure they would have taken us if they had found us there."

I stopped to swallow my tears. "They took them both away, and we never saw them again. Sometime in the night, they shot them in the head. In the morning, they dumped their bodies in the street. We couldn't even come out of hiding to bury them."

I saw the major's face flush. He swallowed hard, then he rose to his feet and walked a few steps away from the desk. "And you've been running ever since," he finally said, with his back turned to me.

I sniffed back a tear. "Fantastic," he said quietly to himself. "You have employed the daughter of an enemy of the *Führer*." The major turned back to me with renewed composure. "What else have you lied to me about, *Fräulein* Dietrich?"

I must have given him a blank stare. He repeated his question.

"Before God, *Herr* Major," I responded quickly, "except for my surname, I have been honest with you."

The major's expression seemed unchanged. He lowered his eyebrows. "What other secrets are you keeping from me, *Fräulein* Dietrich?"

I swallowed hard. "I am not keeping any secrets from you. I have four siblings. We have been living with my aunt and uncle in Sinsheim. Actually, they are my great aunt and uncle, my mother's aunt and uncle. They were kind enough to take us in after—when we had nowhere else to go. He is the one who sent me here to find work."

After I told him that, I wished that I hadn't. I didn't want to get Aunt Frieda in any trouble. The major did not seem moved by my response. There was a long period of silence, and when I looked at the major to try to read his expression, I met his inquisitive eyes.

"I can only think of one thing I have not told you about. The Gestapo picked me up Tuesday afternoon and questioned me about your meeting that morning, but I didn't tell them anything. I told them I didn't know anything about your conversation."

I watched him make his way across the floor and sit down in the chair behind the desk. He leaned back in his chair, and then he folded his hands together. He was still looking at me, but I could see that his mind was busy at work. I couldn't tell what was on his mind, and that only made me fear for the worse. He had said he was going to turn me over to the SS.

At last he spoke. "I'd like to be alone, *Fräulein* Dietrich," he said quietly, not looking at me. I got up from the chair, and although it felt like my shoes were full of cement, I somehow made it out of the study. I closed the doors behind me without a sound.

My next thoughts were only to pack my bag as quickly as I could and to leave. *But where would I go?* He would find me if I went back to the Meissels. *Did I have enough money to get a train ticket back to Sinsheim?*

I sprinted up the stairs to my room and pulled out my bag. It took me less than five minutes to pack up my clothes and you, dear journal. In my rush, I forgot my violin and had to go back for it. By the time I made it to the top of the stairs again, I could hear *Frau* Hoffmann standing at the study door telling the major that supper was ready.

Then, from behind me, I heard a little voice. "Where are you going, *Fräulein* Mauer?"

I snapped my head around and met Annette's bright eyes. My heart sank again. I needed to leave without being detected. "Um, no where. I think it's time for supper, Annette."

I went quickly back to my room and shoved my bag and the violin behind the door. We waited several minutes at the table for the major. *Frau* Hoffmann said that he was talking to someone on the phone in the study. Finally, he came and sat down at the table. The major did not look at me or say anything at all during the meal. Just as we were finishing eating, the telephone rang, and *Frau* Hoffmann announced that the major had another call.

I tried to entertain the children, as I always did after supper, in order to keep them from bothering the major too much, but it was really hard to smile and to put up with their childishness with such an urgency that I felt to leave. When I looked at the children, it only made me sad, thinking that I was about to leave them.

I kept looking at the clock. The major was in his study all evening. I knew that I did not want to stick around to find out what he was going to do with me. Finally, I tucked the children into bed, gave them one last sip of water each, and then I closed their bedroom doors. I slipped on my coat, picked up my bag and violin, and went as quietly as I could to the stairs.

When I got to the first floor, I looked down at the study doors and was glad to see them still shut. However, when I got halfway down the stairs, I saw the major leaning against the doorway to the living room with his arms crossed over his chest and a disappointed look on his face.

I was caught, and I didn't know what to do. My arms and legs seemed to be frozen. The major came over to the staircase, all the while keeping his eyes on me. He mounted the first four stairs and then stood there on the landing with one hand on the banister, not more than a step away from me. I tried to erase the guilty expression from my face.

"*Fräulein* Dietrich," he began after a moment, clearing his throat. "I don't know where you are going to go," he said with a shrug, "but I am not going to prevent you from leaving if that is what you think you must do."

The major was speaking to me in such a gentle way, and his expression seemed sincere enough, but I did not expect to hear these words from him.

"The children are very fond of you, and I don't know where I will find a replacement for you. I think that I can arrange for the 'mistake' on your identification papers to be fixed so that the SS will be satisfied. That will be easier for me than trying to find another nanny. I don't know that you will find this offer of help anywhere else you might go," he added slyly.

This was really a most difficult moment. He was so persuasive with his words that I was confused whether I should go or stay. I had expected him to turn me over to the SS instead of giving me such a choice.

"After what you have been through, I cannot blame you for the distrust I see on your face, but I will give you some good advice. Not every officer of the Third *Reich* is as the SS are. Do not make the mistake of throwing away the baby with the bathwater."

The major paused and looked at me. I was trying hard to decide what to do. I have always had this difficulty. In my mind, everyone associated with the National Socialist German Workers' Party is responsible for the death of my parents. But in that moment, the kindness the major was showing me, the graciousness, began to eat away at my distrust. I felt sure that if he were as evil as the men who killed my parents, he would not now be offering me protection from them. And that is what he was offering me.

I tore my eyes from his, turned around slowly with my suitcase, and took a few steps back up the stairs.

The major called to me again using my assumed name. "*Fräulein* Mauer?"

I stopped and turned around slowly. This was going to be the part where he would tell me the price I was going to have to pay to silence him about my real identity.

"You owe me nothing for this, but for your own sake and mine, you should never speak of this to anyone." The major was looking at me with his inquisitive eyes, waiting for a response from me. I was still having a hard time processing the consideration he was showing me.

I nodded. "Of course," I said hoarsely, and then I thanked him.

I have been sitting here in my room, trying to dry my tears and put away the old memories. I can still feel that July evening. I can hear father's voice in the urgency of the moment. I can see the look in mother's eyes as we hurried down the stairs. I feel Liese in my arms as we went hastily out the garden door. I remember the pale look on the nanny's face when we were safely in the neighbor's basement. I was only ten, but I knew that my world was about to change.

Reiner was certain that we would go home in the morning, but we never went home again. I can still hear Liese crying. She was only six months old. I held her in my arms for the next six months as we were shuffled from relative to relative. No one wanted us. I think they were afraid of the SS. And we were afraid.

Suddenly, there were no more violin lessons, no more well-bred teachers or loving nannies to care for us. There were no more hugs from mother and no instruction from father. All we had was each other and the hope that no one would ever find out who we were.

I don't think the major has any idea what he has offered me tonight—the chance to stop running.

February 10, 1944

Tuesday evening, we spent at least an hour in the cold basement until the long, steady wail of the siren telling us it was all clear. While we were sitting there, I was suddenly seized with the fear that he was going to turn me in to the authorities. All I could see in my mind was the Gestapo showing up at Aunt Frieda's house and dragging my brothers and sister away to some horrible place.

If I am employed by the war production minister for all of Hessen, then I can see now the kind of trouble I might have caused for him. All of the conversations he has with others, all of the communications that have been coming to the house, the documents in his briefcase and papers in his study—they must all be highly confidential. He wouldn't have received that medal of commendation if he were not an important part of what is happening in this city and thus in Germany. I have felt a strange weight on me all week long with these thoughts.

These thoughts haunted me until late yesterday. After *Frau* Hoffmann left for the evening, the major burned my old identification papers in the fireplace in his study and handed me my new papers. He must think that I am not grateful, because I didn't say anything. How can I put the gratitude I feel for what he has done for me into words?

....

February 13, 1944

Dear Journal,

I am writing to you today from Garmish. Annette is sleeping soundly beside me, so I will try not to disturb her. This morning, I woke the children early. *Frau* Hoffmann made us a hearty breakfast. The major took our bags to the car, and then there was a mad scramble to make sure I had everything the children would need for the week.

We left Kassel before nine o'clock. I rode in the back seat with the children on either side of me. They were so excited that it took them a whole hour before they finally settled down. I brought paper and pencils and a few toys to try to keep them occupied. And I remembered to bring the most important item of all—Annette's doll, Otti.

Halfway to Garmish, the children fell asleep. Annette went out soon after she laid her head in my lap. Sepp followed by leaning his heavy head on my left arm. The major looked back at me and smiled at my predicament. I was sandwiched between the sleeping children for at least an hour.

"Have you ever been to Garmish, *Fräulein?*" he asked me.

"No, sir," I replied.

"Ah, then, you are in for a treat," he said. "My father used to take my brother and me there every year to ski. I always looked forward to going."

"Are your parents still alive?" I asked.

"Yes," he responded abruptly.

His response was followed by a long pause. I wondered if he were going to say anything further, but he didn't. I wanted to ask him more, but I didn't want to appear too forward. "Where do they live?" I asked before I could stop myself.

The major took his eyes off of the road for just a second to give me a curious look. "They are living in America," he said with a strange waver in his voice.

I sat still through another long pause. As soon as I decided not to ask any more questions, the major spoke up again.

"My father and I had a parting of ideas around the time that I was at the university in Berlin. That is also when I met my wife, Ida, and she introduced me to the National Socialist German Workers' Party. Her mother has been involved in the movement from its beginning in Munich.

"My parents were probably more along the political lines of your parents. I think they saw the handwriting on the wall in

1937. They left me the house we live in, my father handed over his shares and his position in Henschel to me, and they emigrated with my brother, Rupert, to Sweden first and then to the United States. Of course, with such strong disagreement and now with the war, I have had no contact with them."

I bit my lip to try to keep the surprise from showing on my face. He had told me this with sadness and regret in his voice. I didn't know what to say in return. To my relief, he finally spoke again.

"Tell me about your siblings, *Fräulein*."

I tried to stretch my right leg under Annette's head without waking her. "Klaus is thirteen," I began. "He will be fourteen in June. He is a troublemaker, but he is very thin-skinned. He has always been the most sensitive of my brothers. I have often found it difficult to dislike him even though he does cause trouble.

"Reiner was the most like father—very kind and considerate and gentlemanly. I think Lenz will be very much like that also when he matures. He has my father's talent for arithmetic.

"And Liese is a little like Annette except that she is shy. She was a happy baby, despite all of the turmoil, and she has a contented, easy personality."

I stopped suddenly, realizing that I was talking too freely. Even from the side, I saw a smile creeping up the major's face. "You see them through the kind eyes of a mother," he said, and then he glanced back at me. "That is probably why the children are so fond of you."

I looked down at Annette and brushed a strand of hair away from her sleeping eyes. I wasn't sure how to respond to his comment.

"You may never have been a nanny, but you are much better with the children than anyone I have ever had working for me," he said openly. "I thought that I would need to give you more guidance, but I have found that you need hardly any at all."

When he said those kind words to me, I was surprised and happy at the same time. So many days I have wondered what he thinks of me and how I am doing with the children. He has said so little to me, I wondered if he even noticed.

"You're going to be tired when we get to Garmish, with all of the driving," I said nervously into the silence.

"Actually, I find driving relaxing," he said.

I reached over and played with a lock of Annette's dark hair. Then I looked up at the back of the major's head. He has very light brown hair. It is almost blonde, and he has very blue eyes. The children have darker hair and brown eyes. I tried to picture their mother. I couldn't ask the major what she looked like, but I was sure that she must have been thin and beautiful with dark hair and dark eyes.

Sepp woke up first. He told his father immediately that he was hungry. We had at least an hour more to travel when Annette woke up. Sepp decided that he wanted to crawl into the front seat to sit by his father. On the way into the front seat, he kicked his sister in the ear, and she began to scream.

The major told him to apologize to Annette, and he finally did. I held her and rocked her gently, trying to calm her down. It was a long while before her tears subsided. I wanted to tell the major that I was hungry too, but soon enough, we arrived at the Hotel Sonnenbichl in Garmish.

The Hotel Sonnenbichl was just as I had pictured it in my mind. It is several stories tall and is a grand building set against a hill facing the south. The children were eager to get out of the car as we drove up to the door at the back of the hotel. A porter came out right away to help us with the luggage.

"Major Rager, welcome back," I heard the man at the front desk say to him as we entered the lobby. I watched the major sign the guest book, and then he motioned for me to come over to the desk. "They would like you to sign in too, *Fräulein* Mauer," he said, offering me the pen.

"I'll need to see your identification, *Fräulein*," said the man behind the desk, and then he shrugged. "They want us to check everyone," he added apologetically.

I pulled the new papers Major Rager had gotten for me out of my purse and handed them to the man. I wanted to look up at the major, but I did not. The man at the desk handed them back to me and took the pen from my hand.

"You will be in suite 400." The man behind the desk handed the major the keys to the room. "Oh, and there are two messages for you, *Herr* Major."

I turned around to collect the children. The porter followed us with our luggage into the lift, and we were soon on the fourth floor. The children liked riding on the lift. When I walked into the suite I could hardly believe that this was where we were staying. It was like a room in a palace. I went immediately over to the window and stared out at the snow-covered Alps. I don't think I have ever seen a more beautiful sight.

When I turned around, the major was giving a tip to the porter. As the porter closed the door, the major turned his attention to the two messages. Then he looked up at me.

"I thought you and Annette could have that room. Sepp and I will take this one," he said, pointing to his right.

I nodded and went over to pick up Annette's suitcase.

"I need to make a phone call first, and then we should see if we can find something to eat."

"Yes," Sepp shouted, "I'm starving!"

"Me too," Annette chimed in.

"Why don't we go unpack, children?" I said, shooing them into the girls' room.

The room the major has given us is the nicest room of the two. It has a double, four-posted bed with a fancy wood carved headboard. The wallpaper is a combination of stripes on the lower half and a fleur-de-lys pattern on the top in a pale yellow. There is a beautiful dresser opposite the bed and two very large windows covered by some pale, blue drapes. The view is the same as out in the sitting area.

When the children had seen enough of the girls' room, they ran across to the other room. The major's room has two double beds and is decorated with green wallpaper. I left their room momentarily to bring Sepp's bag in from the sitting room, and then I went back for the major's luggage.

The major was just getting off the phone when the children discovered the balcony off of the sitting room area. The major stood for a moment with his hand on the receiver. He ran his hand along the back of his neck, and then he looked up.

"Let me get that," he said quickly as I bent down to pick up his baggage. "It's heavy." Major Rager took the bag from me, brushing my hand with his in the process.

"Come children," he said, as he disappeared into the other room. "Let's get something to eat."

There is a small restaurant situated on the first floor of the lobby beyond the check-in desk. We had snitzel and noodles with vegetables for dinner. There was so much food on my plate that Reiner and I could have shared the portion. The Third *Reich* certainly does feed her officers well.

The major took the children for a long walk after dinner. He told me I was welcome to come along or take a little rest. I have such a hard time determining whether he would prefer me to go along to help with the children or to stay, but I chose to go back to the room alone.

I stood for a while out on the balcony off of the sitting room just taking in the beautiful scenery. The air was cold and crisp. The sky was a bold blue, and there were a couple of white clouds hanging over the tips of the Alps. I took a deep breath and let it out slowly.

Compared to everything that is going on all around me, the scenery in front of me was calming and serene. I thought about what the major had told me in the car about his family, and I wondered what kind of convictions he must have if he chose to stay in Germany and join the National Socialist Party instead of leaving with his family.

My thoughts turned to mother and father, and I wondered if they had ever considered leaving Germany. Our lives would have been so different if they had.

I watched the sun painting a beautiful picture in the sky and on the mountaintops as it was slipping to the other side of the world. I closed my eyes. The fear and despair of spending hours in the basement at nights during bombing raids began to slip slowly from my mind. I finally got so cold that I came back inside, and soon, they returned from their walk.

The major has been out in the sitting area all evening reading his papers and writing. After the children went to bed, I heard him speaking with someone on the telephone. It sounded like someone on the other end of the line was concerned about the production quota.

I know that the major wants to get up early and go skiing with Sepp, so I am going to put you aside and go to sleep now.

....

February 14, 1944

The major sent Sepp in to wake us up this morning. He launched himself onto our bed and landed on me. I was glad he didn't land on Annette. I got Annette dressed, and then I threw on a dress and headed out to the sitting room. The major said good morning to me, and then he gave me a funny look. I reached up and felt my braid. I hadn't taken the time to fix my hair.

I found Sepp's clothes in various locations next to his suitcase. He had obviously attempted to find his own clothes to wear. Since he was going skiing, I put one layer on him and set two other layers aside for after breakfast.

The major sat reading the newspaper until we were ready to go down to breakfast. Annette was slow at finishing her food. The major and Sepp went back to the room so the major could change and so that Sepp could put on more layers of clothes. They returned fifteen minutes later and handed me the keys to the room.

The major looks like a different man out of his uniform. Sepp was really excited, and he skipped out of the restaurant following the major.

Annette and I spent the entire morning trying to amuse ourselves in the hotel. She doesn't understand why boys get to do all the fun things while girls have to sit around doing nothing. I told her that is exactly how I always felt when father would take Reiner away on some adventure.

After eating some dinner, Annette and I went back to the room, and I tried to interest her in the needlepoint I had brought along. To her credit, she did try it, but I think she is still too young to take any interest. I really need to find a simpler project for her to start on.

Eventually, Annette went to the bedroom, found Otti, and played with her for a while. Then she actually lay down on the bed and slept for a good hour. I took a few minutes this afternoon to write to Aunt Frieda. I think she will be surprised to hear that I am in Garmish.

It was about four o'clock when the major and Sepp returned from skiing. We ate dinner in the restaurant early, but Sepp was almost falling asleep at the table. Annette, however, was wide-awake and told her father every little detail from her day.

Sepp went down to bed early. After I put Annette to bed, I picked up the book I had borrowed from the major's library and went and sat next to the balcony door in the sitting room. The major was sitting across the room doing some calculating in his ledgers.

I must have read for about an hour, and then I looked over at the major. I hesitated a moment, and then I got up and put the book down in my seat.

"Would you care for a cup of tea?" I asked at last.

The major looked up at me. "That would be very nice," he said, drawing out the last two words. Then he looked back down at his ledger.

I took the lift down to the restaurant. Twenty minutes later, I came back with a tray of tea. The major thanked me when I handed him a cup, and he gave me a peculiar look. I found it hard to concentrate on reading my book after that, so I decided to turn in early and write in you, dear journal. Today was such a long day. I hope tomorrow will go by faster.

···

February 15, 1944

Dear Journal,

Today was a lot like yesterday, except for the evening. The major went skiing with Sepp in the morning, but after dinner, he went into town with Annette and left Sepp with me.

After they left for town, Sepp and I went for a hike up the mountain behind the hotel. He had no trouble climbing up the steep path, but I had difficulty keeping up with him. I wasn't wearing the proper shoes for walking in the snow. There was a beautiful view of the Alps at the top. On the way down, the clouds began to cover the sun and that was the end of the sunshine for the day.

Sepp was playing with his toy soldiers on the floor of the sitting room, and I was working on my needlepoint when the major and Annette returned from town. By the smile on her face and the redness in her cheeks, I could see how much she enjoyed the afternoon with her father.

Halfway through dinner, a colonel came over to our table and introduced himself to Major Rager. Major Rager, in turn, introduced me and the children. The colonel asked the major where he was posted. The major responded, "Kassel."

"You serve under the armament's minister?" asked the colonel quite loudly.

"Yes," replied the major softly.

"I hear that our new heavy tank is well into production," continued the colonel. "How many have we rolled out so far?"

I watched as the major shifted uncomfortably on his feet. "I don't think this is something we ought to be discussing in public, *Herr* Colonel," he responded politely.

The colonel looked around him, and then replied "I know most everyone in this room, *Herr* Major. We are all on the same side of the war."

It was true that the majority of the hotel patrons were military officers on leave. I had noticed that the first day we were there, but I could tell that the major was not keen on discussing his business so openly. I wondered how he was going to handle the situation.

"Would you care to join us, Colonel?" asked the major with his disarming smile.

"I don't want to intrude on your family," responded the colonel as he winked at me. I felt my cheeks flush a little.

The major then asked the colonel about his position, and as he showed some interest, the colonel pulled a chair up to our table and went on and on about his duties in Frankfurt.

Although I thought we would be stuck for hours listening to the colonel's conversation, his friends eventually came and liberated us from him. We parted from them as the major was saying something very complimentary about *Herr* Hitler. When we got into the lift, the major turned to me and shook his head. "I thought we would never be free of him," he said.

This time, I put Annette down to bed first. Sepp was close to follow. When I came out of Sepp's room, I saw the major back at his books. I slipped out of the room without asking and went to get a tray of hot tea. When I handed the major his tea, he didn't say anything.

....

February 16, 1944

I will not think of Garmish as a dull place any more after the events of today. Sepp and the major went out skiing again this morning, but they were back in the room shortly before eleven. Without any explanation, the major asked me to wait in the room with the children until noon when we were to meet him down in the restaurant for dinner.

"Please be punctual," he said to me with a stern look, before he turned toward the door.

While I was trying to make sense of his unusual request, Annette spoke up. "Father? Are we going to go into town again?" she asked innocently.

"I'm afraid not today, Annette," the major replied.

"Are you going to see that man we met on the mountain this morning, Father?" Sepp asked.

The major turned and put his hand on Sepp's shoulder. "Remember what I told you, Sepp. Father's business is a secret, and you must never talk of it," said the major strictly. Then he turned his severe gaze to me. "Noon."

After he left, I stood there looking at the door for several moments. I had not understood that he would have to conduct his business while he was on holiday, but I suppose for such a man in his position, during a war, he is never free.

Time went by slowly with the children cooped up in the hotel room. I checked the clock every five minutes for the whole hour before we were to meet the major downstairs. He had been so severe in his request that I did not want to be a second late.

At five minutes to the hour, I led the children out of our room and into the hall. I was hoping the lift would take its time in coming, but it was right there when I called it. We were three minutes early when we arrived in the lobby.

Before we could head to the restaurant, I saw the major talking with a man whose back was to us. When we stepped off of the lift, the major said something to the man. He turned for a moment, just long enough for me to notice the man's dark, intense eyes.

The major reached out and shook the man's hand, and then the man disappeared out the front door of the hotel.

All through dinner, I couldn't help but wonder who the man was. Perhaps the major is working on the secretive, new project for the German air force—the one that will win us the war. *But why did he shut us up in the room for an hour?*

The major's mysterious behavior continued into the afternoon. After dinner, he asked me to watch the children for the afternoon. I don't know where he went, and he didn't say when he would return. The minutes crept by slowly, until about three o'clock in the afternoon.

I was sitting on the couch, trying to interest Annette in needlepoint again, and Sepp was in his room playing war games with his toy soldiers when we heard a knock on the door.

I was half hoping it was the major and half wondering why he didn't just use his key when I opened the door. To my surprise, and to Sepp and Annette's who were also hoping their father had returned, I looked up into the intense eyes of the man the major was with earlier that afternoon in the lobby.

"May I come in?" he asked abruptly.

I nodded automatically and stepped aside. The man darted in and quickly shut the door behind him. His intense eyes shot around the room. "Are you alone? Is Kurt here?"

"I am afraid the major is not here," I began, but the man held up his hand to silence me before I could finish. He bent his head toward the door and listened hard. I watched as his bony hand reached into his coat pocket and pulled out a thin, brown notebook that was no larger than an outstretched hand. He turned the fullness of his intense gaze at me and lowered his eyebrows.

"This is for Kurt," he said almost in a whisper. "Find a safe place to hide it, until he returns."

"I will put it on his dresser," I said innocently as I took the notebook from his bony hand.

"No!" whispered the man emphatically, grabbing me by the arm. "You must find a safer place than that." His eyes darted around the room again. Sepp had already disappeared into his room. I looked over my shoulder at Annette. *What was so important about the notebook that it must be hidden?*

I looked back at the man's dark eyes and tried to smile. He followed me at a distance into the bathroom and watched as I reached up onto a shelf and tucked the thin notebook into the open end of the folded towel on the bottom of the pile. I took a moment to straighten the towels until they looked undisturbed, then I turned back to the man. He opened his mouth to say something, but before anything came out, we heard a pounding on the door.

First, I saw fear in his dark eyes. Next, he raised his finger to his lips and very faintly said, "Please." Without making another sound, the man slipped behind the bathroom door and disappeared from my sight.

The person at the door was pounding harder now. I flipped the light out, closed the bathroom door, and glanced at Annette before I headed for the door.

I had barely opened the door to the hallway when an older man with a scar across his left cheek who was wearing a long trench coat and the hotel manager came barreling in.

"And whose room is this?" he asked abruptly.

Before I could answer, the man wearing the trench coat was halfway to the major's room. The hotel manager wiped a bead of sweat from his forehead and flipped over the paper in his hand.

"Major Rager, his children, and *Fräulein* Mauer, *Herr* Schwartzman."

Sepp appeared at the doorway just in time to run into the man with the scar, who quickly let out a curse.

"Where is Major Rager?" he asked while he was crossing the floor to look into the girls' room.

"He is not here," I replied.

The man with the scar turned abruptly to glare at me. "You did not answer my question. You must listen more carefully. Where is Major Rager?"

"I don't know. He didn't tell me where he was going." I bit my tongue. The force of his questions and his condescending air hit me like a wet snowball.

Just as I had feared, his next move was to dart toward the bathroom. As he tossed open the bathroom door and squinted into the dark, a shot rang out somewhere outside of the hotel. Two more shots pierced the silence in rapid succession.

The man with the scar let out another curse. "I did not give orders to shoot anyone!" he said with his teeth clenched as he threw the door to the suite open and huffed out into the hallway. The hotel manager stood there, dumbfounded—as dumbfounded as I was.

We heard the noise of commotion out in the hallway. I looked over at the hotel manager and then to Annette again. *What was happening?* I thought for a moment. *Where was the major? Had he been on the giving end of those shots or the receiving end?*

The hotel manager was still standing in our room, like a statue, staring at the paper in his hand. I was standing there, like a statue, hoping desperately that the terrible man with the scar would not return to find the man with the intense eyes hiding in our bathroom or the notebook he had brought. And I was hoping, for the children's sake, that the next face I would see coming through the door would be the major's.

The hotel manager cleared his throat but didn't say anything. He moved awkwardly toward the door to the hallway, and bowed halfway, shutting the door behind him on his way out.

"Where's father?" Annette asked.

"I don't know," I replied flatly.

"When is he coming back?" asked Sepp, who was standing in the doorway to his room staring at me.

"I don't know that either."

I don't know how much time went by, but before I could think to move, we heard another knock on the door. Sepp bolted toward the door to answer it, but I stopped him.

This time, it was the colonel from Frankfurt standing in the doorway. His face was red and serious.

"Pardon me for interrupting your afternoon, *Fräulein*, but I was hoping to speak with Major Kurt Rager. Is he available?"

It was only a few minutes before three thirty in the afternoon, but I could tell that the colonel had already been drinking. I looked past him and was relieved to see no one else in the hallway. I shook my head. "He isn't here."

"I'll wait for him," he said as he pushed his way past me into the room.

"I'm sorry, *Herr* Colonel. I don't know when Major Rager will be back."

"He didn't get rounded up with the rest of the traitors, did he?"

I swallowed hard. "I don't know what you're talking about."

"Oh," was all he replied as he sank down in the chair closest to the door. "You didn't hear the shots, then?"

I glanced up at the open bathroom door. The man with the intense eyes was keeping very still. I was feeling a little faint.

"*Herr* Colonel. Shall I tell the major that you called on him?"

"Just tell him I was concerned for him. That's all," the colonel said as he tried to rise from the chair in which he had just sat. "He seemed like such a good party man."

"Yes. Yes, he is. When he returns, I will tell him that you called and that you were concerned."

"Thank you, *Fräulein*. That's so good of you, and I will tell him that you were concerned too."

I drew in a deep breath and prayed that the colonel would just leave. I wasn't interested in having a prolonged conversation with a drunk man. I wished him up out of the chair, and I wished every half step he took toward the door. Finally, he mumbled several words that I did not understand, and then he left.

I started to tremble a little. This horrible war has left so many awful scenes in my mind. I closed my eyes and tried not to think of mother and father, but I couldn't shake the sound of the shots. *Where was the major?*

"Annette! Bring your brush. I want to braid your hair before supper," I called to her in the other room, but my voice sounded hollow and faint to my ears.

Annette came bounding from the bedroom holding her brush and smiling. She loves having her hair brushed. As I sat on the couch, brushing Annette's hair, I saw the man with the dark eyes appear in the shadow of the bathroom. He was very still and stood there for several minutes just watching me brush her hair.

I gathered three separate strands of Annette's lush, dark hair, and I began to weave them back and forth. *The major is in danger.* I tightened the weave. *The major is not in danger.* I tightened the weave. *The major is. The major is not.* "Oh, Annette. I forgot to ask you to bring a ribbon."

Annette smiled and jerked her head sideways. "I brought it. You don't have to ask me." She dug deep into her pocket and produced her favorite, red ribbon.

I looked up at the dark eyed man. *How long was he going to stand there watching me?*

"Good girl," I said, and I reached for the ribbon.

The dark-eyed man waited until I was done with Annette's hair before he moved at all. He crept silently over to the door and opened it a sliver. He hesitated a moment, whispered "*Wiedersehen*," and then he was gone.

Annette sat patiently at my feet while I redid her braid. Now that the dark-eyed man was gone, my hands were a little more steady. I patted her on the shoulder. "There. You're beautiful."

Annette floated back into the bedroom waiving the brush through the air as she went, her braid sailing after her. I had the oddest feeling inside when I came to my senses. I stared out the window and waited impatiently for the major to get back, sure that if he did return, he would ask for the notebook first thing.

And he did. I was a little startled when the major came through the door. I turned quickly and studied his face. He was neither frantic, nor agitated, angry, or disturbed. His eyes were not fearful or inpatient, guilty or doubtful. He seemed to be his usual polished, confident self. He did not greet me or explain his absence for the past three hours. He set his hat down on the table and simply inquired after the notebook.

Something evil seemed to rise in my throat. I wanted to make him wait, just as I had waited—all afternoon.

"The colonel from Frankfurt was just here. He was concerned about you. I told him, I would tell you, that he had called."

The major narrowed his eyes. I moved toward the bathroom. "And before him, a *Herr* Schwartzman and the hotel manager were here. They were also looking for you although I don't know why."

I stood on my toes, reached up between the towels, and slid the notebook out. "And before them, the man you were with in the lobby before lunch."

I stepped back out into the sitting area and looked up into the major's eyes as I handed him the notebook. Although I didn't want to have anything to do with his affairs, I did want to know where he had been all afternoon and what was in the notebook. What else can I think but that he must be involved in something subversive?

"Did you hear the shots?" I asked before I could stop the words from coming out. I wanted to see the look on his face, to be sure he had not participated in what had happened outside the hotel almost an hour ago.

The major turned aside as if he did not hear my question. I watched him flip through the pages of the notebook, and I watched him slip it into his briefcase and set the lock. As he sat down on the couch, he shifted his gaze out the window.

"I heard the staff talking about it. I believe that they concluded that it was a car that backfired," he said, looking back into my eyes.

I sank into the chair across from him and tore my eyes from his. I felt some color returning to my cheeks. If it were true, at least that was better than the thought of an execution.

"*Fräulein* Mauer," he said in a gentle tone, startling me out of my uncomfortable thoughts. "I would like to answer all of the questions I can see on your face, but I cannot."

This must be what drove *Fräulein* Magda to drink. Two days before we left for Garmish, I was searching my room for a safer place to hide you, dear journal. Under the mattress was too obvious a place to keep you. I discovered that a piece of molding on the wall behind the door was a little loose. When I pulled on it, I found a hollow space just large enough to hold two bottles. There was no label on the bottle that was in the space, but when I took the cork off, it smelled like sour liquor. No doubt remained in my mind. I had found *Fräulein* Magda's secret stash.

She probably couldn't stand the pressure of the position, the steady discord between the major's business and his associations, the constant questions from the SS, the never knowing if the major was genuine or playing some dangerous game.

The major cleared his throat. "I have to be back in Kassel on Friday, but I was wondering if you would be interested in stopping by Sinsheim on our way home tomorrow."

I looked back into the major's eyes with disbelief.

"Well," he continued, "you have spent your Christmas and these months with us, without complaint. I think there is time for you to see your family, if only for a couple of hours."

I got up out of my chair and stood by the balcony doors with my back to the major. I couldn't believe what he was offering me. It was such a kind offer, but I was all of the sudden terrified.

"*Fräulein* Mauer? Do you not want to see your family?" I heard the major ask with confusion in his voice.

I must have had a frightened look on my face when I turned back around. "Very much so, sir," I responded. "It is very kind of you to offer."

"Before you attribute too much kindness to my offer, you should know that I have an ulterior motive in offering this to you as this would be a good chance for me to verify your story," he said, looking up at me with a look of suspicion. The gratitude in my heart melted away instantly as I realized that he must still distrust me because I lied to him about my name.

"I figure, if we leave here after breakfast, we can be there by dinner time," he said as he leaned back on the couch. "Perhaps you should give them a call to let them know that we are coming," he added.

The major locked both hands behind his neck. "Come now. What is it?" he said, when he saw that I wasn't moving for the phone. I sat slowly on the edge of the nearest chair.

"My uncle is very disagreeable, sir. There is no one that he is fond of. I have not told them that I am working for a-an officer, someone in such a high position. When he meets you, he will certainly insult you. You will have him thrown into prison, and then I shall be responsible for my aunt and my siblings being thrown out into the street."

It was all the major could do to keep from laughing at me. "*Fräulein* Mauer, it seems that you should give me a little more credit. I am the one who is suggesting this visit, and I can promise you that if he is as bad as you portray him, I may be insulted, but I will not have him thrown into prison."

After a little persuasion, I picked up the phone and called Aunt Frieda. It has been almost three months since I left home, but so much has happened since then, that it feels like a lifetime.

....

February 17, 1944

Dear Journal,

I slept very little at all last night; I was so excited to go to Sinsheim. I was up early packing our bags. I got the children up and dressed, and we were down eating our breakfast by eight o'clock. I took one last look at the beautiful view from the room before we left. The major checked us out of the hotel, and then we were on the road.

As we got closer to Sinsheim, I began to get very nervous. I was wondering why the major wanted to go out of his way to stop at my aunt's house, to meet my family, when he had such important business to attend to elsewhere.

I was also embarrassed at the thought of the major visiting my aunt and uncle's home. The house is very old and modest. I know the type of society he is used to, and they are way below that. The major was staring ahead at the road, with no particular expression on his face, when I stole a glance of him. *Was I leading a wolf into the sheep pen?*

As we pulled into Sinsheim, the major asked me to direct him to their house. The children began to ask where we were going. He told them that we were going to have dinner with my family. They didn't seem at all interested.

But I could hardly contain my excitement as we turned onto the street that their house is on. I saw Aunt Frieda watching for us at the window as we pulled up. I took in a deep breath as I stepped out of the car with Annette at my side. I straightened my dress with my free hand and looked over at the major who was getting out of the car.

"Lead the way," he said as he stepped aside and took Sepp's hand. By this time, Aunt Frieda was standing at the front door holding it wide open. I went to her quickly and gave her a big hug. It was really good to see her. Annette followed me in the door with Sepp right behind her.

"Please come in, sir," my aunt said to the major.

I stepped into the living room to give them room to come inside the house, and there was Uncle Lothar as I had left him, on the couch.

"Well, you're back," he said dryly, and then he looked up at the major. "And who might you be?"

I looked at Aunt Frieda. "Uncle Lothar, Aunt Frieda, this is my employer, Major Rager," I said with a little hesitation in my voice.

Major Rager bowed slightly to Aunt Frieda, and he stepped forward to shake Uncle Lothar's hand.

"Forgive me for not standing, Major. I have this old war wound that gives me plenty of trouble," began Uncle Lothar. I rolled my eyes and hoped that Uncle Lothar wouldn't start his two-hour story about his war wound immediately.

"Where are the children?" I asked Aunt Frieda.

"We are right here," said Annette innocently.

I laughed. "Aunt Frieda and Uncle Lothar, these are the major's children, Annette and Sepp."

"Very nice to have you in our home," Aunt Frieda said with a warm smile. "The children should be here any minute now," she added.

I offered the chair across from the couch to the major. Then I asked Aunt Frieda if there was anything I could do to help get dinner on the table, but she told me it was all ready.

I sat down by Uncle Lothar who was staring unkindly at the major, and Annette came over to sit on the other side of my lap. I think she had a sudden spell of shyness come over her.

"You didn't tell us you were working for a *Wehrmacht* major, Klara," Uncle Lothar said.

"What did she tell you, sir?" asked the major with a teasing smile.

Uncle Lothar was surprised that the major had responded so. I looked down at the floor. I knew that coming to this house was a bad idea.

"Only that you were kind and generous, sir, and that she is fond of the children," Aunt Frieda replied quickly.

"I don't think she likes your Kassel very much, Major," added Uncle Lothar, not realizing what he was saying. "She thinks that there are too many military men there, and it makes her uncomfortable."

I looked up at the major for a second in pain.

"Curious then that she took the position with me," the major replied.

"Yes, very curious, but then she has been known to do curious things before," said Uncle Lothar.

I was mortified at the thought of where this conversation was going, but I was powerless to stop it.

"Like what for instance?" asked the major, encouraging Uncle Lothar on.

"Here come the children now," Aunt Frieda said as she leaned her head to the side to look out the front window.

I stood to my feet immediately. Their arrival was my salvation. Klaus came in first, followed by Liese, and then Lenz last, but they all seemed to reach my arms at the same time. I cried out of joy. It seemed like an eternity since I had seen them, and they were such a beautiful sight.

"You've grown so tall, Klaus," I said in surprise. He is almost taller than me now. "And you too, Lenz," I said as I took his cap off of his head. "And I think you are more beautiful, Liese."

When I wiped the tears from my eyes, I saw that the major was standing.

"Major Rager, may I present to you my brothers Klaus and Lenz and my sister Liese."

The major gave them each a slight bow. I held my breath as Klaus looked at him from head to toe. Of all of my siblings, he is the one who hates military men the most. For a few tense moments, I was afraid he would say something regrettable. Then Aunt Frieda clapped her hands together and told us that dinner was served.

"Who is this man?" whispered Klaus to me as we were heading into the dining room.

"He is my employer," I whispered back, "and you must be civil to him."

Klaus gave me a disapproving look and headed for the chair farthest from the major. We all sat down to eat around the little table, and it was then that I noticed that Aunt Frieda looks worn-out and thinner. Uncle Lothar looks the same.

I took a very small portion of food, because as we began to pass the food around, you could plainly see that there was barely enough for everyone. Sepp and Annette were very quiet and somber as they ate. I know they have probably never had a humble meal like that before. I was just hoping they wouldn't complain. Uncle Lothar would have none of that in his house.

All during the meal, Major Rager kept Uncle Lothar and Aunt Frieda occupied with polite conversation. He really does have quite a manner that puts you at ease and makes you say more than you would to anyone else under the same circumstances.

"How long can you stay?" Aunt Frieda asked, when everyone was finished eating. I leaned forward and looked at the major.

"At least another hour, if you can stand our company," the major replied.

Aunt Frieda laughed nervously. She offered the major a cup of coffee. I asked the boys to take Sepp up to their room in the attic to show him their toys. Liese offered on her own to take Annette up to see her two dolls.

The major watched them leave the room, and then he turned to me. "She looks a lot like you," he said.

I smiled and nodded. As I was picking up the dishes to bring them into the kitchen, Aunt Frieda came out with a cup of weak coffee for the major and one for Uncle Lothar.

"You leave the dishes for me, Klara. I can get them later."

"It won't take me long, Aunt Frieda," I said, knowing that I couldn't leave them all for her to do.

Aunt Frieda soon came back into the kitchen and took up a towel to dry the dishes I had just washed. She leaned over close to me. "I am quite surprised at you, Klara, working for such a man," she said with concern in her eyes. A moment later, she cleared her throat. "He doesn't take advantage of you, does he?"

I gave Aunt Frieda a look of surprise. "No."

"Do you remember Louise Weiss? She was your classmate."

"Yes, I remember Louise."

"She went to Dortmund to work for a colonel there. She has just had a baby, a baby girl."

"He has been very kind to me; very kind and patient," I replied after a moment. All I could think about was that night on the stairs when he offered to get me new papers. I almost told Aunt Frieda about it, but then I remembered that he told me not to tell anyone.

"Well, it wouldn't hurt for you to sleep with a chair on your door."

"Aunt Frieda, please," I said in a whisper as I sloshed some water onto the front of my dress. "He has always been proper."

"He is quite handsome," she said with a hushed voice. I didn't respond immediately.

"He has a girlfriend," I said at last.

"I was so surprised to get your call and that you came, but it is good to see you," she said with her nice smile, trying to work her way out of our awkward conversation. "I hope that Lothar behaves himself."

"I already warned the major," I said when I saw the look of concern on her face. "He is a fair man."

Aunt Frieda told me how much she missed me, and how much more work there was for her to do without me around. She also told me the town gossip while we finished cleaning up. She asked me about Sepp and Annette.

Then she reminded me that she still had some of the clothes Lenz and Liese had grown out of up in the attic, and she asked me if the children might be able to use the clothes. I was delighted at the thought. I was sure the major did not have time to attend to getting them some new clothes. I also thought that this might get him out of some trouble with *Frau* Brandt.

I put the dish cloth down, then I passed through the dining room on my way to the stairs. I wanted to check to see how the children were getting on.

"When would you like to leave, sir?" I asked the major. "I don't want to keep you."

"We can stay another half hour. Your uncle still hasn't told me about his military experience," he said with a persevering look on his face.

We will be here another two hours then, I thought. When I got halfway up the stairs, I was passed by Lenz who was in a big hurry to get downstairs. Then I heard Sepp, who was standing at the top of the stairs, calling him some terrible names. I put my hand over my mouth as if that would stop Sepp's words.

I was wondering what I ought to do as far as Sepp was concerned since there was obviously a disagreement between my brother and him, when I heard the major's voice behind me.

"Sepp Rager! Come down here at once!"

I turned aside so that there was room for Sepp to pass by me on the narrow staircase, but the major had to call him one more time before he responded. I don't know where the major took him or what was said, but from the sound of the major's voice, he was in big trouble.

I proceeded up the stairs and was relieved to find Annette and Liese playing happily in my old room. When I turned around, I caught a cold stare from Klaus.

"Lenz didn't do anything wrong," he confessed to me without me asking. "The boy just got angry when Lenz wouldn't let him play with one of his soldiers."

"I didn't think he did anything wrong," I replied, my words chasing him as he climbed the stairs to the attic. I followed him at a distance and found him lying down on his bed facing the wall. I sat down slowly on the edge of his bed, and reached out for his shoulder.

I don't remember what was said, but finally, Klaus turned around. He asked me pointedly what I was doing working for a Nazi. I tried to explain to him how it had happened and how much better this position was than the one I had at the school, but I could still sense his animosity. I wanted to explain to him the gratitude that I felt toward the major, but I was sure that he would not understand.

As I was retrieving the clothes from the attic, Lenz came back up, and not long after that, Sepp appeared at the top of the stairs. His shoulders were a little sunken. He apologized to Lenz, and then he went back downstairs.

After I took the clothes to the car, I went up to see how the girls were getting along. "I have more dolls than this, Liese. You can come play at my house," said Annette as I came in the door.

This was perhaps the only success of the visit. I was proud of Annette's kind offer to my sister.

Aunt Frieda was looking at the clock when I came down the stairs. As I turned to sit on the end of the couch, I saw Reiner's army picture sitting on the end table. I stared at his face for a moment, and then I reached out and brushed the dust off of the top of the picture frame.

When I sat down on the couch, I saw the major standing in the doorway between the living room and the dining room looking at me. I saw Uncle Lothar behind him, leaning on his cane and struggling to get to his feet. The time had come and gone too fast.

After some tearful good-byes, we left. Aunt Frieda didn't quite know what to say. After this visit, I don't know what they think of me, or what Klaus thinks. Although it did me really good to see them, I almost wish that we hadn't stopped.

I also don't know what the major thinks of me, now that he has met my family. At least now he knows that I am telling him the truth about them. It was very strange to see him in their home. He seemed quite out of place.

Frau Hoffmann was there to greet us when we returned home later that evening. She had several messages waiting for the major. After dinner, I took the children upstairs, bathed them, and then put them to bed. We will start our regular routine all over again in the morning.

March 1944

I am sitting in the basement with the major and the children, waiting for the all clear siren to sound, writing by the light of the lantern. The major is sitting with his arms crossed and his head leaning up against the wall. The children are quiet. So far, there has been no sound of the airplane engines and no bombs dropped.

Today is Monday. The major has been all out of sorts. I woke up at the usual time and got the children up and dressed in some of their new clothes, but when we got down to the kitchen, *Frau* Hoffmann wasn't there. She has been having a lot of trouble with her sister lately, but she always lets the major know if she isn't going to be there.

I got the children their breakfast as quickly as I could, put a pot of coffee on the stove, and got the major's toast going. He has been so busy since we got back from Garmish and so distracted that I didn't want to contribute to his trouble in any way. I looked up at the clock as I came downstairs with the children's jackets. It was just about time to leave for school.

I was putting the major's toast on the table by his coffee when he came into the dining room wearing a wrinkled shirt that was half unbuttoned and a look of frustration on his face. "Where is *Frau* Hoffmann?" he asked me.

"I'm not certain," I responded. "She usually phones if she has been delayed."

The major sighed. "I can't find a clean shirt. This one needs to be ironed, and I cannot afford to be late today," he blurted out.

"Your toast is ready, sir," I said calmly. "If you give me your shirt, I'll iron it right away," I offered, sticking my hand out to ask for his shirt.

"You have to get the children to school."

"I have a few minutes," I said, trying to calm him.

He hesitated only a moment, and then he took off his shirt and handed it to me. I tried not to stare, but even with his undershirt on, you could see that the major has two very prominent scars—one from his collar bone down the top of his left arm and the other on his neck, which is usually covered by the collar of his shirt.

I had to smile while I was ironing his shirt. I wondered what everyone would think if they saw the major eating his breakfast in his undershirt.

Ten minutes later, I handed the major his freshly ironed shirt, and then I pushed the children out the front door. We were late, but I knew that if we hurried, we might be able to make it on time. We met *Frau* Hoffmann crossing the street. Her cheeks were bright red, and she was panting. She said that her bus never came.

I have been working regularly with the children on their music lessons after school. In the evenings after supper, we work on their schoolwork. Then if there is time left, they play.

Sepp has been doing much better with his unkind words since the incident at Aunt Frieda's house with Lenz. Annette has now taken a turn for the worse, with what I can only describe as an attitude of ugly proportions. I have tried to warn her that if she is not careful, she will lose all of her friends.

Yesterday, the major told *Frau* Hoffmann that some very important people from Berlin from the office of the Ordnance Inspectorate will make a visit on Wednesday. He asked her if she could prepare a special dinner for the inspectors and the *Gauleiter* on Wednesday evening.

I don't think I have ever seen the major more nervous. I can see that he is trying to hide it, but he is very anxious about the inspections for some reason. He has been curt with all of us and short with the children lately. I have tried to keep them out of his path. I will be glad when spring comes, when we have more daylight, and I can take the children outside more often.

I got a letter from Aunt Frieda today. This is the first I have heard from her since our visit. She wrote that Uncle Lothar was thrilled to have the money the major gave them and said that anyone who pays his own way is welcome at his house any time. I am going to write Aunt Frieda back and ask her what she means by this. *Why would the major have given them money?*

I do wonder how Aunt Frieda has put up with Uncle Lothar for so long. Perhaps he was much more charming when he was younger.

....

March 9, 1944

Dear Journal,

Today is Thursday. I have just put the children to bed and decided that I must do better in writing what is happening, so I am sitting in bed with my nightstand light on and with you, dear journal, in my lap.

Yesterday was, of course, the big inspection day for the major. He was already up and out of the house when I came down with the children for breakfast. In fact, I don't think we saw him all day on Tuesday either.

After I took the children to school, I came home and went straight to the kitchen. I washed and peeled the potatoes for *Frau* Hoffmann and helped her in every way that I could. She is so distressed about her sister's health. I guess there has been no improvement. She told me, while we were working, that her sister's sickness reminded her a little of *Frau* Rager's.

I didn't ask, but she told me that the major's wife became ill about a year after the major got back from France, just as he was recovering from his injuries. She looked me straight in the eyes and told me that the major sat by Ida's bedside until her very last breath. I can see in her eyes just how highly she thinks of the major.

I hurried the children through their music lessons, through their schoolwork, and then through dinner, in order to have time enough to get them upstairs and into bed before the first of the major's guests arrived.

I put the children to bed early, but told them they could play if they were quiet and didn't leave their rooms. I had just enough time to help *Frau* Hoffmann with the last of the preparations and go back up to check on the children before I heard Heiner drive up with the major and the *Gauleiter*.

I heard the other guests come in as I left Annette's room. I decided that it would be best for me to stay in my room as *Frau* Hoffmann assured me that I had done enough to help her. I planned to sneak down through the hall and into the kitchen in about an hour to see if I could help with the dishes. So, I worked on my needlepoint for a while, and then I went downstairs.

How I wish I had not gone down. When I got to the kitchen, *Frau* Hoffmann told me that the dinner went very well and that they were just finishing up with their coffee. I asked her how the major looked. She told me that she thought he looked fine. I was telling her that I would come back down later to help with the dishes when the major came in from the dining room. He greeted me.

"*Frau* Hoffmann, that was delightful," he said, turning to her. "*Fräulein* Mauer, I would like to introduce you to our guests." The major swung the kitchen door open and held it for me. I breathed in deeply and headed into the dining room. I really didn't want to meet them.

There were eight men seated at the table in the dining room. The major introduced me to the *Gauleiter*, the three inspectors from Berlin, *Herr* Gerhard Fieseler, Dr. Erwin Aders, who is the head of Henschel's Panzer program, and another military man from the general headquarters in Kassel. The last person around the table was Lieutenant Braun. He took my hand and kissed it. I tried not to turn red, but I'm sure that I did. The men all laughed.

"I was telling our guests what a fantastic violinist you are, *Fräulein* Mauer," said the major as he sat back down in his chair at the head of the table.

I turned my eyes to him quickly while my heart started beating faster. I was hoping his comments would stop right there. But they didn't. "I was wondering if you would oblige me and play something for us this evening."

It seemed like I stood there for a long time without answering him. *Had he really just asked me to play for them? Why was he doing this to me?* "Certainly," I finally said with a high, choked out voice.

"But which one of us will accompany her?" asked one of the men from Berlin in jest.

The major smiled and stood to his feet. "She will have the best accompaniment available, *Herr* Colonel—the Leipzig Gewandhaus Orchestra. Gentlemen, if you will follow me to the living room."

I swallowed hard as I went to get my violin and my music. It was no use wishing that I could turn back the clock fifteen minutes. I grabbed the violin and marched back downstairs, resigned to my fate. My only hope now was to get this over with as quickly as possible.

The major met me in the hall.

"Sir," I began in a nervous whisper. "It has been almost ten years since I—"

"I have no doubt you will perform beautifully, *Fräulein*," he said with a confident smile, "or I wouldn't have asked you."

He took a glance toward the living room, and then turned his hopeful eyes back to me. "*Bist du bei mir* (Are you with me)?"

I held his gaze while my mind spun around. *Was he asking me to play the beautiful love song, the first intermediate song that* Herr *Eldering gave me to learn, the song I played from memory at my last recital, the music that even as a child stirred my emotions?*

Or, was he asking for my devotion and support in making this evening a success for him? Bist du bei mir was the question my father would often ask mother when he needed her approval, when he wanted her eyes to light up with affection. Maybe, because of these memories, I couldn't think straight, but the candor in the major's voice and the longing in his eyes told me he wanted both.

The softness in his expression made a hasty retreat as if he suddenly realized what he was asking of me. He tapped on the music in my arms with his finger and finished his question. "Do you have the music for *Bist du bei mir*, and would you play it for us?"

I took in a deep breath. In my distress, I had grabbed all of my music, including the song he was now requesting. I felt my face flush as I managed to look up into his eyes, and then I nodded.

As I followed him into the living room, my hands fumbled for the music that I would stare at as I played. The major went directly to the record player while I hastily tuned the violin. I set my music on top of the piano and stood in the piano's curve. I looked up at the major, then back to the music and raised the violin to my shoulder.

They were all very generous with their applause when I finished, and I heard several compliments. The major thanked me with a rather pleased look on his face. At the first opportunity, I gathered my music and wished them all a good night. On the way out of the room, I caught an admiring look from the lieutenant.

I was headed up the stairs when I heard the men begin to talk about *Herr* Hitler, the course of the war, and what they thought about the Allied bombing campaign. I sat down on the third from the last step at the top and set my violin on the first floor landing.

I stayed there for almost half an hour, my interest captured by the conversation. The men took turns adding their support to the war efforts and strategies and expressing their thoughts about the bright future of Germany. I listened carefully to the major as he spoke. There was something different in what he was saying. In his tone of voice, you could hear his passion and in his eloquence, his intellect. One of the men from Berlin told the major that he was just the kind of man who made the *Führer* proud.

At this point in the conversation, I stood to my feet, grabbed my violin, and headed up the second flight of stairs to my room. A dark sadness came tumbling down on me. I sometimes forget that the major is part of the movement that is responsible for the death of my parents, but in conversations such as this, that are political in nature, there is no hiding that fact. No matter the kindness he has shown me, he is still one of them.

I left the violin on my bed, tip-toed down the stairs, and went quietly through the dining room into the kitchen. I dried the dishes for *Frau* Hoffmann, and then I went up to bed. The men were still talking in the living room.

I didn't see the major at breakfast today, but I was sure from his demeanor last night that the inspections had gone well, and I hoped that he would be more relaxed now that the stress of the past few weeks had passed. But I found out today from *Frau* Hoffmann that the major is to go to Berlin next week to give a report.

March 12, 1944

Friday morning, I walked with the children to school under a beautiful, clear blue sky. Sepp and Annette went with the other children inside, and then I turned to head back to the house. But as I turned, I almost ran in to *Herr* Löning. He was wearing his long, leather trench coat, and he was standing right behind me.

He greeted me and tipped his broad-rimmed hat. Then he asked me if I would accompany him to his office. I told him that *Frau* Hoffmann was expecting me back at the house, but he just replied that it was not a request but a requirement that I come with him.

We walked the two blocks to the Gestapo office at the Goethe *Anlage* in an uncomfortable silence. This at least allowed me time to make up my mind what I was going to say if they asked me about Major Rager. If I really did believe the major was one of them, I had nothing to fear in telling things about the major that make him the ideal, dedicated officer.

As I sat down in a wooden chair in his office, I braced myself for some aggressive questions. But this time, *Herr* Löning employed a kinder, friendlier tactic with me. He asked me first about the dinner with the men from Berlin. I figured he could have been watching the house and could have already asked anyone else who was there, so I answered his questions about who attended and what was said without any hesitation.

Herr Löning asked me several questions about the after-dinner discussion. Again, I thought that he could have heard this from others, so I felt free to report to him that I had overheard most of the conversation. He seemed pleased to hear it. He did not seem pleased when I told him that one of the guests said that the major was just the type of man that made the *Führer* proud. He quickly asked me if any of the men brought any papers to the meeting, but I didn't know.

Next, *Herr* Löning began to question me about our trip to Garmish. He seemed to be asking me as a friend would inquire, but I didn't let down my guard. I concentrated on breathing and stared at his right ear lobe instead of his small, piercing eyes.

Whenever possible, I mentioned the children in my response. I didn't hesitate to tell *Herr* Löning that the major was very careful not to discuss his military business in public, even when others were not so careful. I shared none of my emotions, and I did not mention the long afternoon in the hotel room.

As the questioning continued, *Herr* Löning's patience seemed to be wearing thin, and the smile faded gradually from his lips. Finally, he named several names and asked me if the major was speaking, meeting, or corresponding with any of the persons he had named. I told him honestly that I did not know.

Herr Löning threw his pen down onto the desk, sighed heavily, and shook his head. "You are absolutely useless to me. You may go, *Fräulein* Mauer. But I forbid you from saying anything about this conversation."

Dear journal, I couldn't have been happier to leave that place and to be on my way home. *Frau* Hoffmann asked me why I was over an hour late in getting home, but for some reason, I didn't want her to know why, so I told her that I got stuck talking to someone.

After *Frau* Hoffmann had left for the evening and after I had put the children down, I did what *Herr* Löning had forbidden me to do. I interrupted the major as he was working in the study and told him I had done my very best to tell *Herr* Löning all the right things. Major Rager did not seem surprised to hear that I had been hauled in by the Gestapo, but he did seem a little surprised when I told him that I thought I saw Heiner being questioned in one of the other offices as I was leaving.

"Do you play chess, *Fräulein* Mauer?" he asked.

"No, sir."

"I'm glad to hear it," he said as he turned his eyes back to the papers on his desk. I think, in his own way, that he meant that as a compliment to me. But with him, it is always hard for me to tell.

March 19, 1944

Today is Sunday, and I have so much to write that I don't know where to begin. Heiner took the major to the train station Friday morning. The children were able to say good-bye to him before we left for school. *Frau* Hoffmann left the house after she served us dinner. There was really no reason for her to stick around. I don't know why, but I locked all of the doors after she left. I guess I don't feel as safe here with the children alone as when the major is here.

Annette complained to me, for the first time Friday evening, that her mouth hurt. I found a flashlight and looked in her mouth, but couldn't see that there was anything wrong. I told her to tell me if it got worse. I thought that maybe she just bit into something hard at dinner.

Both Sepp and Annette know how they must behave when their father is around, but when he is gone, I have a terrible time with them sometimes. I finally gave up trying to get Sepp to practice on my violin. When Annette saw that Sepp got out of it, she too refused to practice her exercises on the piano.

I was glad when seven o'clock finally came, and I could put them into bed. I was so out of sorts that I even refused to tell them a bedtime story.

Yesterday was a long day. It was cold and rainy out all day until it got close to dark. By bedtime, I didn't want to see or speak to the children for at least a week. They were so naughty and disrespectful. I suppose I only have myself to blame although I don't remember Klaus, Lenz, or Liese ever treating me this way.

Then it happened. Just before ten o'clock, I heard the air raid sirens go off. The sound is so piercing that it always makes my heart stop. I jumped out of my bed and fumbled around in the dark for my robe. Finally, I turned on the light so that I could find my shoes. I flew down the hall and into Annette's room. She was sitting awake but still in her bed. She threw her arms around my neck, but she wouldn't walk on her own accord. I set her back down on her bed.

"Annette! You must get some warm clothes on. We have to go to the basement for a while," I said. The siren was shredding my nerves. I shouted the same words at her again. When I turned to go to Sepp's room, he was standing in the doorway.

"Go get some warm clothes on, Sepp," I barked. I was thankful that he moved faster than Annette. I scrambled in Annette's wardrobe to find some clothes. Finally, I put her socks and shoes on. By this time, she was crying for her father.

"We're going to be all right, Annette. Please stop crying."

I grabbed her jacket and the cover off of her bed and took her hand, but she just sat down on the floor. I reached down and picked her up like a baby. In the next room, I found that Sepp had actually dressed himself and was struggling with his shoes. I put Annette down on his bed and helped him on with the last shoe.

"Get your jacket, Sepp," I said as I pulled the cover off of his bed.

With two covers, Annette's jacket, and Annette in my arms, Sepp and I hurried down the stairs and into the basement. When we got into the room, I turned on the light and set Annette and the covers down. Next, I lit the lantern.

"Where's the flashlight?" Sepp asked.

"What flashlight?" I asked, a little annoyed at his question.

"Father always brings a flashlight in case the lantern goes out," he said calmly.

I sighed loudly. I had never seen the major with a flashlight. The sound of the air raid siren was beginning to unnerve me.

"I'll be right back," I said. I needed to go get my jacket anyway. It was colder than usual in the basement. I was wondering while I was climbing the stairs how long we were going to have to be down there, because I thought that we might freeze before it was all clear.

When I got back to the basement with the flashlight, Annette was lying on top of the cover I had pulled off of her bed, and she was sucking her thumb.

By the light of the lantern, I made us a nice padded seat on the innermost wall of the room and sat the children down next to me on both sides. Then I covered us all up with the cover from Sepp's bed. Almost as soon as we got situated, the siren went silent.

The children were groggy. It was very cold in the basement, and I just wanted to go back to bed. I don't know how many times we have retreated to the basement when the sirens have gone off, but not once have any bombs dropped on us. I was almost tempted just to go back upstairs, but I decided to stay at least half an hour or until I could stand the cold no longer.

It wasn't long before I heard the cracking of gunfire. I had never heard the sound before. Then I heard the vibrating monotone sound of airplane engines. I pulled the children in closer. Annette looked up at me and told me her mouth was hurting. Quite by accident, I put my hand on her forehead. I noticed right away that she was a little hot.

I put my head back against the wall. *Why did the major have to be gone for my first bombing experience?* I had no idea what to expect or what to do. *Why did the major have to be gone while there was something wrong with Annette?*

A horrible thought sped through my mind. *What if she died before the major got home? What if we all died?* In the distance, I heard whistling sounds and what sounded like dull claps of thunder. I remember thinking that it must be the bombs dropping. In the next few minutes, I thought I would go crazy. Every sound, no matter how far away it was, made me shutter. *What if the sounds come closer? Who or what are the bombs being dropped on? Did they come back to level the rest of Kassel?*

I pulled the children closer and started humming a tune my mother used to sing to us. I was full of fear, but I realized that I needed to be brave for the sake of the children. I don't know how long the bombing lasted, but we stayed huddled together in the cold basement for a good hour until the all clear sounded.

In the morning, *Frau* Hoffmann had the news on what was bombed last night. She said that there were only about a dozen planes and that they hardly did any damage. When she told me this, I was thinking only one thing. I wondered when they would come back.

While we were talking, the telephone rang, and she went to answer it. When she came back to the dining room, she said that the major had called to make sure we were all safe from last night's bombing. That is when I told *Frau* Hoffmann that Annette had a slight fever, and that I thought she might need to see a doctor.

"This is a fine time for the major to be away," she said, shaking her head.

Frau Hoffmann took the flashlight and looked into Annette's mouth, just as I had done. Then we both looked at her face. It did seem that the left side of her face was a little larger than the right side.

"What should I do, *Frau* Hoffmann?"

She shook her head and scratched the bottom of her chin. "I suppose you ought to take her to the major's dentist, first thing on Monday."

I looked at *Frau* Hoffmann with forlorn. The major wasn't expected back until Tuesday evening. I reached over and put my hand on Annette's forehead. She felt hotter to me than last night.

Most of the rest of the day, she has been lying on her bed, uninterested in doing any playing. Sepp has a hard time playing by himself. I am concerned about her, and hope that a trip to the dentist will cure her before the major gets back.

March 20, 1944

This morning, I dropped Sepp off at school, and then Annette and I boarded a bus to Nordshausen. *Frau* Hoffmann had given me instructions on which bus to take, and she had given me the address of the major's dentist. She told me that she thought he had an office in the bottom of his house. I held Annette on my lap the whole way to Nordshausen. I could tell that she was in a lot of pain, and I hoped that the dentist could do something for her before the major got home.

Once we got off of the bus, I had to ask directions to the dentist's house. He was only two blocks from where the bus dropped us off. I was relieved when I saw the dentist sitting at a desk in his office as we stepped inside the door.

He was quite old, and I had to repeat myself several times while explaining what was wrong, but finally, the dentist put Annette in a chair. He tilted it back causing Annette some alarm, and then he proceeded to examine her mouth.

At first, I thought that Annette was not going to let him look into her mouth, but the dentist was gentle with her. At last, he determined that she had a tooth that had rotted and should be pulled immediately. He went to get some of his instruments, and then he tilted his examining chair back a little more.

Annette didn't like what he had done to the chair, and she tried to get out of it. The dentist asked me to come and hold her hand. He apologized to me that he had nothing to give her to help with the pain, and then he told me that he could hardly get any medicine at all any more.

I stood beside her, holding her hand, trying to comfort her while the doctor pulled the tooth. Annette let out a piercing scream, and then she started to cry. Her sad, tearful eyes made me feel sorry for her. He put some gauze in her mouth, and rose up from his stool to leave the room.

A few minutes went by, and then the dentist came back into the room and handed me the bill. I looked up at him in shock. I hadn't even thought about paying the man. I looked at the amount, and then I looked into my purse. Not counting the money I needed for our bus ride home, I had only half of the money the dentist was asking for, and it was all of the money I had in the world.

"I can't pay the whole bill," I said sheepishly, handing him almost all of the money in my purse. "When the major gets back from Berlin, he will have to settle the account."

The dentist sighed and took my money. "That is fine, *Frau* Rager," he said, "but if you would, please ask the major to send payment before the week ends. In this economy, I can't afford to extend credit."

I knew it would be fruitless to correct him concerning my name, so I simply thanked him for his consideration and left with Annette in my arms. We had to wait almost two hours for another bus to take us back to Kassel. Annette would whimper quietly each time the bus jostled her. I could feel some of the people on the bus staring at us.

We had no sooner arrived home and put Annette into her bed, when I had to turn around and pick Sepp up from school. Annette's teacher was waiting with Sepp when I got there a few minutes late. She wanted an explanation for Annette's absence.

For some reason, I don't think she believed me when I told her that I had to take Annette to the dentist, but I don't care because Annette has a big hole on the left side of her mouth to prove it. When we got home, Sepp was quite curious and wanted to look inside her mouth. Maybe he will want to be a dentist someday.

By evening, Annette's fever was gone, and I could tell that she was feeling better. *Frau* Hoffmann made us a nice soup for dinner. We put Annette's soup in a cup.

I am relieved that Annette is better. When the major returns tomorrow evening, the children will have a lot to tell him. I hope that he will be pleased with how I have handled things in his absence. I hope, for the children's sake, that his trip went well and that he can now return to his genteel self.

....

March 21, 1944

The children were very happy to see the major this evening. He arrived home just as I was trying to coax the children into practicing their music. I stood in the doorway to the living room and watched as they almost tackled him with their hugs. Annette began immediately to tell him about her saga. She is talking with a little bit of a lisp. I suppose that will disappear with time. Sepp was trying to tell him all about the bombing and our cold stay in the basement.

Finally, the major looked up at me and smiled as he was trying to listen to two stories at once. I could see that he was glad to be home, whatever the outcome of his trip. After the children had run out of things to tell him, the major sent them both in to tell *Frau* Hoffmann that he was home and would like dinner as soon as possible.

As he disappeared into the study with his briefcase in hand, the telephone rang. Since I was closest to the telephone, I stepped into the hall and answered it. It was *Fräulein* Farber.

I was a little surprised when I announced her to the major and he rolled his eyes. "Thank you, *Fräulein* Mauer," he said, and he headed directly to the phone.

While I was walking back to the living room, I overheard him greet her. Then I heard him say, "I have just now arrived. I haven't hardly even greeted the children." There was a little pause, and then he said, "I don't know if I was going to phone you or not. Hello? Hello?"

I think *Fräulein* Farber hung up on him, but if it upset him, he didn't show it at all this evening. At dinnertime, he listened to the children chatter about what they had done while he was gone. Then he asked me about Annette's tooth. Annette started in with her side of the story followed closely by Sepp, who added his explanation of events. When they were finished, I filled in the details that were missing.

"Oh, and I almost forgot. I have the dentist's bill. I was able to pay half of it, but he wanted me to ask you to send the rest of the payment by the week's end."

The major sighed. "*Fräulein* Mauer, in the future, please don't let me go away without leaving you some money in case something like this comes up. I apologize for the oversight on my part."

I nodded and took another bite of my dinner. As I was taking the children upstairs for the evening, the major stopped me and told me that I had done a good job of handling things while he was away. He also said that he realized that I had gone to some trouble to keep the children out of his way for the past couple of weeks, and he wanted me to know that he had noticed.

I didn't know what to say in return. I am not sure how I can explain this mess of feelings that I have inside every time I encounter him. I cannot imagine a man more devoted to his country and the cause of the *Führer*.

And then there are times that I doubt that he really is. There must be a reason why the Gestapo want me to report on him. I just get this feeling when he looks at me sometimes, that he isn't as evil as the rest. Or, maybe I am just hoping he is not.

....

March 31, 1944

Heiner arrived this morning with some news that the major has said nothing about. I don't know if it is true or not, but it seems that the high command has relieved *Herr* Fieseler of his duties as operations leader at the three aircraft working plants because of low production numbers. I wonder if the major had any part in that decision. I wonder if there will now be additional responsibilities for the major because of this.

Since he has returned from Berlin, things have returned to how they used to be, with the exception that I do not think *Fräulein* Farber has called once since the night he got back.

The air raid siren went off again last night around midnight, jolting me out of my sleep. I put my shoes on and my coat and took the cover off of my bed before I went to get the children. The major was already getting Sepp up, so I went in to get Annette. I followed the major down to the basement, and then I made a nice little place for Annette and me to sit in the corner. The major sat down right beside me with Sepp in his arms. I think the children drifted off to sleep just after the siren went silent.

There was a long period of silence before we heard the hum of the airplane engines overhead. I thought maybe the major had gone to sleep too, but then I heard him sigh. "I'll have to go check on the plants when this is all done," he said quietly into the stillness.

"In the dark? In the middle of the night?" I blurted out.

I heard the major sniffle. "Yes, otherwise, we may lose eight whole hours of productivity. If there is something that has been put completely out of commission, I am responsible to make alternative arrangements immediately. I also want to make sure that my workers are all safe. This was not such a problem until we went to two shifts."

"How did you get to this point, sir, where you have so much responsibility on your shoulders?" I asked curiously.

"How did I get to this point?" he repeated. "I sometimes wonder that myself." The major was silent for a moment, and I thought maybe that was all the answer he was going to give me.

"After I graduated from the university in Berlin, Ida and I got married. It was maybe a month later that her mother arranged for me to get a commission in the army. I went through officer training, and then had my first assignment in Berlin. The children were born there."

The major paused for a moment. "I rose up in the ranks because I was a party member, but when my father left Germany, I had a difficult time of it for a while. After I returned from France, they decided to send me back to Kassel. I guess they figured I knew the inner workings of Henschel better than anyone else because of my father's connections. That's when I got my promotion to major." He lifted his eyes to the ceiling. "Here they come."

"What is that noise?" I asked. It sounded like cannon fire.

"The flak guns," replied the major.

Maybe it was because we were sitting there in the dark that the sound of the plane engines droning overhead intermingled with the booming of the flak guns sounded so threatening to me. The major stopped talking, and we listened to the dull thud of the bombs making impact somewhere in the distance.

Both of the children woke up. I pulled Annette closer, and she started to cry. "Shh. Don't cry, sweet one," I said softly, trying to comfort her. "Shh."

Last time, I was all alone with the children and didn't know what to expect. Although it should have been less frightening since the major was there, it wasn't for me. While we were sitting in the cold basement waiting for death to be dropped on us, a cold, windy chill swept up my back, bringing fear and panic. A very strong thought seemed to paralyze me. *I'm not ready to die.*

"Are they not going to stop until they level the whole city?" I asked, without expecting an answer.

"We're at war," said the major back with somberness in his voice.

To our relief, the distant sounds of the bombs never came nearer, but I couldn't get the thought out of my mind that the bombs were dropping on someone else, and that the major was going to have a mess on his hands when they were all through.

He finally said he thought it was safe for us to go back to bed. At the top of the stairs in the front hall, I took Sepp's hand and told the major that I would put them both back to bed. I knew he had a long, unsavory task ahead of him.

While we were eating our breakfast this morning, the major came staggering in the front door. His hair was a mess, and he looked wrung out. He did manage to give the children each a kiss on the forehead before he sat down at the table. I got up and went to tell *Frau* Hoffmann that the major was home. She sent me back to the dining room with some coffee.

"Is it terribly bad out there?" I asked him. *Frau* Hoffmann had already told me that this was another light raid compared to October.

"They did some good damage," the major said with a sigh. "Fortunately there aren't many casualties."

When I got back from taking the children to school, *Frau* Hoffmann warned me that I should be as quiet as possible as the major had retired to his room to sleep until noon. Just before I was to go get the children for dinner, she asked me to go up and wake the major. At first, I refused, but then she explained that he had asked her to wake him just before noon, and she didn't want to have to climb the stairs with her knees bothering her so.

Reluctantly, I agreed. I knocked on the major's door, but when I didn't hear him stirring, I opened the door. He was sound asleep. When he didn't respond to my voice, I went over to the bed and was finally able to wake him by shaking him gently. I turned quickly to leave, but on my way out the door, I tripped on his boots. By the light from the hallway I could see that they were dirty. Next to the boots on the floor was his polishing box. I picked up the boots and the polishing box and closed the door behind me.

His boots were so dirty from wherever it was that he had gone last night that I knew it would take him a while to clean them. I went down to the basement and washed them off in the laundry sink. Then I sat down on the bottom stair in the hall and got the polish and the rags out of his box. I may not be able to do a lot of things, but the one thing Uncle Lothar did teach us was how to polish his boots.

The major still hadn't come down by the time I got the boots to shine again, so I grabbed the box and went up the stairs. I was just about to set them down in front of his closed bedroom door when the door opened all of the sudden.

There was the major, dressed and ready to go, except for his boots. I opened my mouth to say something, but nothing came out. Instead, I handed him the polishing box and his boots. He looked at his boots and then back to me. I think he was just as surprised as I was to find me standing there with his boots. He still looked tired.

"Thank you, *Fräulein*," he managed to say.

I hurried out of the house as fast as I could, partly because I suddenly wondered if I shouldn't have taken his boots, and partly because I was late.

At dinner, the major told me that he had decided earlier to go to his office with his dirty boots and suffer the consequences, but he wanted me to know that he has never before received so many compliments on how shiny his boots are. He told me that he did not dare tell them that his nanny had shined them, for fear that he would find them all lined up outside of his house when he got home.

The major turned in early this evening and all is quiet. I hope we will not get bombed again this evening. It really sets my nerves on end to be woken up and displaced in the middle of the night. I had a hard time going back to sleep last night after the major left. I guess I will try to get some extra sleep tonight.

April 1944

April 9, 1944

It is Sunday afternoon, and I am free to write. Today has been a beautiful, sunny day all day long. I am not sure if this is the beginning of spring or only a temptation to think so. I have a curious circumstance to tell you about, but first, I will tell you all of the news.

Sepp and Annette are progressing in their music lessons about as much as their complaining has progressed. I have had a hard time with them both lately. Annette has been crying every time Sepp bothers her in any way. Sepp is normally quiet and reserved, but he has been increasingly pesky to Annette.

He has also picked up a very bad habit, I would guess, from the other boys at school. Just yesterday, while they were playing in the garden, I heard Sepp saying some very unkind words to Annette and calling her names. As it was an unusually nice day outside, the major was on the back porch reading the *Kurhessichen Landeszeitung* (newspaper). I know that he heard the whole exchange.

I got up from my chair and went directly to Sepp. "Young man," I said, trying to be patient, "those are not words that are acceptable for you to say."

"But I can say them to a Jew," he shot back at me with defiance in his eyes.

I was so taken back by what he had just said that I was speechless for a moment. Out of the corner of my eye, I saw the major lower his paper and look over toward us. I waited for a moment, but the major said nothing. I was trying to think how I should respond.

I knew what I should say to the son of a German officer. I know what the policy of the Third *Reich* is, but I didn't know if the major bought into the policy so much that he wanted his children to be infected by it.

"You should always speak kindness, Sepp, especially to a stranger," I finally replied. I saw the major take his paper back up, and I sighed quietly. He didn't make me give Sepp the "correct" answer. I was a little surprised.

When I got back up to the porch, I thought that he might say something to me, that I might be in trouble, but he said nothing.

I have noticed that the major has had a lot of phone calls lately. After *Frau* Hoffmann goes home for the evening, I will, sometimes, answer the calls for him. Three days ago, the *Gauleiter* called him very late at night. The major is always polite and well spoken. Although I try not to pay attention to what he is saying, I sometimes cannot help it.

I finally got a letter from Aunt Frieda last week. She explained to me that during our visit with them, the major left some money with her to thank her for the trouble in preparing the meal for us. When I read that, I had to put down the letter for a moment. This was yet another act the major has done that baffles me.

I keep thinking I'm going to get a letter from Reiner, and then I remember. I understand that he is gone, but in my heart, it is as if he still lives. Next week, Lenz will have his twelfth birthday.

I remember when he was just learning to walk. I miss them all so much. I do wonder sometimes what mother and father would think of how we are all growing up.

....

April 17, 1944

I think it is finally going to be spring. I noticed today for the first time that the Linden trees are beginning to break out into a beautiful green. The sun is lingering a little while longer in the sky too.

I heard from Aunt Frieda again. She wrote that they have all been very sick, Liese being the worst of them all. I have been quite upset these past few days, knowing that I cannot go to her and nurse her as I want to. I somehow feel that I am letting her down by not being there.

She was very good at writing to me when I first came to Kassel. Now I hear from her less frequently. Klaus has written me only once since I saw them in February. On my part, I suppose, I have not written them such long letters as before. It is hard to come up with something new to write when you do the same thing every day.

Sepp and Annette have been fairly good about practicing their music lessons lately. I think they will have more incentive when there is still time for them to go outside to play, and it is still light outside. Last Saturday, when the children and I went for a walk, I met a woman who is one of our neighbors. She asked me what my relation to Major Rager is.

When I told her I am his nanny, she asked me immediately what had happened to *Fräulein* Magda. I didn't want to say anything unkind, so I told her that I was not certain. She remarked that the children were growing up beautifully, and then she began to complain about the lack of food at the market these days. She asked me if the major was going to send his children out to the countryside, like all of the other parents are doing. I told her I didn't think so, but I didn't know.

I suppose if it weren't for the children, I might still be there talking with her. They were getting quite antsy. After she told us all about the new electrical "O-Bus" that would soon begin operating between Harleshausen and Kirchditmold, I finally made excuse and said good-bye. I think she is the one whom I have seen sweeping the sidewalks in the morning when I am taking the children to school. She reminds me a little of Aunt Frieda.

The major told me a week or so ago that his mother-in-law has invited them up to Berlin the beginning of June. I am not sure if that means that I will have to go along or not. It has been almost ten years since I was in Berlin. I am not sure how it would feel to go back there.

I am in a rather strange mood today, dear journal, wishing that I were back in Sinsheim. But really I have no complaints about my present situation.

....

April 19, 1944

Today is Wednesday, and it has been one of those days I will not soon forget. Everything went along like a normal day until I was taking the children back to school after dinner. Right as we turned the corner and were in sight of the school building, the air raid siren went off. I ran with the children to the shelter close to school, under the Goethe *Anlage*. There was such panic and pandemonium that I think a bad situation was made worse. It was stuffy inside the shelter, crowded, and dark. I held the children close to me when we heard the booming of the flak guns. Then the bombs started to drop. They have never come during the day before. That chilly, panic feeling came all of the sudden, and my head began to ache. *How much more of this can I endure?*

When the warden finally let us out of the shelter, we could see the smoke rising from the south part of the city. I wondered where the major was. I supposed that he would be very busy for the rest of the day and that we wouldn't see him this evening.

When we got home, *Frau* Hoffmann said that the Americans hit the Branch Aircraft Assembly Factory and Eschwege Airfield, and that they did a lot of damage. I asked her how she always knew what went on with such accuracy, and she smiled proudly. "Heiner," she answered with one word.

"Do you think the major will send the children out to the countryside?" I asked *Frau* Hoffmann when the children were out of earshot. I had been thinking about that question ever since the neighbor had mentioned it.

Frau Hoffmann lowered her voice. "I have already had this conversation with him. The authorities would not allow him to do such a thing since he is in leadership. They want him to set the example and to be fearless. Besides that, I don't think he would be willing to part from them."

I let a silent minute go by and then I cleared my throat. "What do you do when the air raid siren goes off and you're at home? Where do you go?"

Frau Hoffmann looked up at me from the pile of laundry she was folding and shrugged. "Maria and I usually go with our neighbor, Rosine Staude, to the basement of our apartment building."

"You are not tired of all of the bombings?"

"Of course I am," replied *Frau* Hoffmann immediately.

"Do you ever get afraid? Do you worry that you're going to die?" I asked, looking directly at her.

Frau Hoffmann shook her head. "I suppose if it is my time to go, it's my time. Rosine always brings her Bible and reads to us from the Psalms. He father was a minister in Oberkaufungen until he passed away." *Frau* Hoffmann let out a short laugh. "Now there's someone who's not afraid to die. If you want to know about going to heaven, you'd better ask Rosine."

I didn't say anything else to *Frau* Hoffmann, but I wondered why Rosine would know so much since the priest at the church never says anything about it.

The major came home very late. Before he took off his coat, he inquired about the children's safety. I told him that we had made it to the shelter with time to spare.

"What would I do without you?" he mumbled, and then he turned into his study. I will not soon forget the fearful emotions of today, or the look on the major's face when he said that.

May 1944

May 11, 1944

Dear Journal,

Today is the major's thirtieth birthday. Tomorrow, I will be twenty. I was quite surprised to find out that his birthday is only one day before mine. I think that *Frau* Hoffmann has something special planned for dinner tonight. Since I only found out two weeks ago that it is his birthday, I have not had a lot of time to plan anything with the children.

We have had to work very hard getting ready for this day. Heiner was able to help Sepp with his carving and cutting in the small workshop in the basement. Sepp has been down there every afternoon instead of practicing the violin.

I am proud to report that Annette has done a really beautiful but simple needlepoint of a flower. Last night, I stayed up late, finishing it off for her. I was able to place it in the frame that Sepp had carved. I don't know where Heiner found a piece of glass, but it fits Sepp's frame perfectly. I showed the children the finished product this morning before they went to school and then wrapped it up this afternoon. I think the major will be very surprised. I must leave now to go get the children.

I have just come upstairs after having helped *Frau* Hoffmann clean up in the kitchen. We had a most enjoyable meal, and then the children gave the major his present. At first, he just looked at the picture. Then Sepp and Annette, both at once, tried to tell him their contribution. Sepp's frame is carved and notched in symmetrical patterns and is very complimentary to the simplicity of the flower.

"Did you really do this all by yourselves?" asked the major with a mischievous smile on his face, looking to me for an honest answer.

I nodded my head, and then the major raised his eyebrows. "What a talented twosome you are," he said to them proudly. "I think I know just the special place that I will put this."

The children followed him into his study. I think he set it in a prominent place on his desk. The children were beaming with happiness as I put them down to bed. Now I am going to put you aside, dear journal. I am going to go to sleep nineteen and wake up twenty.

....

May 12, 1944

The first thing that I noticed this morning was the giggling outside of my bedroom door. I put my robe on and opened the door. Sitting on the floor outside of my room were Sepp and Annette, and they were sliding a box with a red bow between them on the floor.

"Good morning, children," I said.

"Good morning, *Fräulein* Mauer," they both said in unison.

"This is for your birthday," said Annette, rising to her feet and picking up the box. Sepp got up and tried to help Annette hand me the box.

"Thank you," I said, a little embarrassed. This was something I had certainly not expected. I turned around and went and sat on my bed. Then I beckoned for the children to come in.

When I opened the box, I could hardly believe my eyes. I pulled out a very nice dress that looked like it had been displayed in a store window somewhere. I drew my breath in, and then I held it up.

"It's just beautiful," I said to the children. I thanked them for the present although I knew that they probably had nothing to do with it, and then I sent them to get dressed. I put the dress on immediately and tried to look at myself in the small mirror on the dresser. It seems like a long time since I have had a new dress.

The major was already having his breakfast when we came downstairs. He looked up at me and set his coffee cup down.

"Good morning, *Fräulein*," he said. "Do you like the dress the children picked out for you?"

"Very much," I said. "I don't know how to thank you."

The major nodded, picked up his coffee cup, and took a sip. "I hope you have a very nice day, and I will see you all this evening," he said as he got up out of his chair. He kissed the children, and then he left the room.

It was on the way back from taking the children to school this morning that I remembered that Aunt Frieda had bought me a dress around the time that I turned fifteen. She had managed to save up some money doing some errands for a friend of hers, and she had spent it all on a dress for me. The thought of the sacrifice she had made brought tears to my eyes. I had appreciated it then, but much more so now.

When I got home, *Frau* Hoffmann gave me a vase full of some beautiful flowers from her garden, and she wished me a happy birthday. She asked me where I got the new dress. I told her it was from the children. She laughed.

"Well, it looks very lovely on you, but I wouldn't go outside in it," she said.

"Why not?" I asked.

"You'll turn too many heads, that's why not."

I shook my head at her, but she continued. "How come you never get any mail from your boyfriend, Klara?"

"I don't have a boyfriend," I said simply.

"Such a pretty girl as you? What a shame."

I asked her about *Herr* Hoffmann, and she told me a long but interesting story about her husband, all the time with a look of great admiration in her eyes. He was a heavy smoker, and his lungs finally gave out. He has been dead five years now. I get the feeling that she loved him very deeply, and I can see that she misses him.

The postman brought me a letter from Aunt Frieda this afternoon. Inside were birthday greetings written by Liese, Lenz, and Klaus. I was happy to hear from them and to receive their wishes, but it made me sad too to think that I could not be with them today.

After I read the letter again, I got up and looked at my new dress in the mirror. It is a beautiful light blue, and the material is very soft to the touch. There are several teardrops embroidered into the top of the dress around the neckline. I wonder how much the major paid for it.

Sepp played his violin piece all the way through for the first time this afternoon. I threw my arms around him and gave him a kiss. I don't think he appreciated me doing that, but I couldn't help it. Annette is making progress on her piano piece too. After supper, the major spent some time with the children. They are always so happy to have his attention.

I am twenty now, but it doesn't feel much different than being nineteen. My wish for the day is that someday, Klaus, Lenz, Liese, and I will be together again.

May 20, 1944

Dear Journal,

A very strange event happened today, and I still don't know what to make of it. Today is Saturday. I spent a lot of time outside with the children. The major was in his study almost all day long, working in his ledgers.

About an hour before dark, he stepped out onto the back porch and asked me to come inside. He looked around, as if to make sure no one else was there, and then he turned to me with a very serious, almost pained look on his face.

"*Fräulein* Mauer? Would you be willing to do me a favor?"

I looked up at him, and I'm sure he could see the confusion that was on my mind.

"Would you take a message over to the other side of town for me?"

A message—to the other side of town. Why was he asking me to take it, instead of sending it with his usual couriers? The major was waiting for my response. "The couriers are all busy?" I asked, testing him.

"I can't send this message by courier, *Fräulein*. It's far too important."

"Is it a military matter, sir? Because I don't want to—" The major put his hand up to silence me.

"Please don't ask me any questions, *Fräulein*. That is one of the conditions of the favor I am asking."

I breathed in deeply and looked away from the major. He must know how uncomfortable the encounters with the Gestapo were for me, and yet, he was asking me to risk that for him. I really didn't want to be involved.

"Yes. I'll do it," I said. A moment later I saw relief come over the major's face. He pulled a piece of paper from his pocket and placed it in my hand. The major told me the address and the name of the man to whom I was to deliver it. Then he had me repeat it back to him.

"If anything should happen, it is critical that no one ever find this note or the response that he may send back with you. Do you understand?"

"Yes, sir," I responded.

"And if you suspect that anyone is following you, do not go to his house. I will have to get his answer in some other way."

I nodded and swallowed hard. *Why was he involving me in his business?* "Could not Heiner take this for you?" I blurted out. I was sorry that I had said it when I saw the look on the major's face.

"No," he said quickly. "I don't trust him."

This revelation really shocked me although I tried not to let him see it. *What was wrong with Heiner that he was not to be trusted?*

"You don't have to do this, if you are unwilling."

"I'll go," I said immediately and turned my back to him. I stuck the message in a safe place down the front of my dress and turned back to him with determination on my face. The major was trying to stifle a smile.

"You've done this before, *Fräulein.*"

"No," I responded honestly. "That is where *Frau* Hoffmann keeps her money."

It was plenty warm outside, and there were a lot of bugs in the air. On the way to the other side of town, I was careful to notice if any one was following me. All that was going through my mind was question after question about what type of business this was if the major could not send it by regular courier.

By the time I got to the west side of town, I was so exhausted from going back and forth about the issue, that I wished that I had just told the major no. Before I turned onto the street where *Herr* L. lives, I hesitated a moment and pretended to look at the flowers in the window box of the house on the corner.

As soon as I was convinced that I was not being followed, I knocked on the front door of the address the major had given me. The door swung open after the second knock. I was so surprised that I recognized the tall man with a beard, that instead of saying I had a message for *Herr* L. only a faint, unrecognizable sound came from my mouth. A second later, the man reached for my arm and pulled me inside.

"Is there anyone following you?" he asked nervously as he shut the door behind me. I looked up into the dark, intense eyes of the very one who had given me the notebook and had hidden in the bathroom that long, confusing afternoon in Garmish.

"I don't think so," I responded, still surprised.

"Good," he said with a sigh. "Won't you come into the parlor?"

I followed him to the parlor, and he offered me a seat on the couch.

"Are you *Herr* L.?" I asked.

"Yes, I beg your pardon for not introducing myself to you earlier. Do you have a message for me?"

I turned a little on the couch and reached inside my dress for the piece of paper. After *Herr* L. had read it, his eyebrows turned downward, and he sighed again.

"Would you wait here for a moment while I compose a response, *Fräulein*?"

I nodded, and the man got up, went over to the fireplace, lit a match, and set the letter on fire. He dropped it into the fireplace and left the room. I watched the letter burn until there was nothing left but ashes. Then I sat there for almost half an hour, listening to the hands of the clock on the mantle move slowly to the next minute and watching the daylight shadows fade from the room.

Finally, *Herr* L. came back and handed me a piece of paper. "I'm sorry to keep you. You'd better get going," he said with his low voice. "It's almost dark."

It was almost dark, and I had a long walk ahead of me. If I had known I was going to be so delayed, I would have grabbed my brooch with the light in the center to wear through the dark streets.

I hurried out of his house and down the street. Darkness was falling fast, and I had an uncomfortable feeling in my stomach. First, I was carrying a note that was secretive and could probably get me into a lot of trouble, and second, I was wondering how I was going to make it home without a light, once it was dark.

Ten minutes into my journey home, I crossed the street and started down another block. I was going as quickly as I could. Although it was a little hard to see, the figure coming toward me on the sidewalk ahead looked a lot like Heiner. He was heading my way, and he was the last person I wanted to see. I turned around quickly and headed back to the street I had just crossed.

As I rounded the building on the corner trying to get away from Heiner, my shin caught the brunt of the left, front-wheel of a baby carriage being pushed by a short, stout woman who must have been on her way to the Weinberg bunker to sleep for the night. As I tumbled over the carriage, my face hit the side, and the blankets and other personal belongings of the woman spilled onto the sidewalk. I hit the cement hard, scraping my left knee and elbow.

I looked up in a daze, and by the little light left in the sky, I saw the woman standing over me with both hands on her hips. "Why don't you watch where you're going?" she said, along with some other unkind words.

I apologized to her as I hastily tried to pick up her belongings. My primary concern at that moment was that Heiner would soon be arriving at the scene, and I would surely be discovered. As I picked up the last of the items that had spilled from the carriage, I heard a familiar voice behind me.

"*Fräulein* Mauer? Good evening."

I turned around to face Lieutenant Braun, and winced as the pain shot down my leg from my knee. "Good evening."

"What are you doing in this part of town?"

"I-I was visiting a friend," I replied.

"You don't have a light?" he said with concern.

"I-no. I stayed longer than I anticipated."

"Then it is lucky that I have a light. How about I walk you home?"

"That would be very kind of you." I smiled and turned around boldly. By the time we rounded the corner, there was no sign of Heiner.

Lieutenant Braun told me he had just been to the hospital to visit a friend, and then he began to tell me about his plans for Sunday. We had walked no more than two blocks when my heart suddenly stopped.

I had been so distracted by the fall that I failed to notice that the letter from *Herr* L was no longer lodged in the place I had put it for safekeeping. I stopped abruptly. Lieutenant Braun took a few more steps alone before he realized I had stopped. He turned and aimed the flashlight back at me.

"What's the matter?"

"I have a stone in my shoe," I said as I bent down to remove my shoe. I was glad it was dark because otherwise he would have seen how pale I was all of the sudden. My heart started again, but now, it was racing. If I had lost the letter, I was going to have to go back to try to find it. I didn't even want to think of what the major would do to me if I returned home without it. I felt a little dizzy at the thought.

As I bent down to remove my shoe and shake it out, I felt a slight crunch around my waist. *Had I really felt it, or was it just wishful thinking?* I put my shoe on and stood up slowly putting my arm across my waist. *No. I could feel the letter.*

I took in a quick breath and caught up with Lieutenant Braun. He talked on and off as we walked the rest of the way home, but I didn't hear a single word he said. All of my mental power was focused on keeping the reply letter in place just above my waist. I didn't even feel the stinging pain in my knee any longer.

When I came in the front door, the major was pacing in the hall. He looked at me with eager anticipation and with grave concern in his eyes.

"What happened to you?" he asked while he came to me. I watched his eyes rise from the blood running down from my knee, to the scrape on my arm, and then to my cheek.

"I'm fine," I said, too embarrassed to tell him the truth. "I just need to run upstairs for a moment." I moved around him toward the stairs without giving the major a moment to respond.

When I got to the bathroom, I saw the damage the sidewalk had done to my elbow and knee, and I saw a small gash on the side of my cheek from the baby carriage. Once I took my arm off of my waist, the letter dropped freely to the floor. I closed my eyes for a second and tried to compose myself.

The major was waiting for me at the top of the stairs, outside the bathroom, and he startled me when I opened the door.

"*Fräulein* Mauer, what happened to you? Are you all right?"

It would have been less uncomfortable for me if he had been more concerned about the reply than my well-being, but he had yet to ask for the letter. I extended the letter, and he took it from my hand, but he still wanted an answer to his question. I looked away from his eyes.

"I had to wait for him to answer the letter, and then it was dark. I-I ran into a baby carriage as I was coming around a corner. Lieutenant Braun had a light and he was kind enough to bring me home. I chanced to meet him on his way home from visiting a friend at the hospital."

"Yes, there is a nurse at the hospital that he is fond of." The major ended his thought abruptly and took a long look at me.

"If you will excuse me, sir," I said and turned to climb the stairs to my room.

I don't understand what it was that the major had me do tonight, but I do know that I don't want to have any part in his business. I hope he never asks me for a favor again.

June 1944

Dear Journal,

Tonight, I am writing you from Berlin. This morning Heiner took us to the train station with our luggage. Several hours later, we pulled into Berlin. It does feel strange to be here. The city is quite a mess from all of the bombings. I did not realize that there were other places that looked as devastated as Kassel. If this is what all of the other cities in Germany look like, I am afraid to know what will soon be left of our country.

When we got to our hotel, there was some confusion over the major's reservation and my room. The major had a dinner engagement, and so I took the children to a restaurant to eat.

Sepp and Annette have finally gone to sleep. We are in two separate rooms with an adjoining door between. Sepp is in the other room where the major will stay. They each have a bed. Annette and I are sharing a bed. She is holding onto Otti with all of her might next to me. I almost forgot to pack Otti.

I wonder what the topic of conversation at the major's dinner engagement will be. He mentioned to me yesterday that the Allies have landed in France and that our forces are trying to push them back into the sea. I imagine that this will only increase work for the major.

Tomorrow, I am to take the children to see *Frau* Brandt while the major will be attending some very important meetings. We were going to stay at her house, but then she phoned to say that she had some unexpected visitors. I think the major was relieved to have to make other arrangements.

It seems strange to be back in Berlin after all of this time. It has been almost ten years since mother and father died here. When I think about it, it feels like yesterday, and all of those horrible emotions blow through me like the winter wind.

....

June 10, 1944

Today is Saturday. Last night, we were awakened by the air raid siren. After getting dressed, we were herded with the other hotel patrons to the basement. From our short stay there, we all judged that it was a light raid, but I was still afraid.

When I woke up this morning, I could see that there was a light on in the major's room. I didn't sleep very well last night with the air raid and with Annette in bed with me, so I was up early. I waited until the light went out next door, and I knew that the major was gone before I went in to wake Sepp.

The major had written instructions for me on how to get to *Frau* Brandt's house. After breakfast, I took their hands, and we walked to the trolley stop not far from the hotel. I think the children enjoyed riding on the trolley although we weren't on the trolley long before we came to *Frau* Brandt's neighborhood.

She lives in a very affluent section of Berlin. The streets are very clean, and the houses are large with very fine drapes in the windows. I am sure that my old home was not far from *Frau* Brandt's address. We walked up a very wide staircase to the front door. Sepp was too short to reach the door knocker although he made a good attempt.

A very well-dressed butler answered my knock by swinging the heavy wooden doors fully open. I nodded to him in greeting and gave him our names. He welcomed us in and took us directly to the parlor. I felt immediately that I had been in her house before. Perhaps I am mistaken.

For ten minutes, I tried to keep the children from touching all of the fragile items that seemed to be everywhere in the room. I kept staring at the beige sofa. There were ten pillows on the back of the sofa. All of them were lined up at an angle in perfect symmetry. Finally, *Frau* Brandt appeared in the doorway.

"Children, how good to see you again. *Fräulein* Mauer. How was your trip up yesterday?"

"Very good, ma'am," I responded politely.

"And how do you find our fair city?"

"It is very lovely, ma'am."

"Why don't we all go into the study for a moment? I would like to finish a letter I am writing, and then I thought we might go down to Friedrickstrasse to do some shopping."

Shopping? She took the children by the hand, and I followed them into the study. Over by a large picture window that looked out onto a very green lawn was a grand piano. *Frau* Brandt headed toward a desk against the wall on the right hand side.

Annette headed straight for the piano. I was able to grab her by the hand before she touched the keyboard. I shook my head, and to my relief, she backed away from it.

There were several pictures on top of the piano lid. I looked at one of them in particular. *Frau* Brandt must have seen me staring at it. "That is my daughter, Ida," she said while still writing at her desk without turning toward me.

This was the first time I had seen a picture of the major's wife. She was very beautiful, but I was surprised. Even though the photograph was black and white, I could see that she had very light hair and pretty light eyes.

"She's very beautiful," I said slowly.

"Yes. She was my only child. Such a heartache!" *Frau* Brandt said dramatically. "I still feel that if it weren't for my son-in-law, if he hadn't taken the promotion and gone to Kassel, she might still be alive."

I looked up at the major's mother-in-law in shock. Had she really just blamed the major for her daughter's death? I looked back at Ida's picture. Then I looked over at the children. I wished that *Frau* Brandt hadn't said this in front of them. It hardly seemed like an appropriate thing to say, even outside of their presence.

"That is her piano too," *Frau* Brandt added. "She used to play so beautifully."

I had always wondered why the major had a piano in his house, and this explained everything to me. I smiled at the thought that Annette may someday surprise her grandmother by playing the piano for her.

After *Frau* Brandt finished her letter, after she gave instructions to the butler on how and when to post it, and after she collected her purse and straightened her hair in the hallway mirror, we left the house for Friedrickstrasse.

It was late afternoon before we returned to *Frau* Brandt's house. My arms and hands were tired from carrying the packages, and the children were tired of walking. All day, I tried not to think about the money she was spending. I wonder where she gets it all, but it is really none of my business.

I took a little extra time in the bathroom when we got to her house. I washed my face and relished a brief moment of silence. The streets were crowded with people, and everywhere we went today, *Frau* Brant complained loudly about the lack of merchandise. She seems not to notice that there is a war going on. After all of this, I was ready to go back to the hotel, but I knew we were to stay for dinner.

And what a dinner it was. The major arrived shortly after *Frau* Brandt's guests who were staying the week and right before several others to make an even dozen. Just before the butler came to announce that dinner was served, the major came over and asked me if the children had eaten their supper yet.

When I told him that I understood that *Frau* Brandt wished for them to dine with us, he seemed unpleasantly surprised. He gave me an agitated look. "A formal dinner is no place to display the children." I stood there motionless, unsure if he was displeased with the arrangements *Frau* Brandt had made or if he was displeased with me for not circumventing them. Before I could say anything, we were interrupted by one of the guests.

Quickly, I stooped down and gathered the children into my arms. At that moment, I wasn't thinking that *Frau* Brandt might be wishing to do me harm by proving in such a setting that I had been negligent in my training of the children. I was just hoping to prevent a scene that would cause embarrassment to the major.

"We are going to have dinner now. You must both be on your best behavior. Annette, you must watch me closely and do everything that I do. Don't do anything unless you see me do it. Sepp. Sepp!"

I took his face in my hands and turned it so that he was looking at me. "You must watch your father and do everything that he does. Do you understand?"

I had barely finished my last word when *Frau* Brandt appeared at the doorway to lead us into the dining room. I tried to give the major a reassuring look, but he was firmly engaged in conversation. I sent Sepp over to his side, and Annette and I fell in line on the right side of the table, following *Frau* Brandt's instructions.

Annette slid around the side to sit in her chair, but I grabbed her on the shoulder before she seated herself.

"Why can't I sit down?" she asked quite innocently, looking up at me with her big brown eyes.

"We must wait for our hostess, Annette. We are her guests," I replied softly.

Across the table, Sepp, disregarding everything I had said, reached for his chair. At the last minute, he looked up at me. I shook my head vigorously and gave him a stern look. "Watch your father," I said as loudly as I dared. Sepp looked up at the major, and then he tried to stand up straight.

The butler seated *Frau* Brandt. The man next to my seat, pulled the chair out for me, and I thanked him as I sat down. I saw the butler seat Annette, then I heard a clear thank-you from her lips.

We waited as the men took their seats, and then I watched for *Frau* Brandt to put her napkin on her lap. I slid my napkin onto my lap and opened it halfway. From the corner of my eye, I watched Annette do the same.

"Well done, Annette," said her father from across the table. Sepp lurched back in his seat in a hunch. "Sit up straight, son," said the major.

To my relief, from that moment on, the children behaved as if they had been specially trained to attend a formal dinner party. It wasn't long before the major took a sip of his drink and the tenseness in his jaw slowly melted away.

During the evening, *Frau* Brandt spent a lot of time bragging about the major to her guests. I wondered that she even finished any of the food on her plate; she was talking so much.

The man with the large teeth who was sitting next to Sepp, a *Herr* Siegel, soon asked the major about his Knight's Cross. I looked over at the major wondering how he was going to address the question, wondering myself what the answer would be.

"They gave this to me as a parting gift on my way out of France," he said casually.

Frau Brandt's face twisted, and she let out a nervous chortle. "My son-in-law is far too modest. Kurt served under Field Marshal Gerd von Rundstedt in Poland commanding a Tiger unit. They broke through Polish lines in Bzura and destroyed the anti-tank battery that was bombarding the other Panzer units. Shortly after that, he was awarded the Iron Cross, Second Class."

I looked over at the major. Before that moment, I did not realize that he had seen combat. *Frau* Brandt cocked her head at a funny angle and continued. "Was it in October of that year that you received the Iron Cross, First Class?"

Major Rager wiped his mouth with his napkin and urged Sepp to finish the food on his plate. *Frau* Brandt was not flustered by his lack of response. "Yes, and then in France, in the Ardennes, again with Field Marshall von Rundstedt, he was seriously wounded while leading his men out of a valley where they were well pinned down. Every man in his group got out of there alive because of Kurt's decisive and brave actions, thus, the award of the Knight's Cross. Of course, I am very proud."

Major Rager shifted slightly in his seat but managed a polite smile when *Herr* Siegel said that he was a hero. The major shook his head and stared at his plate. "The heroes are the ones who never return home," he said contemplatively.

There was an uncomfortable moment of silence after which *Herr* Siegel raised his glass. "To all of Germany's heroes," he said boldly. The major raised his glass. My thoughts drifted to Reiner. After that, I wasn't interested in any of the dinner conversation, and it was quite late when they brought out the last course.

Frau Brandt, who was sitting at the head of the table, leaned back and whispered something into the butler's ear, who promptly went over to the major to relay the message. The major looked over at me and motioned that I should bring the children and follow him. When we got out into the hall, he explained to me that she had suggested that I put the children to bed upstairs in her room.

"She wants her war trophy to stay a little while longer," he said. "I don't want to send you back to the hotel alone. We won't stay too late, but do you mind putting the children down here?"

"Not at all," I said immediately although I really did want to leave.

"Good. Go on upstairs with *Fräulein* Mauer, children," he said.

At first, I had a hard time convincing them to lie down on her bed and go to sleep without their nightclothes on and without Otti. I stayed up in *Frau* Brandt's room for a short while, until they were quiet and still, and then I returned to the dining room.

"Is this your first time in Berlin, *Fräulein* Mauer?" asked *Frau* Brandt's guest, who was seated next to me at the table. I looked into his round but kind face, and then I saw the major look at me with concern.

"It is a very beautiful city, sir," I responded vaguely. "It seems like I have been here before."

"There is so much to Berlin, *Fräulein* Mauer," piped up *Frau* Brandt "that the small village you are from could never hold a candle to. I would think someone of your class would feel utterly lost here."

I drew in a breath and looked down at my plate. Everyone around the table was suddenly quiet. What she had said to me was unkind and very presumptuous. I wanted to tell her that I was born in Berlin and that I began my life in a family above her own status, but I was so stunned by her words that I said nothing.

When I looked up at *Frau* Brandt, I saw the major's expression. I think he knew what I was thinking.

"I mean, there is so much culture and high life to this great city. And it is the center of the Third *Reich*. There is nowhere else I would rather live," continued *Frau* Brandt in a weak attempt at trying to tame down her insult of me.

There were several "here, heres" from the other end of the table, and then the conversation around the table slowly resumed. To my relief, *Frau* Brandt's guest did not ask me any further questions.

Around nine o'clock, we all left the dining room for the parlor. *Frau* Brandt's guest had brought his violin and had volunteered to entertain us for a short while. I went upstairs to check on the children. They were fast asleep. When I returned to the parlor, I could see that all of the seats were taken by the ladies, so I leaned up against the doorway.

While her guest was tuning up his violin and applying the rosin to the bow, *Frau* Brandt was busy praising his musical talent and pointing out that he was a fine example of the best that Berlin had to offer although I was certain that I had heard at the dinner table that they had just arrived from Köln.

I watched as her guest began to play. His execution was good, but his bow pressure was uneven. Although he did not play with much expression or interpretation, he did seem to hit all of the notes correctly. From across the room, I saw the major leaning up against the wall with his legs crossed at his ankles, watching me closely. He had a curious look on his face. I wondered whether he would notice the level of skill *Frau* Brandt's guest was displaying.

I clapped along with the rest of everyone when he was done playing his second song. Someone in the room asked him whom he had studied under, and I heard him respond, "*Herr* Bram Eldering."

I couldn't believe it when I heard it. How interesting, that we have both studied under the same instructor. Someone else in the room asked if *Herr* Eldering wasn't from Berlin.

"Yes," I responded at the same time as *Frau* Brandt's guest.

"But he is now in Köln," continued her guest.

As if the night had not been long enough, we had to wake the children, walk them to *Frau* Brandt's car in the rain, and then go back to the hotel and try to put them down to sleep again.

The major waited until we were back at the hotel and out of the earshot of *Frau* Brandt's driver to tell me he was sorry for what his mother-in-law had said about me tonight, and that he knew I could play ten times better than her star violinist.

I told him it was not his apology to make. I didn't know what else to say. Her unkindness to me was really no surprise, and I know that the less I make of the incident, the sooner it will be behind me. What I cannot get out of my mind are the things that *Frau* Brandt said about the major.

I thought about it the whole time we were in the basement of the hotel during another air raid. How did I come to work for such a man as this—a decorated officer who has seen combat and who doesn't even consider the extraordinary things he has done as heroic? Every time I think I have gathered enough parts to piece together a picture, when I turn around, there is a new piece, more intriguing than the last to add to the puzzle. And I am back, once again, staring at a figure that looks only like a shadow.

....

June 11, 1944

I got the children up a little late this morning. While Sepp was in the bathroom, I was gathering up his dirty clothes from the day before. When I picked his pants up off of the floor, a large, round, heavy object fell to the floor with a thud. It sparkled in the morning sunlight on the carpet. I picked it up and put it in the palm of my hand. It was a beautiful silvery brooch with a large pearl in the center and delicate, carved leaves lined with diamonds flowing out from underneath the pearl.

I took a step toward the restroom, intending to ask Sepp what the brooch was doing in his pants pocket when I suddenly realized that he must have taken it from *Frau* Brandt's room. There was no other reason he would have such an exquisite and expensive object in his possession. When I thought of the ramifications that his childish action might have, I decided that it would be better for his father to deal with this.

I returned to my room to check on Annette's progress in getting dressed, and I placed the brooch in the back of the top drawer of the dresser, underneath Annette's nightgown, for safe keeping.

We were two minutes late in meeting *Frau* Brandt for mass. Afterward, the children and I spent the day walking in the area around the hotel. We found a park nearby with beautiful gardens, and the children played for a while by a pond. The sky was clear in the morning, but it began to rain in the afternoon.

We were very wet when we got back to the hotel. I had to help the children change into the clothes they are supposed to wear tomorrow. After I rinsed their wet clothes out in the sink and hung them to dry, I found them staring out the window at the people and the umbrellas on the street below. We are on the third floor.

Between the time that we finished eating our supper and time to put the children to bed, it seemed like an eternity. It was still raining out, and the children had nothing to do.

The only thing worth mentioning that happened today occurred after I had put the children to bed in my room. I put Sepp in there with the intention of transferring him to the major's room once the major returned for the evening and once I had a chance to talk with him about the brooch. In the meantime, I sat in the major's room and read.

Around seven o'clock, I heard a knock on the door. At first I thought it might be the major, but then I decided that he would have just come in because he has a key. I opened the door cautiously.

"Good evening," said the tall man, who was wearing the neatly pressed uniform of a major. "Is this Kurt Rager's room?"

"Yes."

The man looked to his right and then to his left. "May I come in?"

The man stepped right inside, and then he reached over and closed the door behind him. When he turned to me, he gave me a nice smile. "I'm Kurt's cousin, Karl Rager," he said, introducing himself and extending his hand for me to shake.

"He's not here, sir," I said. "And I'm not sure when he will return."

The man looked around the room, and then he gestured toward the adjoining room. "Are Sepp and Annette already asleep?"

"Yes, they are," I said. "I put them down a while ago."

"And you are?"

"I beg your pardon, sir. Klara Mauer. I am the children's nanny."

"Yes, of course. You are just as pretty as your picture. May I sit down?"

While I was wondering what he meant by what he had just said, and before I could answer him, he picked my book up out of the chair I had been sitting in, and he sat down with a thud.

"He told me he would meet me here at seven, so I hope you don't mind if I wait for him."

"Not at all," I said. I was still standing by the door. There were no other chairs in the room, and there was nowhere for me to go. I cleared my throat and played with my hands nervously. There was a long minute where nothing was said. Finally, I sat down on the edge of the major's bed.

I was wondering why the major's cousin wasn't asking me all of the usual questions. Where are you from? How do you like working for the major? How long have you been working for him? How do you like Berlin? What do you think of the major's mother-in-law? What is your real name?

I bit my lip at my last thought and looked over at the other Major Rager. He looked up at me as I turned my eyes back to my hands—still no questions and still no conversation. He leaned forward in the chair, posted his elbows on his knees, folded his hands together, and looked over at me. Maybe he was waiting for me to say something.

"I'm sorry that I cannot offer you anything to drink," I finally said. He had won the silence game, but I didn't care.

"That's all right," he said. "I don't need anything. I wonder where he is," he said, looking at his watch. "We're going to see Elisabeth Schwartzkopf tonight, and I don't want to be late."

I raised my eyebrows, trying to look interested, but he saw right away that I did not recognize the name.

"The really gorgeous opera singer. Kurt met her when he was in France. She's singing tonight." I nodded my head, pretending to understand the significance of his statement. Another minute came and went, and finally, I heard a key in the door. I stood to my feet and faced the major as he came in. He looked surprised to see me standing there right by the door, but he seemed even more surprised to see his cousin.

"Karl! Here you are. I have been waiting for you in the lobby," he said quickly. "I see you have met *Fräulein* Mauer."

"Yes, we have met," said the other Major Rager with half a grin.

The major turned to me and told me they were going out, and that he would be back in two hours or so. Then after some departing pleasantries, they both left.

I sighed when the door shut. If I were going to talk to the major about Sepp, I was going to have to wait up. I picked my book up and resumed reading where I had left off when the other major had come.

I kept re-reading the same page in the book, because my mind kept wandering to the question of what the other Major Rager meant when he said I was prettier than my picture. He must have been mistaken, because I could not figure out a way he would have ever seen a picture of me.

The major didn't return to the room until after eleven o'clock. I think he was surprised to see that I was still up. I waited for him to take his coat off. Before I could say anything, he turned to me. "I am curious, *Fräulein*, what my cousin might have said to you before I came."

I shrugged. "He asked if the children were asleep, and then he asked me who I was. And that was about it."

"That was it?" asked the major, pressing the issue.

I narrowed my eyes. "He told me you were going to an opera, and he told me that I looked prettier than my picture, but he must be mistaken. How would he have seen a picture of me?"

The major turned away from me for a moment and sat down on the edge of the bed to remove his shoes.

"Why are you asking me these questions?" I asked boldly.

The major looked up at me out of the corner of his eyes. "I cannot tell you why, *Fräulein* Mauer, and I must ask you to be satisfied with that answer."

The major took off both of his shoes, and then he looked up at me. I was still trying to decipher what he had said to me.

"Is there a reason you put Sepp down in your room, *Fräulein?*"

"Yes. There is." I felt my face flush as I suddenly realized how inappropriate this looked to the major. I swallowed hard and removed the brooch from my pocket.

"While I was collecting the dirty clothes this morning, this fell out of Sepp's pants pocket." I handed the brooch to the major and watched as confusion came over his expression. "I think it probably belongs to your mother-in-law."

"I don't understand. Why would he take this from her?" he asked, holding the brooch in his hand.

"I don't know, sir. Maybe he just saw it and liked it, so he took it. I'm sure that he knows nothing of its value"

"You didn't take it?" he asked me pointedly.

I drew in a short breath. His question took me completely by surprise.

"I'm sorry," he added quickly. "That is not what I meant to ask. You didn't see him take it?"

"No," I answered immediately, trying to hide the hurt that I felt from the insinuations in both of his questions.

The major set the brooch down on the table between the two beds and rubbed his eyes wearily with his right hand. "Did you ask him about this?"

"No," I responded. "I thought, considering whom it might belong to, that you would want to handle it."

The major nodded. "I'll have a talk with him in the morning, after I have had some sleep. We are to go to her house tomorrow afternoon," he said with a sigh. "I suppose we can straighten this all out then."

"Yes, sir," I responded. I opened the door between the rooms, went into the dark, and lifted Sepp to bring him back to the major's room. He watched me tuck the sleeping boy into bed. I wished him a good night and went back into my room. I heard him mumble, "Good night" before I closed the door.

Although it is very late and I am drained, I cannot sleep. I hope I did the right thing and that the major is not angry with me.

....

June 15, 1944

Dear Journal,

Today is Thursday. We arrived back in Kassel yesterday. I have been in bed all day and am still not well. I don't know how long it will take me to get over this illness or the embarrassment of the past week. What a story I have to tell you.

Early Monday morning, we had to go to the basement again. It was the third night in a row that the bombers came. When the sun was fully up, I heard the major having a discussion with Sepp. I couldn't hear what he was saying, but I could hear his voice. I tried to keep Annette occupied. She wanted to go into their room, but I didn't want her to interrupt their conversation.

The major went out for a meeting that morning, but he returned in the early afternoon and collected us. When we arrived at *Frau* Brandt's, the butler opened the door, but she was already standing right there in the spacious hall waiting for us.

"Kurt, I must speak with you at once—alone," she bellowed out. "And I want you to wait right here in the hall, *Fräulein* Mauer," she said with her teeth clenched.

I was holding the children's hands, and so I just froze where I was. I wondered why she would give such a command, but I thought that perhaps she didn't want the children touching all of her precious, breakable things in the parlor or the sofa pillows. I felt bad for the major, knowing he had a delicate issue to break to her about the brooch and seeing that she was already in a horrid mood.

She and the major went into the study, where the piano was, and she shut the door behind her. But from the middle of the hall where the children and I were standing, we could hear every word that they were saying.

"I have every reason to believe that your nanny has stolen a very valuable piece of jewelry from my room, Kurt, and I want you to do something about it," she said, beginning their conversation.

I rolled my eyes and then looked down at Sepp. His little lip was trembling. There was a long pause, and I thought that maybe I would only be able to hear half of the conversation, but then the major spoke.

"I think I know who took it, Helma," he said. "If you will indulge me a moment?"

The study door opened suddenly, startling me a little.

"Sepp, come," called the major from the doorway.

Poor Sepp. He could hardly put one foot in front of the other. Annette and I stood there as the study door closed with a thud.

"Why are you involving the child in this, Kurt? He didn't do anything."

"Sepp, I want you to tell your grandmother how this got into your pocket," I heard the major say.

Frau Brandt gasped.

Then I heard the tiny, scared voice of the little thief. "I saw this nice flower on the nightstand, and I wanted to play with it when I got back to the hotel, so I took it," Sepp said between sobs.

"There now, Sepp," *Frau* Brandt said. "There's no need to cry. Kurt, you must do something about your nanny. If the children had been properly supervised, this never would have happened."

My mouth dropped open and my blood began to boil. I couldn't believe what I had just heard.

"If I recall correctly, Helma, it was your idea for her to put the children down in your room, was it not?" came the major's response.

I took two steps toward the study, but I did not hear a response. In a minute or so, the study doors flew open, and the major's mother-in-law emerged with her head held high.

"Come, Annette," she said sternly. "There is candy in the kitchen for you."

Annette did not hesitate. The major came out of the study with Sepp. Neither of them looked my way.

Later in the afternoon, Annette and I were in the study alone, and she went over to the piano lid and picked it up. Then she sat down on the piano bench and began to play one of her practice songs. The piano was a little out of tune, but I didn't care. I was so happy to see her playing, even without her music, that I did not think of the ramifications.

I didn't think anything about it, until I saw *Frau* Brandt walk past the doorway in the hall. She backed herself up, cocked her head at a strange angle, and then headed straight for the piano. Annette was so short behind the music stand on the piano that she didn't see her grandmother storming toward us.

For one blissful moment, I thought that her grandmother would be proud when she saw that it was Annette who was playing the beautiful music. But the expression on *Frau* Brandt's face was not a happy one, and it did not improve when she saw that it was Annette who was playing.

"This piano is Ida's. It is not to be played by anyone," she said with finality as she closed the lid on the keyboard with a thud.

Annette slid toward me and burst into tears, burying her head in my side. I looked up at *Frau* Brandt. "I'm sorry, *Frau* Brandt," I said. "I certainly thought you wouldn't mind her own daughter playing it."

"Well, you are wrong, *Fräulein*," she spat back.

It was such a sad scene, with Annette weeping in my arms and her grandmother angry that her granddaughter was playing her daughter's piano. I was relieved when *Frau* Brandt turned on her heels and left the room.

"It's all right, Annette," I said, trying to comfort her. "You were playing so beautifully. I'm sure she didn't mean to hurt you."

That was the second bad scene within the space of an hour that involved me. I wondered what I would do next to cause the major's mother-in-law distress. I was beginning to feel that the major might have to dismiss me after the day was done. I knew if *Frau* Brandt had any say in the matter that he would.

But the worst event of all was yet to come. Right before dinner, I asked the major if he would mind if I went back to the hotel alone. I was afraid I would ruin *Frau* Brandt's dinner just by being there. The major said he would prefer if I would stay to help with the children, so I did.

Frau Brandt's guests from Köln were still there, and they also joined us for dinner. I was listening to the violinist tell me about his music studies in Köln when the butler brought out seven dinner plates. On each plate was a large lettuce leaf, and on top of the leaf was an entire fish.

"What is this?" asked Annette immediately.

I closed my eyes and hoped that *Frau* Brandt didn't hear her question. "It's a fish," I replied softly. "I'll help you cut it up."

"It is cod, Annette—North Sea cod—caught especially for us and brought to Berlin by railcar," said *Frau* Brandt proudly. "I'm afraid you will not get such fine delicacies in Kassel, so you must enjoy them here in Berlin."

I looked down at Annette, who was seated to my left, and prayed that she would not turn her nose up at her grandmother's fine food. I looked across the table at Sepp. He was poking the fish's head with his fork.

I worked quickly at carving my fish up, and then I traded plates with Annette. To her credit, she ate several bites although she hardly put a dent in her fish. The fish had a very strong taste to it, but I was determined not to disappoint the major's mother-in-law. I finished every edible bite.

I was relieved when the major successfully made excuse for us all to leave and go back to the hotel, shortly after dinner. I suppose *Frau* Brandt had had enough of us for one day anyway. Her driver took us back to the hotel in her car.

It was while we were in the car, careening through the streets, that I began to feel very ill. My head was pounding by the time we got out of the car at the hotel. I took Sepp's hand as we went inside, but I was struggling just to breathe. We rode up the lift to the third floor. The major and Annette got out ahead of us.

I think I made it most of the way down the hall to our room, but then I had to stop and lean up against the wall. Everything around me was spinning, and I was feeling faint. I heard Sepp call out to his father when I stopped. Then everything went black.

The children told me later on, with pride, that their father caught me before I fell to the floor, and that he carried me to the room. He put me on his bed, the one closest to the door. At least that is where I was when I came to. The major was on the telephone with the front desk asking for a doctor to be sent up immediately. My head was throbbing, and I found it very hard to breathe.

I saw the concern in the major's eyes, and I heard him say that I was very hot. Then everything went black again. When I came to, Sepp and Annette were hanging in front of my face.

"Step back, children," said the major. I heard a high-pitch squeaking, and then I realized that the sound was me trying to breathe without much success.

"A doctor is on the way, *Fräulein*," the major said. "Klara! Please hold on."

I tried to look at the major, but my eyes wouldn't focus. He had never called me Klara before. *Why did my head hurt so much?*

I don't know how long it took, but the next thing I remember, there was a stranger with a long mustache stooping over me. He pushed his spectacles back and touched me on the cheek.

"Tell me again. What did she have to eat this evening, Major?"

"Cod."

"And did you all have the cod?"

"Yes," the major said.

"My," the doctor said as he rubbed his chin. "I have been treating compound fractures and concussions for so long now that I feel I have lost my medical knowledge, but I once had a case very similar to this. *Fräulein* Mauer, do you eat fish regularly?"

I nodded and tried to breathe in. "From the river," I said, straining for air.

"Where are you from?" asked the doctor.

"Sinsheim," replied the major for me.

"Have you ever eaten fish from the sea, *Fräulein*?"

I shook my head. The doctor put his hand on the inside of my arm by my wrist. "Pulse is very weak. Fever and difficulty breathing," he said, talking to himself. "Open your mouth, *Fräulein*."

I tried to take in another breath, but all I did was choke. After he took a look inside my mouth, there was a long pause.

"Hmm." He felt around the side of my neck. "Swelling. She needs medicine right away." The doctor rose from my side. "She most likely has iodine poisoning, *Herr* Major, or an allergic reaction to the seafood. I am going to go back to my office. We don't have much in the way of medicine these days, but I need to find something for her quickly. Her throat is swelling shut," he said while grabbing his medical bag. "In the meantime, call down to the front desk and tell them you need some milk immediately. Give her a little bit at a time until I return."

"Yes, *Herr* Doctor," replied the major.

"And try to keep her alert. Don't let her fall asleep."

The doctor left. The major phoned the front desk, and sooner than I thought, he was propping me up and trying to get me to drink some milk. The children were sitting still as ever on Sepp's bed, watching me with sullen faces.

"I'm sorry, Klara," he said as he was coaxing me to drink more. "I should have let you come back to the hotel when you asked me. If I had, this wouldn't have happened."

I choked a little on my milk when he said that.

"Don't try to talk now. Just rest," said the major as he put the glass of milk down on the bedside table and put a cold cloth on my forehead. I watched Annette disappear into the other room, and I closed my eyes for a moment. The throbbing in my head was getting worse.

"Klara," said the major when he saw my eyes close. "Klara, have some more milk." I tried to sit back up, and then I felt an object drop into my left arm. I looked down. Annette had put Otti in my arms. My head started spinning again. Then everything went black.

When I came to again, the doctor was back, and he was stirring some sort of powder into the glass of milk. He sat down on the bed and helped me sip a few times. The powder was bitter, but he told me I had to try to keep it down.

"You will need to help her drink this every fifteen minutes, until you see some improvement. You will know when the danger has passed, *Herr* Major. I have checked, but there are no nurses available. They are all attending to bombing victims."

"I will see to her, *Herr* Doctor," said the major.

"Let me leave you my telephone number. If anything changes for the worse, please call me immediately, no matter what the hour. Otherwise, I will check in with you first thing in the morning. I expect that, with the medicine, she should make a full recovery by then."

The major thanked the doctor, and he left after patting me on the hand. I don't know when the children went to bed. I must have fallen asleep. The major put a blanket over me, pulled the chair from by the window next to the bed and sat down. Every fifteen minutes, the major would wake me. Every fifteen minutes, he would make me drink the awful powder and milk mixture. This cycle continued well into the early hours of the morning.

I remember waking up one time and seeing the major asleep in the chair. I don't know what time it was, but I noticed right away that my breathing was easier and that my head had stopped throbbing. I rolled over and went back to sleep. The next time the major woke me, I told him that he should lie down, that I was feeling much better.

The next thing I knew, the morning light was coming through the window, and I could hear the major in the other room trying to get the children dressed. I tried to get up off of the bed, but when I sat up and put my feet on the floor, my head began to swim.

The major must have heard me, because he came right to the door between the two rooms. I saw the children peek out from behind him curiously.

"How is the patient this morning?" he asked.

When I didn't respond immediately, he stepped forward. "You look like you should lie back down, Klara."

"I'm feeling much better, *Herr* Major," I said, and then I did as he said.

The major sat down on the bed and put his hand on my forehead. "I think your fever is gone, but your eyes are still not right."

Sepp and Annette crowded each other on the other side of the bed.

"What do you think, children?" asked the major playfully. "Should our patient have some more medicine and get some rest?"

Sepp and Annette responded in unison.

"No more medicine," I said. "I don't want any more of that powder."

When I looked from the children to the major, I saw that his smile had been replaced by a contemplative look. "I was afraid we were going to lose you, *Fräulein*," he said softly. "Don't worry about the children today. I am going to let them keep my mother-in-law company. She needs to show us all how to properly supervise them anyway," he added with a hint of sarcasm in his voice.

The doctor came by to check on me and seemed pleased with my progress. The major and the children left with the doctor. I was all alone the rest of the day. I don't know how the major made it through his day on the little sleep he got because he was tending to me. I slept most of the day away, and by the time they returned at eight o'clock that evening, I was up on my feet.

Yesterday morning, I packed up all of the suitcases, but when I had finished that task, I had to sit and rest for a good long while. I let the major go to breakfast with the children without me. I still didn't feel much like eating.

The major gave me his arm on the way to the train, but he told me that he would not be able to do so once we got to Kassel. He didn't want people talking.

Our train ride home was uneventful, but by the time we pulled into Kassel, I was exhausted. Heiner met us at the station. I was actually glad to see a familiar face.

Frau Hoffmann commented on my lack of appetite at dinner. The major, after asking my permission, relayed the whole unpleasant situation to her, ending with strict instructions never to serve me codfish.

"You don't have to serve me cod either," piped up Annette.

"Me too," added Sepp.

I turned in early last night and got a lot of sleep, but I am still weak today. I think I will put you away, dear journal, and get some more rest.

....

June 17, 1944

This Saturday morning, the sun was shining and I am actually feeling well again. This I attribute to a most puzzling act of kindness.

I stayed in bed all day Thursday, not even feeling well enough to eat. *Frau* Hoffmann kept her eye on the children for me while tending to her normal tasks. Around two in the afternoon, I heard a knock on my door. *Frau* Hoffmann came in carrying a tray with a bowl of soup, a freshly baked roll, and a cup of ginger tea.

"I know you don't feel like eating, but here's something special, Klara. My neighbor, *Frau* Staude brought this over for you. I told her what happened to you in Berlin. She was so concerned. Rosine told me that this is the soup that her mother used to make for her when she was ill." *Frau* Hoffmann smiled. "You will never taste better soup than Rosine's, and it is sure to heal you."

I looked up at *Frau* Hoffmann as she set the tray in my lap. *Did I understand correctly that someone I have never met was concerned about me, took the time to make me something to eat, and bothered to come all the way to the other side of town to deliver it?*

"Eat up, Klara."

"Yes, *Frau* Hoffmann. Thank you."

Even though I was not hungry, I did eat. I ate the whole bowl of soup and the wonderful roll. And it worked its healing charms on me almost immediately. Still, I am perplexed by the kindness that *Frau* Hoffmann's neighbor showed to me by this deed. I don't know how I am to repay her.

We didn't do much of anything Friday. The children played outside for most of the day, and I unpacked our suitcases. I did interrupt the major in his study to let him know that I expected him to deduct the doctor's bill from my wages. He wouldn't hear of it and told me he didn't have time to discuss such nonsense.

Tomorrow is Klaus's birthday. I will have to close now so that I can write him a birthday greeting.

July 1944

July 8, 1944

Sepp, Annette, and I went to watch the major play football today. It turned out to be a beautiful day for it, even if it was a bit warm. The major said that every year the men at the military headquarters draw lots and divide themselves into two teams, and they play a match at the stadium on the south side of town where they used to hold the federal veteran's day parades.

Sepp has been looking forward to this for some time. He and the major have been passing the football out in the backyard every day since we returned from Berlin.

I didn't really know what I expected, but there was a good crowd of people who came to watch the game, including *Fräulein* Farber, who sat down right next to me and the children just before the game began.

She has a very pretty smile and a very pretty hat. I learned today that she is the niece of the *Gauleiter* and has lived her entire life in Kassel. I asked her how long she had known the major. She replied, "Forever." There was a sadness in her eyes when she talked about the major, and I felt badly, because I can see quite plainly that she loves him.

I saw her on the field before the game started. She went over to the major and greeted him. He was polite to her, but it is clear to me that however high he may have held her in his heart at one time, she is not there any longer.

I saw Lieutenant Braun, or more to the point, he saw me and waved with a big smile. He and the major ended up on the same team. I have to say that as the game progressed, I gained a little more respect for the lieutenant. He and the major both played with impressive skill. The men on the other team displayed some un-sportsman like conduct toward the end of the game, but this behavior was not returned by the major's team.

Sepp and Annette enjoyed cheering for their father, and in the end, the score was tied three to three. After ten more minutes of hard playing and maneuvering, the major made a pass to the lieutenant who scored a goal. We all cheered as loudly as we could. The game was over.

Some of the children took flowers out to the members of the winning team. I went down to the field with *Fräulein* Farber. While she was congratulating the major, Lieutenant Braun came over to me with a flower bouquet in his hand.

"These are for you, *Fräulein* Mauer," he said as he handed them to me.

I was so surprised when he handed them to me that it took me a moment to thank him. "You played very well," I said enthusiastically.

"You have a beautiful smile," he replied.

I looked down at the children in order to try to hide a blush that was rising in my cheeks. They were eager to be free from my side and run off with the other children onto the field. "Go ahead," I said to them. "But stay together."

I looked back up at the lieutenant. He cleared his throat and put his hands on his hips. "I was wondering if I might come by and see you this evening or maybe next Saturday?"

This was another surprising thing from him that took me off guard. "I-I don't have Saturdays off," I replied.

"When are you free, *Fräulein?*" he asked softly.

I looked past the sweaty lieutenant to the major who was standing in the distance behind him, talking to a crowd of people.

"Sunday afternoons," I replied, twirling the bouquet of flowers in my hands.

"May I call on you tomorrow afternoon, *Fräulein?*" he asked with a look of hopefulness in his eyes.

"Yes," I replied. I didn't want to disappoint him.

"I'll come by around two o'clock. Perhaps we can go for a walk."

I nodded, and as I did, someone came to congratulate the lieutenant on his performance.

I have been thinking about the lieutenant all afternoon, wondering if I should have said yes to him. I have never had a suitor before, and I really don't know how to act. I find that although I am a little apprehensive, I am also looking forward to it.

July 9, 1944

I went to mass with the major and the children this morning. I had a hard time concentrating on the homily as I was thinking about my date with the lieutenant.

Two o'clock finally came, and the lieutenant showed up right on time. The major answered the front door as I was coming down the stairs. I think he was surprised to see the lieutenant and even more surprised that I left with him.

We walked down by the Fulda, over the stone bridge by the old part of town, and along the river. It was a beautiful day for a walk, with a nice, gentle breeze blowing. The lieutenant told me a lot about himself. I listened with interest, trying to find something we had in common.

He asked me about my family and where I grew up. He started by telling me that I did not sound at all like I was from Sinsheim. He said that my accent was not like someone from the Swäbish region. I told him that my parents were from Berlin.

He asked me how long I had played the violin, and we talked about music for a while. He was surprised to hear that I began playing the violin when I was five. I didn't tell him, but I was the youngest student *Herr* Eldering had ever accepted.

We stopped at the stone bridge on the way home and threw some rocks into the river. Lieutenant Braun can make the stones skip on the water just like Reiner used to. He also has a characteristic in his laughter that reminds me of Reiner. Our conversation was easy, and the three hours I spent with him passed as if they were only ten minutes.

The awkward part of the day came when we got back home. I wasn't sure if I should invite him in or not, but then he said he had to get going. So we said good-bye.

I thought that the major might say something to me about going out with the lieutenant when I came in, but he did not. He seemed to be in a bad mood.

In the morning, I plan to take the children up to the *Bergpark* Wilhelmshöhe. Lieutenant Braun said that the grounds are beautiful and that there is a wonderful view of the city from the statue of *Herkules*. I think that is the brooding castle that I have always seen up on the hill.

....

July 16, 1944

This whole week went by slowly. On Tuesday, I got a note from Lieutenant Braun saying how much he enjoyed seeing me. He asked if he could call on me again this Sunday. The major had a lot of paperwork this morning, so I took the children to church. I was starting to get nervous as the clock got closer to two, but then the major came out of his study, and I was free to get ready for Lieutenant Braun.

The major gave me a peculiar look when he saw me leave with the lieutenant. I think he may not like not having my help with the children on Sunday afternoon as I have always spent my afternoons off in the house.

The lieutenant gave me his arm, and we walked all the way to the *Karlsau*. It is a beautiful park that, except for the Orangerie, has escaped destruction from the bombings. All of the trees and the grass are very green, because we got quite a bit of rain this week. This afternoon, however, was beautiful and sunny.

When we were at the temple by the *Schwaneninsel*, Lieutenant Braun told me he really liked my reply to his letter, and then he renewed his request to me to tell him a secret about myself. I tried to distract him by pointing out all of the beautiful swans.

I don't know why he keeps asking me for a secret. I wanted to tell him about my family. He has asked me about them too, but I somehow feel uncomfortable telling him anything, so I keep changing the subject when he brings it up.

From the way he tells it, the lieutenant has a normal family except for a great aunt who is in an asylum. He has one brother and one sister. He even told me about his favorite memories of growing up. He seems like a decent young man. I found out today that he is twenty-five years old. I think he has a lot of ambition and optimism for someone of his age.

It is also clear to me from our conversations how much he admires the major. I wonder if the major is aware of the influence he has on the lieutenant.

On the way home, the lieutenant took my hand instead of offering me his arm. I liked holding his hand, but I do wonder if it isn't a little bold for him to do that. I could see that the major was in a bad mood when I came into the house after the lieutenant left.

I hope I will get another invitation from the lieutenant for next Sunday, for I really enjoyed our conversation and his company.

....

July 18, 1944

Today is Tuesday, and it rained almost the entire day. I spent almost two hours, first with Sepp on the violin and then with Annette at the piano. I only had two years of piano lessons, and they were so long ago that I sometimes wonder if she isn't going to have to have a different instructor if she is going to improve.

Sepp, on the other hand, is making good progress on my violin. Toward the end of the lesson, however, he broke one of my strings. I am not sure how I will get a replacement, and I am quite upset about it.

I did not get a note from Lieutenant Braun today, as I had hoped, but I did get a letter from Aunt Frieda. Klaus is away at the Hitler Youth summer camp. Lenz misses him terribly. She has been teaching Liese how to make a quilt. Aunt Frieda says that Liese is very good at sewing.

Aunt Frieda's letter inspired me to take on a project with Annette. Otti is in need of a new dress, and Annette is in need of something to do. We spent the afternoon in the dining room cutting out a pattern for a doll's dress from some of the major's old newspapers. Sepp was in his father's study, drawing pictures of airplanes until the major got home.

The major has been very quiet lately at mealtime and has said very little to me about anything at all. I don't know whether I have done something to displease him, or whether he is preoccupied with his business.

....

July 19, 1944

Frau Hoffmann came out onto the back porch this afternoon, just after dinner, and told me that the major had just phoned and asked her to ask me to meet him at his office at the general headquarters before two o'clock this afternoon.

"Before two o'clock?" I asked her.

"Yes," *Frau* Hoffmann said.

I wrinkled up my nose and looked out over the garden. "Am I supposed to bring the children?"

"I'm not certain," *Frau* Hoffmann replied, "but I would suspect so. I don't think he would have you leave them with me. Oh, and he specifically wants you to bring your purse."

Although I found the major's request quite strange, I called to the children. We would have to leave immediately if we were to get to the major's office before two.

We ended up waiting longer than I had hoped for the yellow trolley on Wilhelmshöher Allee. When we arrived at Rundstrasse, Annette tripped getting off of the trolley and scraped her knee. I didn't spend too much time consoling her, because we were late.

Four Nazi flags were hanging from the top story of the four-story headquarters building, covering the columns on the east side and whipping in the breeze. We hurried up the stairs, passing the statues of the men and the horses, and stepped inside the hallway. The last time I was there was the day the major received his medal, but I have never been to his office. I asked directions to the major's office, and after I explained to her who I was, the woman at the desk on the first floor offered to take me there herself.

She led us across the courtyard, down a wide hallway, up two flights of stairs, and into an office on the right hand side. The first person I saw was Lieutenant Braun. He was sitting at a desk right inside the door. I smiled at his surprised expression when he saw me. "What are you doing here?" he asked.

I shrugged. "The major asked me to come," I said.

The lieutenant narrowed his eyes. "I hope you're not in any trouble," he said.

I laughed nervously.

"Before I tell him that you're here," said the lieutenant, lowering his voice, "can I see you on Sunday?"

"Certainly," I said. I was already wondering when I could see him again. The lieutenant came close to me and whispered something funny in my ear. I laughed just as the door beyond the lieutenant's desk opened.

There stood the major, with a most serious look on his face. I stopped laughing immediately and swallowed hard, but I could see that the major was unimpressed at the sight of the lieutenant flirting with me. That was when the feeling that he is somehow displeased with me returned.

The major looked from the lieutenant to me. "Children, would you wait out here for a moment? *Fräulein* Mauer, would you step inside, please?"

Lieutenant Braun turned aside, and I followed the major into his office. He shut the door behind me immediately, and then he walked over to his desk and opened a drawer on the left hand side. First, he removed a pistol and set it carefully on the side of his desk. Then he took out a small stack of papers.

I tried to look around his office without looking too interested. The room was quite large. His desk sat at an angle next to the window. The books on the shelves flanking the window were all neatly arranged. He had several piles on the corners of his desk, and there was a mound of papers covering the rest of it. I noticed that there were no pictures on the wall, just a giant map of Kassel.

The major looked at me as I was standing at attention before him. Then he reached over to his telephone, disconnected the cord from the back, and took the telephone off of the receiver. "*Fräulein* Mauer, would you be able to take these papers over to my friend this afternoon?" he asked after clearing his throat.

I am not sure whether there was a look of relief or confusion on my face when I heard his question. I stared down at the telephone for a moment, and then I met his eyes. A moment later, I realized what he was asking, but he had asked me with no such acknowledgement of a favor as he had before. *Did he think I was now his personal courier?*

"Yes," I responded automatically.

The major reached down and folded some papers into a small square. "I would suggest you carry this in your purse, *Fräulein*," he said, handing me the papers. "You remember his address?"

"Yes, sir," I said as I opened my purse and shoved the papers inside.

When I looked up, the major was looking at me with his inquisitive eyes. Then he took a couple of steps toward the window turning his back to me, rested his left arm on the window frame, and stared outside.

"Will that be all, sir?" I asked, after a full moment of silence.

The major looked back at me as if I had startled him out of a bad dream. "No," he said quietly.

My heart began to pound as he looked as if he were going to deliver some dreadful news to me, or as if he were about to do something very difficult. He looked at his watch, and then he moved quickly toward his desk.

There were two identical ledgers sitting one on top of the other in his top, middle drawer. As he pulled out the one on the top, the gold writing on the front cover of the one that was left in the drawer sparkled in the sunlight. He closed the drawer with a thud. Then he walked around the desk to where I was standing.

"I need you to take this home. But you must get it out of the building without anyone seeing you do so."

I narrowed my eyes and stared at the major.

"Please don't ask me any questions," he said in a tone of desperation. "I can see them in your eyes."

I looked down at the ledger. The one he was asking me to take home had bronze letters on the cover. I tried to think of how I could accomplish what he was asking me. The ledger was too large to fit in my purse. I reached around my back and tugged on the belt around my waist. *Why was he asking me to smuggle the ledger out of the building?*

I took the ledger from his hand and asked him to turn around. At first the major just stood there, and then he complied with my request and turned back toward the window. I unbuttoned the two top buttons on the front of my dress and slipped the ledger down the front until it rested on the top of my belt. After I had buttoned my dress back up, I adjusted the ledger until it was wedged just slightly underneath the belt against my stomach.

"There," I said as I swung my purse onto my arm and drew it up to my waist. "Will this work?"

The major turned around and looked at me. "I think it will do," he said although the nervousness was not completely gone from his eyes. "If anything happens to that ledger, Klara, I am a dead man," he said candidly.

The whole situation was so strange from the moment *Frau* Hoffmann told me the major wanted to see me at his office. He was in such an odd mood when we got there, and his requests were even more baffling to me. But I understood the pale look that he gave me when he said he would be a dead man.

Before I could assure him that I would take care of it, the lieutenant popped his head in the door. "Excuse me, *Herr* Major. The inspector general is here to see you."

I looked back at the major in an attempt to reassure him, and then I left his office, pressing my purse to my waist.

"Let's go, children," I said walking right past the lieutenant's desk and the inspector general. I didn't even stop to take the children's hands.

It was quite an uncomfortable walk to *Herr* L.'s house with Annette constantly wanting to hold my hand and the ledger constantly shifting inside my dress as I walked. Halfway to *Herr* L.'s house, I decided that I was going to have to remove the ledger from my dress and carry it with my purse the rest of the way home. And that is exactly what I did, once I got to *Herr* L.'s house.

After delivering the papers, I took the children home. They ran out the back door almost as soon as we got in the front door. I went up to my room. The first thing I did was to place the ledger behind the molding in the hole in the wall where *Fräulein* Magda used to keep her booze and where I now keep you, dear journal.

Even though I have not seen the Gestapo men again, nor have I been asked to tell anyone what the major has been doing, I decided not to look in the ledger. I really don't want anything to do with the major's business. He keeps telling me not to ask him any questions. Truthfully, I have a hundred questions in my mind from the things I have seen and heard. He may well be the most gracious man I have ever met, but he is also the most mysterious.

The major got home late this evening. He found us all in the living room, and the first thing he asked me was for the ledger. I didn't tease him but went straight up to my room and produced it for him.

"Did you look in this ledger, *Fräulein* Mauer?" he asked as soon as I handed it to him.

"No, sir," I replied, looking him straight in the eyes.

"Good," he responded and turned around to leave my room. "Thank you for getting me out of a very uncomfortable position this afternoon," he added, turning back around.

I never know what to feel when he looks at me the way he does sometimes. I don't know whether to feel like he has used me, like I have done the right thing for a good cause, or whether I will some day be in trouble for aiding in a great conspiracy.

July 21, 1944

I am not sure what is going on in Germany, but something has happened that has caused quite a stir. *Frau* Hoffmann told me this afternoon, that Heiner told her, that someone tried to kill the *Führer* yesterday with a bomb. Now it seems that there is chaos in the cities with some reporting that he was killed, and others claiming he is still alive. Heiner says that the SS and Gestapo are trying to round up all of the conspirators. I know what will happen to them next.

I didn't see the major at all yesterday or this morning. I was beginning to think that he might have been someone they were going to round up, because of all of his secretiveness, but when I went downstairs this evening to get a glass of water, I found him sitting in the living room in the dark, listening to the radio. He nearly scared me out of my skin. From the look on his face when I turned the light on, I could not tell whether he was mourning the loss of his comrades or relieved to hear the voice of our *Führer* on the radio.

....

July 23, 1944

Dear Journal,

I don't think, in all of the time I have had you for a companion, that I have ever felt so mortified as today. A most horrible set of circumstances has happened, and I don't really know where to begin to sort it all out.

I went with the children, but without the major, to mass this morning. He made a special point to help us get out of the house on time. He seemed preoccupied at the dinner table, and by the time two o'clock rolled around, I was left to wonder again if he was ever going to come out of his study so I could get ready to go out.

Finally, the major emerged and took the children out to the garden. I ran upstairs, changed my dress, and brushed my hair. But none of my preparation mattered. I sat on the stairs by the front door for over an hour waiting for Lieutenant Braun. He never came.

At first, I convinced myself that some important matter that couldn't wait had probably delayed him. Then I began to think that perhaps he was not feeling well and could not send me word that he was unable to come. But as the clock chimed three, I began to imagine that something awful might have happened to him.

I was about to get up and go up to my room when *Frau* Hoffmann came out of the dining room on her way to the living room. She gave me a piteous look as she passed by. Then she stopped all of the sudden and turned back to me.

"You needn't wait any longer, Klara. It seems that he's not going to come," she said.

I narrowed my eyes. *How did she know who I was waiting for?* "How do you know that?" I asked curiously.

Frau Hoffmann tilted her head and the edge of her lips curled up a little.

"What do you know, *Frau* Hoffmann?" I asked, reading her face. "Did he call?"

"No," she said at last, drawing her answer out. *Frau* Hoffmann looked around the corner toward the back porch, and then she looked at me directly. "I probably shouldn't say anything to you about it as I normally would not. But since the major will never tell you what he has done for you, I suppose I will have to."

"What do you mean?" I asked, by now completely baffled.

Frau Hoffmann set the linens down on the table in the hall and came over to the stairs where I was still sitting. "The major called Lieutenant Braun to his study this morning," she said half in a whisper. "They were having a pleasant conversation when I left him there, but when I passed by the study a little later on, I heard the major tell him why he had really asked him here on a Sunday morning."

I leaned forward as *Frau* Hoffmann continued.

"He told the lieutenant that he thought that they had always worked well together, and for that reason, he felt obligated to point out that the lieutenant was engaging in a very risky endeavor that was likely to affect the major in a most unpleasant way."

Frau Hoffmann paused for a moment and tilted her head toward the back of the house as if she heard someone.

"Go on," I said, trying to coax the story out of her.

"Well," she finally continued, "the major told the lieutenant that he didn't mind if he was seeing you, if he really cared for you and treated you honorably. But if he was only toying with you and if he broke your heart, it would cause distress to the major's household. He made it very clear to the lieutenant that if that happened, the lieutenant's career would equally be in jeopardy. He told the lieutenant that it was his choice how to proceed and that the major would never bring the subject up again."

I couldn't help it. When I heard her words, my mouth hung open. Then I bit my tongue and breathed in deeply. How could the major interfere in my personal affairs in such a way? *Frau* Hoffmann must have seen the disgust on my face.

"He did you a favor, Klara," she said defensively. "That young man does not have a good reputation."

I looked up at *Frau* Hoffmann, surprised at what she had just said. Was that what the major meant when he said at the Christmas party that the lieutenant could not be trusted?

"Have you ever been in love, Klara?" asked *Frau* Hoffmann with a look of pity in her eyes.

"Not in that way," I responded. "I have only given my love to children, and they do not always return it."

"When it is the right time and the right one, you will find that it will be returned to you and in good measure. You will never have that from the lieutenant."

I stood to my feet and headed toward the front door. Now she was making me angry. "Don't wait on supper for me," I said, turning back to *Frau* Hoffmann.

I didn't know where to go, but I knew that I wanted to get away from there as quickly as I could. The news from *Frau* Hoffmann had crushed me. I couldn't believe what the major had done.

After wandering around for over an hour, I sat down on a bench overlooking the Fulda and looked down the empty path where I had strolled with the lieutenant last Sunday.

I was angry with the major. What right did he have to scare off the lieutenant like he had, all because he didn't want his household interrupted? I closed my eyes and let a couple of tears fall. I had fallen a little for the lieutenant. I had listened to him flatter me and tell me how beautiful he thought I was. I had even let him steal a kiss from me.

But none of this mattered now, because he didn't come for me this afternoon. Nor did he send any explanation as to why he wasn't coming. If *Frau* Hoffmann hadn't told me, I would still have no idea.

As time went slowly by, I wasn't sure whether I should feel angry at the lieutenant too, or just sorry for myself. While I was trying to decide this, I got up and walked toward the old stone bridge. If I hadn't been so preoccupied with my thoughts, I might have noticed what a lovely afternoon it was. I realized this when I saw a couple ahead of me, crossing the bridge arm in arm, enjoying the afternoon.

All of the sudden, I turned around and headed back down the path where I had just been. To my relief, when I looked back over my shoulder, the couple ahead of me turned down the path on the other side of the bridge and went the opposite direction. I didn't know who the girl was, but when the man reached over and planted a kiss on the girl's cheek, I saw at once that it was Lieutenant Braun!

The lieutenant had not even given me the courtesy of a rejection, and there he was strolling with someone else when he was supposed to be with me. I collapsed on the nearest bench. I couldn't believe this was happening. It was all so unbelievable.

It must have taken me quite a while to sort this new circumstance out. When I did, I was angry with myself for being taken by the lieutenant, for reacting in such a childish way, and for not appreciating what the major had done for me.

There was no way around it. Now I was going to have to admit that the major had done me a favor. *How could I go back to the house and face him, knowing that he had to step into my personal affairs to protect me, like a child, from my own foolishness? What must the major think of me?*

I sat on the bench, watching the water flow by until it was time for the sun to set. There was no peace in my thoughts, and I had an awful feeling in my stomach, but I knew that I had to be back before dark. So, I picked myself up and started home.

I did not see the major when I came in. I am glad, because I don't know how I can face him now. The doors to the children's bedrooms were shut when I sneaked upstairs, so I know the major put them to bed. I came straight to my room and sat in the dark until I decided I should get you out and tell you all about it.

I don't feel any better for having done so, and I don't know how in the world I will get through tomorrow when I am sure to have to face the major.

....

July 24, 1944

Last night, I didn't sleep very well. I heard Annette screaming early in the morning while it was still dark. I went to her room as quickly as I could. She was lying in her bed crying hysterically. I sat down on her bed and put my arms around her.

"What's wrong, Annette?" She clung to me immediately. "What's the matter?" I asked again.

"The dogs," she sobbed.

"What dogs?"

"The dogs were eating me," she cried.

I looked up as I heard a noise in the hall and saw the major's figure in her doorway.

"She's had a nightmare," I said as I was stroking her face. "I'll stay with her."

The major hesitated a moment in the doorway, and then he went back downstairs. It was at least another half hour before Annette was calm enough to go back to sleep. I tried to make myself comfortable next to her. I was afraid that if she woke up and didn't find me there that she would start screaming again.

When I was brushing my hair this morning, I noticed dark circles around my puffy eyes, and then I remembered all of my troubles. I decided that I was going to pretend that nothing had happened. After all, I am not heartbroken over the lieutenant. Now that all is said and done, I find that I am only ashamed of myself—of my hope and of my ignorance.

I got the children dressed, and we were sitting at the table when the major came downstairs. I sat up straight and tried to look pleasant. He glanced at me, and then he greeted the children, paying special attention to Annette.

"I used to have bad nightmares when I was a boy," said the major as he sat down with his newspaper in hand, "usually after a very bad thunderstorm."

"Mine always involved officers," I mumbled after a moment, wondering if the major would understand what I was saying.

The major looked up at me suddenly. "Lieutenants or majors?" he asked quick-wittedly.

"SS," I said in all seriousness.

"You and I have more in common than you think," replied the major as he took a sip from his coffee cup.

I have been thinking about his comment all day long. I am relieved that between Annette's nightmare and the major's comment, I do not feel as horrible as I did yesterday.

It was so hot today that I took the children down to the *Flussbad* to play. While I was sitting in the shade watching them splash in the water, Heiner came walking down the path with two men. They were very well dressed. My immediate thought was that they were Gestapo, and I wondered what Heiner was doing in their company.

I smiled as I greeted Heiner and rose to my feet as he introduced me to the two men as Major Rager's nanny.

"Ah, then you have the enviable job of shaping these young, impressionable children," said the older man with the brown hat.

I nodded politely.

"I was just telling them about Major Rager, Klara," began Heiner. "There are very few men like him."

I looked at the two men who were standing on either side of Heiner.

"What is your opinion of Major Rager, *Fräulein?*" asked the man with the crooked nose.

"I-I agree with Heiner," I said.

"Yes, but that is just as well," said the man with the crooked nose. "Heiner may say what he will, but you are undoubtedly more intimately acquainted with the major. How long have you been working for him?"

I squinted into the sunshine and shifted on my feet before I responded. "About eight months now."

"And what is his opinion of the change in the Kassel *Wehrmacht* command?" asked the man with the brown hat all of the sudden.

"I don't know, sir," I responded immediately. "He never speaks with me of such things."

The two men shifted their gaze to Heiner, asking for a response from him. He shrugged. "He has said nothing to me on the subject."

A few awkward seconds were followed by a long silence. I looked Heiner in the eyes as I remembered that the major said he did not trust Heiner. I wondered why Heiner was keeping company with these men, and I wondered what they meant by "a change in the Kassel *Wehrmacht* command."

From out in the water, I heard Annette scream. Sepp either pushed her or accidentally bumped into her, and she was struggling in the water.

The man, who did not have the brown hat, stepped aside as I took off toward the water. My heart was beating fast as I helped Annette come onto dry land. The fall into the water had scared her, and she was sobbing uncontrollably as she was gasping for breath. I laid her on the ground and turned her over on her side so that I could pat her on the back. When I finally got her calmed down, I saw that Heiner and the two men were gone. It was almost as if they had vanished.

I shook my head and looked down at my soggy dress and wrung out my hair. The first thing I was going to tell the major when I saw him next was that he was right about Heiner. He was right about Heiner, and he was right about Lieutenant Braun. Maybe that was why I wasn't having such a hard time trusting him any more.

After the children were done with their baths, *Frau* Hoffmann asked me where I had gone yesterday afternoon. I told her I went down by the river by myself. Then I tried to change the subject because I did not want to talk about it. I asked her how her sister was doing, and somehow, the conversation came back around to the major's wife.

"How did she die?" I asked all of the sudden although I had been wondering since that day in Berlin when *Frau* Brandt had blamed her death on the major.

Frau Hoffmann put down the wooden spoon that was in her hand and shrugged. "She just got sick and two months later, she was gone. I think the doctor said it was meningitis." She looked over at me with a curious expression.

I looked down at the floor. She was wondering what business I had asking such a question. "When we were up in Berlin, *Frau* Brandt said that Ida would still be alive if it hadn't been for the major."

"Don't you believe a word of it," said *Frau* Hoffmann immediately, pointing the spoon at me. "He had nothing to do with her sickness. The doctors didn't know what to do for her until it was too late. She died of meningitis, not from anything the major did. He couldn't have been more devoted to her."

I put my hand on my chest as the air left my lungs. I was surprised at the relief I felt at hearing this. *Frau* Hoffmann might have said more, but at that moment, the major stepped through the door into the kitchen. *Frau* Hoffmann turned red for a moment until the major spoke, and it was clear that he had not overheard our conversation.

I wanted to tell him right away about Heiner and the Gestapo men, but I ended up waiting until *Frau* Hoffmann left the house for the evening. After I put the children to bed, I went downstairs. I did not find him in the study, and he was nowhere in the house. As a last resort, I went out onto the back porch.

At first, I didn't see him. He was standing in a shadow, leaning against a column, staring up at the moon. The view from the porch that evening was clear and beautiful. The landscape to the south was covered in soft moonlight, the kind of night that bombers relish. I cleared my throat. The major looked over at me, and then he looked back at the moon.

"I wanted to tell you, sir, that I think you are right about Heiner," I said.

"What do you mean?"

I stepped toward the major. "I took the children down to the Fulda this afternoon, and I ran into Heiner there. He was walking with two men. They started asking me about you."

The major turned to me, and in the moonlight, I could see that I had his attention. He asked me for a full account of the conversation, and when he had heard it all, he tipped his head back and let out a slow sigh. "I think those are the same ones who showed up at one of my plants today. I wonder what they want."

"I hope they didn't find it; whatever it was they were looking for," I said stubbornly.

The major brought his right hand up to his forehead.

"Are you to be transferred?" I asked, finally getting up the courage.

The major glanced over at me quickly. "No. No," he said. He let out a forced chuckle. "Berlin has finally decided that Kassel is important enough to have a higher ranking officer in command of production. It remains to be seen how this will affect my position, but I know that it primarily depends upon the disposition of the new commander."

I looked out into the darkness. I wasn't sure, from the tone of his voice, whether he was glad for the change or not.

"For your sake, I hope he is a reasonable man," I said.

The major looked back at me again, but in the shadow of the moon, I could not see his expression.

"I hope so too," he said slowly.

"Good night, sir," I said, at last.

"Good night, Klara."

I left the major out in the evening. I cannot help but wonder what secrets he is hiding. In public, I always see the model Third *Reich* officer, one in whom *Herr* Hitler has not bestowed his trust in vain. In private, I get the sense that his loyalty is otherwise. It is almost as if the two are always in conflict inside of him, and I am not sure where his heart really stands.

July 29, 1944

Today is Saturday, and I am sitting out on the back porch in the sunshine, watching the children play in the garden. I am glad to see that the trauma of the past couple of days seems to have worn off completely, and they seem to have all but forgotten it. I have not.

On Wednesday, I went with Sepp and Annette down to Frankfurt on the train. My primary reason for going there was to get my violin restrung. Sepp has fallen behind in his violin lessons, and I wanted to get back to them as soon as possible. The major told me that I should take the children along, and so we made a day of it.

I have never been to Frankfurt before, but I have to say that it is looking a lot like Kassel and Berlin, with bombing damage nearly everywhere you look. I had trouble finding my way around in the streets. We spent an extra hour just trying to locate the shop of the man who restrung my violin. I was relieved when we were finally on our way out of town with my violin fixed.

Our return trip started out uneventful, except for the conductor who came through the car asking for our tickets. He had thick eyebrows, and as he moved from person to person, he kept glancing back at the children. As time went on, I became quite uncomfortable, wondering why he should be so interested in them. I was relieved when we pulled into the next station and the conductor got off the train.

There have often been delays as I have ridden the trains, and there was a particularly long delay at this station. We must have sat there for close to fifteen minutes. The children were becoming restless. I got up and went to the exit to look out onto the platform. That is when I saw the man with the bushy eyebrows and several soldiers boarding the other end of our car. When I got back to

Sepp and Annette, I met the soldiers, who immediately raised their guns at us and demanded that we off board the train.

My heart began to beat so fast. I have never had someone point a gun at me. Everyone in the car was staring now. In my confusion, I grabbed my violin and the children and went straight out the back of the car. I had no idea why we were being treated this way, but it only made me angry when I saw how scared the children were. They were clinging to me. The soldiers marched us into the train station and locked us in a room in the trainmaster's office, without answering my question, "What's going on?"

Everything happened so quickly and made no sense to me that I am not sure what happened next, but it was not long until they put us back on a train to Frankfurt. The soldiers with the guns guarded us the whole way. When I tried to ask them where we were going and why they were taking us, they just told me to be silent.

I kept the children close to me and tried not to look as scared as they were. All I wanted to do was call for the major. I was sure that some horrible mistake had taken place, but in the back of my mind, I was wondering if someone had found out my true identity.

I don't know what time we got to Frankfurt or when we got to the awful building they took us to, but they took my violin from me, and then they literally threw me and the children into a cell with no bed, no chairs, and only one light bulb hanging from the ceiling. There was a tiny sliding hole on the door that one could use to peek inside our room. Despite my efforts of pounding on the door, no one ever came to check on us. The room smelled damp, and it was dirty. The children began to cry.

I was trying to understand what was happening to us, but the more I thought about it, the more things got twisted around in my mind. I pulled the children close to me and tried to comfort them, telling them that we were going to be all right. I don't think they believed me. I had a hard time believing myself.

Inside the whitewashed room with the light bulb, I lost all sense of time. I figured we should have already been back home by now, and I began to wonder how long it would take for the major to miss us. It was very hot and stuffy inside the room, and I hoped that whoever had put us in there would take us out before all of the oxygen was gone.

Just as I had lost hope that anyone would open the door, an officer came in, flanked by two guards with their guns. He demanded to see my papers, and then he asked me my name and the names of the children. I told him our names and explained to him that I was Major Rager's nanny.

He laughed at me and handed my papers to one of the guards. "That's a very good story," he said with a sneer.

"Why are you holding us?" I asked boldly. "Major Rager will be very upset when he gets home and we are not there."

"Major who?"

"Rager," I responded.

"And who is he?"

"The children's father. The war production minister for Hessen," I said.

"Right," said the officer in a tone of unbelief. "We're putting an end to your child smuggling operation, *Fräulein*, and we are not fooled by your phony story."

"You'd better call Major Rager," I said with fire in my eyes. "You're making a big mistake."

The officer narrowed his eyes, and then he smiled devilishly. "Make yourself comfortable. You're going to be here a while."

The officer turned and left. One of the guards threw two blankets at me, and then they slammed the door shut. I drew in a quick breath. Child smuggling? *Had I heard him correctly?* This was all some big mistake, and there was nothing I could do. There we were, hungry, and without a single comfort in life. I picked up the two blankets and sat down on them in the corner by the door with the children.

It was all I could do to speak calmly with them and to try to make believe that we were not in such a horrible situation after all, when I knew that we were. Sepp and Annette both began to complain that they were starving. Despite my efforts to assure them that I knew, they kept complaining. I think they thought there was something I could do about it.

Finally, I snapped at them and told them both that we had to do without food, and that they should just go to sleep. We were stuck there.

It was the most miserable night of my entire life. When I would drift off to sleep, the light bulb seemed to wake me up, and I would stare in disbelief at the white walls. I have never been in prison before and never dreamed that I would ever be in such a horrible place. I tried not to think of how angry the major would be with me even though I had done nothing wrong. Then I thought of Uncle Lothar. I could picture the look he would have on his face when he found out.

A graver thought entered my mind as I remembered that they had taken my papers. I hoped that they wouldn't find out what the major had done for me. I hoped that they wouldn't find out my real identity, and I hoped that when morning came this whole nightmare would be over.

But it wasn't. The night went on and on. The children would wake up shivering from being on the concrete, and they cried. I would try to pull them closer to me and calm them. I don't think they got much sleep, but I got even less.

I figured that it must have been morning when someone slid a dish with some stale, black bread and a small tin of water through the door. Sepp was the first to get to the bread, and he nearly knocked over the water getting to it. I grabbed the bread from his hands and divided it up between us. Then I helped them each take a sip of water.

Annette nearly spit out the bread, but I held my hand up to her mouth and told her that she had to eat it. I didn't know how long it was going to be before we had anything else to eat. Before I could prevent him, Sepp drank down the rest of the water. I was still parched.

An hour or so passed, and then someone came and dragged me out of the cell to an interrogation room. The children were screaming as I left. I didn't want to leave them, for fear I would never see them again, but I had no choice.

A gruff looking, Gestapo-type man came in with my papers in his hand. He asked me the same questions that the officer the night before had asked me. I gave him the same responses, and at every chance I pled with him to call the major. He peppered me with questions about the children, but there was nothing more I could tell him than that we lived in Kassel at Terrassestrasse 1 and that Sepp and Annette were the major's children.

I remember when I was fourteen when I said something disrespectful to Uncle Lothar, and he slapped me across the face. It took me a while to admit it, but I did deserve it. The backhanded slap the Gestapo man gave me—I didn't deserve, and it hurt much more than Uncle Lothar's. Maybe it stunned me more than anything, but it stung so bad, my right eye began to water, and I whimpered a little.

At last, the Gestapo man leaned into my face and told me that he knew they were Jewish, and that we were going to rot away in that cell until I admitted it and told them where the rest of the children were hiding. I begged him humbly to call the major, and I said again that he would verify my story. The Gestapo man called the guard, and the guard threw me back into the cell with Sepp and Annette.

I sat down against the wall opposite of the door fully stunned. Then I looked up at Sepp and Annette who were staring at me with frightened eyes. By now, my right eye was starting to swell shut.

"They think you're Jewish," I mumbled. "That's what this is all about. God help us!" I pulled the children onto my lap, and I put my arms around them. I had done my very best to convince the Gestapo man that this was a mistake. There was nothing more I could do. All that was left to do now was to pray that the major would somehow find us.

For the next couple of hours, I gathered the little strength I had left, and I told the children stories. We made up a little game to play, and I tried to keep them occupied in the stale room with the one light bulb. The right side of my face still hurt and it felt bruised, but I didn't want the children to know I was in pain. Dinner finally came. It was the same as breakfast. This time, Annette didn't spit it out.

We spent another horrible night on the concrete and ate the same stale bread for breakfast and lunch the next day. I couldn't tell how much time had passed that afternoon, but just about the time I thought I would go out of my mind, Annette came over to where I was sitting against the wall, and she sat down on my lap.

"I love you," she said, and she put her little arms around my neck. Although I knew that I had to be strong, I couldn't stop the tears that came to my eyes. Suddenly, I heard keys at the door, and I turned to watch as it lurched open. I wasn't ready to go to another long session of interrogation, nor did I want to receive another beating.

I don't think I have ever been so relieved to see anyone in my life as I was at that moment. Standing there with the guard was the major. I will never forget the look of horror and relief that spread across his face when he saw us. The children let out a shriek. Sepp was the first to head for him, but Annette was not far behind. I scrambled to my feet, wiping the tears away and with a dozen questions in my mind.

The lieutenant, who had opened the door for the major, became concerned when he saw the children charge toward them, and he raised his gun. In one defensive move, the major pinned the lieutenant and his gun against the wall.

"You point that gun at my children again, and I'll have your rank! Where is your commanding officer?" demanded the major.

"I don't know, sir," the lieutenant blubbered.

The major slowly released him. "Go and find him and bring him here. I must speak with him at once. Move!"

"Sir, I-I cannot leave without securing the prisoners," the lieutenant said apologetically.

"I will take their charge, Lieutenant. Go!" said the major firmly, crossing his arms.

The lieutenant hesitated, but then he left. As soon as he was gone, I stepped out of the cell and leaned up against the wall in the hall. The major stooped down and gathered the children in his arms.

After a moment, he stood up and came to me with a mixture of confusion and concern in his eyes. "What on earth happened to you?"

As he reached for the right side of my face, I cowered away from him and closed my eyes. "Interrogation," was all I could say.

The major breathed in deeply and let out one word, calling my captors an offensive name. "Did they lay a hand on the children?"

I shook my head back and forth and lifted my eyes to his.

"What is going on? Is this about your identification?"

"No. They think I'm smuggling Jewish children," I said.

"What?" he shot back in disbelief.

"We were on the way home on the train, when the conductor had us arrested. I told them they are your children, and I begged them to call you, but they didn't believe me. Neither did the Gestapo."

His eyes dropped slowly to the floor. I have never seen the major lose his temper, but I think that he came close to it at that moment. He clenched his jaw tight, and his face went almost red. He had very little time to compose himself, because a moment later, there were steps in the hall. The lieutenant had returned with his superior.

"Lieutenant, what are the prisoners doing out in the hall?" asked the captain when he saw us standing with the major.

"Captain, these are my children and my nanny, *Fräulein* Mauer, and I demand to know why they have been arrested and why you are holding them like criminals."

The captain was a rather short man. He looked up at the major with a blank stare. "You will have to take that up with the Gestapo, *Herr* Major. I cannot release them without their authority."

The major sighed, and then he ran his hand through the side of his hair. "Then get the Gestapo down here right away, Captain. You are wasting my valuable time. I am supposed to be running the production of Germany's military equipment, not trying to figure out why some idiot has imprisoned my children and my nanny," said the major through his teeth.

"Right away, sir," said the captain with a deferential bow. "Nevertheless, they will have to remain here until the Gestapo releases them."

The major glanced at me, and then he looked back at the captain with an impatient sigh. "Then leave the lieutenant here with them. But I won't have them put back in that cell."

The captain hesitated, and then he nodded. "Very well."

The major stepped forward to follow the captain down the hall, and the children both began to follow him, but I caught them by their arms and drew them back to where I was standing. Sepp struggled to get free, but I squeezed his arm tightly.

"You must stay with me, Sepp," I said firmly.

I looked up at the lieutenant. This was clearly a deviation from his normal routine. I was afraid that he would try to make us go back into the cell, but I think that the major had sufficiently intimidated him.

An apologetic captain and the major returned in less than an hour, and we were free to go. I asked the captain for my violin. Although the major was anxious to leave, we had to wait for him to locate it.

At four o'clock in the afternoon, we were at the train station and boarding the train for Kassel. When we got settled in our seats, I finally had the courage to look up at the major. He was staring out the window, resting his chin on his knuckles.

"I am very sorry, sir," I said.

He turned his head and gave me a reassuring look. "I would very much like to have someone to blame, but this was none of your fault, Klara."

The train jolted slightly as we passed over multiple tracks. I closed my tired eyes and rested my head against the back of the seat. I wanted to say more, to talk about it, but I could sense that the major did not.

Heiner met us at the train station and drove us back to the house. He didn't say anything about my face, but he did stare at my eye. *Frau* Hoffmann was so relieved to see us that she gave us all hugs. Then she found some salve and put it on a cloth for me to hold on the side of my eye. She had supper on the table for us in less than an hour. We were extra thankful for the food. I don't remember her cooking ever tasting so good.

After I put the children to bed, I went into the kitchen to help *Frau* Hoffmann finish with the dishes. She insisted on taking a careful look at my face, and then she said she thought that it already looked a bit better. She told me that she started to worry about us when we didn't get home for supper, and then when the major got home and we weren't there, he started calling to try to find us.

No one at the Kassel train station had seen us, and no one at the Frankfurt station remembered us either. *Frau* Hoffmann said that the major was gone by the time she got to the house in the morning, and that he didn't sleep in his bed either night. The major had called her just before he left for Frankfurt around noon. Apparently, the Gestapo man had finally contacted him to disprove my story.

I don't think there is any bed in the world as comfortable as my bed. I was asleep by eight o'clock, but I woke up in the middle of the night in a sweat, and then I had a hard time getting back to sleep.

The children seem to have suffered no ill effects. It is clear that the major does not want to discuss the matter. I am not sure whether he is embarrassed by the whole situation, or whether he just wants to put the whole unpleasant affair behind him. I did hear him tell the children that they were not to mention it to anyone.

I am still afraid. The whole time I was sure that they were after me. My fear was not altered when I realized they were after the children, because they have become so much a part of me now, that the danger to them was no different than my own. I have never felt so secure in my life as the moment I saw the major at the cell door. Nor have I seen the love he has for the children, like I saw in his eyes and in his actions.

August 1944

August 9, 1944

Dear Journal,

It is late on a Wednesday evening but I am not very tired, so I will tell you all about the past couple of days. Major Rager decided, at the last minute, to take Sepp and Annette with him to Düsseldorf to visit a friend. They left Kassel yesterday in the early afternoon with the plan to stay overnight and return today. My instructions from the major were to have a quiet day off.

After they had left, *Frau* Hoffmann finished up her work for the day, and I sat down and wrote a letter to Aunt Frieda. As she was leaving for the day, *Frau* Hoffmann called up the stairs. I thought she might have some further instructions for me.

"Why don't you come to our apartment for tea tomorrow, Klara?" she said as soon as I arrived at the top of the stairs. "You could finally meet my sister."

I smiled. "That sounds lovely. I would like that very much."

She wrote some instructions for me on how to get to Oberkaufungen, and then, although it was not necessary, she repeated everything she had written down. I locked the door behind her and turned around to face an empty house. I stopped to listen for a moment, but there wasn't a sound to be heard.

After supper, I took a long bath. But the trouble started when it began to get dark outside. It had been very nice to have the whole house to myself all afternoon, but darkness served up a tepid cup of fear. It seemed that I could hear noises coming from downstairs. I went down twice to check that the doors were locked. *What would I do if the air raid siren went off?* The last place I wanted to go was to the basement, where all of my fears would certainly get the best of me. The thought of dying there alone made me shiver.

I didn't sleep very well last night. I was glad when the sun finally came up. With a light step, I made my way to the main train station where the buses from the outlying areas still congregate.

I stared at the wispy clouds in the sky while I waited to board the bus to Oberkaufungen. It was a beautiful day, the kind of clear day that the Americans like to use to spread terror and fear with their airplanes and bombs.

I took a seat in the middle section of the bus by the window and tried not to think about the bombs. I had thought enough to choose six very beautiful roses from the garden to bring along for *Frau* Hoffmann's table. They were peeking up at me from the bag on my lap. We crossed the Fulda, and I watched eagerly out the window as we crept slowly out of Kassel.

Sooner than I thought, we were passing into a valley. The day was warm, the sky was blue, and the fields were green and yellow. Just as I was about to forget about the bombs, we passed an industrial site. Light gray steam was puffing out of the tall, twin towers at the back of the property, but the building at the front of the property was a tangled, charred, twisted ruin.

I closed my eyes for a minute and let the sun beat down on my face through the open window. Maybe it would wash away some of the gray of war. I tried to turn my mind to *Frau* Hoffmann's apartment and her sister. I have heard so much about her sister for the past nine months that I am sure I already know her.

Much to my surprise, the big brown bus swung into Oberkaufungen less than ten minutes later. Just before noon, I was knocking on *Frau* Hoffmann's door. They live on the ground floor of a three-story apartment building close to the market. I stared down at the roses in my bag and thought that I should have brought something else for her.

Frau Hoffmann's cheerful smile greeted me as she swung the door open. "Please come in, Klara," she said happily.

"I've brought you some roses," I said as I lifted them out of the bag for her to smell. One of the thorns poked me.

"Those are my favorite ones too," she said as she made her way down the hall. I didn't have time to look at them, but I noticed that she had picture frames full of beautiful embroidery hanging on the pale yellow walls. I almost ran into her back as she turned abruptly into the kitchen.

"Here is my sister, Maria Noll. Maria, this is *Fräulein* Klara Mauer."

As I turned into the kitchen, I saw her sister sitting there at a table. She was a large woman, her face was shriveled up with wrinkles, and her hair was a dull gray. She looked a good ten years older than *Frau* Hoffmann, and I have to admit to you, dear journal, that she is not at all what I had pictured in my mind. In this one thing only, I could tell that they were related; she has *Frau* Hoffmann's eyes.

"It is a pleasure to finally meet you," I mumbled as I extended my hand to her to shake. She was struggling to get to her feet, but I told her she didn't need to stand. All I could picture was some sort of accident happening and then *Frau* Hoffmann would have even more trouble.

"Won't you sit down, Klara," said *Frau* Hoffmann when her sister did not offer me a chair. "Rosine should be by soon. She is going to join us."

"Your neighbor? The one who made me that delicious soup?"

"Yes," Maria answered. "I call her the 'prophetess' and we'll be in for an earful today, just as always."

I looked up at *Frau* Hoffmann, hoping that the sour comment from her sister didn't mean that we were in for a troublesome afternoon. *Frau* Hoffmann seemed to be immersed in her final tea preparations over at the sink. I looked down at the elaborate china settings on the table and smiled. She had probably gotten up early in order to have enough time to get her best tableware and china out, to wash it up, and to set the table for us.

When I heard the bell ring, I offered to go to the door for *Frau* Hoffmann. My first glimpse of Rosine Staude came when I opened the door. She leaned back in surprise when she saw my unfamiliar face. She was a petite, brown-haired woman with a long delicate nose and bright eyes, set close together on top of some rosy cheeks.

"You must be Klara Mauer," she said, a friendly smile creeping up her lips. I shook her bony, delicate hand and then invited her to come in. Before we got to the kitchen, I stopped and thanked her for the delicious soup she had brought me when I was so ill.

"Yes, that is my mother's recipe, and it never failed to cure me when I was unwell. I suppose the love she put in it was probably what did me good."

Frau Hoffmann greeted her with a kiss, and we all sat down around the table. The afternoon was filled with conversation on all sorts of topics. *Frau* Hoffmann's sister did most of the talking, and she is the one who eventually brought up the topic that caused the most heated of the discussions of the day—religion.

I don't know how *Frau* Hoffmann's sister behaves normally, but she has a most skeptical mind. She began the discussion by asking *Frau* Staude whose side of the war she thought God was on. Then *Frau* Hoffmann's sister turned to me and whispered loudly, "Rosine thinks she has all of the answers because her father was a minister."

Frau Staude sat forward in her chair and placed her cup of tea back in the saucer. "He is on the side of righteousness and justice. But as I have told you before, when it comes to man, the Bible says that there is no one who is righteous."

"What about priests and nuns, Rosine?" *Frau* Hoffmann's sister shot back. "If anyone lives righteously, they do."

Frau Staude shook her head slowly. "The blood of Jesus Christ was shed to cover their sins also. And if the bombs fall on them, they must answer to the same God to whom we will answer. They must trust Christ, the same as we must. He is the only one who can forgive our sins and give us eternal life."

Frau Hoffmann's sister crossed herself twice and then took another bite of her bread while *Frau* Hoffmann rolled her eyes. "Maria insists on having this same conversation every time Rosine comes to visit," she said in an apologetic tone.

"It cannot be that simple, Rosine," said *Frau* Hoffmann's sister with her mouth half full. "I cannot believe it, and that is not what the church teaches."

"But it is that simple, Maria. I have read the Bible through many times and that is what it says. 'God so loved the world that he gave His only Son. Whoever believes in Him, will not perish, but will have everlasting life.' You can argue with me all you want, Maria, but peace will only come when you have settled this matter with God by faith. He wants you to come directly to Him. You do not need to go through a priest or through Mother Mary."

There it was. I could hardly believe it. This woman, who had more the frame of a girl than a woman, had just answered three of my recurring questions in the space of a minute. Here was a woman who spoke of things that none of the priests ever discussed. *How did she know these things? How did she know these were my questions?*

The blood dripping from the body of Jesus on the cross, the repetition of the Lord's prayer, the burning of the candles, the nauseating fear that always lurched through my heart as the bombs were dropping—she made it sound as if none of this was necessary.

None of this was going to bring peace on the earth or an end to the war. What I wanted to know, but never heard at mass, was that God would forgive my sins and that, should I die in the next bombing raid, I would be with Him.

Her words on the subject sounded so foreign to my ears. Her words sounded strange, but also somehow true. But there was still one problem. Something in that moment snapped in my mind, and I spoke for the first time since we sat down to tea, interrupting whatever argument Maria was making.

"How can I trust Him when He allowed my parents and my brother to die?" My own bitter question seemed to echo in the room, and I wished, for a moment, that I could take it back. *What part of my dusty heart had stored that question?*

Frau Staude closed her eyes for a second and shook her head. Slowly, her lips curled up in a sympathetic smile. "Klara, God never intended for us to experience sorrow and heart break. That is what sin has brought into life. He does not. He will not allow these tragedies to break us although it sometimes feels as though they will. He allows these things to teach us, to draw us to Him, and to mold us into something better—to accomplish His purpose. He has a purpose for each one of us."

I don't remember anything else she said all afternoon. I didn't hear any of the further arguments that *Frau* Hoffmann's sister had with her. I was struck with an emotion that is hard to describe as if I had eaten two meals in one sitting and could hardly move.

On the way out the door, I thanked *Frau* Hoffmann for the lovely tea and told *Frau* Staude that I hoped we would meet again. She asked me simply to think about the things she had said, and I promised, with a feeble voice, that I would.

The bus ride back to Kassel seemed quite short. The sun was slowly sinking in the sky. The rays of light through the walls of the bombed-out buildings made ghostly shadows across the sidewalks as I headed back to Terrassestrasse. And waiting for me, when I got home, were two children who couldn't wait to tell me all about their trip to Düsseldorf.

....

August 22, 1944

The children are back to school, and we are back to our routine. *Frau* Hoffmann says that her sister is feeling better, and she has been in brighter spirits lately. I have heard very little from Liese, Klaus, or Lenz, but on my part, I have had very little time to write. I can hardly believe I have been away from them this long. The next time I am in Sinsheim, I hope we have time to go and have a picture made. I would like to have one to put on my dresser.

The major has been very busy lately and has taken several trips out of town since the new *Wehrmacht* commander has arrived. I have not seen Lieutenant Braun since the day at the *Karlsau*, but I am glad for it.

Tomorrow, I will go with *Frau* Hoffmann to get some groceries. She asked if I would be willing to help her. She said it would be faster if she had someone else to stand in the long lines for her while she went to pick up other items. I must put you aside now and go to get the children.

September 1944

September 22, 1944

Dear Journal,

It has been over a month since I last wrote. I am sorry for neglecting you. The days have gone so quickly. The leaves on the trees are starting to change, reminding me that the summer is gone and that winter will soon be here.

I knew that the peace and silence could not last, and it did not. On the way home from bringing the children back to school after dinner, the air raid siren went off again. This is the second time this month we have been bombed, but this was the worst. I was too far from home to make it there in time, so I went to the shelter at the Goethe *Anlage*. I was the last one to get inside the door before the warden closed it.

We were crowded in there for over an hour and a half. First I heard the anti-aircraft guns and then the droning of the airplane engines that went on and on. This time the sound of the bombs dropping came from every direction and seemed to never end. And the ground shook and kept on shaking.

No one inside the shelter was saying much, but as time wore on, you could sense that morale was declining quickly. About midway through the bombing, maybe in the most intense part, an older woman deeper in the room began shouting and waiving her arms as if she were fighting a ghost.

Everyone around her was scampering to get away. The warden and several others rushed over to see what was going on. I only saw part of it, but they must have injected her with something, because soon she went limp. They carried her to the back of the shelter and all was quiet. The woman beside me pulled her sweater tight around her. "The bombings are going to make us all crazy," she muttered. This was the longest and hardest pounding I have ever experienced.

I tried not to think about Sepp and Annette, about the major, or *Frau* Hoffmann, but I must have worried about them a hundred times over. It is difficult to think any happy thoughts with the sound of explosions and chaos above you and when the air you are breathing is full of despair. The woman on the other side of me kept crossing herself, and that only made me think of what Rosine had said. I wonder if God cares that I am afraid.

From the sound of it, I imagined that the whole city would be in ruins when we finally saw daylight again. There was a lot of smoke in the air. Normally, everyone is subdued when coming out of the bomb shelter, but this time, the people were starting to panic when they saw the damage. One woman even fainted.

My instructions were to pick the children up as soon as possible following a raid. When I got out of the shelter, I went back to the school as fast as I could. As I passed some burning buildings, I prayed that the children made it safely to their shelter.

I must have held my breath all the way there, and what a relief it was to see the teachers and the children out in the front of the school. I finally found Annette, and then we saw Sepp. I gave them both a long hug.

Our journey home was a little longer than usual as there were several sections of houses that had taken direct hits. I tried to hurry the children along as I was starting to get anxious to see that our house had survived.

Frau Hoffmann met us at the front door with anxiety on her face. She was relieved to see us, but she was still in a nervous state as she was worried about her sister. I finally told her that she should go and see to her. I knew her sister would also be worried about her.

She made excuses and hesitated for a while. Finally, I assured her that I would see to the meal at the end of the day. I knew that the major would not be home anytime soon, because he had to make the rounds to all of the plants, and from the looks of it, he might not have any plants left.

Finally, *Frau* Hoffmann put her coat on and shuffled out the front door. We were without electricity, and either clouds or smoke were obscuring the sunshine, but I made the children practice their music anyway.

Toward the end of the afternoon, they both were asking me when their father would be home. I could see that they were worried about him. I wondered if they knew just how fragile their existence was. If they were to lose him, they would have no one but *Frau* Brandt. What a horrible thought!

I pulled out some meat, cheese, and bread to feed the children around suppertime. I glanced at the clock. We had not seen the major since breakfast. I imagined it was going to be a very long night for him, and the thought that he hadn't had anything to eat since morning made me feel weary for him.

I left the children at the table, went into the hall, and picked up the telephone. I was surprised that even in all of the chaos, I got an operator at the telephone exchange. When I asked for the general headquarters, she put me through to the major's office. I recognized Lieutenant Braun's voice immediately.

"Is Major Rager there?" I asked boldly.

"No, he is not. Who is asking?"

"This is Klara Mauer," I said.

"*Fräulein* Mauer, I believe he will be back here to report within the hour. Is there a message I should give him?"

"No message," I said. "Thank you."

I put the receiver down and went back into the dining room. "Children?" I said. "Should we take some food to your father?"

"Yes," they both said enthusiastically. We finished up our meal in a hurry. I found a basket in the corner cupboard in the kitchen and filled it with bread, cheese, and meat. Then I covered it up with a napkin. As we were on our way out of the house, I wondered for a moment if we ought to be going out into the chaos.

There were no trolley cars on Wilhelmshöher Allee, so we had to walk. Halfway to the general headquarters as we were trying to avoid the fires and the rubble, I was thinking that we should turn back, but I held the children's hands and we soon arrived at the headquarters unscathed.

The building seemed almost vacant. We walked across the courtyard, up the stairs, and into the major's office. I was relieved that Lieutenant Braun was not at his desk when we got there although I had prepared myself to see him. I set the basket on the major's desk, and we turned to leave. When I turned around, Lieutenant Braun was at the door.

"What are you doing in here?" he asked, clearly surprised to see me.

"We brought some food for the major. There is plenty if you are hungry too," I added.

Lieutenant Braun managed half a smile. "How kind."

"Good day, Lieutenant," I said as I grabbed the children's hands and stepped toward the door.

"Klara?" he said in a subtle tone. I turned around and looked at the lieutenant. He looked like he wanted to say something important, but at that moment, the phone on his desk rang. He didn't say anything further to me, nor did he reach for the telephone. Finally, he picked up the phone, and I left with the children. I wanted to get home as quickly as possible.

After I put the children to bed, I went downstairs to the living room with my violin and the flashlight. I didn't bother taking any music because the electricity was still out. I stood by the piano and played a couple of songs from memory. It has been a while since I took the time to play, and I can feel that I am out of practice.

I wasn't sure how long I played, but it was very late when I heard the major's car. I met him with the flashlight when he came through the front door. He closed the door behind him and locked it. Then he turned to me, and I handed him the flashlight.

"Klara, please tell me that you did not drag my children through all of that terribly dangerous mess just to bring me food," he said to me immediately.

My heart fell to my feet. "I did," I confessed.

"Your first concern must always be the children," he said with a weary and tired voice. I swallowed hard. This was really the first time he has ever scolded me for doing anything wrong. "You never want to be out there after the kind of raid we had today. It is very dangerous."

I bit my lip to keep the tears from coming. "I'm sorry, sir." I wished that he would, but the major said nothing in return. I just stood there, frozen like a statue until he went into the study, taking the light with him. My feet somehow found the stairs in the dark, and I stumbled along the hall. When I got to my room the tears came fast. I collapsed onto the floor behind the closed door. My head felt heavy as if it were trying to hold up under the pressure of all of the anxieties of the day.

Under normal conditions, I consider myself to be level-headed. But today, after the bombing and with concern for the major's welfare, I extended myself too far. I know I deserved to be called down for going out into the chaos. I only hope that the major doesn't realize that my rash thoughtfulness for his well-being has clouded my better judgment. I don't want him to know that I care.

September 23, 1944

Today is Saturday. When I woke up, it was raining. At least the electricity has been restored. I got the children up and dressed, and we went down for breakfast. *Frau* Hoffmann told me that the major was already gone. She also told me that the Americans had hit the marshalling yard, Henschel's armourment plant, and the ordnance factory. I had to sit down when I thought about the effect this would probably have on the major. No wonder he was upset with me last night.

It rained all day long, and all I could think about was how much difficulty the major must have to deal with to get the factories up and running again—and in the rain. Sepp and Annette were like two animals in a cage all afternoon. We played games, cut out figures from the major's old newspapers, and listened to some music on the radio.

Frau Hoffmann went home in the afternoon, and I started a fire in the fireplace. The major came home around suppertime. The children ran to greet him, but he was dripping wet from the rain. I took his coat from him and went to the basement to hang it up by the furnace.

When I got back upstairs, I saw that he had left his dirty boots by the front door. I took them down to the basement and wiped them off. From downstairs, I heard the major talking with the children, and I was glad to hear him interacting with them. Sometimes, I think that he doesn't know how much they want and need his attention.

I climbed the stairs and put his boots back by the front door, then I went through the dining room and into the kitchen. *Frau* Hoffmann had set the table for us and left the food for me to serve. When I had put it all on the table, I went into the living room to call them for supper.

"Children, why don't you go sit down at the table," said the major as they were sliding down off of his lap. "I'll be right there."

I turned to leave with the children, but the major called my name. I watched him stand to his feet, and then he came over to me.

"I want to apologize," he said slowly, "for what I said to you last night. I-I should have thought it through more carefully. I also neglected to thank you for the reason you went out in the first place."

When I looked into the major's eyes, I could see that he was sorry. I didn't expect an apology from him, and because of this, I was unprepared for the tears that began to form in my eyes.

"You should know, sir, that I would never put the children in harm's way. But, I know very well that if they don't have you, if no one cares for you, then they have no one. And that is a concern of mine."

The major looked away from me for a moment as if he had never thought about what I had just said. Then he looked back at me and swallowed. "Klara, have I made you cry? I can't take the thought that I have hurt you on top of this awful day."

"No, sir," I said, lying. I turned away from him so that he couldn't look at my puffy eyes. What had caused this sudden tenderness in the major, I do not know, but I do know that my heart seemed to mend instantly when it heard his apology.

I laugh now when I think that the major thought the lieutenant would break my heart when he never had my heart. It is the major who seems to hold that kind of sway over me.

....

September 27, 1944

Dear Journal,

Today is Wednesday, and I am back in Sinsheim. Since you will never guess how this has come about, I will tell you.

Yesterday afternoon the children were up in the nursery playing, and I was in the kitchen with *Frau* Hoffmann when Major Rager arrived home.

He greeted *Frau* Hoffmann, and then he asked me where the children were. When I told him they were in the nursery, he replied, "I would like a word with you and the children, upstairs, *Fräulein* Mauer."

I looked at *Frau* Hoffmann, and then I set the dishcloth down and followed the major to the stairs. I thought maybe the children were arguing, but when we got to the hall, he stopped and turned to me.

"Would you like to go to Sinsheim? Do you think that your aunt and uncle would be willing to take you and the children for a few days?" he asked me out of the blue.

I stumbled on my answer. "Yes. Yes, it would be nice to see them again. I could write and ask them if they would mind a visit."

"There's no time for a letter," said the major without hesitating. "Perhaps you could give them a call."

I gave him a blank look. *Why was there no time for a letter?* "When-when should I say we will visit?"

"Tonight," he responded with a most serious look on his face. "I would like you to call them and make sure they will have you and the children. Then you will need to pack in a hurry. The train leaves in an hour."

I opened my mouth, but no words came out. I didn't understand what was going on. The major sighed.

"I know. I know," I said. "No questions."

The major nodded. He seemed pleased that I had finally caught on to him. "The train arrives in Sinsheim at eleven," the major said. "I will call ahead and have someone meet the train so that you will have an escort to their house. Tell your aunt that, so she won't worry."

I moved around him and picked up the telephone. When I was finally connected to Aunt Frieda, I stumbled over my words.

The major looked on, waiting impatiently for an affirmative response. Aunt Frieda was just as confused as I was, and she was asking me questions I couldn't answer.

"I don't know," I responded when she asked how long we would be staying. "I have to go, Aunt Frieda. The train leaves here shortly. No, I am well. Everything's just fine. I will see you very soon. Good-bye."

When I hung up the phone, I nodded to the major.

"Pack as quickly as you can, Klara."

The phone rang, and the major answered before the second ring. As I went up the stairs, I heard him say something about a briefing they had. I listened carefully, hoping to find some reason for the major's urgency.

"We just got word an hour ago," he said into the receiver. "Yes, my instructions are to disassemble as quickly as possible. We don't want to keep all that equipment in one place. Oh, and lieutenant, I'll be back in an hour."

I packed my bag first, but while I was packing, it occurred to me that I didn't even know how long we would be away. I remembered to pack you, dear journal, but I hesitated when it came to my violin.

Quickly, I moved on to Annette's room and then to Sepp's. Then I heard the major come upstairs and talk with the children. There were so many questions in my mind, but I knew it was useless to expect any answers from the major, so I concentrated on packing. This time, I didn't forget Otti.

I put my suitcase and the suitcase for the children at the top of the stairs, and then the major came out of the nursery with the children. He took a look at the bags and me holding Otti.

"Are you going to take your violin?" he asked.

"I don't think I will be able to carry all of this and the children too," I said.

The major nodded and headed down the stairs looking at his watch. "I think we have time to eat something before you go. Come, children."

I could hardly eat anything, but I tried. All I could do was think about the trip we were about to take, in the dark, at the last minute. *What must Aunt Frieda think of me, calling her up so suddenly and asking to be taken in?*

I put the piece of bread from my plate into my bag for later and made sure the children were bundled up. Annette had Otti in her arms. The major took the two suitcases to the car. He had to drive us to the train station on the south side of town because the bombing last Friday has damaged the main station again.

Annette was full of questions about our trip on the way. The major didn't answer any of them, and I thought that his patience might run out, but he finally told her that she needed to be a brave girl and talk as little as possible during this adventure.

He carried Annette and Otti and the larger suitcase to the platform when we got to the station. I followed him, carrying the other bag in one hand and holding Sepp's hand with the other. The wind was blowing in gusts, and it was almost dark when we got to the platform. The major set the bag down and reached into the inside of his coat, pulling out our tickets and a white envelope.

I set down the bag I was carrying, took the tickets and the envelope from his hand, and put them into my purse.

"I am sending you with some money and food stamps to give to your aunt to help with any expenses while you are there," he said as an explanation of what was in the envelope.

When I looked up at the major, he was brushing the hair out of Annette's face. I saw his jaw tighten up, and then he looked at me. "I know you will take good care of them, Klara. I will call you when it is safe to return."

When it is safe to return? My eyes grew big, and I swallowed hard. In the distance, I could hear the clickety-clack of the train rolling toward the station.

Major Rager kissed Annette and put her down on her own two feet. Then he stooped down, winked at Sepp, and put his hand on Sepp's shoulder. "You're the man now," the major said. "Make sure you take care of the ladies."

"Yes, Father," Sepp responded. The major grabbed both bags, and I took the children's hands as we boarded the passenger car of the train. There was only one other person who boarded with us. The major took the luggage into the compartment and stowed it for me. Then he kissed the children, tipped his hat to me, and left.

Sepp raised the blind on the window, and he and Annette both crowded together to wave good-bye to him. In the process they began to shove one another, and before I could stop what was going on, I saw Otti fly out of the open window. Annette screamed. I pushed past the children and stuck my head out the window.

"Otti!" I shouted to the major who was still standing a few feet away on the platform. "Sepp threw Otti out! Do you see her?"

I heard the conductor's whistle, and I prepared myself to leave without Otti, but the major was quick to locate her on the ground. He reached up and handed her back to me just as the train lurched forward.

"Thank you," I shouted back to him. There was enough light still in the sky that I saw the major clearly, standing there on the platform—all alone. For just one moment, he seemed to let down his guard, and I saw the look on his face. It was the look of a man who thought he might never see his family again.

I hung out the window until I could no longer see him. Then I drew the window up and pulled down the blind. Annette was relieved to have her dolly back in her arms. I should have scolded Sepp, but I was too overwhelmed. I sat down in the seat next to Annette and tossed my hair over my shoulders. We had the compartment all to ourselves, and I was glad for that, because I felt like such a wreck.

The major could have had many reasons for sending us to Sinsheim, but it all happened so quickly that I think I was in shock. I should have been excited that I was only a few hours from being home and seeing my family again, but instead, I was simply baffled at the reason we had been sent away. Whatever the reason, he did it with reluctance, because I could see in his eyes that he didn't want us to go.

The children were full of energy for the first hour and a half, but after that, they went fast asleep. Sepp was sprawled out on the seat across from me. Annette was sleeping with her head in my lap. I had to wake them when we got to Würzburg, because we had to transfer trains there.

It was a nightmare to get them, the bags, and Otti off the train and onto the other one. The train to which we transferred was carrying a carload of soldiers, and there was little room for us. Someone gave me a seat, and I held Annette on my lap while Sepp sat unhappily at my feet on the floor. It wasn't long until Annette was fast asleep again, and then Sepp laid his head on my feet and was gone.

Not long after Annette went to sleep, the soldier next to me put his arm on the back of the seat behind me and the men sitting across from us started to snicker. He was sitting uncomfortably close to me, and I was on the edge of the seat already, so there was no where I could go. He tried to start a conversation with me, but I just told him I didn't want to wake the children. I think that Annette and I were the only girls in the whole car. I was glad that the distance to Sinsheim was much shorter than what we had already traveled.

Just after eleven o'clock, the train pulled into Sinsheim. I could not wake Annette, and she was very heavy, but one of the soldiers carried my bags down to the platform for me while I dragged Sepp, who was still half asleep, and carried Annette off of the train. I tried to smile and thanked him.

There was a dim light on in the station. I stood there for a moment, wondering how I was going to get the bags and the children over there. I let go of Sepp's hand and took a hold of one of the bags.

"Let's go, Sepp," I said. He began to whimper. When we got inside the station, I set the bag down and told Sepp to stay with it. Then I carried Annette back to get the other bag. When I returned to the station, Sepp was sitting on the other bag rubbing his eyes. A soldier came out of the door by the conductor's office and headed straight for us.

"Ma'am," he said as he came up to me. "Major Rager phoned down with a request for someone to meet you."

"Yes," I said, hoping he would also be able to help me with the suitcases.

"Here, let me take the bags, ma'am." I looked up at the soldier. He looked familiar.

I don't remember much of anything he said to me as we were walking through the streets, because I was carrying Annette, and she was getting so heavy that I thought my arms were going to break. Sepp kept blubbering about being too tired to walk. Aunt Frieda's house is only seven blocks from the train station, but it seemed like farther. At last, we arrived.

Aunt Frieda opened the door immediately when I knocked. I thanked the soldier for the escort, and then I stepped inside with the children. Aunt Frieda lifted the suitcases inside the door, then she took Sepp by the hand.

"They're so tired," I said.

"They're bound to be," Aunt Frieda said. "It's almost midnight." She gave me a look that mirrored the questions in my own mind. "I have a bed ready for Sepp on the floor next to Lenz. I thought Annette could sleep with you and Liese," said Aunt Frieda in a whisper as she started up the stairs in front of me, dragging Sepp behind her.

I sighed a little as I climbed the stairs. Sleeping with two girls in a small bed wasn't going to work too well, but I didn't want to say so since I was the one imposing on poor Aunt Frieda. I headed first into my old room and set Annette down on the bed next to Liese, who was curled up in a ball on the right side of the bed. Otti fell to the floor when I put Annette down, but I picked her back up and set her in Annette's arms.

Sepp was standing at the door looking completely dazed and just about ready to cry. I picked him up and took him upstairs into the boys' room, nearly stumbling over the bed Aunt Frieda had made for him on the floor.

"Good night, Sepp," I said quietly. "If you need me at all during the night, I am right downstairs where I just put Annette."

To my relief, Sepp lay down immediately, and when I pulled the cover over him, he closed his eyes. Aunt Frieda was waiting for me in the hall downstairs, and I collapsed into her arms.

"Thank you for taking us in on such a short notice," I said.

Aunt Frieda pulled away from me and touched me on the nose. "You are always welcome," she said with a tired smile. "We will talk in the morning."

I said good night to her, and when she went into her room, I went back downstairs and brought the two bags up to my room. I pulled two summer covers out of the wardrobe and put them down on the floor by the left side of the bed. With the last ounce of energy I had, I pulled off my dress and slipped into my nightgown.

I don't remember laying my head down, but the next thing I knew, the sunlight was coming in the window above my head, and Liese was staring down at me from on top of the bed.

"I thought you were dead," she said to me in a whisper.

"Is Annette still asleep?" I asked. Liese nodded.

"Come here and give me a hug," I said. I had waited a long time for this.

It was a hectic morning. I helped Annette dress in some clean clothes, and then I ventured up to the boys' room to help Sepp. Uncle Lothar was sitting on the couch in his usual spot with his cane at his right hand when we came down the stairs. I took a second look at him. I think he trimmed too much off of the right side of his mustache. He didn't say anything to me or the children.

After Klaus, Lenz, and Liese left for school, I served breakfast to Sepp and Annette. Before we left for the market, I went upstairs and dug into my purse for the white envelope the major had given me. On my way down, I kept it close to my dress so that Uncle Lothar wouldn't see it. Then I handed it to Aunt Frieda.

She gasped when she opened it up. "What is this?" she exclaimed.

"The major asked me to give it to you for our expenses," I said plainly.

"Does he expect that you'll be staying until Christmas?"

I narrowed my eyes and stepped closer to Aunt Frieda so that I could look into the envelope. I was surprised at the amount of money and food stamps the major had put in there.

Aunt Frieda looked up at me. "I will use what I need and give the rest back to you to give back to him," she said in a whisper. "If Lothar finds out about this, he will put it all in his pocket."

I nodded in agreement. If I had known I was carrying around that much money in my purse, I would have been nervous the whole trip long.

Uncle Lothar stopped us as we were going up the stairs to get our jackets. "Why did Major Rager send you down to Sinsheim, Klara?" he asked, followed by the typical twitch of his now lopsided mustache.

"I'm not certain," I replied.

Uncle Lothar shook his head. "Let me tell you something about military men, Klara. They do what they do only after careful calculation."

"Yes, Uncle Lothar," I replied, trying not to roll my eyes. "I'm sure that is the case."

"No. I am convinced that he has sent you here for a very specific purpose."

I shrugged. "I don't know what that would be, Uncle. He only asked me last evening when he arrived at home if it would be possible for us to impose on you."

"How long will you stay, Klara?"

"I don't know. He said he would call and let me know when we should return."

"I hope he doesn't expect for me to pay the costs to board and feed his children," said Uncle Lothar, raising his voice at the end.

"No, Uncle Lothar," I said calmly. "He sent money enough to cover our expenses."

"Good," he said, rubbing his mustache in a satisfied way. "Then he must be a good man."

I sighed and climbed the stairs with Annette and Sepp at my heels.

"I don't like him," Sepp said as I was helping him on with his jacket.

"Me either," Annette said.

I closed my eyes, and then I bent down to look them both in the eyes. I knew that if I did not try to sway their opinion of him that it would be only a matter of time until some colossal event would happen and there would only be a big mess to clean up.

"He is my uncle, children, and he has been very kind to me. I can see how he may seem old and mean to you both, but please be courteous to him. We are his guests. Besides that, he does not have many friends, and I think that makes him very sad."

I am not sure what was going through their heads, but when we went downstairs and out the front door, they both just stared at him as we went by. It was nice to be out in the fresh cool air and to walk on old, familiar streets where there was not the first sign of bombing damage.

This has been a long day with going to the market, helping Aunt Frieda with dinner and supper, and trying to keep the children occupied. The house was an absolute zoo once my brothers and Liese got home. I am glad to see that Liese and Annette get along very well. Even Lenz and Sepp seemed to have a good time with one another despite their prior disagreement and despite the almost five-year age difference.

I wasn't able to have a good talk with Aunt Frieda until after the children were all in bed and Uncle Lothar retired to his room. We ran into some of her friends at the market, and they asked what I was doing back in Sinsheim. I gave them a polite answer, but now, Aunt Frieda wanted to know how I was really doing.

It was hard to tell her how things have been for me. I have tried to be positive in my letters to them. I don't want them to know that the days are long, that the bombings scare me, and that I feel in constant conflict, working for a military man. Least of all, do I ever say anything about the major or his political games. I have never told her what I think of him, or that I spent two nights in a Frankfurt prison with his children.

But for all that I am hiding, I feel rather safe. It is pretty clear that Aunt Frieda thinks that the major is just as he presents himself—an important and well-qualified officer of the Third *Reich*. She has gone out of her way not to say anything amiss, even to me. These are difficult times, when no one is free to speak his mind.

She has always told me that my mother was her favorite niece. I suppose that is why she finally was able to convince Uncle Lothar to take us in. I suspect that she might hold some disdain for the Third *Reich* and for what they have done to my family, but she has never said anything. And Uncle Lothar would not allow it. Still, there is something awkward in her voice when she mentions the major.

I wonder when he will call and tell us it is time to come home. It is really crowded in this house with eight people. Sepp and Annette had a difficult day, primarily because they are in a strange setting. I don't think Uncle Lothar will be able to stand us much more than a couple of days.

I will be sleeping on the floor again tonight, but before I lay my head down, I am going to say a prayer for the major. I keep seeing the look on his face as he was standing on the platform at the train station, and I keep wondering why he sent us away.

....

September 30, 1944

Today is the last day of September, and it is late on a Saturday evening. I just said good night to the children and tucked Liese in. I have so much to share with you.

First, I will tell you that the days have been going by slowly. After Klaus, Lenz, and Liese leave for school, I have been going to market with Aunt Frieda and then spending time reading with the children. I am concerned that they are going to fall behind in their studies, and as I do not know how long we will be away, I think it best for them to have some school work to keep them occupied.

In the afternoon, I let them play while I have been helping Aunt Frieda clean her house. I do not want to offend Aunt Frieda, but I think she is too tired to look after her house like she once did. It is a difficult thing for me to see what a burden my siblings are on her, even if she never complains.

This morning, we all went to market, except for Uncle Lothar. He rarely leaves the house. I think that he was glad for the silence for a little while. I don't think he is bearing our visit too well although I am surprised he has done so well so far. The children have not said a word to him, and he has only felt the need to correct them a handful of times.

After we left the market, we walked past the crooked beamed house and down along the riverfront in town. I had a good chance to speak with Klaus. He was always the quiet one who stores all of his emotions in a powder keg. Now that he is fourteen, he is no different. But I do see a difference. I see that he is half boy and half man. I had never seen the man part until today.

I wish that I did not understand some of his struggles. He is distressed at having to pledge his allegiance to the government that is responsible for the death of our parents, and he is far from eager to follow in Reiner's footsteps.

I tried to console him by telling him that we sometimes have little choice in life, but at least we still have one another. I told him how hard it was for me to be away from them, and how much I missed them. I told him that our situation is no more his choice than it is mine. I think he understood what I was trying to say, because he looked me straight in the eyes and told me that he did.

When we got home, I followed him up to the attic. I had one more thing I wanted to say to him. I told him, with a lump in my throat, that he was almost a man, and that part of being a man was doing the hard things. For some reason, all I could think of when I said that to him was the major.

October 1944

October 1, 1944

This morning, Aunt Frieda, Liese, Sepp, Annette, and I went to mass. In Sinsheim, you can hear the church bells ring for miles around calling everyone to service. It was a cloudy day, but it did not rain until the afternoon.

I confess that I did not pay much attention to the homily as I was thinking instead of how much longer I thought we could stay with Uncle Lothar and wondering how long it would be until we heard from the major.

Quite by accident on the way out of the church, which was very crowded this morning, I overheard a conversation between two ladies that I did not know. I wouldn't have paid any attention, except that I heard one of them say something about Kassel.

I know that it was quite rude of me to interrupt them, but after I excused myself, I asked them what the news from Kassel was.

"Why do you ask?" inquired the older woman with the large, dark hat.

"I live in Kassel," I responded. "We are just down for a visit."

The countenance of the older woman fell. "How long have you been in Sinsheim?"

"Since Tuesday last," I said.

"Then you have not heard? My husband's sister lives in Fuldatal, on the north side. She phoned us yesterday to tell us that they were all well." The woman paused, and I held my breath. I could tell by the look on her face that there was more to come. "But she did say that all of Kassel seemed to be on fire. They have been bombed continuously since Wednesday."

My heart dropped all the way to the floor. I looked up ahead where Aunt Frieda was standing with the children waiting for me. Sepp and Annette were standing there so patiently.

I turned back to the women and cleared my throat. "Thank you for the news," I said, "and again, I beg your pardon for interrupting." My legs felt as if they were going to give out from under me.

"What ever is the matter?" asked Aunt Frieda when I reached them. "You look as if you have seen a ghost!"

I waited until the children had run ahead of us a little before I repeated what the woman had told me. I think the news did not hit Aunt Frieda as it did me.

"Then it is good that you are here, safe, with us," she said. I was silent the rest of the way home.

When we got back to the house, I went immediately to the bathroom to be alone. I felt a sickening feeling in my stomach. I closed the door behind me and leaned with my back against it. Then I covered my mouth with both hands to keep the cries from coming out. I was shaking all over.

I had the worst feeling about the major. First, I could not get his sorry look out of my mind. Then, all I could do was wonder if he and *Frau* Hoffmann, and everyone else I knew in Kassel were still alive. If the whole city were on fire, then there would be thousands of casualties. I had seen what devastation the British one-night raid, three weeks before I ever arrived, had done to Kassel. I couldn't imagine what continuous bombings might have done. *What was I supposed to do with Sepp and Annette if the major was dead? Would I ever hear his voice again?*

I crossed my arms and tried to talk sense to myself. *What was wrong with me that I had gone from feeling utter disdain toward the major and all he stands for, to fearing for his life and for the trouble I knew he was going to have because the military factories were destroyed?*

I tried to breathe in deeply and to calm myself as I remembered what he had said on the platform. He had said that he would call us when it was safe to return. *How did he know the Allies were going to raid Kassel?*

I washed my face and straightened my hair. When I returned to the living room, Aunt Frieda and Uncle Lothar just stared at me.

"Are you all right, dear? You look very pale," said Aunt Frieda as I sat down on the couch.

"She's just sad that she missed out on all of the excitement," said Uncle Lothar carelessly as he flipped the page in his newspaper. Aunt Frieda had clearly relayed the news to him.

"It is not exciting to be in a bomb shelter, wondering if you are going to die or live," I shot back.

"Perhaps not, Klara. But you must consider that your major has spared you and his children any of this trauma. Has he not?"

I opened my mouth to respond to him, but I did not say anything. Then I looked over at Aunt Frieda.

"That's nonsense, Lothar," she said. "He couldn't possibly have known this would happen."

"Is it nonsense, Frieda?" asked Uncle Lothar, looking up from his paper. "I think it is too coincidental that he put them so suddenly on a train, the night before these bombings began. He hasn't called you home yet, so, perhaps it is not over yet."

After hearing this from Uncle Lothar, I threw my head back and stared at the ceiling. I didn't even want to think of the possibility of more raids.

"He couldn't have known," I said quietly.

"Let me tell you something about military men, Klara. Military men get intelligence reports, and they know things. Either that or your major is a spy for the Allies. They have told him ahead of time, and he has used that information to protect his own family." Uncle Lothar chuckled. "He knew that you would be safe here in Sinsheim. There is nothing here to bomb."

I rolled my eyes at what Uncle Lothar had just said.

"It does seem rather peculiar," added Aunt Frieda as she got up slowly out of her chair. "I should start dinner," she said, heading for the kitchen.

"I need to check on the children, and then I will help you," I called after her.

As I was climbing the stairs, I decided to say nothing to the children about the bombing. There was no sense in causing them distress when I had no information whatsoever about what had really happened to their city, their home, or their father.

I found Annette playing happily with Liese's dolls. Upstairs, Sepp and Lenz were arguing, but Klaus was trying to intervene. I sat down on the stairs and listened to the sounds of the children playing, while my mind imagined the horror that must be taking place in Kassel. I shook my head and tried to stop my thoughts. It would do me no good to guess. I needed to hear from the major. Finally, I went down to help Aunt Frieda and to try to get my mind off of the most disturbing news.

After supper, I played games with the children Liese and Lenz, trying hard to enjoy their company and not to think about Kassel. I almost jumped out of my seat when I heard the phone ring. It was around seven o'clock. Aunt Frieda answered it, and then she came and got me from the dining room immediately. I was so relieved to hear the major's voice.

"How are the children?" he asked me first.

"They are well," I replied. "Would you like to speak with them?"

"Not unless you think I should," he said.

"Are you all right, sir?" I asked. I could hear the strain in his voice.

"I'm fine," he said after a pause. "You have heard the news?"

"I only heard this morning. Is it true that the whole city is on fire?"

The major let out a sorry laugh. "No, just the important buildings. It is quite a disaster right now, but we'll just have to get back up on our feet."

"Under the circumstances, when should we return?" I asked anxiously.

"I think it best that you stay there at least another week," he replied. "Will that be all right?"

"Yes, sir."

"Please give my love to the children."

"They miss you, *Herr* Major."

"I must go now," he said softly. I wanted to tell him that I understood now why he had sent us away, and that I was grateful that he had, but before I could say anything, the major said good-bye.

I stood there in the living room holding the receiver for more than a few seconds until I put it down. At least he was still alive, and the children still have a father. I was surprised at the relief I felt. I took in a deep breath, and then I returned to the table.

"Was that father?" asked Annette hopefully.

"Yes," I replied with a smile.

I noticed that Sepp sat up in his chair. "Are we going home?" asked Sepp eagerly.

"Not just yet, children." I watched their countenance fall, and Sepp even groaned. I looked over at Uncle Lothar, but thankfully, he didn't seem insulted.

"There's more to come," said Uncle Lothar from the living room.

"Lothar!" scolded Aunt Frieda. "Not in front of the children."

And not in front of me, I thought. I didn't want to hear his gloomy prediction either.

I don't remember much more about the evening, but I can say that I feel quite exhausted from the emotions. I was devastated to hear the news of the bombings from the woman at church, and then so happy to hear the major's voice.

The major sounded so far away and very weary. He must miss the children very much. I have often seen him lighten up, after a hard day, when they come to greet him. Whatever the reason he sent us away, he has clearly spared us the horror, and for that, I am thankful.

....

October 8, 1944

Dear Journal,

This morning, we said good-bye to Uncle Lothar, Aunt Frieda, Klaus, Lenz, and Liese, and we rode the train from Sinsheim to Würzburg. I was a little nervous when the conductor came through the car, but he didn't pay any particular attention to us. As we got closer to Kassel, the train slowed quite a bit. I thought we would never arrive. It looks like the Allies have dealt a severe blow to the most important transportation center for Germany.

The major had to drive several stations out to pick us up. I am not sure who was happier to see whom—the major or the children. The first thing I noticed when we got off of the train was the smell of smoke in the air although I didn't see anything burning. I sat in the backseat with the children and stared out the window all of the way home. I noticed quite a bit of damage, but there are still buildings standing, and I could see that the reports of the entire city on fire had been exaggerated.

The major got an ear full of trivial details from the children all the way home and all through supper, including a most scathing report on Liese's sorry doll collection. After supper, *Frau*

Hoffmann apologized to me for the meager amount of food. She told me there has been a severe shortage, and she thought we should have stayed in Sinsheim longer because things have been so bad.

When the major was out of earshot, she told me that the motor works and one of the ordnance depots had been almost completely wiped out. A thousand people are now homeless. She said that they had just restored water and power earlier this week, but that it was knocked out again yesterday with another raid.

At one point, *Frau* Hoffmann lowered her voice and told me with a mischievous look in her eyes that *Frau* Brandt kept calling while we were gone, asking to speak with the children. She heard the major tell her that the children would be no safer in her highly targeted Berlin than here. For some reason, that made me laugh.

"Do you think he knew the bombings were going to happen?" I asked *Frau* Hoffmann suddenly. As soon as I said it, I wished that I hadn't. She looked at me peculiarly, and then replied discreetly, "I don't know what the major knew."

All I know is that I am somewhat glad to be back in Kassel. It was very good to be able to be with my siblings and to spend some time back in Sinsheim. I even got to see some old friends and had a chance to visit with the neighbors one afternoon. Sometime soon, Aunt Frieda will be sending me the picture she took of me, Klaus, Lenz, and Liese, and I will be able to put that on my dresser. Liese insisted on holding Otti in the picture, much to Annette's distress.

It is a good thing that we did not have to stay any longer, because I am sure Uncle Lothar could not have stood our company for another day. Before I retired this evening, I handed the major the white envelope containing the money and food stamps Aunt Frieda had not spent while we were there. I can only describe the look on his face as one of surprise when I explained to him that it was left over from what we had not used. I guess he did not expect to get any of it back.

I am going to return you to your usual hiding place in the wall, turn out the light, and get some much needed rest. I have the feeling that things are going to be very different around here. Everyone seems to be on edge, and since we are on cut-back rations, things will become that much more difficult. The major hasn't said anything to me, but I can see the stress on his face. I only hope that the balm the children seem to be to him will be able to soothe some of his distress.

....

October 9, 1944

Today is Monday. When I took the children to school this morning, Sepp saw right away that the buildings just down the street from the school had been hit by a bomb. For some reason, Annette was reluctant to go into her classroom. I had to coax her in.

Their teachers both wanted an explanation for why the children had been out of school so long. I didn't know what to tell them, except that we had been in Sinsheim the whole time. I think I am beginning to understand why the major never answers my questions. It is easier for me to tell others that I don't know anything, if that is the truth.

Frau Eichel made a smart comment about the major leaving town during the bombings. I didn't hesitate to inform her that the major was here the whole time.

Frau Hoffmann is distressed because there is hardly any food at the market to buy. I asked her how long she thinks this will continue, but she just shook her head. She told me that she doesn't even remember this kind of trouble when she was younger, not even during the Great War. That is the first negative comment I remember hearing from *Frau* Hoffmann.

This afternoon, after the children had practiced their music, I had them draw some pictures for *Frau* Hoffmann. I hope the drawings will cheer her up. The major did not get home until late. He asked me to tell him when the children were ready for bed. He wanted to tuck them in.

I can see the strain in the faces of the people I passed on the street today that didn't seem to be there before. There was no bombing yesterday and none today. I don't know how long it will take to rebuild the factories and to get them working again, but I know enough to know that the major's career hangs on what he is able to accomplish despite these dire circumstances. I only hope he is up to the task.

....

October 13, 1944

Dear Journal,

You were almost taken away from me today. I am still in shock from what has happened. It was a normal Friday, except that the children were extra tired and grumpy when I picked them up from school this afternoon.

I was not happy to see that the major was home and in his study when we got to the house, because I had planned to have the children go to the living room to practice their music for at least an hour. They have already missed so much practice since we were in Sinsheim nearly two weeks.

I decided to go upstairs and get my violin and their music. While I was coming down the stairs, I made up my mind to interrupt the major long enough to get his consent for them to practice. I knew that if he minded, he would tell me. I knocked on the door, and I heard him call me to come in. The children must have seen the study door open, because later, I found that they had followed me in. I was sorry that I had interrupted the major when I saw that he had his ledger open, and that he was hard at work.

I cleared my throat to ask him about the music lessons, but before I could speak, I heard a loud knock at the front door.

"Yes?" asked the major, looking up at me impatiently. Then I saw him look beyond me and out to the hall.

"Would you like me to get that?" I asked nervously.

The major shook his head as I heard *Frau* Hoffmann's footsteps out in the hall.

"I'm sorry to bother you, sir, but I was wondering—"

I don't think I got the rest of the sentence out of my mouth before I saw the major's eyes dart away from mine. In one quick motion, he closed up the ledger on his desk and stood to his feet in alarm. I heard commotion and footsteps in the hall behind me and turned my head to see the two Gestapo men I had met last December, along with several SS men.

My heart stood still. They were rushing too aggressively into the room for me to think that they were here on a social call. From deep in the basement of my memory, the feeling of panic that surrounded me that awful night they came and took father and mother, flooded my chest, almost choking me.

I glanced down at the major's desk and finally took in a short breath. There, in plain view, was his precious ledger—the one with the bronze lettering, the one he has always treated with such secrecy. I looked up at the major, but he was standing there poised and had already carefully replaced the look of concern with his normal, hospitable and confident expression. My eyes flew back to the ledger, bare and vulnerable on the desk. As I turned to face the intruders, I picked up the ledger and slid it underneath the music in my arm.

Frau Hoffmann followed *Herr* Löning and *Herr* Knappe into the study. Behind her, I saw the SS fanning out into the other rooms in the house.

"I'm sorry, sir, but they insisted on showing themselves in," said *Frau* Hoffmann apologetically.

"That's all right, *Frau* Hoffmann," said the major with great composure. "Come on in, gentleman."

Neither the Gestapo nor the SS moved further into the room at the major's invitation. I looked down at the children who were now standing between me and the men.

"Good evening, *Herr* Major," began *Herr* Löning, with his broad rimmed hat and small eyes. "My apologies for dropping in on you like this, but—"

Before *Herr* Löning could finish his sentence, I stepped to the side. I thought that if I were careful enough, I might be able to slip out of the room undetected while they were engaged in conversation.

But I was wrong. I did not hear *Herr* Löning finish his sentence, but I did see him remove his broad rimmed hat from his balding head and cast a suspicious glance at the items I was cradling in my arm. He wasn't even facing me, but his next sentence was aimed at me.

"Where do you think you are going, *Fräulein*?"

All eyes in the room seemed to turn on me at once. "If you will excuse me, sir," I said boldly, "I must see to the children's music lessons." In that moment, I thought of something I had heard the major's mother-in-law say about her guest from Köln. "They may one day play for *Herr* Hitler, and I don't want them to fall behind in their lessons."

I continued toward the door, pushing the children in front of me, but the man with the balding head reached out and stopped me.

"What is that you are carrying, *Fräulein*?" he asked warily. Panic rose from my heart, jamming itself into my throat. I tried to swallow it while I held the music out just far enough so that it was displayed for him to see. I looked over at the major. *Why had I grabbed his ledger? Now he was going to lose it, and it was my fault.* The Gestapo man sniffed, and then he looked back at me.

"They are playing only music from German composers?" he asked, expecting a positive response.

"No, sir," I responded coolly. "They also play music by German speaking composers from Austria." I saw almost immediately that the Gestapo man was satisfied with my answer. I tried to steady my heart. I was hoping no one in the room could hear how hard it was beating. Finally, he gave me a swift nod of his head indicating that I had his permission to leave.

"Come, children," I said with a faint voice. I left the room as calmly as I could with the children following me. When we got out into the hall, I turned around and saw that *Herr* Löning had sent one of the SS men after us.

"Sepp, would you get my violin? It is next to your father's desk," I said, suddenly remembering that I had left it in the study. I looked up at the SS man and tried to smile, but he didn't smile back.

While we waited for Sepp, I listened to *Herr* Löning in the study. "I am afraid that I must ask you to step out into the hall while we search your house, *Herr* Major."

"Why?" Major Rager exclaimed. "What is the meaning of this, *Herr* Löning?"

As soon as Sepp appeared with my violin, I shuffled the children into the living room. As I pulled the bench closer to the piano, I lifted the seat slightly and slipped the ledger and the last piece of music on my pile into the piano bench. Then I sat down on the bench and called Annette over to the piano while I set some music on the stand for her.

"Go ahead and get the violin out, Sepp, and get it ready to play," I said sternly. With the way they had both been behaving today, I was praying that they wouldn't give me any trouble now. I gave a particularly firm look to Annette, then I pointed to her music and asked her to start playing. I felt pity when she looked up at the SS man and then to me. I could see that she was as scared as I was.

"It's all right, Annette," I said. "He won't mind your playing."

I bit my tongue to keep the relief from showing on my face when she started to plunk out her notes. She was not even distracted when one of the SS men came in and started searching the room.

From the piano bench, I could see that they were swarming all over the house. To my left, I saw *Frau* Hoffmann come in from the kitchen and sit stiffly on the couch. Then, when I looked straight in front of me beyond our guard and out to the hall, I saw the major standing there with *Herr* Löning. The major turned away from my glance quickly.

I don't know how long it took her to play the song I had put up on the stand, but at one point I looked up, and *Herr* Löning was standing next to our guard with both hands behind his back. He had a scowl on his face.

"*Fräulein* Mauer," he said. I couldn't believe he remembered my name. "I don't believe that you are really giving music lessons to these children at all."

Annette stopped playing. I looked up at him in disbelief. "Would you like to hear them play together?" I asked with a smile.

Herr Löning raised his eyebrows, daring me.

"Sepp, may I have the violin?" Sepp got up from the couch and brought me the violin and the bow. I asked Annette to give me the notes, and I tuned it up, playing a few difficult bars of music from memory to make sure it was tuned.

I got up from the bench, handed the violin to Sepp with a reassuring look, and then I set out the music for him and Annette. Before we had fled to Sinsheim, I was working with them both on a piece that they could play together. I was just about ready to surprise the major with a concert when we left Kassel.

"Children, do your very best now. The gentleman would like you to play for him."

I nodded to Annette to start playing. Sepp raised the violin to his shoulder reluctantly. Annette stumbled on the first two notes, but she played on. I was so proud of Sepp when he started playing at the correct measure. For almost an entire page, they played on—not flawlessly, but together.

I looked over at the doorway to the hall. The major was watching his children perform with a carefully measured expression of restraint on his face. I looked back at the children. This is not the debut I had planned for their father to hear.

It wasn't long, dear journal, before the mini-concert was interrupted as one of the SS men came down from the bedroom holding you! The children stopped playing. *Herr* Löning asked if they were done searching upstairs.

"This is all we found, sir."

I took in a deep breath. "That's my personal journal, sir," I said as I reached over and put my hand on the piano to steady myself.

The Gestapo man flipped through your pages, dear journal, and for a moment I thought he was going to take you. I swallowed hard and prayed that he would not read any words that I had written in you about the major's business.

I watched *Herr* Löning closely. Finally, he closed your lid, let out a sneer, and tossed you onto the pile of cold ashes in the fireplace. "I could care less about your hopes and dreams, *Fräulein.*" He looked up at me with his small eyes. "You and Major Rager's children went to Sinsheim a couple of weeks ago on the evening train. Why did you go to Sinsheim?"

"To visit my family," I responded.

"Did Major Rager send you there?"

I tried not to flinch. "He was very kind to allow me to visit them. I hadn't seen them in a long time," I said slowly.

"Why did you take the children?"

The Gestapo man was firing his questions at me so quickly that I was afraid I would give him the wrong answer. I swallowed hard. "His work and his devotion to it leave him with no extra time to look after the children. I would never presume—I could not impose on him to do his duties and mine while I enjoyed the luxury of visiting my family."

I braced myself for another question. He stared at me for a moment with an unsatisfied look. Then he turned to the other SS men. "Are you all done with your searches?" he barked out.

After receiving a positive response from all of his men, *Herr* Löning turned with a swish of his coat and went back into the hall.

"*Herr* Major, again, my apologies for disturbing your evening."

"And am I to receive no explanation for this disturbance, *Herr* Löning?" I heard the major ask.

"None whatsoever," replied *Herr* Löning firmly. "Are you all through in the study?" he asked the man with the crooked nose.

"Can I expect this same pleasant interruption at my office on Monday?" asked the major coolly.

"No, *Herr* Major. We have already searched your office," said *Herr* Löning arrogantly as he put on his hat and headed for the door. "*Heil* Hitler!"

"*Heil* Hitler," returned the major without hesitating.

It took a good minute for all of the men who had invaded the major's house to leave out the front door, but they were quick, like roaches. The major was still standing in the hall in the same spot, when the last one out closed the door. I looked back at the children. Annette was still sitting at the piano, and Sepp was still standing with the violin in his hand. We all listened to the car engines start, and then we heard them driving away.

The major disappeared into the study. I walked over and picked you up out of the fireplace. As I tried to dust you off, he came into the living room and headed over to the window at the back of the house. He stood looking out at the view for a good minute, his right foot ahead of the other, and all his weight on the left.

"Father?" Annette said.

"Silence," the major said abruptly as he turned around. *Was he worried that someone was still in the house?* I looked over at *Frau* Hoffmann.

The major brought his left hand up to his chin. "*Frau* Hoffmann, would it be possible to have dinner ready in an hour?"

"Yes, sir," she replied, and she rose and went directly into the kitchen.

"Children, run and get your coats," he said at last. "I think you should go outside and play while it is still light out."

Sepp set down my violin and bow as he wrinkled his nose. "I don't want to go—"

"Do as your father says," I said sternly, looking him directly in the eyes.

While Sepp and Annette left the room, I stood as still as possible, waiting for my instructions. The look on the major's face told me that he was like a ship by a rocky coastline, trying to navigate in heavy fog.

With everyone else gone from the room, the major took a couple of steps toward me until he was standing directly in front of me. He turned his distressed eyes to me and whispered softly, "Did I see you take the ledger?"

I nodded.

Then he wanted to know what I had done with it. I raised my hand to point to the piano bench since he didn't seem to want me to speak, but he was quick to grab my hand to stop me from pointing. I looked into his eyes. "Piano bench," I whispered, my words barely audible.

The major was still holding my hand, and I could see something like machinery working in his eyes. He shook his head slowly. "Are you sure?" Then he looked at me for reassurance. I nodded confidently.

The major's world had just been turned upside down, but he was yet to feel the full brunt. In the next few minutes, he made a careful search of his study. It wasn't long before he found a small listening device on the top of the light next to the fireplace. The cord for the device, hid cleverly in the paneling, came to an abrupt end at the floorboard.

The major's next stop was the basement. I followed him to the work bench. Soon I realized that we were directly underneath his study, and there the thin chord came down along the wall into a cabinet on the side of the bench that was well hidden in the corner. The major stooped down and tugged on the locked cabinet door. He bit his lip as he rose to his feet.

Then he spoke one word under his breath. "Heiner."

The major was still not done with his discoveries. Up in the hall, he unscrewed the mouth piece of the telephone and pulled out a small, square, black box. He shook his head and placed it back in the mouthpiece. I watched from the study door as he produced an identical black box from the telephone receiver in his study.

The major held the telephone in his right hand and stared at the fireplace. I watched his chest rise and fall slowly as he measured his breath. "There is only one thing to do," he said, at last. He pressed the telephone down, lifted it to his ear, and asked the operator to connect him to General Major Erxleben.

"He is? Yes, please. This is very important."

While he was waiting, the major turned and looked at me. I didn't know whether I should stay or go outside with the children. I didn't understand what was going on, and I didn't understand why the major was making a call on a telephone line that he knew was tapped.

"General Major? I apologize for disturbing your dinner, sir. I just had a visit from *Herr* Löning and his men. He informed me that they have already searched our offices. I wanted you to know that this has taken place."

The major listened carefully to the voice on the other end.

"No, sir. He has nothing, and he will find nothing. Everything is as it should be. I have been very careful over the years to follow the instructions I am given and not to operate beyond those parameters."

Major Rager leaned against the desk and rested the telephone on his leg.

"I won't see your reputation jeopardized just to prove my innocence, *Herr* General. Before you find yourself entangled in a painful inquisition, I am fully prepared to offer my resignation. And when Berlin calls, you can tell them that I will deliver it to them personally on Monday should they wish it. I will not stand in the way of *Herr* Löning's personal ambitions, and Berlin does not need an officer in charge of their military production in whom they cannot have full confidence."

I had to put my hand over my mouth. *Was this to be the end of the major's career?*

"He has no truthful accusations to make, but in cases such as this, the next step is always to fabricate. *Herr* General, I am certain that you will hear from Berlin soon enough, and I am sure they can find someone else to place in my position who will be more satisfactory to *Herr* Löning."

There was another long pause, and to my surprise, something like a smile spread slowly over the major's lips.

"I await your instructions, *Herr* General. Please accept my apology for interrupting your dinner. Good evening and *Heil* Hitler."

The major set the telephone down slowly, then he turned to me with a peculiar look on his face. "*Fräulein* Mauer? Do you know where the children are?"

"Yes, *Herr* Major," I replied. "They are outside."

"Would you go and see to them, please?"

He was acting so strange, but I wasn't surprised when the major followed me out the back door and into the garden. I watched as he walked the entire length of the garden wall, then he returned to where the children were. He put his arms around them and told them how proud he was of their behavior this evening and how impressed he was with their performance.

I watched as proud smiles lit up their faces. The major stood up and adjusted the hat on his head as Sepp picked up his mallet and sent his ball flying toward Annette. Major Rager turned his restless eyes to mine.

"I don't know what possessed you to take the ledger, but I can't thank you enough for hiding it, Klara," he said softly.

"Will you, are you forced to resign because of this?" I asked with a tremble in my voice. "I don't understand what is going on."

Major Rager shook his head. "I don't know what's going to happen, but I wanted to get to the general major before *Herr* Löning did. In any case, Berlin is going to have to be involved, and I'll have to walk the tight rope."

"But the ledger is safe," I sighed.

"Yes, thank God for that. But *Herr* Löning has been after me like a hound ever since my family left, and it seems that he won't stop until he ruins me. In 1930, my father purchased this house from the Rosenzweig family, a Jewish businessman. My father paid them full price, and *Herr* Löning has never forgotten it." The major shook his head.

"What does the ledger have to do with any of this?" I asked curiously.

The major hesitated a moment, and I thought that he wasn't going to answer my question, but then he looked down at me. "It is a record of everything that I have done right, and there are some who would use it to feed me to a firing squad."

I drew in a quick breath and looked at the children.

"If you hadn't hidden it, that is where I would be tonight."

My heart sank. He should have stopped at telling me about the ledger, but his mention of a firing squad only served to confirm my uncomfortable suppositions about the nature of his business.

"I wonder how long Heiner has been taping my conversations," said the major as he looked away. For a moment, I saw the unmistakable sign of hurt and betrayal in his eyes.

"You can cut the wire," I suggested.

The major shrugged. "If I do, they will just find some other way to eavesdrop. I'll just have to be careful." The major sighed. "I need your help, Klara."

The way he said it—the look in his eyes—I knew he was about to ask me to do something that I shouldn't. Then the wrestling started, the back and forth in my heart. I had already gone too far in concealing the ledger from the Gestapo. Now he was going to ask me to do something further. *Where was this all going to end?*

"I have got to get a message to a couple of people, to warn them. That'll be an impossible task for me now that the Gestapo is likely to follow me around. After supper, will you take some apples from the basement and make a couple of social calls?"

I hesitated a moment as my breath was caught in my throat. Then I looked into his eyes and gave in again. "I'm not very hungry. Perhaps I should go while it is still light."

The major nodded. "I didn't want to ask that of you."

"*Herr* Leitner?" I asked, anticipating that he was one stop I was to make.

The major pulled his head back slightly. "Yes. Tell him that the Gestapo was here and that my phone line is tapped."

"Anywhere else?"

"Make a couple of stops. It doesn't matter where. Do you know where Kölnischestrasse is?"

"Yes."

In an unusual gesture, the major rubbed his palms together as if he were nervous. "Besides *Herr* Leitner, go to Kölnischestrasse 175."

I looked away as he met my gaze. "Who am I to meet there?"

The major rolled his bottom lip in. "I believe he lives alone. You will know it is the right man if he grunts before he speaks. Tell him the same thing you tell *Herr* Leitner."

He paused a moment and a disturbing look came over his face. "Klara, they may be watching the house. If you suspect at all that you are being followed, don't go." The major shifted on his feet. "I never wanted to involve you in any of this."

"It's too late for that, *Herr* Major. But you don't have to worry about me. I don't know what you are involved in."

The major narrowed his eyes. "Then, why are you helping me?"

I looked away from the major for a moment, because the answer that came to my mind was not an answer I could share with him. "Please don't ask me any questions," I said, parroting his own words.

A slow smile spread over the major's face, and then he chuckled nervously. "I deserve that answer, Klara. I have given it to you often enough." The major looked up at the sky. "We had better go inside. Trude should have supper ready."

Before he sat down for dinner, I saw the major secure his ledger. I went directly to the basement, and then left the house with a basket of apples. When I closed the gate behind me, I saw two figures sitting in a car parked down the street from the house. I swung the basket of apples in front of me and looked down at the sidewalk. I had to think fast.

The first call I made was to the neighbor lady on the corner who always sweeps the sidewalk. She looked quite surprised to see me. I asked her how she had been doing with all of the bombings. Then I asked her which kind of broom she prefers. After that, I ran out of things to ask her, but she took up the conversation quite well, and I was forced to stay longer than I wished.

When I left her house, I headed down Amalienstrasse toward Wilhelmshöher Allee, praying that the car down the street wouldn't follow me. But they did.

By the time I reached the corner at Wilhelmshöher Allee, I could hear the jingle of the trolley bell. If I were to confuse them, this would be the best way to do it. I pulled the basket close to me and took off running. I was out of breath by the time I boarded the yellow trolley with my basket of apples. I held on tight as the trolley lurched forward, and I searched the street for the black car.

The black car stayed with the trolley for two stops, but then I lost sight of it. At the fourth stop, I got off with several other people. I decided not to waste any time. I headed directly to *Herr* Leitner's house. After circling the entire block, I stopped in a doorway to an apartment building across from his house and read the names of the tenants while I tried to scan the street for the car.

When I was certain that no one was following me, I crossed the street. A feeling of uneasiness came over me as I was walking up to his house. I turned up the stairs to his neighbor's house instead and pretended to knock on the door. Then I leaned over as if I were looking in the window to see if anyone was at home. When I turned around, I didn't see anyone who might be following me, but the feeling of uneasiness persisted.

My heart was pounding as I climbed the stairs to *Herr* Leitner's door. I rested the basket of apples on my left hip. It seemed like a long time before *Herr* Leitner opened the door, and I met his dark eyes.

"The Gestapo has searched the major's house and they have tapped his telephone," I said as quickly and softly as I could. "Is your neighbor at home?" I asked, pointing to the house next door. "Shake your head no and bid me good day," I said, trying to coach him.

Although a look of confusion clouded his face, he complied with my request. I took another long look at the neighbor's house before I left his block. If anyone were following me, I hoped that all they would see was that I had been unsuccessful in visiting *Herr* Leitner's neighbor.

For good measure, and because it was on the way to Kölnischestrasse, I stopped by the Meissel's house next. Neither one of the Meissels was at home, but I did at least give greetings to Inge. She wanted to know how much the major was paying me. I didn't tell her, but I did leave her with one apple.

It was a good ten minutes before I arrived at my last stop. I had to knock three times before a gruff man cracked the door and grunted at me. The smell of cigarette smoke came rushing out as if it were trying to escape. "What do you want?"

I had to swallow before I could speak. "Major Rager's house has been searched by the Gestapo and his telephone line has been tapped," I finally said.

I could only see a part of his face through the crack in the door, but I thought I saw a look of surprise in the one eye that was visible.

I heard another grunt. "Did they find anything?"

"No."

"Did they arrest him?"

"No."

"Then what do I care?" he said as he pushed the door shut.

I took a step back, and it took a moment before I realized that I should leave. What a rude response to my message. I had intended to leave a couple of apples with the man, but he never gave me the chance.

On my way down the sidewalk, I glanced at the large house. I wondered what kind of man this was and what connection the major has with such a person.

As extra precaution, I took a round about way back home. It was almost dark when I got to Terrassestrasse. But as I glanced up the street from the house, I saw the black car. I was already tired from all of the walking, but I turned around quickly and went around the block so that I could try to slip in the side gate undetected. I came in the back door and put the basket of apples down in the kitchen. As I was turning to go find the major, he came through the door.

We both looked at each other but neither of us spoke although I wanted to tell him and he wanted to know. It is a strange feeling to know that someone has been listening in on your conversations. I opened my mouth to say something just as the major moved over to the sink and turned the water on.

"I didn't find anything in here, but just in case," he said softly. "How did it go?"

"Fine," I said quickly. "But they are watching the house, and they did try to follow me. I think I lost them somewhere along the way, but they are back. I saw them as I came in."

The major closed his eyes for a moment. "Thank you, Klara. *Frau* Hoffmann saved you some supper," he said, pointing to a plate on the counter. "The children are in the nursery."

I took a long look at the major because I dared not ask. I was wondering what he was going to do now. I do not know what it feels like to be betrayed as he seems to have been today, but I know how I felt watching it happen to him.

After a moment, he turned and left. I reached for the facet, turned off the running water, and watched the water disappear down the drain. I didn't speak another word to the major all evening. It is an odd feeling to live in a house that has been bugged and then ransacked by a bunch of SS men. Even though there was no treasonous conversation and no great divulgence of secrets before they came, the only place I feel safe talking is outside. You, dear journal, are secure for the time being, but I must find a better place to hide you from now on.

....

October 15, 1944

Today, I went to mass with the major and the children. I thought about Rosine today and the things that she had said about God. I never hear anything that makes sense from the priest.

The major seems to be in some sort of depression. His sadness has a most undesirable affect on the children and on me. I wish that their bright smiles and childishness were able to cheer him as they always have.

As far as I know, there has been no word from the general major or Berlin about the major's resignation, and he has said nothing further to me. Of course, I can write of none of this in my letters, and so there is little about which I can write back to Sinsheim. I haven't received the photograph yet from Aunt Frieda or heard much from them lately.

I have found a better place to keep you, dear journal. And this time, I am confident that no one will find you.

....

October 16, 1944

Last night, the air raid siren went off just before eleven o'clock. This time we had hardly reached the basement before the anti-aircraft guns started going off. It must have only been a couple of airplanes, because there was little noise and little damage done in the end. The major was only gone for an hour or so afterward.

It was difficult to get the children up this morning, and there was a really cold wind blowing from the north, making our trips to and from school quite miserable. I did lie down and sleep a little this afternoon. I have been feeling really tired.

After my nap, I found a package waiting for me from Sinsheim, but when I looked carefully at it, I realized that someone had already opened it. I guessed immediately that it must have been the Gestapo. I was relieved to find that Aunt Frieda has finally sent me the picture of me and my siblings. I put it right up on my dresser in the frame of the mirror. I can see so much of my father in Lenz but hardly any in Klaus. Liese looks like I did at her age, and I think we both favor mother. I wish I had a picture of mother and father. Before I left for Kassel last year, I asked Aunt Frieda if I could have the picture she has of them, but she wouldn't part with it.

Frau Hoffmann has only bad news about her sister these days. Her sister's health is declining. From *Frau* Hoffmann's descriptions of her infirmities, I am surprised that she has lasted so long. She has seen every doctor in the region, but they all say there is nothing more they can do for her. I have a lot of respect for *Frau* Hoffmann and the care she has given to her sister, especially because I know first hand that she is such a disagreeable person. *Frau* Hoffmann said that Rosine has been coming every day to read the Bible to her sister and that seems to do her good.

I have been unable to get Sepp and Annette to play their piece together with any success. I am about to give up on the whole idea. Maybe when they are older or have progressed a little further in their studies they will be able to play together. Maybe it was a miracle, not to be repeated, that they were able to play for the Gestapo man that day.

The major is going out of town tomorrow, and he won't be back until Wednesday. I don't know where he is going, but I am afraid for him.

The major told *Frau* Hoffmann and me this morning that Berlin would not accept his resignation until *Herr* Löning submits a formal report and until after the inspections. The inspectors from Berlin are coming back to see what progress the major has made in reinstating their production lines next week. This time, I am going to stay in my room until I am sure they are gone. I don't want to get stuck playing for them or answering any questions about the major.

....

October 18, 1944

Dear Journal,

I am not ashamed to write in you that I am tired of hiding in shelters and waiting for the last bomb to drop. We have had another raid today, this time around noon before I went to pick up the children. *Frau* Hoffmann has given me a piece of paper with several Bible verses on it that Rosine wrote for me. I keep it in my pocket so that I have it to read during the bombings. One of the verses says, "Fear not them who are able to kill the body, but are not able to kill the soul, but rather fear God who is able to destroy both body and soul in hell." The other verse says that I am to cast my cares on the Lord because he cares for me.

I went to get the children as soon as the all clear was sounded, and they have been running around the house screaming all afternoon. I don't know when the major is expected home, but he is bound to be delayed as the bombs always seem to drop on the rail lines.

I am preparing myself for a long evening and a long week ahead until the inspection is over. I remember how nervous the major was the last time they came to town, and this time will be even worse with everything that is going on. I hear Annette crying, so I had better go see what Sepp has done to her.

....

October 20, 1944

Last night, the major seemed quite agitated at the supper table. On the way to put the children to bed, I asked him if he was feeling all right as he seemed to me to be quite pale. He was standing in the hallway by the telephone, and we were on the stairs. He did not respond to my question, but instead asked if he could speak with me once I put the children down. Every time he gives me that kind of look, it makes something in my stomach churn. I put the children down with no story and hurried back downstairs.

The light was on in his study, but he was not in there. I went through the living room and finally found him in the kitchen. He was pouring himself a cup of coffee. There was a package wrapped in brown paper, tied with a string, sitting on the counter next to the sink.

The door to the kitchen went *swish* behind me, and I stood there in silence watching the major sip on his coffee. I thought he was going to tell me something about his resignation.

"I hesitate to ask you, Klara, but since there is no one else I would trust and because I feel that I have no choice, I was wondering if you would be able to deliver this package for me tomorrow morning?"

I didn't respond to the major's question as I was hoping he would see how uncomfortable his requests make me. It has only been a few days since I ran all over town to deliver the "important" messages for him, and I don't know how much more my conscience can stand.

"I think it may be some time before the Gestapo gets tired of following me around. In the meantime, I am late in delivering this to the superintendent. I had planned to meet him tomorrow morning at ten o'clock at the plant, but I cannot do that while I am being watched."

I drew in a deep breath. For my eighth birthday, my mother gave me an illustrated book about a sea captain who, through indifference, failed to steer his ship clear of a rock while trying to make port one night. The ship did not sink immediately, but over the course of several hours, it began a slow but steady descent into the depths of the ocean. I can still see the drawings in that book. The very last page was a picture showing the captain standing on the bow of his ship on the bottom of the ocean.

I feel like I am sinking, that I have been sinking. Every time the major asks me to do another thing, I am sinking deeper into the depths of his world. And I am a stranger in his world. Each time he asks, I am determined to say no, but the major's eyes always tug at my heart.

"What do I have to do?" I responded while I vowed to myself that this would be the last time I gave in.

The major looked at me, and for a moment, I thought I saw his eyes mist up. He took another sip of his coffee.

"I really don't trust anyone but you, and this is very important to me," he said, putting his cup down and looking at me with those inquisitive eyes. I tried to maintain eye contact with him, but I always have such trouble when he looks at me the way he does.

"You'll need a pass, but I can write one for you tonight." The major cleared his throat. "You will find Superintendent Vogler at the Henschel tank factory on the north side of town. Take the bus to the Marien *Krankenhaus*. Henschel's factories are right across the street from the hospital."

The major picked up the package in the brown wrapping and handed it to me. Then he told me I would have to show my pass and check in with the guard at the gate. After cautioning me not to say anything in his study, I followed the major there, and he wrote out a pass for me.

I took the pass and the package directly to my room. While I was trying to shove the brown paper package into my purse, one of the ends began to rip, and I saw what was inside. I looked up at the door to my room. It was closed. Then I sat down on the edge of my bed. There was more money in the brown paper sack than I have ever seen in my entire life.

I took in a deep breath and closed my eyes. *What was the major asking me to do?* I opened my eyes and shoved the money into my purse. I didn't really want to face it, but how could I deny it any longer. It is bad enough that I am working for a Nazi officer, but what is worse is that it is clear to me now that he is a crooked Nazi officer. There is no other explanation.

We left the house this morning for the school building on time, passing the nice neighbor who was sweeping the sidewalk on the way. It looked like it might rain, so I grabbed *Frau* Hoffmann's umbrella on the way out of the house. I'm really glad I did. Just before I dropped the children off, the sky let go of its tears.

I caught a bus to the north side of town and got off on the stop right in front of the hospital. I waited for a minute or so, and then I crossed the street and walked toward the gated entrance. The factory is on a large piece of property close by the railroad tracks. The grounds have obviously suffered from multiple air raid attacks. I could see several smaller buildings and two large buildings before me.

I straightened my shoulders and walked directly up to the guard shack at the gated entrance. My eyes followed the barbed wire all along the top of the fence line. A short, thin soldier slid open the door to the shack and asked me to state my business. I told him that I was there to see Superintendent Vogler. He looked me up and down, from head to toe, as if he didn't believe me. The wind was whipping at *Frau* Hoffmann's umbrella. I reached into my purse and pulled out the pass the major had given me, and then I told him my name.

The guard slid the door on the shack closed with a thud. I watched as he picked up his telephone and made a call. I looked around nervously and tried to remember all of the major's instructions to me. The guard made me stand out in the rain for quite a while after he put the receiver down. Finally, I heard his phone ring back.

"Someone will be right out to see you," said the soldier, sliding his door open only a crack.

I waited in the pouring rain for over ten minutes. At last, a man in a gray overcoat came toward the guard shack from between the large buildings in front of me. He was carrying a big, black umbrella. I swallowed and tried not to look nervous, but the money in my purse was causing me some distress.

The guard opened the gate for me, and the man in the gray coat greeted me as I stepped inside the compound. "You are here to see the superintendent, ma'am?" the man asked. He had jet black hair.

"Yes, sir."

"Is there something I can help you with?"

I held my breath for a moment. The major had given me strict instructions not to give the money to anyone but the superintendent. "No, sir," I responded as calmly as I could. "I am to see Superintendent Vogler directly."

"Is he expecting you?"

"I don't think he is expecting me," I replied honestly, "but he was expecting Major Rager, and I have come on his behalf."

The man with the dark hair nodded and then asked me to follow him. We walked in the pouring rain between the two big buildings. We passed another large building on the left, and then headed into the building beyond that one that was marked "3."

Once we were inside the building, we both took our umbrellas down and shook the water out on the floor. My feet were soaked as was the coat and the skirt I was wearing underneath.

"What a downpour!" shouted the man in the gray coat. "If you will come this way, I will show you to the superintendent's office."

It was hard for me not to notice the myriad of activities that were happening inside building number three. I saw gigantic chunks of steel, machining equipments, motors, and lots of men making a great deal of noise at their work.

I followed the man in the gray coat past a large table of parts and through a doorway to the right. We went down a short hallway, and then he motioned for me to step inside the last door on the left. He asked me to wait in the office while he tried to locate the superintendent.

The walls of the office were covered with government work posters, and there was a large portrait of *Herr* Hitler right behind the desk. Although there was a seat by the desk, I did not sit down in it. I set my umbrella by the door and held my purse close to me. I was determined that if I got out of the tank factory alive, I would never do anything like this for the major again. It was all I could do to keep my hands from trembling.

The footsteps in the hall got louder, and at last, a large man, who looked like he had eaten well through the good times and the bad, came through the door. He gave me a look of surprise when he saw me standing in his office. Before he spoke, I heard a grunt. "What can I do for you, *Frau?*" he asked as he moved behind his desk and sat down.

"*Fräulein* Mauer," I said, supplying him with my name. "And you are?"

"Superintendent Vogler," he responded as he stuck a cigarette into his mouth and lit it. "And you are in my office."

This must be the man who lives at Kölnischestrasse 175. My eyes grew big. He didn't seem to recognize me. "Major Rager sent me," I said with a little tremble in my voice.

The superintendent looked up at me with a start. "Close the door," he commanded abruptly.

After I closed the door, I stepped forward, rested my purse on the corner of his desk, and pulled out the brown paper package. When I handed it to him, he took it and immediately slid it into one of his desk drawers. Then he took a long puff on his cigarette.

"Tell Major Rager that everything is in order," he said, sitting back in his chair.

I nodded, and then I turned to leave. Just as I was opening the door, the superintendent stopped me. I could hear footsteps in the hallway coming toward his office.

"Look, I'd like to help you out, but I don't know where your brother is, and if he does show up, he's not going to have a job here anymore," said Superintendent Vogler in a rather harsh tone. I looked back at the superintendent in confusion.

"Holger, will you show this ferret out?" he asked the man in the gray coat, who was now standing at his office door.

The man in the gray coat gave me an intimidating look as I grabbed *Frau* Hoffmann's umbrella from beside the door. When I looked back at the superintendent, he had already buried his head in the paperwork on his desk. He didn't even give me the courtesy of a good-bye.

The man in the gray coat escorted me all the way back to the front gate in the pouring rain, and then he threw me out. I was still shocked at the way the superintendent had treated me, and that was all I could think about while I was waiting to catch the bus back to the south side of town. The scene played over and over again in my mind. Finally, I decided that maybe he had to be harsh with me to put on a show in front of the man with the gray coat. It shouldn't have mattered to me, because I would probably never see him again, but it did.

I didn't see the major until that evening when we sat down for supper. After *Frau* Hoffmann had set the food on the table and had gone back into the kitchen, Major Rager asked me if I was able to deliver the package. I told him between bites the message the superintendent had given me. He didn't say anything, but I thought I saw a look of relief on his face.

"I don't know what to expect tomorrow," he said as he rolled his eyes. "Last time the inspectors were here, we were at ninety-three percent capacity. We have just now arrived at fifty percent, thanks to the Allied bombings in September."

The major shrugged. "It doesn't matter anyway although I must pretend that it does. We are running out of fuel to power our equipment, and because of the bombings, soon, we will be without the manpower or means to build the equipment. How we expect to win the war, I do not know." The major shook his head, took another bite of out of his bread, and then he looked up at me.

While he was speaking, I was just looking at him and listening politely to his words. I have never heard him speak so negatively, and he has never shared his thoughts with me. Part of me thought that maybe he was just saying those things to see how I would react.

Major Rager set the bread down on his plate and crossed his arms. "What is going on in that mind of yours, *Fräulein* Mauer? You say so little that you always leave me to wonder."

I looked down at my plate and tried to think of an answer. "I don't see how what I think should matter to you at all," I replied at last.

"Then you are not aware of the confidence I have in you," he responded, "or how much I rely on you."

I swallowed my next bite almost whole. I wish I didn't, but when the major says things like this to me, I feel awkward, and I don't know what to say in response. I looked up at the children who were consuming their food in utter contentment. None of our conversation was bothering them.

After dinner, I played a while with the children, but my mind was on the subject on which I had pondered all afternoon. I was going to talk to the major, and I was determined to do it that night. What he had said at the evening meal only made my determination to have the discussion more certain.

At nine o'clock, I went to the top of the stairs on the first floor. I could still see the light on in the major's study. I knew I couldn't have a conversation with him in there, so I paced the top of the stairs until I heard the major in the hall.

I was so nervous. I breathed in deeply and bit my tongue. As the major came up the stairs, my heart began to pound. He noticed I was standing there when he got about halfway up, but he had no idea what I was about to say to him. I could see curiosity in his eyes.

"What is it, Klara? Is something the matter?" he asked me as he stepped onto the landing. I looked up at him, and then I looked away for a moment. I was losing my nerve. I closed my eyes for a second.

"I'm sorry, sir," I began putting the fingers of both of my hands together in front of me, "I don't know what it is that you are involved in, but I just can't do it any longer. I can't take any more messages or deliver your bribe money," I stammered, and then I turned around to go up the stairs to my room. Although I tried not to look the major in the eyes as I was turning, I did see the surprised expression on the major's face.

"Bribe money?"

Before I had made it to the first step, the major reached out, grabbed me by the elbow, and pulled me back around toward him. Then, as if he was surprised that he had touched me, he let go of my arm. By this time, I was looking up into his eyes. They looked as if I had just injured him with my words.

"Klara," he said softly. "I won't have you thinking evil of me, at least not when I don't deserve it."

I tried to turn away from him as I felt my cheeks flush, but he pulled me back again.

"Please hear me out," he said with desperation. I looked at him, daring him to explain. When he saw that he had my attention, the major ran his hand through his hair, and then he looked up at the ceiling for a moment.

"The money is mine," he confessed at last. "It's not bribe money. I don't know if he takes any of it for his trouble in keeping the books so that they are just as they need to be for the inspectors, but most of it, anyway, is for paying the workers."

I looked back at the major with surprise in my eyes. I hadn't expected this explanation. Now I was trying to decide whether I believed what he said or not. On more than one occasion, I have had trouble trying to reconcile his less than straight actions with who he seems to be.

"I would have thought that by now you would know what kind of man I am."

At hearing this, emotions surged inside of me like a huge wave. Then, in frustration, I said too much. "You are so good at always being what you should be that I cannot tell whether you are cold and calculating, or a man of true principle. I know I am not supposed to ask any questions, but if I am caught helping you, what cause can I tell myself that I have given my life for?"

For a moment, I thought I saw in his eyes that he wanted to tell me everything. I watched his face as he gathered what he was feeling and put it all carefully away. His response came after a full minute of silence. "I have demanded of you that you ask me no questions because it has been necessary, but I can see that it is unfair of me to ask this of you. I value your service and your loyalty to me, Klara. Perhaps it is time for me to trust you the way you have trusted me."

Those were his words to me before he said good night. I am sitting here now, sorry that I told him that I didn't want to help him anymore. But after almost a year of working for him, I feel like I still don't know him.

The truth is that I am frightened for him, for the children and for us all. I wish that we did not live in the world of the Third *Reich* with its tanks, bombs, Gestapo, and SS. But we do. And no matter where I go, there is no escape. Can it be that the major feels the same way?

....

October 24, 1944

Dear Journal,

Today was a cold and dreary Tuesday in Kassel. The children have been sick with influenza since Saturday. Annette came down with it first. Sepp succumbed on Sunday. I have gotten little sleep during the nights and have gone between Sepp and Annette's rooms more than a hundred times. At least, they both seem to be on the mend now. This morning, neither one had a fever, and last night, they were both able to keep down the little food I fed them.

I have seen the major twice every day since Saturday, briefly in the morning and then in the evening when he has come to inquire how the children are doing. This morning, he looked worn-out and worried about the inspections. I anxiously awaited his arrival home this evening, hoping that he would have good news to share that the inspections went well and hoping that the good news would lift his lagging spirits.

The children felt well enough to play in the nursery this afternoon but only for a short time. By three o'clock in the afternoon, they were both back in bed. After a short nap, I went downstairs and played my violin in the living room until I heard the front door open.

My heart soared when I saw the major smile. "Is it all over?" I asked.

"Almost," he said, clearing his throat. "And I think they are pleased with our progress. I knew it would go well when I heard one of the inspectors remark that we had recovered so much quicker than Frankfurt, under worse circumstances."

Frau Hoffmann took his coat, and he came into the living room and sat down on the couch, picking up his newspaper on the way. "How are the children?"

"I think they are almost recovered, sir," I replied. "They played for a couple of hours this afternoon, but I think it is probably best for them to remain home another day from school."

The major looked up at me for a long moment. "Are you ever disagreeable, Klara?"

"Pardon me?"

"You have been up all day and all night since Saturday, and still, you are so pleasant."

I looked down at the floor a little embarrassed. I was surprised that he even knew that. "I won't deny, I'm very tired, sir. I would like to feed the children, and then go to bed myself, if you will excuse me from supper."

The major's brow turned down with concern. "I hope you are not feeling ill."

"No, sir, just tired."

"I'll feed them, *Fräulein* Mauer. You go to bed."

I opened my mouth to protest for a moment, but I gave up immediately when he gave me a firm look. Just as I turned to go upstairs, the major called my name.

"And Klara, I've been summoned to Berlin tomorrow."

"To Berlin?" I asked as I felt my chest freeze up. This could only mean that *Herr* Löning has submitted his report.

"Yes, and I will tell *Frau* Hoffmann the same thing. If I must give my resignation, I will make it perfectly clear that you both left my employment weeks ago because of some disagreement. If I am not back by Thursday afternoon, you should pack your bags and leave."

I tried to keep my mouth from dropping open, but it didn't matter. He opened his newspaper and started reading it as if he had said nothing to me at all.

I am sitting now underneath my comforter, and I will try to go to sleep shortly, but before I do, I have to say that there is something very strange happening in my heart. I feel as if my heart has been divided right down the middle, and I don't know which side of my heart to side with. *What is to happen to Sepp and Annette? Does he really think I could just leave?*

....

October 26, 1944

Dear Journal,

Yesterday must have been the longest day of the year. Heiner came by in the afternoon, unannounced. He was eager to tell *Frau* Hoffmann that something big was about to happen, but he wouldn't say what. He did say that he thought the major might be up for a promotion. When Heiner said that, I shook my head and wondered how he had fallen so behind in knowing what was going on.

I didn't sleep very well last night. The agonizing wait finally ended this evening just after nine o'clock. Despite the major's instructions, *Frau* Hoffmann did not leave the house until after she had served us supper. She gave me a particularly concerned look as she glanced at the clock in the hall before she put on her coat, but she didn't say anything.

I played with the children all evening, finally putting them to bed at eight o'clock. This time, I was the one pacing the floor in the hall. Never once did I consider packing my bag. *Where would I go?*

At last, I heard a car pull up to the front. My heart began to beat hard. I was so happy to see the major come through the front door, that I couldn't hold back a smile.

He handed me his briefcase, and then I took his coat. He took off his hat and set it on the table by the phone. I stared at him, waiting for him to speak.

"You didn't leave," he said, his voice barely audible.

Before I could explain to him that I felt it was my duty to stay through the good and the difficult times, his lips curled up a little. "Would you make me a cup of tea?"

"There's hot water on the stove," I said, moving toward the kitchen.

The major came through the kitchen door as I was pouring the water into his cup. I set the cup down on the table, and he sank down onto the nearest chair.

"Can I get you something to eat?"

The major shook his head, and then he raised his eyes to mine. "I will be content to never have another day like this," he said, and as he spoke my heart fell.

"*Herr* Löning's report?"

The major took a sip out of his cup. "I don't think we will be hearing anything further from *Herr* Löning." The major gave me a particular look that told me all I needed to know about the demise of *Herr* Löning. I reached up and grabbed the collar on my dress and swallowed hard.

"I have been recommended for promotion to lieutenant colonel, which I don't think will go through since I have not been a major long enough, and, effective today, Heiner is to take *Herr* Löning's office."

"What?"

"I always suspected he was Gestapo—something in his manner." The major took another sip of his tea. "They gave him a very convincing disguise and placed him in just the right places to hear and to observe everything he shouldn't have. I am beginning to think that I may owe this unsuspected outcome to him."

"No," I said immediately. "You have earned their respect and Heiner's good opinion. He sees, and surely by now, Berlin knows that they could not find anyone as dedicated and competent to take your place."

As I finished my sentence, I folded my arms across my waist. *Did I just say that out loud?* The major looked at me as if he were looking at a ghost. Slowly, he lowered his eyes to his cup. After a long silence, when it was clear that the major wasn't going to say anything else, I told him that it was getting late and that I was going to turn in for the evening.

The major rose from his seat. "Would you stay, stay with me while I finish my tea?" he asked, pulling out the other chair for me.

I hesitated only a moment. "Certainly," I said as I sat down and folded my hands in my lap. It was very quiet in the kitchen, and I wondered why he would want me to stay. After he shifted in his chair, he asked me how my family was. My eyes darted to his.

He smiled. "Don't worry. I'm not thinking of sending you to Sinsheim."

I stumbled over my first sentence. Then I told him the news from Aunt Frieda's last letter. I don't remember what I told him, just trivial things, but when he was done with his tea, I took his cup and set it in the sink. After that, I wished him a good evening.

This has been such a torturous day wondering what would happen to the major. It seems to be a cruel thing in life that my own well-being is so wrapped up in what happens to others that I am exhausted from emotions that don't even really belong to me.

....

October 28, 1944

Today is Saturday, and although it was not a warm day, after breakfast, the major asked me if I thought the children could stand a walk down to the Fulda since they have been ill most of the week and cooped up in the house. Because they were quite energetic yesterday, I told him that I thought they could. I was surprised when he asked me if I would get my coat and join them.

The morning sun felt good on my face as we walked through the streets of Kassel on our way down to the *Karlsaue*. The air was crisp and clean. After ten minutes of silence, the major cleared his throat.

"A few days ago, you said that you did not know where I stood. I would very much like to explain myself to you, but I have been keenly aware of the compromising position this might cause for you and the obligation that you would have to report me to the authorities as has been requested of you."

I looked up at the major with surprise. I had called him "cold and calculating," but I saw in that moment that I couldn't have been more wrong. He had obviously considered the trouble it would cause me to be caught in between him and the authorities.

"I think you might be surprised that you may not find anything in our conversation that requires any such disclosures to the authorities, but out of the abundance of caution, I should ask if you are willing to keep what I say in the strictest of confidence as I assume you always have."

"*Herr* Major, it is not necessary for you to explain—"

"Will you keep what I tell you in confidence? Please consider carefully before you answer me."

I opened my mouth to respond, but I closed it again and swallowed hard. "Of course, I will."

The major paused and took Sepp's hand as we crossed the street and started down the path along the Fulda. There were others walking close to us, so the major waited until they were out of earshot before he continued.

"I have been trying to find a place to start, but I have come to realize just how painful and complex the whole situation is for me to explain. It comes down to this, I have made a couple of very foolish choices, and now, I am living with the consequences.

"When I met Ida, I was disillusioned with the direction Germany was headed, and it didn't take me long to embrace the ideas that *Herr* Adolf Hitler was promoting. I, like my father, was interested in seeing Germany prosper. But unlike my father, I was also interested in seeing us break out from under the provisions of the treaty that were keeping us from getting back on our feet.

"I am conservative in my politics and a nationalist at heart. With everything that I have, I supported the idea of protecting our country from the communists, in building our defenses and military, and in growing our economy. I wanted nothing more than to see a strong Germany."

The major sighed. "Between Ida and her mother's enthusiasm for this new movement and the breath of fresh air that National Socialism was going to be for Germany, I got swept away in it all. It wasn't until Operation Hummingbird, in fact the night your parents died, that I began to see that there were radical factions in our movement. I remember that night so clearly. I remember thinking that I was sure that these tiny sects would be rightly checked by someone."

The major let go of Sepp's hand and the children ran ahead of us on the path.

"But that is not what happened," he continued as we headed toward the pond. "Over the years, I have watched that faction gradually take over the whole party like an infection, and now, the movement that held so much promise is guarding *Herr* Hitler's interests and not Germany's. And my country is being destroyed from without by its enemies and from within by my own party."

Major Rager paused as we arrived at the *Schwaneninsel*. I was trying to listen to the major, but what he was telling me was so far from what I had expected to hear, that it was all I could do to keep my mouth from dropping open.

"Father, can we toss stones into the lake?" asked Annette with an eager sparkle in her eyes. The major smiled and shooed the children toward the water. Then he looked back at me.

Major Rager lowered his voice. "I was an enthusiastic party member until a couple of years ago when I started adding things up—all of those things that happened in Poland and France that I have tried to forget. Then I saw just how much they valued their loyal, dedicated party members when they threw our former *Gauleiter* out of office after last October's bombing. He spoke up one time too many.

"I don't want you to have the wrong idea about me, Klara. I love my country, and I still stand for the same things for which I have always stood, but sadly, my party does not. And they have such a stronghold that, as we all know, anyone who fights against such a tide either disappears for good or ends up with a bullet in the head."

The major paused and looked away from me for a moment. "There's a bench over there," he said, looking down the path not too far from the pond. "Would you like to sit down?"

"Yes," I responded numbly. I was having a hard time taking in everything the major was saying to me, and it only made it harder that I could see that he was struggling to tell me. I followed him over to the bench, and we both sat down. He looked out at the water and crossed his legs before he continued.

"I decided a long time ago that I was going to fight for the Germany that should be, that I was going to act as a German officer should act, even if everyone else does not or cannot do the same. If others want to take Germany in the wrong direction, to cast off dignity and to spite humanity, I cannot follow. That will do nothing to strengthen our country or to ennoble our people. I can stand— I must stand for what I know is right, even if it costs me. All of my enigmatic actions, all of the hidden messages, the ledgers—they are all to accomplish this noble and good goal."

I looked up at the major. Although I did not understand exactly what he was saying, he was telling me all of this at great risk. I felt a heavy weight in my chest knowing he trusted me enough to share these thoughts.

"My father was right about the Nazi party, and he was right about Ida. Ida was the other bad choice I made. She was beautiful, charismatic, and enchanting, and everyone told me how lucky I was to have her—everyone but my father. Somehow, he could see past it all. What a nightmare she was to me. Still, I loved her."

I looked away from the major as he clenched his jaw, and I thought I saw tears coming to his eyes. It was more than I could bear to watch the major cry.

"But you have the children. You have done so well with them, sir," I said, trying to turn the major's attention to something more positive. "It is very difficult to grow up without one or even both of your parents, and yet, they are very healthy and happy."

The major looked at me with determination in his eyes. "Since last October, I have had one goal and one purpose in life, and that is to get us through this war honorably, together, and alive. Tell me, Klara," said the major after a minute of silence, "does your conscience allow you to support such a man with such a cause?"

I remember that feeling of pride that I always had for my father because of how he conducted himself as a high ranking member of the government although I did not fully know or understand it all at ten years old. Perhaps a lot of my respect for him was due to the fact that mother loved him and supported him completely. I felt a tear drop from my eyes as I looked back at the major.

"Yes," I said resolutely. "It does."

The major turned his gaze to the children by the water's edge and sighed. "It is such a helpless feeling to watch Germany fail. I know that everything they are telling us in the papers and on the radio is just the opposite. Despite what our propaganda minister is telling us, we won't make it six more months, Klara. And I am afraid there will be nothing left of Germany when it is all said and done."

"Is there no hope at all?" I asked.

The major shook his head and sighed. "Not as long as the *Führer* is in command."

I looked over at the children, gleefully enjoying themselves, and then I looked at the major. This must be the heavy burden he has been carrying all alone, all of the time I have known him. This must be the cloud that has always hovered over his spirit. I wished, at that moment, that there was something I could say or do to erase it.

The major rose to his feet and extended his arm to me. "Would you walk to the bridge and back with me?" he asked. I smiled and took his arm as he called to the children.

Something happened in those moments this morning that I cannot seem to explain. Something between us changed. It was as if he had opened up the door of his world and invited me in. And he seemed relieved to let me in—to tell me what was on his mind. He gave me no great revelation of the things he does in secret. Instead, he told me the reason, and that is more than enough for me.

Frau Hoffmann scolded us when we arrived home late for dinner. I noticed that the children's appetites have returned.

Instead of closing himself up in the study as I expected, the major spent the afternoon with us, listening to the children practice their music and playing games with them.

After I put the children to bed, I came to my room, laid down on my bed, and stared up at the ceiling. All I could do was think about the conversation I had had with the major this morning. The tears rolled down my face one after the other.

From the first time I ever saw him, I thought evil of him, and I have always found it hard to trust him. But when I think of all of the things he has ever done to help me, to rescue me and to protect me, I am ashamed. Then to hear him tell me his heart at the risk that I might have him arrested for treason is more than I can take. Until today, I did not know that he was not a loyal Nazi party member. Before today, I thought he had been happily married to Ida.

I am afraid this strange feeling in my heart is something more than respect for him.

November 1944

Dear Journal,

Early last night, we found ourselves huddled in the basement as the air raid siren blared above us. I held Annette in my lap. Sepp sat next to the major. From the sound of the anti-aircraft guns, there were only a few planes. We heard several bombs drop, but then, the all-clear siren went off.

I carried Annette up to her bed, and the major carried Sepp. I met the major in the hallway and followed him down the stairs. He went to get his hat, and I went for his coat. While he was putting on his coat, he told me that he didn't think it would take him long to check the factories.

I shut the front door behind the major, but when I turned around, my eye caught sight of his hat on the table by the stairs. He always takes it with him. I grabbed the hat and hurried back to the front door. He must have realized that he forgot it, because when I opened the front door, he had already turned back to the house. He smiled when he saw that I had his hat in my hand.

Just as I was handing it to him, an unexploded ordnance went off down the street to the north of the house. I heard a shriek come from my mouth. The hat dropped from my hand to the ground as he pulled me into the safety of his arms to shield me from the flying debris. When I opened my eyes at last, I was resting against the major's chest and holding on to him with all my might.

My lungs filled with several quick gulps of air as if I had just come up out of the water. It had happened so unexpectedly that my heart had stopped beating for a second and then bolted like a wild horse. I stayed still while my heart slowed down, and it suited me just fine that he wasn't letting me go.

I remember the feeling, when I was a child, of slipping my fingers into my father's big, strong hand as we would walk down the street. That feeling of being loved and protected came back to me like a gust of wind. As I was there in his arms, I felt it, as if I were a child again—that innocent sense of trust and security.

Without releasing me, he pulled back slightly, and I felt his hand gently turn my face to his. By the light from the lamp on the table in the hall streaming through the front door, I looked into his concerned eyes.

"Are you all right?"

I tried to nod my head because no words came out of my mouth when I tried to speak. My eyes fell to his chin.

"I have to go," he said somberly.

I dared to look back in his eyes, but it took me a while to find my tongue. "Please be careful, sir."

My fingers loosened the grip they had on his arms, but he was still holding me. He looked at me as if he wanted to speak, his clear eyes filled with something tender. The major tipped his head toward me until his forehead gently met mine. I closed my eyes and tried not to breathe.

"I will," he whispered as he ran his thumb slowly across my cheek. His arm loosened from around my waist, he stepped back, and then he left me standing alone on the doorstep. After he retrieved his hat from the ground, he got into the car. I folded my arms across my waist and watched as he drove away. I was sure. He came very close. I wonder if he was going to kiss me.

The children and I were sitting at the table when the major came down for breakfast. He sat down in his chair and picked up his coffee cup before he looked my way. After that, I tried not to look at the major and was relieved when the children finally finished up. I told them to run and get their schoolbags, or we would be late.

The major caught my hand as I got up to leave. "About last night," he began as he looked up at me with hesitation.

"I-I apologize for running into you." I had already rehearsed my lines, but the major was quick to interrupt me.

"Please don't apologize."

Just as *Frau* Hoffmann came through the door with the major's toast, he let go of my hand. We both watched her set the toast down. The sound of the children charging down the stairs filled the uncomfortable silence.

"If you will excuse me, sir, I need to get the children to school."

"Klara?" said the major as I reached the doorway. The gentle way he said my name made me turn back immediately.

"We need to talk," he said earnestly. "I am gone all day today, and I won't be back until late. I am having breakfast with General Major Erxleben in the morning, but I was wondering if I could meet you and the children at the fountain at *Schloss* Wilhelmshöhe at half past ten. The children seemed to enjoy our outing last week, and I thought that perhaps it was worth repeating."

By this time, the children were heading out the door. "Certainly," I said with a smile.

All the way to school, I could feel that my cheeks were burning. What could the major possibly want to discuss with me? Had he not already told me everything I needed to know?

When I got back to the house, the major was gone. *Frau* Hoffmann sent me to the grocer on Kohlenstrasse with some food stamps to buy some butter and some eggs. I came back with only half of what she had hoped I would get, but it was all that the grocer had left.

Frau Hoffmann left for home in the early afternoon as she said that she had developed a terrible headache. The house was quiet, and I was alone for a good hour and a half. I sat down in the living room in the sunshine and wrote a longer than normal letter to Aunt Frieda, Liese, Lenz, and Klaus. I made sure to let them each know how much I loved them and thought of them.

When I went upstairs to my room to see if I had any more envelopes and opened my bedroom door, I saw a note lying on the floor as if it had been shoved under the door. I sat down on the bed facing the window and unfolded the paper. I didn't recognize the handwriting, but soon I knew exactly who had written it.

The note read:

Dearest Klara,

I have shared only part of my heart with you, and now, I find that I cannot bring myself to share the rest while looking into your lovely eyes. I cannot remember how empty it was before you came to live with us, and I don't want to remember. I realized as I held you in my arms last night that this could not continue.

When I asked you to come to work for me, I did not know that you would become so much a part of me that I feel that I cannot do without you. You are like the soft light of a full moon on a cloudless summer night. Many times, you have been the only one I could trust, and you have stood by me through some lonely and uncertain hours. Do you know that it is your smile that I look forward to at the end of every impossible, unbearable day?

And I am not alone in this sentiment. I think you know that the children adore you. I have never had to worry that they were not in good hands, and that is how I feel whenever I am with you. I cannot express what it means to me that you show me nothing but respect in front of the children.

I realize that I may be asking too much, but I must know how you feel. I want to know if there is any place in your heart for me. Sometimes, I think I can see it in your eyes, but I will not allow this to go any further if this is not something you want. You need only say so. Your interest has always been and remains the first thing on my mind. Until Saturday morning.

I am very truly yours,

Kurt Rager.

My hands were trembling by the time I had read the whole letter. I laid it down in my lap for a second, and then I read it again. I couldn't believe my eyes. Had the man that I loved just told me that he loved me? I wanted to run straight into his arms.

The chiming of the clock in the hall reminded me that I was late in going to get the children. I must have been in a daze all of the way to school and all the way home, because while we were sitting in the dining room working on homework, I couldn't remember leaving the house.

After I put the children to bed, I went down to the living room and sat by the fire for a while. When I think about how much I care for the major, it is as if I am sitting next to a warm fire on a cold day. Now to know that he cares for me is a feeling that I cannot describe to you. Aunt Frieda and Uncle Lothar have cared the best they could for us over the years. But I cannot remember the last time I felt like this; maybe because it has been so long since I felt loved.

....

November 11, 1944

There was fog hovering outside my window when I woke up this morning, but the sun came out and shooed it all away. I helped the children dress, and we went down to eat. *Frau* Hoffmann has served us rice porridge for three days in a row now. I suppose I should have scolded him, but when Sepp complained about it, I just kept silent.

When the clock in the hallway struck ten, I went to get the children's jackets, hats, and mittens, and soon after that, we were on our way to catch the streetcar. Annette was skipping along beside me the whole way. Sepp was always half a block ahead of us. We passed a couple of his classmates halfway between the house and Wilhelmshöher Allee, but I didn't want to stop long to talk.

I had tried not to think about the major all morning long, but as we got closer to the *Schloss* Wilhelmshöhe, I began to get anxious about seeing him. I laughed out loud when I thought of how much had changed since he had tracked me down in the park across from the Meissel's house almost a year ago.

When we got close to the pond with the fountain, on the west side of the *Schloss*, Sepp took off like a lightning bolt. I let go of Annette's hand, and she tried to catch him. She ran after him with her coat waving in the wind like a cape.

I looked out over the grass, still littered with bright gold, red, and orange leaves and up to the *Herkules* at the top of the mountain. Then I turned my eyes to the path coming up to the fountain from the *Schloss* and shielded them from the morning sun. Although he was still quite far away, I could see the major coming toward us. I bit my tongue to try to still my heart.

Sepp had found a branch and was dragging it through the pond, and Annette was dropping leaves into the water trying to make them float when the major reached my side. He smiled when I looked at him—that disarming smile.

"How was breakfast?" I asked nervously.

"It was good," he said, looking over toward the pond at the children. "I do feel sorry for the general major, though. This is his first *Wehrmacht* command," the major said, looking back at me. "He is a communications expert, and he knows very little about military production. I can tell that he is uncomfortable in his position."

"Is his family here with him?"

"His wife is here, but I get the sense that she would rather be back in Bielefeld."

The major shifted on his feet nervously, and then he looked at me as if to ask for a response to his deep question.

I cleared my throat, and then I looked down at the ground. *Why was I so nervous?*

"Did you get my note?" the major asked at last.

"Yes," I said looking up into his hope-filled eyes.

His eyes, clear like a lake on a cloudless day, seemed to reach into my soul. "*Bist du bei mir* (Are you with me)?" he asked almost in a whisper.

He had asked me this question before, but this time, I was sure of his meaning. "Yes," I replied without making him wait another second, "with all my heart."

I watched that charming, pleasant smile spread over his countenance, but there was something else there too that I had never seen before—happiness. I had to look away from his gaze.

"Have you been through the park?"

I cleared my throat. "I came with the children once, intending to go up to the *Herkules*. But we only made it to the fountain here. They were too tired to go any further."

The major turned away from me and called to the children. "Should we go up the path a little ways?" I nodded and took his arm. Sepp brought his stick along and Annette grabbed a whole pile of leaves to deposit on the trail as we went past the white temple.

"Please don't speak of this to anyone, Klara," said the major after a few minutes of silence. "It is not that I am ashamed of my love for you, but I need time to figure out how this is all going to work. I guess I am concerned that your closer association with me might put you in some jeopardy, and I don't want to see any damage done to your reputation."

I looked up at the major in confusion.

"I can see that you don't understand what I am saying, and that is to your credit, Klara," he said. "I am afraid that it wouldn't appear proper for me to be courting someone who resides in my own house," he said plainly.

"Of course," was all I could think to say. I was too embarrassed to admit that that kind of thought never crossed my mind.

What did cross my mind was that I have been in Kassel a year now, and I have had, as you well know, dear journal, a total change of heart about the major. I leaned proudly on his arm while we headed up a curved path. The road made a steady, weaving climb toward the *Herkules* on the hill. At last we rounded a corner and a garden set back in a cove came unexpectedly into my view. An arched, iron bridge sat high on top of a pile of mossy rocks, its gingerbread teeth jutting out below the arch where the water fell like an open mouth.

"What is this place?" I asked with wonder.

The major stopped for a moment. "The Devil's Bridge."

"Ah, yes. I can see it now."

"This is a special place," he said with a far away sound in his voice. We stopped on the *Teufelsbrücke* with its teeth hanging down toward the waterfall.

During the next half hour, the major opened up like a tightly wrapped rose unfolds to bathe in the sunshine. He spoke of his past and shared memories with fondness and reverence. He talked about his childhood in Kassel, of skating on the lake in the winter and swimming in the *Flussbad* in the summer, of riding his sled in the *Rodelbahn* in the *Schloss* park and rowing up the Fulda.

"I'm not sure, but I think that this is where my father proposed to my mother. And when I was ten, I dropped my brother Rupert off of this bridge by accident."

I gasped, and the major laughed.

"Rupert was always the carefree one, oblivious to any danger that life might hold." Major Rager shook his head. "He insisted that I lower him by rope over the edge, but the weight was too much for me to handle."

I looked over the edge at the rocks below. "Did he?"

"He landed at the top on the rocks, about there, and thankfully only had bumps and bruises to show for it. Needless to say, I got a good scolding from mother."

I watched Sepp and Annette weaving in and out of the woods and playing in the leaves, and I thought about the fact that we were both without our parents. All too soon, the major called to the children.

He touched me gently on the arm. "You look like you're getting cold. We should probably go back."

I nodded although I really didn't want to leave. It seemed like we had just arrived. On the way down the path, the wind wiped at the remaining leaves on the trees and blew them horizontally across the path. As we walked, I could almost sense the major close up tightly as the flowers do when darkness falls.

Although I want to tell the world what has happened, I have kept my mouth shut, even in front of the children. You are the only one, dear journal, who knows.

December 1944

December 4, 1944

It is snowing gently outside my window, and I am under the covers at last. Today is Monday. Sepp, Annette, *Frau* Hoffmann, and I had to huddle in the basement this afternoon as there was another bombing. We had just arrived back from school when the siren sounded.

The bombs must have dropped close by because the earth kept shaking. I pulled out Rosine's verses and read them over and over. *Frau* Hoffmann sat across from me, and I noticed she did not cross herself as she always has in the past. The major arrived in the basement halfway through the bombing. I was so relieved to see him.

By one o'clock, the all clear siren sounded. The major went out immediately to survey the damage. The children remained home for the rest of the day.

I have been quite happy and contented lately. The major has been spending more time with me and the children. He has been much more open with me. I am finding that the more I learn about him, the more I love him. At times, I feel that I cannot get enough of him. The time when we are apart seems like an eternity.

It is a strange feeling to me to have gone from such dreariness in life to such delight. Although it is winter, in my heart it feels more like spring. The only thought that dampens my happiness is what Uncle Lothar, Aunt Frieda, and Klaus will think of this attachment I have for the major.

And I feel guilty for feeling such happiness when there is such dreariness all around. When the major got home from his inspections, he told me that the Americans had hit the marshalling yard and that there were a lot of casualties.

Tomorrow, we leave for Garmish. There will be no time to go for Sepp and Annette's birthday as some new production begins in the tank factory in January, and the major will have to oversee it. I think the major is looking forward to getting away from Kassel for a few days. I am just looking forward to being with him.

....

December 5, 1944

Dear Journal,

I am writing to you tonight from the four-posted bed in suite 400 at the Hotel Sonnenbichl in Garmish. The beautiful view that I remember from last year was here to greet us when we arrived. Annette is sleeping soundly next to me with Otti in her arms. The major is out in the sitting area working on some papers.

The new driver, who is probably also a Gestapo agent, had to drop us a couple of stations down from the main train station early this morning. It took us all day to get here. Once we were on the train, the major took off his coat, and then he sat down next to me. He held my hand in his almost the whole trip.

He is very tired, and I can see that he has a lot on his mind. I wish there was something I could do to take his concerns away. I hope that the next couple of days will be restful and happy for us.

....

December 6, 1944

Dear Journal,

Even if I gave you a thousand guesses, you would never guess what has happened today. My heart is so full; I hardly know where to begin.

I woke up early and went out to the sitting area. I was looking at the beautiful view of the mountains when the major came out of his room.

"Good morning, Klara," he said with a sleepy smile.

"Good morning."

"What are you looking at?"

"The mountains are so beautiful, the way the morning sun hits them," I said, looking out the window.

"Yes, but not anywhere nearly as beautiful as you," he said softly in return. When I turned to look at the major, he looked away from me quickly, and I sensed that something was bothering him. I hoped it wasn't me.

"Are you and Sepp going skiing this morning?" I asked cheerfully, fully expecting a confirmation for a response.

"No," the major said. "I thought we should have breakfast and then take the children out for a walk."

And that is exactly what we did. It was rather cold out, but the sun was shining, and the air was pure and crisp when we ventured out for our stroll. We went around the hotel grounds until we came to a path in front of the hotel that leads toward town. Not too far from the hotel building is a gentle hill, free from trees, that is covered with a nice blanket of snow and was shimmering in the morning sun.

There were already several children on their sleds, sliding down the slope. We all stopped to watch them, but Sepp and Annette were particularly interested. Just then, the hotel manager came toward us on the path. After he was past the major, he stopped and turned around.

"I have an extra sled if you would like to borrow it," he offered. The major looked at the children. Sepp started jumping up and down. "Please, Father. Can we?"

Annette seemed less enthusiastic about the prospect of sledding, but she didn't want to be outdone by her brother. When the manager got back with the sled, Sepp took the rope, thanked him, and then started up the hill immediately.

"Wait for your sister," called the major. Annette struggled up the hill behind her brother. Sepp was less than patient with her when they reached the top, and he ended up leaving her flat on her back on top of the hill as he took off at a fast pace down the hill on the sled.

I sat down on the stone fence on the other side of the pathway in a small patch of sunshine to watch the whole scene. After the major had scolded Sepp and sent him back up the hill, he came and sat down next to me. Sepp was more careful on the second run. I watched Annette's face turn from fright to delight as they reached the bottom of the hill. They both got up and scrambled back up the hill.

I looked over at the major, hoping he was enjoying their fun, but instead, he was staring off into the woods with a contemplative look on his face.

"You're very quiet," I said.

The major sat unmoved for a moment, and then he turned and looked at me with a most serious expression.

"It is no use, Klara," he said finally. "Every way I figure it, it won't work." The major looked up at the sledding hill with glassy, sad eyes.

"What doesn't work," I asked, suddenly afraid that he was talking about us.

I watched him clench his jaw, and then he looked back at me and shook his head. "I-I want to make you mine. I want to ask you to be my wife, but every way I figure it, the proposal would be to my benefit and to your decided detriment."

My heart stopped for a moment, and then I breathed in again, trying not to let what I felt in my heart show on my face. I was happy to hear that he wanted me to be his wife, but I did not understand why this seemed to cause him such distress. I waited for the major to explain himself.

"I cannot be married to you publicly, Klara," he said at last, "as much as I want to be."

I breathed in deeply and wondered why.

"The minute *Frau* Brandt finds out that I have remarried, she will stop sending the money she has been giving me for Sepp and Annette, and I have been using all of that money to sustain the lives of sixteen men. And if I am ever caught, you will be in danger too."

I felt my eyes grow bigger as he finished his sentence. "I don't understand," I said.

The major breathed in deeply, and then he sighed and looked me straight in the eyes. "I could marry you tomorrow, if it were kept a secret, but I can't ask you to do that. So, I am stuck. I am stuck fast in circumstances of my own making."

He paused and let out a sigh. "Sure, it would be the happiest day of my life to have you for a wife, to have someone who would care for the children if anything would happen to me, to be able to hold you. But for you, it would mean no wedding ceremony with your family, no blessing of the church, and nothing but the responsibility of my children and the prospect of widowhood once the enemy rolls into town."

I swallowed hard when I had thought about what he was saying, and then I reached over and took his hand in mine. "Even considering all of that, isn't it my choice to make?" I asked.

The major looked at me in surprise as if he had not considered it so. "The last thing I want to see is for you to make a choice that you will regret the rest of your life," he replied.

"I would more likely regret not marrying the man I love—the one who has always shown me such kindness and the one for whom I have the greatest respect."

The expression on the major's face shifted from contemplation to affection. Then, as if he could not get rid of his dark thoughts, he ran his hand through the side of his hair. "The Russians are coming from the east, the Americans and British from the west. I don't know what is going to happen when they reach Kassel. They will probably shoot me, and then you will be left alone."

"Should that happen, I would be no less devastated if I am not your wife," I said.

"You deserve to be my wife in public and in private, but it cannot be so," concluded the major with his pointed objection.

"If it cannot be so, for the reasons you have said, then I am content with that. I would still be yours in private, and that is all that matters to me."

The major shook his head. "And the children?"

I smiled for the first time since our conversation began. "The children have a very special place in my heart," I said, looking up at the top of the hill where they were climbing onto the sled again. "I think you know that."

The major got up from the stone wall and took a couple of steps away from me. When he turned around, I could see determination in his eyes.

It was only a moment, but in that moment, I felt as if my life were hanging by a tiny thread. There, so close to my grasp, was the happiness for which I longed—to be his. There also was the chance that he could not stand the thought of burdening me with such happiness. I felt a little faint.

In that small patch of sunlight on the path that led to Garmish, the major removed his hat from his head, took my hand in his, and looked me directly in the eye.

"Klara Dietrich? Will you be my wife?"

His words sounded more like music than words to me. I stood to my feet as I felt my cheeks flush. "Yes," I replied, looking up into his eyes with a smile. "I will marry you today, or tomorrow, or whenever you think we should."

I don't know if there was anyone on the path, or if anyone was watching, but the major pulled me close, cradled my face with his hands, and with my eyes closed tight, he gently pressed his lips to mine.

He kissed me again, more earnestly as I seemed to melt in his arms. "I love you, Klara," he said softly. "I have wanted to kiss you for so long." I drew back a little so I could smile and look him in the eyes. Then he drowned my smile with another kiss. The major ran his hand along my cheek. "Would you really marry me tomorrow?"

"Yes," I said resolutely.

The major let go of me. "You're certain?" he asked.

"Yes," I replied, nodding my head.

"Because if you are certain, I will go back to the hotel and phone down to Innsbruck. If we are to be married, it would be best that we do so in Austria. It will take longer for the paperwork to get to Berlin."

By this time, my heart was pounding hard. "I'm willing to do whatever you think is best," I responded.

The major smiled, and then his brow turned down a little. "Sometimes, I think you are only a dream, Klara," he said solemnly. "I will be honest with you. Ida was always so consumed with herself that there wasn't room for anyone else in her life. You are just the opposite."

I looked away from the major for a moment. I felt awkward hearing him talk about Ida. I always had. But I also felt badly for him. The more I learn about the major, the more respect I have for him. The more I know about Ida, the less I think of her.

The major called to the children and told them to take their last run on the hill. His request was met with dismay and denial, but he was firm with them. As soon as we had returned the sled to the manager and were back up in our room, the major phoned down to the magistrate in Innsbruck. I sat on the couch staring out at the Alps while he asked for the information he wanted.

When he set the receiver down, he looked around to see where the children were, then he came over and stood by the window.

"If you haven't changed your mind, we can go down to Innsbruck first thing in the morning," he said.

"What about the children?" I asked.

The major breathed in deeply. "I don't think it is best for them to know," he said seriously. "I will tell them we have some business to conduct."

I leaned back on the couch. I certainly hadn't thought that we would have to keep this a secret from them. The major must have seen the uneasiness on my face. He sat down next to me and put his arm on the back of the couch.

"I was serious when I said it would have to be in private. If word of this gets to my mother-in-law, I will have the lives of sixteen men on my conscience."

"Who are these men?" I asked, and then I shook my head. "You don't have to tell me," I said, remembering that I shouldn't ask him any questions.

The major looked out the window and then back to me. "No, if we are going to do this together there are some things you are going to need to know."

Just then, Sepp came out of the green bedroom. "Are we going skiing today, Father?" he asked, interrupting our serious conversation.

"No, son," replied the major, turning himself on the couch. "I think we will have dinner, and then perhaps we will go into town together."

Sepp wrinkled his nose and cast his head down. I thought he was going to protest, but then he turned and went back into the bedroom.

"There will be plenty of time for me to explain later, Klara, and I will. For now, I would like to enjoy your company. And I don't want to frighten you away," he said with a mischievous grin.

After dinner, we did go into town. On the way the major told me that he wanted to get me something special. We went into several stores and looked around, but at the jewelry store he bought a gold wedding band that fits perfectly on my finger.

The children get quite tired and bored with shopping, and today was no exception. I can't help but think that they must sense something is going on between us. I wonder how we are going to be able to keep this all a secret. And what will Aunt Frieda say when she finds out?

After I tucked Sepp into bed, I went to get some tea for the major. I was standing by the bedroom door getting ready to come to bed, when he set aside his papers and came over to me. He leaned with his shoulder against the doorpost and took my hand in his.

"There is still time for you to change your mind, Klara," he said, his deep blue eyes full of concern. "I don't want you to do this unless you are absolutely certain this is what you want."

"I am," I said back, almost immediately. Then the major reached for me. My heart feels like water when he kisses me.

I said you would not guess what has happened today, because I can hardly believe it myself. If I am making the wrong decision, I suppose I will soon know it. I only hope that I am able to be the kind of wife the major deserves, and that we will be able to be happy together despite everything that is going on around us.

....

December 8, 1944

Today is Friday. This is our last day in Garmish. Kurt, at my insistence has gone skiing with Sepp, and Annette is sitting next to the picture window, where the light is good, working on a needlepoint. I am filled with happiness I have never known.

Yesterday, our wedding day, Kurt woke me up early. He got Sepp up and dressed while I put on my blue dress and brushed my hair. I got Annette up and dressed, and then we went out into the sitting area where the men were waiting for us.

"You are beautiful," Kurt said. Before he offered me his arm; he looked me straight in the eyes. He wanted to be sure I hadn't changed my mind.

We boarded the train just as the sun was starting to light up the sky. As we were passing by the Olympic stadium, I suddenly started to get nervous.

"Will I have to sign papers?"

"Yes," Kurt replied, "the marriage license."

"How do I sign it? What name do I use?" I asked him almost in a whisper.

"Klara Mauer," he responded. Kurt cleared his throat as he scanned the car for listening ears. "The night you told me your real name, I called up to Berlin and had my cousin check your record."

I must have looked at him in horror.

"I had to be sure you weren't lying to me," he said defensively. "At first, he couldn't find your papers. Then he found them. Your file and your siblings' files were in a watch folder. He phoned me back to say that he had found them there. I knew you were telling me the truth when he told me the girl in the picture was very beautiful, and he wanted to meet you."

"What is a watch folder?"

Kurt turned his gaze out the window. "They were looking for you. But you don't have to worry about that anymore. I had him remove your files and put them back in the general records. And just as a precaution, he sent me your new papers."

All of my nervousness and any doubt that I might have had about marrying him vanished in that moment. I wanted to thank him for what he had done, but nothing came out of my mouth.

All I could see in my mind were the events of that night. I could still hear him telling me that I owed him nothing. Now, I feel like I owe him everything.

I held onto his hand a little tighter and listened to the screeching of the wheels against the rails as we descended into the Tirol valley. Sepp sat across from me, yawning every couple of minutes, while Annette's feet were dangling energetically from her seat. She wanted to know why we were going to Innsbruck.

It was very cold and cloudy, but by the time the train pulled into Innsbruck, the sun was peeking through the clouds and adding some warmth to the day. We had several blocks to walk from the train station. You could see clearly the majestic white peaks of the mountains rising above the unscathed buildings as you walked down the street.

The magistrate's office was on the second floor of a brown stoned building in the newer part of town. Kurt sat the children on a bench outside of an office door in the hallway and told them sternly that they were not to move off of the bench and that we would be back out in a few minutes.

Then he took my hand, and we went inside the office. An older, dark-haired woman greeted us. Kurt told her we were there to be married. He was very calm. I suppose that it was his serenity that helped still my heart. She took some papers, and after those were all filled out, she went and got the magistrate. We signed the papers in front of him and his secretary, and then he married us.

I left the magistrates office as *Frau* Rager, clinging to Kurt's arm and smiling, but inside, I was wondering now how I was going to hide the fact that I was married to him. Sepp and Annette were slouching and squirming on the bench as we came out into the hall.

"Let's go get some breakfast, children," said Kurt as he winked at me.

"I'm starving," said Sepp, dragging himself to his feet.

I had always dreamed that I would be married in a church, and I wanted to hear the bells ring for me afterward, but the Nazi party, the war, and circumstances not of my making had successfully done away with most of my hopes and dreams. But as we stepped out into the street and turned onto the sidewalk, the bells in the steeple of a nearby church began to ring. It was nine o'clock. Kurt leaned down and kissed me.

We had a very nice breakfast at a restaurant in a hotel near the train station. Then we took our time getting back to the platform. We had a long wait for the train back to Garmish. When we were almost back to the hotel, Sepp asked his father, impatiently, when they were going to go skiing. Kurt told him firmly that this was a special day, and that we were going to spend it together.

My new husband brought his camera with him to dinner, and after we were all finished eating, we stood out on the balcony of the restaurant with the beautiful mountains in the background and the waiter took our picture alone and then one with the children.

It was in the early afternoon as we were walking on the hotel grounds when Kurt reached into his pocket and presented me with the wedding band he had bought for me. I didn't know it, but he had also purchased a necklace. With a timidity I had never seen in him before, he suggested to me that I might wear the wedding ring around my neck until I could wear it publicly. That was when I began to realize how hard it was going to be to be married to him only in private, but more than that, how hard it was going to be on him.

The whole day was filled with good memories, but the best part came after we put the children to bed. Annette kept fretting about sleeping in the green bedroom with Sepp. Finally, Kurt told her plainly that she needed to go to sleep without any more complaining. He kissed her on the forehead, and then he took me by the hand, and we left them in the dark.

When we got into the other room, Kurt took me into his arms. There and then he wrapped me in his love. In a world where there is evil and death all around and where the darkness closes in on you until you can hardly breathe, for one incredible night, the war and everything associated with it dissolved, and I felt happiness as never before. It was as if my heart was sealed together with his in a tight bond that was never meant to be broken. I am amazed, but this binding that I feel and the strange power he has over me does not frighten me. Instead, I feel like a crooked bone that has been set straight as if I have finally found my way home.

In the morning, the children came bursting into the room without warning. Kurt sent them out of the room immediately.

"Go back to your room and hide, children," he said to them. "I am going to come and try to find you, after I count to twenty." Sepp beat Annette out the door. Kurt turned and winked at me. It was all I could do to keep from blushing at the situation.

The men should be back from skiing soon, and I need to see to packing. Tomorrow, this whole beautiful dream will come to an end as I know that I must resume my stale and distant role as his nanny. I am really not looking forward to going back to Kassel.

....

December 9, 1944

Dear Journal,

We are back in Kassel, and I have finished unpacking our luggage. I am in a most humble and sober frame of mind. On the train ride home, Kurt tried to warn me that he might be short with me or might ignore me, but that I should not be hurt by it. He wanted me to remember that it was imperative that our marriage be kept a secret. I only hope that I don't let him down.

The reality of it all sank in as he put my hand back in my lap and let go of it. I could sense him tensing up as we pulled closer to Kassel, and he snapped at the children when we got off the train.

It was a strange feeling to walk back into the house, knowing that it was now my house but that it could not be known that it was mine. *Frau* Hoffmann wanted to know all about our trip. I held my breath as the children told her about our time in Garmish. I was just hoping they wouldn't mention that they had found us in bed together.

I am sitting on the top of the stairs by Sepp's room, waiting for Kurt to come upstairs for the night. He had several messages waiting for him when we got home. I don't know where I am supposed to sleep tonight, but I definitely don't want to go to sleep unless I am by his side. My heart just wants to be near his.

....

December 17, 1944

Today has been a cloudy and gray Sunday. This morning, I went to mass with Kurt and the children, and tonight, we will light a candle on the Advent wreath. It has been a most tumultuous week for me. Garmish and the happiness of it seems so far away.

Around noon on Friday, while we were trying to set up for the Christmas party, we had to take shelter in the basement for an hour. *Frau* Hoffmann sat in the corner muttering prayers. On the way up the stairs afterward, she was mumbling to herself that she thinks they won't stop until they have killed every last one of us. I am starting to think she might be right.

Yesterday evening was the Christmas party. Although *Frau* Hoffmann has economized, scrimped, and saved our food stamps for this occasion, it was not a large spread of food as last year. There is just not enough food to be found at the markets. It turned out to be not all bad as it was much less work for us.

Besides the lack of food, there seemed to be only half the crowd as last year. I did see Lieutenant Braun, but he went out of his way to avoid seeing me. *Fräulein* Farber, however, came and took her usual place beside Kurt.

I didn't have to do as much running back and forth as last year, but every time I went out to the hall, I saw her leaning on him and sticking to him like glue. I saw the uncomfortable look on his face, but this didn't really matter to me. I was having a hard time understanding why he was allowing her to hang on his arm.

I retreated to the kitchen and tried to calm myself. I was just as jealous as last year, only worse. *Frau* Hoffmann had gone to the basement to get something, and I was glad for a moment alone. Then I heard the *swish* of the kitchen door. When I turned to see who it was, my husband was standing there with a mixed look of regret, dismay, and frustration.

I looked away from his stare as quickly as I could. I didn't want him to see the jealousy in my eyes.

"Klara, don't look at me like that. It's not as if I am enjoying this," he said, trying to defend himself. When he stepped closer to me, I tried to pass by him. I thought it would be best if I went upstairs for the rest of the evening. But he grabbed my arm before I could pass by him.

"Klara!" he said, trying to plead with me. Just then, *Frau* Hoffmann came back into the kitchen. Kurt let go of my arm quickly, and I looked up at him.

"I'll see to it right away, sir," I said to him, trying to bluff my way out of the awkward situation. *Frau* Hoffmann was already staring at the both of us. She must have felt the tension in the air.

I went as fast as I could up the stairs and straight to my room. This was the first time since we were married that I have felt so far away from him. I was surprised at the way I had acted. I could have relieved his mind on the matter as I knew he did not welcome her attention, but instead, I made him think that I was angry with him.

The moments couldn't have gone by slower. I went down to Kurt's bedroom and watched in the dark as the guests left the house, one by one. I wondered how long it would be before he would come upstairs, and I could apologize to him.

At last, Kurt opened the door and turned the light on. When he saw me standing by the window, he shut the door behind him. Then he went over to the bed, sat down, and began to take his shoes off. I couldn't read the expression on his face with his back to me, so I walked across the room and knelt down at his feet by his shoes.

I swallowed hard and reached up for his hand. "I'm sorry for the way I acted," I said, looking into his eyes.

"I never want you to have any cause to think that I am unfaithful to you," he said slowly and deliberately.

"I don't," I responded immediately.

"Then what was that look in your eyes all night long?"

I looked down into my lap, ashamed. I really didn't want to tell him. "I-I think it was jealousy," I said softly.

"Who could you possibly be jealous of?"

"I am jealous of the love you had for Ida. I thought that it wouldn't bother me, but when you talk about her, it does. And I am jealous of *Fräulein* Farber. I had this same feeling last year at the Christmas party."

When I looked up, Kurt was looking at me with confusion. I watched him breathe in deeply and then he sighed. "My love for Ida died with her, and in the end, it was only obligatory anyway. As for *Fräulein* Farber, I have known her since I learned to walk, and, at least on my account, there has never been anything between us but friendship."

"She loves you," I blurted out.

"If she loves me, it matters very little as you have my heart, and you are the one I have married."

I looked away from his unwavering eyes for a moment, ashamed at the thoughts I had all evening. "I am sorry for feeling this way, and I think you should pay no attention to me," I said at last, rising to my feet.

Kurt pulled me down on the bed beside him. "No! This is the way marriage works, Klara. You work through the confusing, the mundane, and the difficult times together. Otherwise, you grow apart."

My eyes were fixed on his hand that was enclosing mine, when he reached up with his other hand and lifted my eyes to his. "Now, I have been wanting all evening long to hold the most beautiful girl at the party. Let's go to bed."

I am glad that it seems that Kurt has so quickly forgotten about my foolishness. Keeping our marriage a secret is already starting to wear thin on me, but I know that I must find the strength to bear it, because I promised him that I would.

December 25, 1944

Dear Journal,

I can hardly believe that today is Christmas. This was the first year I can remember that I did not make a gingerbread house. I had hoped to make cookies and the gingerbread on Saturday, but there is not enough flour at the stores, and there is no sugar, honey, or molasses to be had in all of Kassel. Annette and I were only able to bake a few unsweetened cookies.

Yesterday evening, I put the cookies on a plate under the Christmas tree. I helped Kurt put the children's presents in the living room, while he was lighting the candles on the trees. On our wedding day, we had purchased a small wood working set for Sepp and a tea set for Annette in Innsbruck while the children were looking at other toys. After Kurt made a fire in the fireplace, we let the children into the living room.

Although it wasn't much compared to last year, it seemed that the children were happy with their presents. The evening was quiet until Kurt asked me if I would play a little music on the violin. I was happy to play for my little audience.

I don't know what Christmas has been like for Lenz, Liese, and Klaus, or if they are feeling the effects of war like we are here in Kassel, but I hope that it was a happy time for them as it was for me.

January 1945

January 19, 1945

Dear Journal,

It seems that this new year will be worse than the last. We have had one bombing raid after another since the day after Christmas. We even had to leave mass on New Year's Day to go to the bunker at the Goethe *Anlage*. On days where there was cloud cover, we used to be safe. The worst part is, now they are coming on the cloudy days too.

Kurt's mother-in-law arrived yesterday afternoon with eight suitcases for her annual birthday visit. I don't think she was happy to see that I am still here, but this time, I am determined that she will not fluster me, and this time, I know that I am not in peril of losing my job.

Last night, I slept in my old room, and we all had to get up in the middle of the night to go to the basement. Although Kurt tried very hard to make her comfortable, *Frau* Brandt was clearly not happy with the situation. She complained the entire time about being too cold, and she insisted that the light be kept on. She kept asking Kurt if we shouldn't all go to a bunker instead, for safety's sake.

I always thought it was odd that Kurt would light the old lantern instead of leaving the light on, but now, I understand. It is somehow more nerve wracking to watch the light flicker on and off with every impact of a bomb, than to sit quietly by the consistent light of the lantern.

After all of that, I slept very poorly. I guess that I am used to sleeping with my husband, and I missed him being there beside me although he wouldn't have been anyway, because he was out inspecting for damage.

I know that I must be on my best behavior while she is here, and I am determined to try very hard. I don't want to cause any trouble for my husband. She wants to take the children to have their photographs taken tomorrow. I hope I don't have to go along.

....

January 24, 1945

I am breathing a sigh of relief today as *Frau* Brandt has gone back to Berlin. After I picked the children up from school, I made them practice the violin and the piano for an hour, and then we sat down to work on their homework. I was there in the hall when Kurt came home, on time, since *Frau* Brandt is gone. I have tried every night to greet him with the smile that he looks forward to, whether or not he acknowledges me.

He looks very tired tonight. I know that he has been working very hard on a new project at the tank factory and this has taken a lot of his energy. We had another air raid, the night before last that also set him back. I don't know if I will have the opportunity tonight or not, but I feel that I must speak to him.

I got a very disturbing letter in the mail today from Klaus that has upset me. They are calling him and the other boys in his unit up for duty. He thinks they will be sent to Berlin. I have a grave feeling in my heart. I remember well the day Reiner left, and that was the last time I ever saw him alive. Klaus is only fourteen! What are they doing calling boys into the war?

....

January 29, 1945

Something has happened in the last couple of days that has shocked me more than all of the bombings that I have lived through up until today. I suppose that it all began on Saturday when I went into the kitchen to get a cup of coffee for Kurt. I had poured him a cup and was turning to leave, when *Frau* Hoffmann suddenly caught me on the sleeve.

"I don't think I can stay silent any longer, Klara. I must speak with you."

I was standing right by the kitchen door, but I turned to her because I could hear the distress in her voice. I was afraid that she was going to tell me that her sister had died, and I was preparing myself to comfort her.

"I know that you are not sleeping in your bed, and I can only think of one other place that you are sleeping," she said to me without looking at me. "You're playing a very dangerous game, child. Nothing good comes of having an affair, and sleeping with your boss will get you nowhere."

I was astounded at what she was saying to me and at her frankness. I had expected a totally different conversation, and it took me a moment to realize what she was saying. Then I was in trouble. I closed my jaw and tried to think fast. I wanted to tell her that she was mistaken, but she was too wise for that. She already knew I was sleeping with him.

"It is none of my business, Klara, but I don't want to see you hurt. The last thing we need around this house is more illegitimate children."

I had turned my gaze to Kurt's coffee cup, but at hearing those words, my eyes bolted back to hers. "What?" I said, trying to process her words. "What children are you talking about?"

Frau Hoffmann turned toward the sink and picked up a dishcloth. "Sepp and Annette," she said reluctantly.

"They are not Ida's children?" I blurted out.

"They are Ida's," *Frau* Hoffmann said. "They are not the major's," she said with raised eyebrows, correcting my confusion.

"How do you know that?" I asked in amazement.

Frau Hoffmann turned back to me with a ghastly look on her face. "I have never said a word to anyone about this, but if it keeps you out of trouble, so be it. I came back to the house one night to get my umbrella. I was on my way to a friend's house, and I heard the major and Ida arguing."

While I stood there in utter shock, *Frau* Hoffmann moved past me toward the kitchen door. "I must see to the laundry," she said. "You be careful, child."

She left me in the kitchen, holding Kurt's cup of coffee, rattled to the bones by what she had just said. Eventually, I went to the study and handed Kurt his coffee. He thanked me for it, but he didn't even look up at me, or he would have seen that I was in distress.

I went up to the nursery where Sepp and Annette were playing and sat down in one of the small chairs by the door. When I looked up at them, I couldn't help but wonder if what *Frau* Hoffmann had told me was true. I was also disturbed by the fact that she knew I was sleeping with the major.

I tried to convince myself that I didn't care that she thought I was that kind of a girl, but a part of me did care. I wanted to tell her that we were married so that she would not have to trouble herself with the thoughts she had for me, but I had at least made it through that conversation without telling our secret. This has turned out much harder than I thought it would be.

I went through the rest of the day without saying more than two words. I was still in shock when we sat down to eat supper. Kurt kept glancing over at me, but he didn't ask me any questions, nor did he break the silence.

I went straight to my old room after I put the children down for the night, and I crawled into my old bed for half an hour. Then I got up and made it back up, imperfectly, so that *Frau* Hoffmann would think I had headed her advice, and then I went downstairs to Kurt's room and got ready for bed. I was lying there, staring at the ceiling when he came up for the evening.

I watched him take off his shoes, his belt and his coat, and then he turned to me. He must have felt my piercing eyes. "Is something bothering you?" he asked as he proceeded to undress.

I waited until he had crawled into bed before I started. "Why didn't you tell me that Sepp and Annette aren't your children?" I asked slowly.

Kurt whipped his head toward me and gave me a look that must have been the same one I gave *Frau* Hoffmann when she told me. "Who told you that?" he asked immediately. "Did *Frau* Brandt say so?"

"No," I responded. "*Frau* Hoffmann told me this morning."

"*Frau* Hoffmann?" he repeated, looking quite confused. "How does she know?"

"She told me that she has never told anyone, but she said that she heard you and Ida arguing one night."

I had expected Kurt to be relieved to hear this, but he was not. He turned his eyes away from me and stared at the ceiling. I was still waiting for an answer. I lay there beside him for a good five minutes, listening to him breathe in and out.

Finally, he spoke, in a soft but strained tone of voice. "We were married for almost a year, when she told me she was three months pregnant. I hadn't seen her in five months, because I was away at officer training," he began, and then he stopped for a moment.

"I took full responsibility for it and, in order to demonstrate to her just how deeply I loved her, I agreed to claim the child as my own. In this way, I hoped to save us, particularly Ida, any embarrassment. I wanted desperately to save our marriage."

He shook his head back and forth. "We didn't expect two children. But it wouldn't have mattered anyway. She couldn't even care for one. It was hard enough to sort through everything, with two babies always crying and Ida a wreck. But on top of that, it wasn't long until I discovered that, despite her assurances, she was still carrying on with her affair."

I could feel my throat tighten as he was talking, and I sensed that he was telling me something he had never shared with anyone.

"After I got back from Poland, I volunteered to go into France with the invasion force, figuring that I had nothing to lose by going. When they shipped me home, I was barely alive. In an odd sort of way, I think it was the children who were responsible for my recovery—the children that weren't even mine.

"Not too long after that, Ida died. Sepp and Annette were the only part of her I had left. I knew that they had no father, no mother, and no hope for a future. The only prospect for those innocent children was for them to be raised by their grandmother to be just as selfish and unfaithful as their mother had been. How could I allow that to happen?"

"Oh, Kurt," I said with tears in my eyes. As I laid my head on his shoulder, I felt a tear drop from his eye. I had not anticipated this response from him. I hadn't anticipated a single thing he had said. "I am so sorry I asked," I said although it was far too late.

"Klara?" he said with emotion in his voice. "Now can you see why you are such a bright spot in my life?"

"Do the children know?"

"No. I have never told them. I don't think it would serve any purpose. As far as I'm concerned, they are mine."

"What happened to their father?" I asked.

Kurt looked away from me and a daze seemed to cloud his eyes. "He was sent to concentration camp," he replied after he cleared his throat.

"Concentration camp? What did he do?"

After a long moment, Kurt replied simply, "He's a Jew."

I took in a quick breath.

"That is why my heart nearly stopped when I found you in the prison in Frankfurt and you told me why they had arrested you. It was true that they're Jewish. I only prayed that the Gestapo would believe that they were mine."

"*Frau* Brandt knows that they are Jewish?"

"Yes," Kurt said. "Until today, I thought we were the only ones who knew. I have never said a word to her about it, but as soon as Ida was buried, Helma started sending me money. I think she was afraid I wouldn't claim the children. And if I were to say anything, things could get very difficult for her. She doesn't want her dirty secret known. It would certainly be the end of her high position in the Nazi party if word got out that she has Jewish grandchildren."

I slept very restlessly Saturday night. All day Sunday, all I could do was look at the children and wonder at them. This morning, after I walked the children to school, I took the trolley out to the *Bergpark* and climbed up the hill by the *Schloss* to a spot where I could sit and look down over Kassel. I felt like I needed to sort out the mess of thoughts that were twisted around in my head.

Kurt's revelation to me on top of *Frau* Hoffmann's disclosure was difficult for me to take. I suppose that Kurt never told me about the children because he didn't want them to be in danger. He has risked everything and saved their lives by claiming them as his own.

As for Ida, I knew when he told me about her affair that the letter in the attic must have been from her lover. I closed my eyes and let the winter sun try to warm my face. I could not imagine the pain and heartache that she must have been to Kurt. My eyes welled up with tears, and I reached up to wipe them away. My heart was breaking for him. Although he had tried on several occasions to tell me about his choices and his life with Ida, I never put the pieces together until then.

The piercing sound of the air raid siren jolted me out of my sad contemplation. I jumped to my feet and ran as fast as I could down the road toward the city. The last place I wanted to be when the bombs started dropping was out in the open.

I must have run for twenty minutes straight, but I was still nowhere near home when the anti-aircraft guns started shooting. I heard the dull roar of airplane engines, and I caught a glimpse of several enemy planes high in the sky as I ducked into an apartment building. I tried to catch my breath as I searched for the stairs to the basement. When I got to the bottom stair, I could see that there were already too many people jammed into the small space below. I sat down on the last stair, pressed my shoulder against the wall of the staircase, closed my eyes, and prayed.

It wasn't long before the ground all around the building started to shake violently. The sound of the bombs dropping was almost deafening. Dust and bricks started falling all around us, and there was the sound of desperate screams mixed with prayers. If I have ever thought my life was going to end, I thought it today. One after another, came the whistling of the bombs, the sound of explosion, and then the violent shaking. I put my hands over my head and tried to curl up on the stairs.

Then, as if a miracle had suddenly happened, the sounds dissipated and the ground stopped trembling. I looked up cautiously. People were coughing as they breathed in the dust that was heavy in the air. The all-clear siren sounded. I got to my feet, buried my face in the crook of my arm, and climbed the stairs.

When I stepped outside, I realized just how close death had come. All around me, the apartment buildings were on fire or completely leveled. I stood in horror for a good minute, and then I realized that I had to hurry to find the children. I went through the streets toward the school in almost a panicked state.

By the time I got to their school, there were no children there. I stood there for a moment wondering where they could be, and then I finally came to my senses and headed for home. I have never been happier to see those two children than when I came through the front door.

"Where have you been?" I asked as I entered the living room and saw them sitting on the couch. "I have been looking all over for you!"

"The teachers sent us home when the air raid siren went off," Annette replied. "Where have you been?" she said back to me with a laugh as she was pointing to my head. "Is that lipstick?"

I wrinkled my noise, and then I went to the mirror in the hall by the telephone. I breathed in deeply as I saw my figure in the mirror. My head was covered with dust, and the dust had colored my hair gray. Blood was dripping from a small gash on my forehead. I didn't even feel it.

I went back to the living room and asked the children to practice their music. Then I went upstairs and drew a bath for myself.

Kurt came home earlier than I expected. He said that the Americans had done little damage to his plants but had hit the Wilhelmshöhe Palace and had done great damage to the residential part of Wilhelmshöhe. I didn't tell him that that was where I had been today.

After *Frau* Hoffmann left for the evening and after I read two stories each to the children and tucked them into bed, I found Kurt sitting by the fire in the living room. He looked up at me as I came over to him and sat down by his side.

He put his left arm around me. I leaned my head on his chest and watched him for a few minutes while he was reading through his papers. I lifted my eyes up to his, and then he stole a kiss from me. Quite on purpose, I kept my eyes closed, and he kissed me again.

"You're very distracting, Klara," he said in a playful tone.

"And?" I responded.

"And if you don't stop distracting me, you may find out what the consequences are," he replied in a more serious tone.

His tone of voice and the look on his face only made me reach for him and kiss him. It wasn't long before we went upstairs. I feel like my heart is so full of love for him that I cannot give him enough of it. Every tear, every sorrow, every fear goes away when he touches me. And I know of no better place in all the world, than to be in his arms.

February 1945

February 20, 1945

Dear Journal,

A week ago Kurt told me that he had gone to General Major Erxleben last month and convinced him to petition Berlin to send the company of Hitler Youth from Sinsheim to Kassel for security detail at the plants. He said that Berlin had approved their petition, but he was not sure if they would get the company from Sinsheim. Although he cautioned me not to get excited at the prospect, he did say that there was a small chance that he had been successful in diverting Klaus's detail to Kassel.

This afternoon, almost without warning, Klaus showed up at our front door. I almost knocked him over when I flew into his arms. After a moment, I pulled back to look at him. He is taller than I am now, and in his brown uniform, he looks quite handsome.

"I am told that I am to billet here," he said as he picked up his rucksack and his travel bag. I smiled and led the way into the house. Before Kurt got home and while the children were attending to their homework, Klaus told me that their company has been assigned to plant security detail. He is to report for duty first thing in the morning.

Frau Hoffmann came in, and I introduced my brother to her. She seemed very surprised but pleased to meet him. Then I asked him how everyone was in Sinsheim.

We were sitting in the living room, still talking, when Kurt got home. Kurt came straight to Klaus and extended his hand to welcome him.

Klaus shook his hand half-heartedly. Then he reached into his pocket and took out his papers. "I understand I am to billet here, *Herr* Major," Klaus said in a businesslike tone.

Kurt nodded his head as he reached for the papers in Klaus's hand. "Yes, I thought you should like to stay with your sister," Kurt replied.

I looked down at Klaus's papers, and I saw immediately that the last name on his identification was "Mauer." My mind froze up for a minute, and then I spoke before thinking. "Your identification papers. The last name—"

"Yes," said Klaus before I said too much. "We all received new papers in the mail about a year ago. Uncle Lothar must have ordered them for us." Klaus gave me a funny look and then turned back to the major for further instructions.

My eyes rose slowly to my husband's. Uncle Lothar had nothing to do with it. A year ago, Kurt had told me he had wanted to visit my family in Sinsheim because he wanted to "verify my story," but what he had really done after the visit was to arrange for my family to have new identification papers. He had done more than have our files removed from the watch folder; he had made sure no one would ever find us, and he had done this long before he loved me. *Or was it long before?*

"He is welcome to stay in the guest room, Klara," said Kurt, giving me a look that told me he knew that I had just realized what he had done. "Would you like to take him upstairs so that he can get settled?"

"Thank you, sir," said Klaus as he headed toward the hall. I hope Kurt did not miss the look of utter admiration I gave him as I passed by him.

It seemed odd but very nice to have Klaus at our table for supper. At least he is not a stranger to the children. Klaus answered Kurt's particular questions about everyone in Sinsheim succinctly and politely as they were asked.

Before Klaus retired for the evening, Kurt offered to take him to his post in the morning. Klaus nodded his head and then said good night. I have been away from Klaus for so long that I don't know why he is behaving in such a distant and almost hostile manner. It disturbed me to see his cold reception to Kurt.

"Is he always like this?" asked Kurt after Klaus had gone.

I shook my head. "He didn't used to be, but," I continued, "he has always disliked military men, and I'm sure that he has no idea that you are any different."

Kurt scratched his head. "He will get into big trouble with that attitude around here, and there won't be anything I can do to help him."

"You have done so much for him already," I said quickly. I was desperately hoping that my husband would not take offense at Klaus's ungrateful manner. I hope that I will have a chance to talk with Klaus before he gets himself and Kurt into any trouble.

....

February 24, 1945

Today is Saturday, and it has been my first chance to spend any substantial amount of time with Klaus. He has been quite withdrawn and has kept to himself since he arrived.

A most unsavory scene happened at the dinner table just after noon. After *Frau* Hoffmann had served us, Kurt tried to hold a conversation with Klaus. He asked Klaus how he found his assignment and how he got along with his company. I was surprised at the impolite answers Klaus gave him.

"Where did you learn to speak so rudely, Klaus?" I finally said as I felt that I had had enough of his caustic attitude. The children looked up from their plates when they heard my tone of voice.

"It's all right, Klara," said Kurt, trying to calm me down.

I stood to my feet. "No, it's not! I need to speak with you, Klaus, out on the back porch," I said, pointing toward the kitchen. "Now!" I added when I saw that Klaus was just sitting there, looking at me.

With his eyes now glaring at me, Klaus rose to his feet, threw his napkin onto his seat, and headed toward the kitchen. When I passed by the children, they were sitting up straight in their chairs, looking at their father.

By the time we both stepped out on the back porch, I was ready to explode. But before I could, Klaus let me have a piece of his mind. "How do you expect me to behave, Klara? I am only treating them the way they have treated me."

"Oh, Klaus, I don't know where to begin with you. You cannot treat the major with such disdain. You cannot treat any of the officers with such disrespect, or they will put you in front of a firing squad. Is that what you want?"

"Your major is no different than the rest of them," Klaus shot back.

"Oh, yes, he is!" I responded definitively. "I think you need to understand what is going on here, Klaus. He is the one who stuck his neck out and convinced his superior to put in a request to Berlin for your unit to be transferred to Kassel. The major says that there is going to be a big battle for Berlin, and he didn't want to see you in the middle of it. He is also the one who has opened up his home so that we can be together again."

"I don't understand you, Klara. Why are you defending him? Are you on their side now?"

I closed my eyes and breathed in deeply. "He is not what you think, Klaus," I said more calmly. "Please listen to me, because it has taken me a year to see things as they really are. He is not like the other officers, the other men in his party."

Klaus was searching my face as he seemed to be searching his heart. "Why are you in his room late at night, Klara?"

All I could do when I heard his question was to close my eyes and hang my head. I couldn't bear the thought of my own brother wondering about such a thing. I looked back into his accusatory eyes. No matter how much pain it gave me, I had to keep my promise to my husband.

"That is none of your concern," I said softly at last, "but I promise you that it is not what you think. Klaus, I know you don't understand what is going on, but I can tell you that the major is the most gracious man I have ever known. I cannot tell you everything he has done to protect and to help me."

The bitter, distrusting expression on Klaus's face remained unchanged. I drew in another breath and tried again. "Now he is trying to help you, but he cannot do that with this hostility you have in your heart. Please reconsider your position, Klaus, for my sake and for your own. There are those who deserve your disdain, but he is not one of them."

Klaus drew his arms across his chest and stared out into the distance. "If you have ever trusted me, you must trust me this once," I begged.

Finally, Klaus shifted his feet and wiped his brow. "If he is as you say, then I do owe him an apology."

I took a deep breath and opened my arms to him. He has changed so little since he was just a boy, but I have always been able to count on him coming to the right conclusion in the end.

Kurt and the children were just finishing up their meal when we came back into the dining room. I took my seat by the children, but Klaus stood behind his chair, next to Kurt.

"I owe you an apology, *Herr* Major. I can give you no excuse for my rude behavior, but I can promise you that it won't happen again," he said.

Kurt looked at me for a second and then back to Klaus. "Apology accepted. Please, finish your dinner."

All I can do now is hope that Klaus will keep his word, and that he will show my husband the respect he is due. I am ashamed that it wasn't so long ago that I felt the same way as Klaus.

March 1945

March 12, 1945

It has been several weeks since I have been able to sit down and write in you, dear journal. Things around us are not improving, but rather are declining quickly. There is a palatable sense of uncertainty in the air. Since last I wrote, several events have happened that have brought change into our lives.

Last Friday evening, we had to shelter in the basement while we listened to the engines of what sounded like hundreds of airplanes and the whistling of bombs as they were dropping. This was the first time I ever saw fear in Kurt's eyes. He seemed to grow more and more restless as the bombing went on and on.

He took Klaus out with him to do the inspections afterward, and I put the children down to bed. At two o'clock in the morning, Kurt woke me and asked me to get dressed. He explained to me that Klaus had seen *Frau* Hoffmann in the street on their way back from one of the factories. He told me that her apartment building was bombed, that she had survived along with the others who were in the basement, but that her sister had died right next to her. He thinks her heart gave out.

I quickly put on a dress and hurried downstairs. I found *Frau* Hoffmann weeping quietly in the living room. She was covered in soot and dust, and her coat was torn. I did not hesitate to throw my arms around her. What else could I do for the woman who has always been so strong and kind and had cared so long for her ailing sister?

We stayed up with *Frau* Hoffmann for a while, trying to comfort her, and then Kurt told her that he wanted her to stay with us until she could find a suitable place of her own.

She looked up at Kurt in unbelief. "But there is no room for me here," she protested as she blew her nose into her hanky.

"There certainly is!" Kurt insisted. "You can have the guest room. We can move Klaus to Klara's room so that you won't have to do the extra flight of stairs."

Frau Hoffmann shot a disapproving glance at me.

"Before you worry any further, Trude, it has been long overdue for me to tell you that Klara and I are married," said Kurt at last. "We were married in December."

I breathed in a big sigh of relief as I watched a careful smile come over *Frau* Hoffmann's tear stained face.

"How about that?" she said, looking a little surprised. "Bless you both, and I accept your kind and gracious offer to stay, *Herr* Major," she said.

"We have told no one about our marriage, not even the children, and that is how it must remain," Kurt said.

"Of course," replied *Frau* Hoffmann with a discrete nod.

In the morning, after I walked the children to school, I went with *Frau* Hoffmann to the ruins of her apartment building. She wanted to see in the daylight if there was anything she could salvage. By some miracle, as we were picking through the rubble, she found a photograph of her husband blowing in the wind. I found one of her teacups charred but miraculously intact.

Frau Hoffmann pulled out her handkerchief and blew her nose. I thought she might be happy to have recovered her teacup, but she was thinking of something else. "I'll see Maria in heaven, Klara," she said through some tears. "She told me a week ago that she had done as Rosine had said and trusted Christ to save her. And I have done the same."

I looked at *Frau* Hoffmann quite stunned. Her sister was so antagonistic toward Rosine. Now I am the only one around the table that summer afternoon who has not made peace with God.

"That's good," I managed to say. "And Rosine?" I said, looking around. "Was she in the basement with you?"

"No. She left two weeks ago to attend to her cousin in Marburg who is very ill. Now she'll have nothing to come back to, and she has lived her whole life here."

"Does she have family here?"

Frau Hoffmann shook her head. "She is an only child. Her grandparents were part of the German Baptist movement that settled in Oberkaufungen a hundred years ago. When most of them left for America, her father remained behind to pastor the ones who stayed. Her father married one of the elder's daughters, and then they moved into the apartment next door to us. Of course, her parents are long gone. I hope she took her father's Bible with her to Marburg. It is the only thing she really treasured."

Frau Hoffmann turned back to sifting through the rubble and after a moment, I returned to doing the same. When she had seen for herself that there was nothing else left, I went with her to make the burial arrangements for her sister.

We accompanied *Frau* Hoffmann to the graveyard for the burial on Sunday afternoon, and then we brought her home. I can see how hard it is on her to lose her home and her sister in one blow. Although I think that she will now have some relief from the constant care she had to give her sister, I am worried because she seems to be quite disoriented.

Now we are six people in the house, and although it is a large house, it is beginning to feel crowded. Klaus has been working long hours guarding the tank factory. I don't think he is happy to be here or happy to be in the military, but I am glad to see that he has been more civil to Kurt.

For at least a week now, I have been dropping the children off at school, walking to the train station, and then taking the train a couple of stops to the south into the country. Food stamps are beginning to do us no good. There is hardly any food that can be purchased with them, but I am able to buy food directly from the farmers. So, everyday, except for Sunday, I will go to buy what I can for us. This was *Frau* Hoffmann's idea. Although it is a lot of trouble, so far it has worked well.

Kurt says he does not know how much longer this war will go on. I hope for all our sakes that it ends very soon, but I dread what the end will bring.

***

March 24, 1945

Last night, Kurt came home with news that the Americans have crossed the Rhine and will soon arrive in Kassel. He is in such a state of mind that I cannot tell whether he is relieved, anxious, or devastated by the news. I was glad when he suggested that we go for a walk this morning, but I was surprised when we left without the children.

We walked up to the woods around the *Herkules*, just above the *Teufelsbrücke*. He told me that he and his brother often would play war games there, and that he knows the woods like the back of his hand. It made me a little sad to listen to his stories, because I could see that he was in a nostalgic mood, but the good memories were overshadowed by a sense of impending doom.

We stopped at a nicely shaded part of the woods that had an expansive view over Kassel and sat down on a green patch of grass. I looked out at the charred ruins of the palace and to the hollow structures beyond that now dominate the city skyline, having no idea what Kurt had on his mind.

He started by saying that he was glad the Americans were coming and not the Russians, because he felt that he had half a chance of living if he were taken prisoner by the Americans. He told me that the end was coming soon, and that I needed to be prepared to say good-bye to him. This was when I began to cry.

I expected him to scold me, but instead, he took me in his arms. "I don't know whether I will make it out of this alive or not. If I don't, I want you to know that loving you has been the happiest part of my life," he said to me.

I looked up at him with tears in my eyes, but none of the words that were in my heart came out. I didn't want to hear him talk about dying.

"I know this will probably be the hardest thing you have ever done, but you are going to have to be strong for me and for the children. Whatever happens, you need to make it through. Sell the house, sell everything we own if you must, but make it through. If anything happens to me, and you know that I am dead, I want you to take the children, go to America, and find my parents. I am sure they will help you."

"Please, don't talk this way," I said, choking back the tears.

"Klara, you're going to have to face this. They are going to arrest me, or I will be surrendered. Either way, I will be gone, and you are going to have to carry the load. I will do everything thing I can to get back to you as soon as I can, but all of that effort will do me no good if you don't make it, however long it takes."

I stood up on my feet and took a couple of steps toward the charred and bombed-out palace, then I crossed my arms. I was trying to stop the tears, but it was no use. I felt his arms slip around my waist, and I leaned back on his chest.

"It is just that I love you so much, that sometimes I feel like my heart will break open. And the last thing I want is for you to be in any danger, or to be away from you," I said.

"Klara, the separation will change nothing unless you let it. My love for you will remain the same. I am not worried for my sake, but I am concerned for you, because you will have the children, and only God knows what will be left of Kassel when this is all over."

I turned around in his arms and looked into his unwavering eyes. "I promise you that I will be strong and that I will do my best to make it through," I said with as much determination as I could muster.

"That's all I needed to hear," replied Kurt with a smile. "Now, listen carefully," he said, pulling an old oilcloth and tin box from his rucksack. "I am going to bury the ledger up here in a safe place. But before I do, I want to explain to you what it is and what I have done. If I am ever to be held accountable, this ledger will be my only defense."

We sat down on the grass again, and Kurt opened up the ledger. In the next few minutes, all of the scattered details came to focus in a daring and frightening picture. I would have thought he was telling me a tale if were not for the fact that I knew it was all true. There was no other explanation for the bronze gilded ledger.

"I met Ibraham Spuler at the airplane engine factory in early 1941. By then, most of the Jews in Kassel were forced out of work, but he and several others like him were very skilled and their experience was particularly valuable in the factories. Ibraham was an engineer by training and education, and so we had that in common.

"Before he was forced to sell his business, he had a dozen employees in his shop, so it was no surprise to me that the factory manager had set him over the forced laborers. Despite how he was treated as a Jew and the deplorable conditions under which he was now forced to live, he assisted us with solving some baffling problems.

"I wasn't supposed to acknowledge him because he was a Jew, but Ibraham was a good man, and he quickly earned my respect. I was relieved to find him and his former employees still at the factory following the first transport of Jews to the concentration camps, but I knew it wouldn't be long until the next transport."

I looked up at my husband as he wiped his brow. He hesitated a minute, and then he continued.

"I don't know when it happened, or how it happened, but I couldn't turn a blind eye anymore to their plight. I kept asking myself what excuses I was going to give to Sepp and Annette when they were grown and they wanted to know why I didn't do anything to help their fellow men."

Kurt swallowed hard and then continued. "It occurred to me, one day, that I was in a choice position to act, but I had to wrestle with the potential consequences, should I be caught. My only real hesitation was what would happen to the children. I finally decided that it was more important for me to lose everything, including my life, than to stand by and do nothing.

"I knew that my cousin in Berlin, whom you met in June, often 'fixed' identifications and 'discrepancies' for other officers for a price. He is in charge of the *Reich's* official records bureau. I drew up a list of Italian names, and then I asked him to send me replacement identifications for these invented free Italian laborers who had 'lost their papers.' All he wanted in exchange was an introduction to Elisabeth Schwartzkopf, which I was finally able to do when we were in Berlin.

"One of my very good friends since childhood, Hans Leitner, is Kassel's mortician, to whom you have delivered several messages. We were having dinner once when he expressed to me some open disgust about the *Reich's* policy with respect to the Jews. I suspected that *Herr* Leitner would be more than willing to sign a few death certificates for me. He has always trusted me. I also knew that *Herr* Vogler at the tank plant cared little for Nazi politics. His one and only concern has always been profit and production."

Kurt paused for a moment and looked out over the city. A gust of wind rustled the branches above our head. I pulled the hair back out of my eyes.

"So I did it, first with Ibraham's nephew. *Herr* Leitner signed his death certificate without asking me any questions, and Ibraham delivered it to the supervisor at the engine factory, who could care less if one of his Jewish laborers had died.

"It didn't take me long to convince *Herr* Vogler to add Ibraham's nephew to the work roster at the tank factory because he was highly skilled and *Herr* Vogler always needed more laborers. He never asked me where I found him. Once I saw that the whole scheme worked, I did the same thing with a couple other men.

"We went for a long period of time without a bombing or any event that would allow me to ask for some more death certificates, and I felt that it was too dangerous to move anyone else without some reason for cover. Also, some of the men, including Ibraham, still had wives and children here, and they were reluctant to go underground, to leave their families.

"One night in late August, just before the last Jewish transport, the British came. They hit the Henschel works. They hit the hospitals, and they hit the airplane factory. It was utter chaos. The Jews were never allowed in the shelters, but Ibraham and six of his men somehow made it out alive.

"The next morning, I found them all huddled together in the forest, south of the *Herkules*. I had pre-arranged with Ibraham to meet them there should a bombing occur. They lay low for another two days while I got their death certificates signed and buried them, and then they reported to the tank factory with their new identifications.

"*Herr* Vogler agreed to arrange for them to be housed and fed with the other free laborers, but his only insistence was that he wouldn't pay the foreign workers from the *Reich's* payroll. I think he wanted to skim that money off for himself. So I told him I would try to find some money in the "armaments production" fund. That is when I started giving him the money that my mother-in-law was sending for the children, and that is when I had to start keeping the ledgers.

"Each time we were bombed was another opportunity for me to act, and over time I was able to transfer a few others that Ibraham had thoroughly vetted from the slave labor pool over to Henschel. But it became more and more work for me to keep track of everything. I now had to trace the new identities and log their payroll, so that when it came to the production records and employment rosters at the plants, they always matched perfectly."

I looked up at Kurt with confusion. "So the records at the plants are what the inspectors wanted to see, but your ledgers are what really happened?"

"Exactly," Kurt replied. I looked at Kurt with a blank stare. I was trying to take in all of the information he had just given me, but in the end, it seemed to add up to one thing. Kurt, at risk of his life, had smuggled the men listed in his ledgers from the concentration camp transports and the labor camps and was paying their wages out of his own pocket. I looked down the page in the ledger at the list of names.

"Most of them are still working at the tank factory and still alive," he said proudly. "I only had two of them disappear on me. They have been housed all of this time in the worker lodging, and they have had a decent daily food ration and a place to go during the air raids. None of them would be alive if—"

"How could you do this?" I asked, looking up into Kurt's eyes. "You've risked everything for them."

Kurt looked away from my glance and closed the ledger. "I haven't done enough," he said with regret. "If you only knew."

Off into the woods a little ways from the trail by the upper lake, Kurt dug a hole with a hand trowel he had brought in his rucksack. After he tightly wrapped the ledger in the oilcloth and placed it in the tin, he buried it in the hole. I helped him cover over the freshly dug hole with dirt, sticks, and dead leaves and tried to note exactly where the spot was.

There were several emotions swimming around inside of me. I didn't say a word on the way back to the house. I was overwhelmed at my husband's bravery, daring, and seemingly endless amount of compassion.

All of the nights that he poured over those ledgers, all of the times he must have feared that he would be found out, and all of the machinations he had to go through to help these men made me feel faint. I had, up and until that moment, very poorly underestimated the driving force behind Kurt's actions, his work, and his life.

I was relieved when I thought that he had shared none of this information with me until now, because I know in my heart that I never would have been able to bear the pressure of keeping it secret or the stress of never knowing when he would be caught. Now I am torn between wishing that the Americans would come tomorrow so that it would all be over and wanting another lifetime to spend with him.

....

March 27, 1945

Frau Brandt has been calling every evening for two weeks now, demanding to speak with Kurt. Last night, she called again while we were eating supper. Kurt rolled his eyes, put his napkin on the table, and told *Frau* Hoffmann he would speak with her.

I looked up at *Frau* Hoffmann as Kurt answered the phone and said hello to *Frau* Brandt. We both listened intently to the one-sided conversation.

"Yes, Helma, it is true that the Americans are on their way to Kassel. No, I do not agree with you that the children would be safer in Berlin, not as long as the *Führer* is in hiding there.

You will be next to be invaded, and it is looking like it will be the Russians who will overtake you."

There was a little pause, and then Kurt sighed. "Well, on that front, I have good news for you, Helma. I have gotten rid of *Fräulein* Mauer as you insisted," he said with mischief in his voice. "Yes, she is now *Frau* Rager."

Even from our seats in the dining room, we could hear the echo of her shouting on the telephone in the hall. Then we heard Kurt laughing uncontrollably.

"Calm down, Helma," he said when the shouting ceased. "Now you needn't worry what will become of the children when I am taken by the Americans. Klara will care for them."

There was a slight pause, and then Kurt replied. "I thought you would be happy for me, Helma, and for the children. She will take good care of them, and at any rate, they will be much better off with us in Kassel than in the hands of the Russian communists, and I think you know that."

The conversation ended abruptly, and then Kurt took his place back at the table with a smirk on his face and a look of great satisfaction. He didn't say anything to us about the conversation, but I think that now he will finally be rid of her. At least, I hope that is the last we will hear from her.

After supper, Kurt sat down with Klaus, the children, and me in the living room. He told them that we were married. I don't know what I expected the reaction of the children to be, but there were more questions on their faces than anything else. Annette seemed amused by it, and then she asked if she could go back to playing with her dolls. Klaus was visibly surprised.

"When did this happen?" he asked, directing his question to me.

"In December," I replied. "It had to be a secret, until now."

His reaction to this information was so odd that I could not tell whether or not he was happy for me. I took my wedding ring off of the necklace last night and put it on my finger. I'm going to wear it there from now on. There is no point in keeping it a secret any longer.

The news for today is that the Americans are in Frankfurt, and our days in Kassel are numbered. Before Kurt and Klaus got home this evening, there was a knock on the front door. The children and I were in the dining room, working on homework, and *Frau* Hoffmann was in the kitchen. So, I went to answer the door.

I was surprised to see Lieutenant Braun. He greeted me warmly and then asked for the major. I told him he wasn't home yet. Lieutenant Braun looked slightly over his right shoulder, and then he asked me to step outside for a moment. I hesitated. Then I shut the door behind me and stepped down next to the lieutenant.

He leaned in close to me. "Can you give him a message?"

"Sure," I said, wondering why he was acting so secretive.

"Tell him, please, that I have contacted everyone he asked me to and all but one have agreed to meet him tomorrow night."

I narrowed my eyes.

"That's the message," the lieutenant said. "Will you give it to him, *Frau* Rager?" he asked, drawing out my name.

I swallowed hard. I was so used to it being a secret that I was surprised to hear myself referred to that way.

A sly smile lit up the lieutenant's face. "And for the benefit of the men who are following me, you will forgive me for this," said the lieutenant.

Before I knew what he was going to do, he reached for me and pressed his lips against mine. He turned with an evil laugh and left me with a look of shock on my face.

I was about to say something after him, until I thought I did see someone behind the bushes across the street. I opened the door and went inside where I couldn't be seen, and then I wiped my mouth with my arm. What a disgusting thing for him to do.

Kurt looked quite agitated when he got home. He seemed only a little relieved when I told him the lieutenant's message.

He wondered out loud who the one person was who wouldn't be coming. I wondered what kind of meeting Kurt had called, but I didn't ask. I didn't have to wait long to find out.

We were all at the dining room table eating in silence when Kurt spoke up. He told us all that the Americans would probably be here in less than a week, that we were just finishing up on thirteen new Tiger Tanks, and that the Heavy Tank Battalions were going to attempt to defend the city along with the *Reichsarbeitdienst* paramilitary members and an armored infantry division.

Klaus asked him if he thought they would be successful in defending Kassel. Kurt laughed at him, and then he shook his head. "They won't last three days against the Americans," he responded. "Not even with thirteen Tigers. We have no fuel."

I watched as the color left Klaus's face, and he swallowed hard. "What are we going to do?" Klaus asked.

Kurt sat back in his chair and dismissed the children from the table. "*Herr* Himmler has declared Kassel a fortress city. General Major Erxleben has orders to resist to the last round, and then to leave the city burning. And those were the orders that were given today at the defense command meeting. All of the factories are to be destroyed—Fieseler, Wegmann, Junkers, and Henschel. I have been trying to convince the general major and others to save the lives of their men and the lives and property of what is left of Kassel—to surrender."

"Are they listening to you?" asked *Frau* Hoffmann.

Kurt shook his head. "They are intent on following out their orders," replied the major. "But I have asked Lieutenant Braun to gather certain men together that I think may listen, and I will meet with them tomorrow evening. Perhaps together, we can convince the general major to save Kassel."

A sudden shiver went up my spine. He was taking a big chance convening such a meeting. If anyone told the authorities, if he were caught in such a meeting, that would be the end. Part of me wanted to beg him to keep silent, but I knew it would be no use.

I was going to help *Frau* Hoffmann with the dishes, but Kurt sent the children up to the nursery to play, and he asked me and Klaus to follow him up to our bedroom. I sat down next to Klaus on the edge of the bed, and we watched Kurt pace the floor for a minute.

"After giving us all a rousing speech about defending Kassel to the last round, the *Gauleiter* has left town. He won't be back. The situation in Kassel is going to deteriorate quickly. If they don't listen to sense and surrender Kassel, we are in for a losing battle. But I will not see us killed in the last moments of this war, and will not stand by and watch my city destroyed."

"What can we do?" asked Klaus in a defeated tone of voice.

Kurt looked up at him with piercing eyes. "Do you trust me, Klaus?" he asked pointedly.

Klaus leaned back when he heard the question. "Yes," he responded at last with more conviction than I thought he had.

"Then I need your help," Kurt said. "I know what must be done."

"Why don't we just leave, like the *Gauleiter* did?" I asked.

Kurt took a couple of steps to the right, and then turned back and paced again. "That wouldn't solve anything," he replied.

"Yes, it would," I said. "We would all be out of harm's way, and you and Klaus wouldn't be captured."

Kurt sighed heavily. "It would only postpone the inevitable, Klara. Germany is falling apart. And besides that, where would we go? To the east? To the Russians? No. At some point in time, you have to stop running and face your due."

"I agree with him, Klara," said Klaus immediately. I looked at Klaus in shock. I had hoped for my own brother's support in my proposition.

The more Kurt talks about the Americans coming and the closer we are to the surrender of Kassel, the more I want to run away and the sicker I feel. Neither Kurt nor Klaus would be moved from their position, so I am stuck with the prospect of losing them both and being alone with the children. And that is only if we survive the battle for Kassel.

April 1945

Dear Journal,

Today is Thursday. It has been gray and raining, off and on, all day long. I am sitting in the attic on a mattress. *Frau* Hoffmann is sleeping next to me. Sepp is on the floor at the foot of our bed, and Annette is on the floor next to me. I am writing by the light of the lantern tonight.

It is all over, and I cannot seem to stop crying. I feel that my heart cannot stand to beat another moment, and I really don't know if I can go on.

On Friday, the tank alarm, which I had never heard before, sounded early and wailed for over five minutes. We heard that the Americans were less than five kilometers from the city. Saturday, we could hear the fighting in the distance. Kurt and Klaus were gone from sun up until almost midnight. Kurt came home exasperated, muttering something about the Gestapo killing eighty of the laborers who had broken into a boxcar looking for food to eat.

The neighbor came by Sunday morning to ask us if we were going to go to the Weinberg bunker to wait out the battle. She said that all of the civilians in the city were going there.

The rest of the morning was eerie and hurried. I saw Kurt exchange some words with Klaus as Klaus was preparing to leave. Then Kurt told me that I should say good-bye to him. I looked at my husband with unbelief in my eyes. I didn't want to accept that the time had come, but I tried to be brave. I had promised him I would be so. As if the good-bye to Klaus wasn't hard enough, I had to do it all over again with the children when Kurt left a half hour later.

Before he left, Kurt instructed me not to go the bunker, but instead to wait it out in the basement where he thought we would be safer. He said that he hoped when the Americans came they would treat us well. I just looked at him and pled with him. "Just this once, will you tell me where you are going and what you are going to do?"

We were standing alone in the hall. At first, Kurt looked at me impatiently, and then I saw pity come to his eyes. He took me by both arms. "I'm going to the command bunker for a meeting. I must then come up with an excuse to leave, because I plan to meet Klaus in my office just after noon. If he is willing, I will take Klaus, and we are going to have to find a way to get into Grossenritte without being shot. I am going to surrender myself to the Americans."

I took in a quick breath. "Today?"

"Yes, today. And my goal is to get there before dark."

I looked away from him and swallowed the tears that were coming. Kurt lowered his voice. "When they ask, I'm going to tell them where each and every one of our defensive positions are."

My eyes shot to his. "You're going to betray your country?"

Kurt narrowed his eyes. He didn't like my question, and I wished I hadn't said it. He shifted all of his weight to his back foot. "There is nothing left of our country to betray except for senseless orders that will only lead to more military and civilian casualties and the complete destruction of what is left of Kassel. The general major is determined to blindly carry out these orders. How can I stand by and watch more people die for no reason while what is left of Kassel is destroyed? This insane war has gone on long enough, Klara."

After he said that, I realized that there was no use in trying to talk him out of it. He had made up his mind. Kurt asked me to find *Frau* Hoffmann, and then he called for the children. He shook *Frau* Hoffmann's hand. Next, he gathered the children in his arms, told them that he loved them, and that they should mind me. Then he pulled me close and told me he would never stop loving me.

After he kissed me, I looked into his eyes. At that moment, I knew he needed my support, not my doubt. I reached deep inside for all of the courage I had left. "I am with you, my darling," I said almost in a whisper as the tears began to fall. "Please be careful." He drew slowly away from me, took a look around the hall, and then he left for the command bunker.

The large anti-aircraft guns were firing constantly throughout the day. We listened to the sporadic sounds of fighting all morning long from the basement. The children were restless and full of many questions. I was glad that *Frau* Hoffmann was there with me, or I would have felt more alone.

Sometime during the day, we heard a large series of explosions. Later on, we found out that our soldiers had blown up the Fulda bridge. In the early afternoon, we heard the telephone ring. I ran upstairs to answer it, hoping it was Kurt. But my heart sank when I heard Lieutenant Braun on the other end. He wanted to know where Kurt was.

"I-I haven't seen him since this morning when he left for a meeting," I said as calmly as I could.

Lieutenant Braun told me they were all looking for him, and I was to phone him if he showed up at home. I promised I would.

As darkness began to fall, I got more and more restless. I was struggling with the thought that I might never know if Kurt and Klaus had made it to Grossenritte safely. We slept down in the basement, all four of us, but I didn't really get much sleep. I kept hoping that Kurt and Klaus would come home, but they never did. Early in the morning, I hurried out to the wash basin and threw up. I can't remember the last time I felt so sick.

Monday, we spent another long day in the basement. I don't remember when, but Lieutenant Braun phoned again looking for Kurt. I told him honestly that he never came home.

Late on Tuesday afternoon, we heard someone pounding on the front door upstairs. I hushed the children and pulled Annette close. The moment had come. We heard movement upstairs, and it wasn't long until there was the sound of footsteps on the basement stairs. The door to our shelter flew open, and in came two American soldiers with their guns drawn.

After such a long wait, I don't remember feeling much, but the children were scared. When the soldiers saw that we were only women and children, they motioned for us to follow them.

As we came into the hall, we saw other American soldiers searching the house. I don't know what they were looking for, but when they returned to the hall, they all had a discussion. Ten minutes later, a gruff, important-looking, hefty man with scruffy facial stubble and wrinkled clothes came sauntering through the front door. A shorter, dark-haired soldier followed him in. They were both drenched from the rain.

Initially, the dark-haired soldier spoke to us in German. He asked us to sit in the living room and told us to stay out of the way. After an hour had passed, he came back to us.

"*Frau* Rager? Our unit will be setting up in your house. You should take some clothes, bedding, and whatever valuables you might have and move up to the attic."

I looked at *Frau* Hoffmann and then back to the American. "How did you know my name?"

The American looked down at the ground. "Your husband specifically asked us to look out for his family."

My heart soared at hearing these words. "Did you speak with my husband?"

The American shifted uncomfortably on his feet.

"Yes."

"And was there a young man with him?"

The American nodded.

At that moment, I couldn't have asked for more. I had confirmation that Kurt and Klaus had made it to the Americans alive, and I didn't have to worry about them dying in the skirmishes that were taking place in Kassel at that very moment. But the tears came like a flood when I realized that after all of the difficult, heartwrenching things my husband had done on Sunday, he had one thing on his mind—the safety of his family.

Before dark, the Americans had set up a base in our home, and there were men coming in and out. The activities intensified until Wednesday morning. The German speaking, dark-haired soldier was kind enough to relay the news to *Frau* Hoffmann at breakfast that General Major Erxleben had finally surrendered. When I asked what would become of the soldiers, he told me that they were rounding up all of the military men, and that they would all be sent to prison camp.

There are no less than fifty men sleeping in our house now. *Frau* Hoffmann, the children, and I are living in the attic. Since Tuesday, we have been collecting the soldier's rations, and *Frau* Hoffmann has been cooking them up for every meal. In exchange for her services, they have shared their food with us.

The children have been eating well and seem to be taking all of this in stride. I haven't been very hungry and have been feeling quite ill. Sometimes, I go down to the basement and curl up in a corner in our bomb shelter room and cry. The children keep asking me when their father will be home. I do not know how to answer them. I miss my husband so much that I sometimes feel like I would rather die. I wonder if he is well, and I wonder if I will ever see him again.

May 1945

May 13, 1945

Dear Journal,

The war is finally over. As unbelievable as it sounds, we have heard the news that Hitler has committed suicide, and Germany has surrendered. As for me, I have had little to write and little motivation to do so. Kurt's birthday and mine have passed. I did not get my wish, for I have heard no word from Klaus or from my husband. Every day seems to be more difficult to bear than the last.

We are living from moment to moment now, hoping to survive. I have been out of the house only enough to see that Kassel is in ruin. Those who have survived the war are walking around like dead men with their heads down, passing silently by the American soldiers who are trying to keep order. Although the rumor is that the Americans are going to set up feeding stations, for the time being, there is little food and no water.

At least on that account, we have much for which to be thankful. The soldiers who are living in our house have been kind to share their rations with us, and we have plenty of water from the well that Kurt's father dug in the 1930s. The Americans have introduced us all to a new sticky American food they call "peanut butter." The children are wild about it, but I don't care for it.

Frau Hoffmann keeps occupied preparing meals for the Americans. As for the children, Sepp has been collecting the soldier's dirty laundry and bringing it to Annette and me to wash. Annette does quite well with the iron. I am proud of how they are both taking these difficult times. Occasionally, they will whine and complain, but, for the most part, they are bearing it well.

I cannot say the same for me. Although I try to be strong in front of the children, I am having a terrible time of it. I suppose that it does not help that I feel exhausted all of the time. Oh, dear journal, I am afraid to tell you. I haven't told a soul, but I am certain that I am pregnant.

This news, that should be happy news, only seems to make me fearful and sad. I want to reach out and feel Kurt next to me. I want him to hold me and to assure me that everything will be all right. I sometimes wonder if he will still be alive to see his child although I try hard not to think about it. I wonder how long it will be until I cannot keep this a secret any longer. I hope Sepp and Annette will be happy to have a brother or a sister.

....

May 28, 1945

I have heard from Aunt Frieda for the first time since the beginning of March. She says that things in Sinsheim are even bleaker than she ever thought possible. She is desperate to hear from me and wants to know what has happened to Klaus. She says that Liese and Lenz have been shut up in the attic lately as Uncle Lothar has been in despair. He has been telling Aunt Frieda that he cannot bear the thought of going through the humiliation of another treaty, and he keeps his pistol right next to him on the couch.

I wrote her a letter this afternoon. I don't know how she will receive it, but I have asked her if Lenz and Liese could come to stay with us. At least we have food. I told her I didn't know anything about Klaus, and then I told her that I had married the major. I hope that she will not be too angry with me, and I hope that Uncle Lothar will allow Lenz and Liese to come to Kassel.

....

May 30, 1945

Dear Journal,

I am sitting on a bench by the *Schwaneninsel* at the *Karlsaue*, watching the children throwing rocks into the pond. My heart flows with emotions—familiar and unfamiliar—as I think back to all that has happened since Kurt and I walked the paths in the park together.

Gone are the frightening nights of cowering in the basement wondering when death would arrive. Ever present is the emptiness in my heart because of Kurt's absence. But this morning, I awoke with a new found hope. I have finally made peace with God.

Yesterday, *Frau* Hoffmann received word from Rosine's cousin in Marburg that Rosine had died peacefully in her sleep after battling a respiratory illness for six years. I asked, but *Frau* Hoffmann said that she did not know Rosine was so ill. *Frau* Hoffmann said that Rosine never spoke a word of her own problems.

All the rest of the day, I thought back on that August afternoon when we had tea. I thought about her kindness in making and bringing me soup and bread when I was ill. I thought about the little notes of Bible verses she would send me through *Frau* Hoffmann. And I thought about the fact that it was those verses that had given me comfort when nothing else did.

Rosine was the one person who shattered all of the hope I had of getting to heaven. I have always thought that I would be accepted by God if my good works outweighed the bad. But Rosine had told *Frau* Hoffmann's sister plainly that not even the nuns and priests were exempt from having to put their trust for forgiveness and eternal life in God's Son.

I thought on this all evening. I didn't hear a word that *Frau* Hoffmann spoke as she read the Bible to me and the children last evening. I was thinking instead that if Rosine, with all of her good works, had to ask for God's forgiveness, how much more would I.

Rosine, Maria, and *Frau* Hoffmann had all believed in Him. Why was I waiting to make my peace with God? I kissed the children good night, and *Frau* Hoffmann put out the light. The darkness seemed to press down on my chest.

I have hidden from everyone since I was ten years old. When Uncle Lothar would go into one of his rages, I would hide in the attic with my brothers and sister. When I came to Kassel, I had to hide in the basement every time the air raid siren sounded.

Although I have questioned the things I heard at mass and though I have wanted to know that God would take me to heaven, I have never been willing to come out of hiding to take His hand. As I lay there in the dark, the tears began to fall from my eyes. We have made it through the war, but I felt in the bottom of my heart that I do not want to hide from God any longer.

I do not know what time it was, but I finally closed my eyes and prayed with all of my heart that God would forgive my trespasses. I told Him that I trusted in Him, just as Rosine said I must.

I lay on the mattress in the attic. *Frau* Hoffmann was snoring softly by then, and the children were asleep at my feet. In that moment, the crushing darkness lifted from my chest and a peace and quietness flowed into my soul, like a cool stream of water trickling over pebbles in a stream.

As soon as I could this morning, I told *Frau* Hoffmann what I had done. She smiled, her crooked smile, and then she hugged me. "We will have to teach the children now," she said.

I cannot pretend that the bleakness all around us and the uncertainty that lies ahead does not discourage me, but now at least, I don't have to hide any of this from God.

June 1945

June 19, 1945

Today, for the first time, there was a market at the *Königsplatz*. We all went, just to see what they had to offer. As *Frau* Hoffmann said, at least this is a sign that life is trying to return to normal.

It has been an unbearably hot day, but I seem to be feeling better. Lenz and Liese came on the train last week. Although there are now six of us living in the attic, at least we are all together again. Now, if only Kurt and Klaus will be released, we will be complete.

Two days ago, I got a letter from Klaus that was dated over three weeks ago. He didn't say much, but he did say that he was in good health, and he asked me to let Aunt Frieda know that he is still alive.

And I finally got a letter from Kurt. It was written on a single piece of paper, and it was short, but I drank in every word. He said that this was his first opportunity to write, that he has been told that he will be able to write one such letter, once a week, and that he will be allowed to receive one such letter, once a week. He wrote that he has been treated well, but that he does not know anything about when or if they will release him. He told me he loved me and said that I should give his love to the children.

I sat down immediately to write him, but I had to rewrite the letter two times for it all to fit on one page. I did not tell him about the baby. It didn't seem the right way to tell him—on paper. Tomorrow morning, I will go and try to post the letter.

Frau Hoffmann has discovered my secret, but I think it is best for her to know. She has been like a mother to me, and I have been so thankful for her company and her steady spirit these past few months. I told her so today.

August 1945

August 10, 1945

Dear Journal,

Yesterday was a bittersweet day, and I am tired from all of the emotions. I have been receiving Kurt's letters regularly, except for the weeks when he told me he was going to write to his parents in the United States. About a month ago, he told me that the Americans were going to allow each officer at his facility a five-minute visit.

Yesterday was my chance. I got up early and rode the train down to Frankfurt. It was quite a long walk from the train station to the prison, and it was very hot. By the time I reached the front gate, I thought I was going to faint. Immediately, I recognized the prison as the place they had taken Sepp, Annette, and me over a year ago.

I joined the line of over a hundred other women and waited to be processed. Once inside, they put us all in a large assembly room, and then they began to call out names at ten-minute intervals. I kept staring at the clock on the wall. I had arrived at half past nine in the morning, but by two o'clock they still had not called Kurt's name.

By the time they did call, I was so nervous, that I was shaking. They led me down a series of halls, and then into a small room with a single chair. A fine mesh, metal screen was stretched across the length of the wall opposite the door. The man who led me into the room told me I would have five minutes to visit with my husband, and that I was to sit in the chair. I did exactly what he said, and then I waited. My heart was pounding hard.

I heard a clanking sound on the other side of the wire mesh, and when I leaned forward, I saw the door on the other side open. I couldn't help but smile when I saw Kurt, and he smiled back at me. The guard instructed him to sit in the chair. I reached up and put my hand on the mesh, but when he put his hand up to mine and I felt his touch, the guard on the other side told him to put his hands at his side.

"How are you, Klara, and how are the children?" he said as he took his hand down. "It is so good to see you."

I took in a deep breath and put my hand on my stomach as I felt a kick.

"What's the matter?" asked Kurt with concern in his voice. I looked up into his eyes, and then I saw him looking at my stomach.

"The baby started kicking when he heard your voice," I said with a smile.

"The baby?"

"Yes, we are going to have a child in November," I said proudly. Kurt closed his eyes and sat back in his chair.

"Why didn't you tell me?" he asked, sounding as if he were displeased.

"I-It didn't seem right to tell you in a letter. I didn't want to worry you." I looked down at my hands. The time was slipping away. "We are all doing well, and the children are doing good. They miss you so and are always asking me when you are going to come home."

I looked carefully at Kurt. He looked better than I expected him to look, but I could see the distress on his face. "Is there any word on when they will release you?" I asked, hoping for a positive response.

"No," he said, "but I have been told that they will soon be assigning me a defense lawyer. The next step after that, as I understand it, is a classification hearing to determine whether or not I fall into a category that they have decided to send to the military tribunal for prosecution."

"I hope it won't take forever," I said.

"When is the baby due?" asked Kurt.

"November," I said although I had already told him. Kurt sighed. "Have you heard from Klaus?"

"He is in a de-Nazification program," I said. "He is due to be released in October."

"That's good. And the children? Will they be starting school soon?"

"Yes," I said cheerfully. "The Americans have been working to open up the schools by October. They have treated us very kindly."

"Good," Kurt said. "And how is *Frau* Hoffmann?"

"She is well," I said. "She sends her greetings."

"And you have had enough to eat? I have heard that is a problem."

"We have enough to eat," I said after a moment. "And your family has been sending us care packages. We wouldn't be doing so well without them."

I watched as the guard behind Kurt moved to his side. It was already time to go.

"I love you, Klara. Please take care of yourself," he said, "and the baby." I stood to my feet. He took one last look at me, and then he was gone.

I rested my head against the window on the train on the way home and closed my eyes. All the way home, I could see his face in my mind, marred only by the wire mesh. I curled the fingers on my right hand. I could still feel his touch. I think that the tears that were rolling down my cheeks were tears of relief and joy. My husband is still alive, and he still loves me. At this moment, I can ask for nothing more. There are too many people who did not make it through the war, and I know of too many widows. How can I complain?

....

August 21, 1945

Dear Journal,

This morning, I woke up to the sound of twenty birds singing. When I looked out the window, I saw that they were all perched in the tree in front of the house. I think they were sent by someone to try to cheer me up.

Since I was down to Frankfurt to see Kurt, I have been thinking a lot about the love I have for him and how, even though we are separated, it is growing. It is a distressing feeling not to know when I will see him next or when we will be able to resume our life together. But I am trying to be content with what I do have. I am not ashamed to say that I stand at the door like a child, waiting for the post to arrive. With the weekly letter writing, I am getting to know another side of my husband. I have found that there is a lot that can be said in one page.

He is ever present in our thoughts. *Frau* Hoffmann is careful to remember him as she says the prayer before we eat, and every night as I put the children to bed, we say a prayer for him. Since there is nothing we can do to help him, we are leaving his care in the hands of God.

Yesterday, *Frau* Hoffmann convinced me that I should alter two of Ida's dresses from the trunk in the attic to fit my ever expanding waistline. Today, she is going to help me pin up the hem and the sleeves, and then I will need to find some thread and start sewing.

It is humbling to see how God is caring for us. So far, we have had everything that we need. A week after the Americans moved out of the house, we began to receive care packages from Kurt's mother and father in the States. I am afraid to say that without these packages, we would be starving. I have written to them several times to thank them, but it is hard to put such gratitude into words.

October 1945

Dear Journal,

Just after the children had come home from school, Klaus surprised us by knocking on the front door. We all ran to hug him. I think I even saw a tear in *Frau* Hoffmann's eye. He seemed to be shocked to see me. I am getting very big.

While I was trying to get the children settled down to do their homework, Klaus wandered around the house, finally ending up on the back porch. That's where I found him, staring out at the view to the south. I gave him another hug and told him how glad I was to have him home.

He didn't say much from the time he arrived, during our meager supper, or through the rest of the evening. By the time I got back downstairs after putting all of the children to bed, it was a little late. And I was surprised to find him still sitting in the living room.

Frau Hoffmann was mending some socks, nestled quietly in her favorite chair next to the light. I sat down on the couch next to Klaus and stretched my back and my legs out. All of the sudden, he broke the silence by asking me what had happened to the major.

After I told him that he was still in prison awaiting a trial, he sighed. "I thought that he would be released by now because of what he did."

I turned my eyes to Klaus.

"What do you mean?"

"When we left here, on the last day," he added.

Frau Hoffmann looked up from her mending, over her glasses. "What did happen that day?"

Klaus folded and unfolded his hands. Then he got up from the couch and walked over to the picture window. After he had stared out into the darkness for a good minute, he cleared his throat.

"He told me to go to the factory, as usual, but to try to steal away at noon to meet him at the general command headquarters. He said he had an important mission he needed my help with. On the way to his office, he wanted me to check at the motor pool to see if they had a motorcycle.

"I did as he said, but when I got to his office, he wasn't there. I waited for him for over an hour, and just about the time I thought I had better get back to the factory, he came in. He was in a big hurry. He thanked me for waiting for him, then he tore the map off of the wall, put it on his desk, and started scribbling on it.

"While he was writing on the map, he asked me pointedly if I was willing to go with him to the Americans. He wanted me to know there was a good chance one or both of us would get shot on the way. He told me that he would go alone, but thought an extra pair of eyes would be invaluable.

"After I understood what he was asking me and after I told him I would go, he showed me everything he had drawn on the map. He wanted to make sure that if anything happened to him along the way, I would be able to tell the Americans everything. I watched him fold the map up tight, and then he rolled it up against his leg and shoved it down the inside of his boot."

Klaus left the window, came back to the couch, and sat down slowly. I looked at him carefully, waiting and wanting to hear more.

"What happened then?" asked *Frau* Hoffmann when he did not continue.

Klaus looked up from the floor with a start. "Uh, we went to the motor pool and took a motorcycle. Then we headed west and turned south. When we got to the Dönche flak guns and they were booming away, I started to think it wasn't a good idea to go. I wasn't sure how he thought we were going to dodge all of the flak, artillery, and bullets coming from both sides.

"We ran into a Panzer unit on the south side of Brasselsburg. The major thought they were in retreat since they were supposed to be in Altenritte. There was no getting around them, so we stopped. The major knew the man in command and walked around with him inspecting their position. He inquired, besides manpower, if they had the equipment they needed to defend Kassel."

Klaus let out a quick laugh. "The commander just looked at the major like he was crazy. The major asked him about the defense positions in front of them, and then told the man he would report their request for backup to the general major the next time he saw him.

"They let us pass to the south, and then we headed up into the forest. It wasn't long after we turned off the main road before we ran out of gas. The major ditched the bike and said that we would have had to go the rest of the way on foot anyway, so as not to be detected."

Klaus shook his head. "We walked a long way through the woods and fields. The panzer unit had said there was a hard defensive line at Altenritte, so we went to the west through the forest to try to go around them.

"We came down out of the forest, just above Elgershausen. The major looked the situation over carefully, but we couldn't tell who had control of the village. We went forward cautiously but soon, ran into the right arm of our front line. We made a hasty retreat back into the forest and turned west.

"We came out of the forest again, but just as we were about to cross the road, I pulled the major back. Out of the corner of my eye, I had seen something moving to our right. We dove down into a ditch and tried to be still while a German scouting party went past.

"After we were sure they were long gone, we crawled over the road. There must have been an American unit in Elgershausen, because while we were crossing the fields between the villages, there was artillery fire being exchanged between Elgershausen and Grossenritte, and the pass just north of Altenritte.

"At one point, it got too intense. The major didn't want to wait any longer, but we sat there in a ditch for a while, waiting for the fighting to subside. Then we heard the sound of tanks rolling toward us. The major said they were Shermans, and he tossed his pistol into the grass. He pulled me up, and we stood by the side of the road with our hands up.

I took in a big breath and shifted on the couch. Klaus brought his hand to his mouth and chewed on one of his fingers for a moment.

"The men in the tank didn't know what to do with us, but soon, these jeeps drove up, and they started shouting and pointing their guns at us. They took our watches and the major's empty gun holster. All the while, we had our hands up. The major was telling them that he needed to speak with their commander; he had important information for them. I don't think they understood a word he was saying.

"They set an armed guard on the back of the jeep and made us march behind them into Grossenritte. When we reached the center of town, they sat us down against a wall under a dim light at the post office and left us there with three armed guards. It was over an hour before this captain came, who spoke very good

German. He and the guards took us over to one of the houses and sat us down in the kitchen in front of some other officers.

"A big man, with a deep voice, started asking us questions. The captain asked the major for his name, rank, and serial number. Then he asked him what his position was and where he was posted. After the major answered these questions too, the big man looked pleased. Then he asked the major whom he reported to. When the major said Berlin, the one in charge almost fell off of his chair.

"He turned to me and asked who I was. The major told them my name, and then he said I was the only one brave enough to come with him. I think they were baffled. They kept stopping to have these side conversations. Next, he asked the major what a war production minister was doing on the road to Grossenritte.

"The major said he had been waiting to greet them since they landed in France. He sat up straight and waited for the captain to interpret. Then he breathed in deeply and said that he had come to deliver the defensive plans for Kassel as discussed that morning in a meeting with General Major Erxleben. The major said that he thought they might be useful to them."

Klaus took in a deep breath, and then continued. "I could see that the men in the room were all very skeptical and didn't believe him, but the major worked on them. He told them he had a map in his boot. He said that there would be information on the map that they did not already have.

"Before the captain reached into his boot and took the map, the man in charge laughed and asked the major why on earth he would want to share that information with the enemy. I will never forget the major's reply. 'Kassel is my home. My wife and children are there. It is in everyone's best interest for this war to be over—friend and foe. The sooner you take the city, the sooner we can all go home.'

"The captain did take the map and after the big man looked at it, he had one of his lieutenants leave to make a call. Before the captain who spoke German left the room, the major stopped him. The major said he had one request. When the captain turned back, the major said that there was an X on the map where his family lived. He said that you were all in the basement and if at all possible, he asked for them to spare your lives."

My eyes began to flood with tears. This must have been the same man that came to our house on the night the Americans got to Kassel, the one who told me he had spoken with my husband.

"The captain turned back and narrowed his eyes at him. Then he asked the major if that was a condition of him giving them the information. The major shook his head and said that he realized that he was in no position to demand any conditions. It was only a plea—gentleman to gentleman."

I wiped away another tear and looked over at *Frau* Hoffmann. She was shaking her head up and down. She already knew my husband would act so bravely.

"Another hour went. Some other officers came in, and when they took me away, the major was answering their questions. He stood to his feet and shook my hand. That was the last I saw him."

Klaus leaned forward and rested his arms on his thighs. "A few days later, the other boys from my unit showed up at my prison camp. They were talking about the fighting they saw in Kassel, and a couple of them were missing. When I asked, someone told me they had died at one of the barricades. They asked me what had happened to me, but I kept my mouth shut. It was then that I realized that by taking me with him, the major had spared me the fighting and maybe the dying."

Frau Hoffmann resumed her mending. I listened to Klaus breath in an out, lost in thought.

"How did the Americans treat you?" asked *Frau* Hoffmann while tugging on her thread.

Klaus shrugged. "Not bad. And I learned some English." He asked us next about how the Americans had treated us. I told him all about the day they came into town. He was surprised to hear that the Americans had moved in and stayed in our home for several months. When I told him they were now stationed at the old air force base, he seemed to cheer up.

"I may be able to get a job there," he said.

"A job?" I said.

"Yes, I am going to have to do something to support us," he said back.

I looked closely at Klaus. I have always thought of him as a boy, but now I can see that the boy is all gone.

....

October 19, 1945

I had a terrible nightmare last night and was screaming and crying. Klaus woke me out of it, and then he held me and tried to get me to stop crying. My dream was so awful that I couldn't tell Klaus right away what it was. I had dreamed that I saw them shoot my husband and that he fell into my arms.

Before Klaus left for his job at the American military base, he told me that he thought I should spend the day in bed. *Frau* Hoffmann agreed. Lenz took Sepp, Annette, and Liese to school, and I stayed in bed. Just after one o'clock, *Frau* Hoffmann came upstairs with a letter from Kurt. I read it over and over again, and then I cried.

> My Dear Klara,
>
> I know that the time is getting close for the baby to arrive. I can only pray that God gives you the strength you will need. You cannot know the joy that is in my heart when I think of you and the baby, nor the sadness as I long to be with you. You are in my thoughts constantly, dear Klara. Know that if I could, I would wrap my arms around you and never let you go. I eagerly await news from you about the baby. You remain my utmost concern and my true love.
>
> Your loving husband,
>
> Kurt Rager

December 1945

December 23, 1945

Dear Journal,

You will never guess where we are this evening, so I will tell you. Klaus, Lenz, Liese, Sepp, Annette, little Hans, and I are in Sinsheim for Christmas.

Baby Hans came to us early in the morning on November 12. If it wasn't for *Frau* Hoffmann, I would never have made it through the delivery, and I would never have made it through the last couple of weeks. I hope that she will have some rest while we are here with Aunt Frieda and Uncle Lothar.

My dear husband has written me several times the past couple of months as I had insisted that he choose the child's name. He finally settled his mind that if it were a boy, he should have Kurt's father's name. Had little Hans been a girl, he would have been called after my mother.

Little Hans Reiner Rager is small, but he is the most beautiful baby I have ever seen. It is a little too early to tell, but I think that he has his father's handsome eyes and forehead, but he definitely has my chin. Sepp and Annette adore him, I think even more so than Lenz and Liese, although Liese likes to carry him around like he is her own. Lenz gets irritated easily with his crying.

Now, he is getting acquainted with Aunt Frieda and Uncle Lothar. Although Uncle Lothar has declined to hold him, Aunt Frieda is always there to take him out of my arms. I am so happy to be back in Sinsheim and to be able to spend Christmas with Aunt Frieda. All of the activity and the crowded house take my mind off of the one I am missing the most.

I wrote to Kurt on our anniversary and told him that I loved him more than when I married him. I sometimes feel like he isn't real, but now, I have a living reminder that he is.

Tomorrow is Christmas Eve. I have no gifts for the children, but this year it doesn't seem to matter. We are all just grateful to be together and to have the war behind us.

February 1946

February 19, 1946

It is late at night and cold. I am sitting up with little Hans. Something has finally happened with Kurt's situation, and I am brimming with hope. Two weeks ago, I received a letter in the mail from his defense attorney explaining that the review committee was in the middle of examining the major's case and would like to see the ledger that the major had told them about.

The next morning, I left Hans with *Frau* Hoffmann and went up into the woods to try to find the ledger. Following a half hour of frantic searching and digging, I finally found it. The next day, I took Hans, and we boarded a train to Nürnberg. After a long journey, we finally arrived at the Palace of Justice. It is such a large building that I had difficulty finding the temporary office of the defense attorney, *Herr* Schaefer. A kind gentleman was finally able to give me the proper directions.

It was just about two o'clock, and little Hans was crying, when I walked into his office. His secretary told me, however, that *Herr* Schaefer was not there. Further, she told me that I should have made an appointment. I asked her how long I would have to wait to see him. She said that he might be back by four o'clock.

So I waited. Hans and I sat down out in the hall on the hard wooden benches. We waited until almost a quarter to four. A shorter, older gentleman in a pinstriped suit came ambling down the hallway beside a taller man in a dark gray suit. They stopped before the door to *Herr* Schaefer's office and finished their conversation. Then they exchanged parting words. I watched the shorter man go into the office.

I looked down at Hans. He was finally sleeping. I stood to my feet, but before I could pick up my bag with the ledger, the man in the pinstriped suit opened the door and stepped back out into the hall. He came directly to me.

"*Frau* Rager?" he said, extending his hand. I shook his hand and tried to smile. "*Herr* Schaefer," he said, introducing himself. "I-I didn't expect that you would trouble yourself to come all the way to Nürnberg. You could have just mailed me the ledger."

"No, sir!" I responded quite strongly. *Herr* Schaefer was clearly taken back by my definite response. "My husband has risked his life and all that he has. This ledger is the proof of that. I could never forgive myself if it did not get here safely," I said, trying to sound calm.

Herr Schaefer scratched the back of his head and looked at little Hans.

"This is the major's son, Hans," I said proudly.

"As long as you are here," said *Herr* Schaefer with a look of pity on his face, "I should ask you a couple of questions."

Herr Schaefer held the door for me, and I followed him past his secretary and on into his office. He offered me a seat, but before I sat down, I handed him the ledger. *Herr* Schaefer sat down in his chair and opened to the first page. He flipped through the pages for a minute or two, and then he looked up at me.

"I understand, from an interview that I conducted with your husband a few weeks ago, that this ledger contains information on some transactions that he made. Can you explain this to me?"

I took in a short breath and shifted little Hans carefully in my arms. Then I told him, the best that I could recall, exactly what Kurt had explained to me before we buried the ledger. *Herr* Schaefer raised his right eyebrow as I finished my explanation.

"This Ibraham Spuler, do you know where he can be found?"

"No, I don't, sir," I responded. "I don't even know him."

Herr Schaefer shook his head. Then he leaned on the left arm of his chair. "So, if I understand correctly, he went to some trouble to make this scheme of his work, and he invested a great deal of his own money in doing so?"

"Yes, but what you cannot see in the ledger, is the hundreds of hours that he spent to ensure that he and the ones involved in this were never caught. The ledgers were his whole life."

"Do you know of any other activities your husband was involved in that would be to his favor? In other words, not in line with his position as a Nazi officer?"

"Yes. I do," I said. "He helped others who are not listed in that book."

"For example?"

"Well, I am one that he helped."

Herr Schaefer leaned back in his chair. "But you're his wife."

"I wasn't at the time," I responded. "My maiden name is Dietrich. My father was the former vice-chancellor and minister of finance under Heinrich Brüning." *Herr* Schaefer sat up in his chair. "When I came to work for the major, and he found out who I was, he helped remove my file and my siblings' files from the watch list."

"And were there others?"

I looked down at Hans and wondered if Kurt would care if I told *Herr* Schaefer about Sepp and Annette. "He has harbored, the entire war, two children of Jewish descent," I said at last, "claiming them as his own."

Herr Schaefer looked at me in disbelief. Then he searched his desk for a pad of paper and pen. After he had scribbled some extensive notes, he looked up at me.

"And now, perhaps a difficult question for you, *Frau* Rager. Do you know of anything he did as a Nazi officer that they can use against him to prove that he committed or assisted in any questionable activities?"

I shook my head.

"Do you know if he ever shot anyone?"

I shook my head again. "I don't know."

"Did he have any shares in any companies that may have profited from the war effort?"

I thought for a moment. "I know that he had shares his father gave him from Henschel, but I believe he told me that he sold them around the time that we invaded Poland."

Herr Schaefer closed the ledger on his desk and cleared his throat. "I will look through this ledger and glean what I can from it," he said.

"You will take care of it?"

"Very good care," *Herr* Schaefer replied.

I breathed in deeply. "Thank you, *Herr* Schaefer."

"Do you have any questions for me?"

"What will happen next?" I asked.

"Ah, yes. The review committee is to meet again in two weeks. We are then to submit to the prosecuting attorneys' inquiry committee our summary and recommendations for the disposition of the persons in custody, including your husband. After that, they will issue a proposal. Some of the prisoners will be slotted into blocks for trials to follow the War Criminals trial that is taking place as we speak. For some, they may have hearings for cause, and some of them, it is our hope, will be released."

I looked away from *Herr* Schaefer for a moment.

"Are you all right, *Frau* Rager?"

"Yes, sir" I responded standing up. "I should be getting back to the train station. We have a long ride home."

"Yes, of course," he said, standing to his feet.

"There is no one more kind and less deserving of prison or punishment than my husband, *Herr* Schaefer. He has done everything in his power to help the innocent in this war, and I beg you to do what you can for him," I said with tears welling up in my eyes.

I saw the older man swallow hard. "I assure you that I will try," he said sincerely.

Little Hans must have cried the whole way back to Kassel, but I didn't care. The ledger was safely in the hands of the defense attorney, and I am hoping that all of Kurt's hard work to keep the information will now either help his case or save his life.

April 1946

April 3, 1946

It is springtime again, and it has been one whole year since they took my husband away. In many ways, it seems like an eternity ago.

If it weren't for *Frau* Hoffmann, I don't know how we would have gotten through this past year. She has stuck with us through everything and all with no compensation. I hate to say this, but she is a much better grandmother to the children than *Frau* Brandt ever was.

Speaking of *Frau* Brandt, we got a postcard in the mail last month from her. It was addressed to Kurt, and it was postmarked from Argentina. She wrote that she intends to settle down in South America, and that when she is settled, she is going to send for the children. I laughed out loud when I read her message. I have put the postcard away in Kurt's desk.

Klaus has been working at the American base cleaning dishes in the kitchen ever since he got out of prison camp. He has been able to use the English he learned at the prison camp in his job. If it were not for the money that he has been making and the extra food he has been able to bring home, we would be as bad off as everyone else in Kassel. In January, he applied to go to the United

States, but he has just received his rejection notice. I have to say that I am relieved. I do not know what we would do without him.

Lenz is entering a very difficult time of life. I think that he needs a father, and there is no one here to fill those shoes. I try to help him the best I can with his struggles, but there is only so much I can do. At least, he seems to be doing well in his schooling. Next year, he will be in the class above Klaus, because Klaus has missed two years of school already.

Liese is a bright spot for me. I enjoy her easy personality, and she has been like a nursemaid to Hans. I smile when I see her caring for him as I was her age when I held Liese in my arms and cared for her.

Sepp and Annette have been like displaced children since Kurt has been gone. I can see it in their eyes, how their world has been shaken, and how they miss him. At first, I thought that bringing Lenz and Liese here was a mistake, but now, I think that having them here has helped distract Sepp and Annette so they don't miss their father so much. I have tried to pay special attention to them ever since little Hans arrived. I know they feel misplaced.

And little Hans is such a wonderful baby. He is turning over now on his own and babbling on and on. He has a charming smile. I try to tell him about his father even though I know he cannot understand.

Tomorrow, Hans and I will go to Nürnberg. There is to be a hearing on whether or not Kurt will be placed into a trial group. *Herr* Schaefer has promised to get me a pass so that I can be there to watch the hearing. A friend of *Frau* Hoffmann's has a daughter who has an apartment in Nürnberg, and she has offered me a place to stay. I am very nervous about the whole trip.

April 9, 1946

Dear Journal,

Today is Tuesday, and I am back from Nürnberg. I can hardly believe what has happened. Hans and I left for Nürnberg last Thursday. Once we were on the train and settled in, I began to get very apprehensive, thinking about how the hearing was going to end up and knowing that whatever happened was going to affect us all very keenly.

I closed my eyes and thought through all of the memories I have of Kurt. I still remember how happy my heart was when he told me he loved me for the first time, and how wonderful it felt to be in his arms.

Hans's piercing, hungry cry woke me out of my pleasant thoughts. Soon after that, we were in Nürnberg. It took me more than half an hour to find my way to *Frau* Theiss's apartment building. She lives on the second floor, and although her apartment is very small, she welcomed us in warmly. She is taller than me and very thin. She introduced me immediately to her two girls, Beate and Mila.

We had a pleasant evening getting to know each other, and then she took the girls into her bedroom. I put Hans down to bed in the lid of a trunk and lay down on the couch to sleep. I said my prayers, but I had a hard time getting to sleep. I was thinking about *Frau* Theiss and the sad story she had told me about her late husband.

I was awake early, because I did not want to miss the hearing. I prayed all the way to the Palace of Justice. *Herr* Schaefer had told me to meet him promptly at eight thirty. *Frau* Theiss offered to keep Hans for me, and so I left him there in the apartment with her, promising to return before noon to feed him.

By eight thirty, I had found the Palace of Justice and was standing with a mob of people outside the courtroom. I wondered why all of the people were there. Finally, I saw *Herr* Schaefer. He was searching the crowd for me. I straightened my blue birthday dress and pushed my way over to him.

After he took me around the corner to a quieter spot, I saw how nervous he was. He handed me a pass to get into the courtroom. "Now, don't you tell anyone who you are. There are people from the press here, and they will try to get you to say something that may harm your husband's case."

I nodded.

"I'm not sure when during the hearing your husband's case will come up, but don't signal to him or wave, or do anything of that sort. You must keep still and perfectly quiet the whole time."

"Yes, sir," I responded, noting how seriously he was lecturing me.

Herr Schaefer sighed. "Truth be told, *Frau* Rager, I don't think there is much chance that I can keep your husband out of being placed into one of these subsequent trials. This is all just a big show and has very little to do with justice."

I must have looked at *Herr* Schaefer with surprise, because he let out a slight laugh, and then he led me by the arm back to the mob at the door of the courtroom. When they opened the doors to let everyone in, I lost track of *Herr* Schaefer.

After I showed my pass to the guard at the door, I ended up sitting in the gallery next to a reporter from Munich. When he sat down in his seat, he reached for a pair of headphones, and then he asked me what paper I was with. I just shrugged.

"You're welcome to share my headphones, if you'd like," he offered. "There is only one other set for German."

I did not know it, but the entire court session was in English. There were translators sitting in the far corner of the room, and as the hearing unfolded, they would translate. The people who were lucky enough to have the headphones could hear the proceeding in their own language.

Right before the judges came in the door in front of the room, the door on the left hand side opened, and in filed twenty men under military police guard. I gasped when I saw Kurt among them.

The reporter from Munich looked down at me. "There's the criminals," he said sarcastically.

As soon as they had all taken their seats, we were ordered to rise and the judges came in. The reporter from Munich told me that the judges were the alternate judges who were currently trying the major war criminals as part of the International Military Tribunal—one from Russia, one from America, one from Britain, and one from France.

When we sat down, the reporter from Munich brought one of the earphones up to his right ear, leaving the other one free for me. I leaned over and put the other earphone up to my left ear. Although I tried to shift in my seat, I could not see Kurt. He was seated in the far corner facing the judges, and unless he turned almost completely around, there was no chance that he would see me.

I listened all morning long as the judges went back and forth with the lawyers, hearing one argument after another as to why the individual in question should or should not be tried. As the clock on the wall began to get closer to noon, I began to get nervous. I had told *Frau* Theiss I would be back by noon. To my relief, I heard in the headphones that the judges wanted to break for lunch, and that they would resume with the remainder of the cases at one thirty.

I rushed back to *Frau* Theiss's apartment. When I got to her door I could hear Hans crying. I must have apologized a dozen times to her for being so late and leaving her with a crying baby, but she was gracious and told me again and again that she didn't mind the crying. I think she expected that it would all be over by now, because she was surprised when I told her they hadn't heard his case yet.

I barely made it back to the Palace of Justice before one thirty, and rushed into the courtroom to find that another man had taken my seat next to the reporter from Munich. I found one empty seat in the very back row of the gallery and sat down out of breath. I sat through one more hour of the proceedings without the benefit of understanding a single word.

Then, we were asked to rise, and the judges left. I made my way up to the reporter. He told me they were just taking a break. When the man who was in my seat next to the reporter left, I sat down in it immediately.

It wasn't long until I heard Kurt's name called, and then I saw *Herr* Schaefer stand up. My heart began to pound, and I leaned closer to the reporter so that I could hear better.

First, the judges spoke about the report that was issued, and then an American got up and said the same things he had said against all of the other men. The American prosecutor finished by charging Kurt with belonging to the Nazi party, committing war crimes and crimes against humanity by participating in the enslavement of concentration camp inmates for use in slave labor and of profiting from the war. When he was done, I held my breath and hoped that *Herr* Schaefer would soon have his turn to set the record straight. It was all I could do to sit still.

Finally, *Herr* Schaefer got up from his chair and made his way to the lectern. "I have been listening carefully to the charges and to the defenses brought by my predecessors here today, but you are about to hear something that is unique and merits your utmost attention," he began as he shifted on his feet at the lectern. "While it is true that Major Rager was a member of the National Socialist German Workers' Party, as were the other defendants who are charged here today, that is where their commonality ends."

The reporter next to me let out a snicker. I looked over at the judges and was glad to see that they were paying attention.

"As I understand it, this court seeks to properly place each one of the accused into a like class in which subsequent trials will be held and like evidence will be presented. By so grouping these individuals, the idea is that judicial economy, and therefore justice will be rightly rendered." I watched as the judges nodded.

"That being the case," continued *Herr* Schaefer, "I must bring to your attention as is also contained in the report that there is ample evidence available that Major Rager's actions and disposition toward these counts against him are definitely contrary to those of the other defendants."

Herr Schaefer continued, "While the other defendants participated in some way, however innocently, in the use of slave labor, Major Rager devoted himself to the liberating of numerous individuals from the concentration and labor camps. You have heard, and are hearing in the current trial, of the responsibilities of individuals in high command for the concentration camps, but I dare say you will not hear among the assembly of the individuals charged here today of anyone who used his rank and position to consciously remove any of the laborers from their pitiful plight. Major Rager is the only one here today who took such bold action.

"While it is possible that the other defendants here have profited from the war, in one way or the other, I submit to you that Major Rager, contrariwise, spent his own money to pay the laborers he had rescued and to hide the fact that the laborers had been removed from the slave labor pool and the concentration camps. Again, you will not hear testimony of this sort regarding any other defendant.

"For these reasons and more, I respectfully request that Major Rager be removed from the classifications for subsequent trials. His actions, his deeds, and his motivations for doing the things that he did, certainly do not rise to the level of the others accused. His defense will certainly be tainted and compromised by association with others whose actions did not align with his."

I sat back in my seat and breathed in deeply. *Herr* Schaefer had done a good job. Before he could leave the lectern, one of the judges asked *Herr* Schaefer what evidence he had. *Herr* Schaefer mentioned the ledger, and then one of the judges asked the American prosecutor to respond.

The American prosecutor repeated his previous arguments and ended by asking the judges not to spend any more time on his case but to let all of the evidence be sorted out at trial.

Herr Schaefer jumped to his feet. "I do not know whether or not the court is so inclined to inequitably include Major Rager in a subsequent trial, but before such a decision is made, I would like to make a motion for a section thirty-four hearing for my client."

After the words had been translated to the gallery, I heard a quiet expression of astonishment come over the courtroom.

"No one has evoked that section before," whispered the reporter from Munich to me as he scrambled to write down some notes in his notebook.

"What is section thirty-four?" I asked, but before the reporter answered me, the presiding judge spoke.

"I have consulted with my colleagues, and if you are requesting a section thirty-four hearing for your client, we are inclined to grant your request, contingent on your exchange of evidence with the prosecution this afternoon and your willingness to agree to an abbreviated hearing on Monday morning at nine o'clock. We must have a decision on these cases to the president of the court by Wednesday as the tribunal is currently in recess and will resume the trial of major war criminals at that time."

None of this made any sense to me until I was able to speak with *Herr* Schaefer after the hearing was over. He told me that in order to keep the major from being lumped in with the other men, who may have done some awful things during the war, he had used an obscure provision in the powers given to the court to get a separate hearing for the major. He hoped that if the judges could hear the evidence, they might acquit him.

After he promised to try to get me a pass for the Monday hearing, I went back to *Frau* Theiss's apartment. I could hear Little Hans crying again before I got to the apartment door. He was happy to see me, and I was happy to see him. It was supposed to be all over, and we were supposed to be on our way home, but I knew that I didn't have the money to go home and then come back again on Monday.

After I explained it all to *Frau* Theiss, she offered to let me stay. I looked at her with tears in my eyes. For some reason, I felt that it was very important for me to be there at the hearing, even if Kurt didn't see me or even know I was there.

So, I stayed with *Frau* Theiss. On Saturday, I offered to stay in the apartment with Beate and Mila while she went to do some errands. On Sunday, we went out for a walk with the girls. It seemed like a very long two days.

I didn't sleep much at all Sunday evening, but this time, it wasn't little Hans that kept me awake. I met *Herr* Schaefer at the courtroom door a little after eight thirty. He was pacing the floor nervously and hardly said two words to me. He looked like he was under a lot of pressure.

This time, there were less people waiting outside the courtroom, but I was glad to see the reporter from Munich, because I was hoping he would share his headphones with me again. I followed him into the courtroom and sat down next to him. We waited a long time before the military police brought Kurt in through the door on the left.

When I saw him, I put my hand to my mouth to keep the shriek from coming out. Everyone in the courtroom suddenly got quiet. Kurt was walking bowed over at a funny angle, and there were two large bandages on the left side of his face. I squinted my eyes. It looked like someone had beaten him.

I wanted to run to him, but I just sat there shaking. The reporter from Munich made a smart comment about how the Americans are treating the German prisoners. A short, dark-haired man with a pointed beard scooted in front of us and took the last chair, two seats away from me. *Herr* Schaefer glanced back at me and then turned back to shuffle some papers on the table in front of him.

Once the judges came in the door and we were seated, I leaned over and pressed my ear to the reporter's other headphone. The judges looked over at Kurt and wanted to know what had happened to him.

Herr Schaefer stood to his feet and told them that he was told that word had gotten out among the prisoners about the major's attempt to surrender Kassel to the Americans. He had been attacked for this while eating his breakfast on Saturday, leaving him with bruises and a broken rib.

I looked up at the reporter. It wasn't the Americans that had done it to him after all. The judges asked if he was in good enough health to continue the hearing, and *Herr* Schaefer said that it was his wish to proceed.

The presiding judge gave the prosecutor ten minutes to speak. The prosecutor got up and said the same things he had said on Friday, ending with the same charges.

Then *Herr* Schaefer stood up and went to the lectern. "All of these charges are valiant indeed, but they do not apply to Major Rager; they are not supported by the evidence, and the learned prosecutor has failed to cite to a single incident or document that would prove his case to you," began *Herr* Schaefer.

"As I stated before, Major Rager is guilty, not of crimes against humanity in using slave labor, but in rescuing the slave labor from the concentration and labor camps. Nor did he profit from the war effort. Instead, he spent his own money to pay the wages of laborers that he helped to smuggle out of the labor camps. That is what the evidence concerning Major Rager shows. None of the charges the prosecution is bringing against my client should stand, and I respectfully request that they be dismissed in total."

Herr Schaefer took his papers from the lectern and made his way back to his seat. I looked at my husband. He was sitting as tall as he could in his chair with no discernable expression on his face. I took in a deep breath.

The presiding judge asked the prosecutor if he wanted to call any witnesses. The prosecutor called my husband's name. The presiding judge looked directly at Kurt and asked him to take the witness stand.

"This should be good," said the reporter from Munich in a whisper.

I watched my husband wince and hold his side as he rose slowly out of his chair to go to the witness box. When he got to the witness box, he turned around and stood to take an oath. The witness box was directly in front of me although it was quite a distance across the room.

At the moment he stood to attention to take the oath, he saw me seated in the gallery. I smiled, and then the pained, serious expression on his face softened. He looked up at the man who was administering the oath and spoke out clearly.

I had already come to dislike the prosecutor as he seemed to be arrogant, and he acted as if he was the most important person in the room. My feelings toward him did not improve as he proceeded to question my husband.

"Can you tell the court what position you held in Kassel?" the prosecutor began.

"I was the war production minister for Hessen," the major replied.

"And in that capacity you reported to whom?"

"I reported to the assistant to *Herr* Albert Speer, in Berlin."

"So you were reporting directly to Berlin?"

"Yes," Kurt replied.

"And your rank is a major?"

"Yes."

"How did you come to be in such a high position as to be reporting directly to Berlin although you are holding the rank of only a major?"

I saw Kurt narrow his eyes. "I don't know," he said at last.

"Let me start at the beginning," said the prosecutor in a condescending tone. "You were awarded the rank of major primarily because of your connection with a high-ranking person in the Nazi party. Is that not so?"

"I am not entirely sure what influence my mother-in-law had on my position in the army, other than she arranged for me to get a commission for entrance to officer training."

"Getting back to your position in Kassel, you were given pretty much free reign to do whatever you wanted to do. Were you not?"

"I was entrusted to do the job of the war production minister," Kurt replied.

"And that job included oversight of the laborers in the factories in Kassel?"

"Yes."

"So you were aware of the use of slave labor in the factories?" asked the prosecutor.

"I became aware of it, yes."

"You became aware of it. Did you visit or inspect the labor camps on a regular basis?"

"I never visited or inspected them."

"So as part of your responsibilities as war production minister, which included oversight of laborers, you never visited the labor camps?"

"I never had occasion to. The labor camps were not part of my responsibility."

"So, how is it then, that you allegedly became concerned about the condition of the slave laborers?"

"I talked with the laborers on a regular basis when I visited the plants. I wanted to make sure that they were being treated appropriately and properly taken care of. If the laborers weren't taken care of, production would logically suffer."

"So your concern was primarily production?" asked the prosecutor smugly.

"My concern as war production minister was production. My concern as a human being was the laborers," responded Kurt.

The prosecutor shuffled some papers on the lectern, and then he cleared his throat. "Did you own shares in Henschel, Major Rager?"

"I did own shares that my father transferred to me, but I sold them in 1939, just after we went into Poland."

The prosecutor shook his head. "And as part of your position as war production minister, did you receive compensation from the heads of the factories to doctor reports to Berlin on production quotas?"

Kurt narrowed his eyes and shook his head. "No. I did not."

"So the entries in this ledger, that you allegedly kept, are not recorded entries of monies given to you in order to falsify records?"

"No!" replied Kurt emphatically. "Those are entries that detail the money I paid to the head of the factory for worker wages."

"And this ledger, that is supposedly so important to your case, how are we to know that you did not simply fabricate it?"

I watched closely as Kurt took in a painful breath. I could see he was trying to stay calm. "No man in his right mind would have given up nearly every free moment he had, instead of spending it with the ones he loved, in order to fabricate such a thing," Kurt said at last.

"So you expect us to just take your word for it?"

"Every man listed in that ledger can tell you that it was not fabricated. Those are not just names and numbers listed in a book. These are lives we are talking about."

"But again, all we have is your word as a Nazi officer—a disloyal Nazi officer." The prosecutor left the lectern and sat down without asking any more questions.

Herr Schaefer stood to his feet and went slowly to the lectern. "Major Rager, can you please tell the court why you served as war production minister of Hessen?"

Kurt shifted in his seat. "I was serving my country like every other officer."

"And in this wonderfully powerful position of war production minister, as the prosecutor has painted it, did you feel that you had the latitude to do whatever you pleased?"

"I had some latitude, yes. Berlin did put a great deal of trust in me, because I produced for them. And I used whatever latitude I had to help the laborers."

"This ledger that I am holding in my hand, is this solely your writing on these pages?"

"Yes."

"And does this contain a list of the men whom you rescued from the transports and concentration camps?"

"It does."

"And does it also contain record of the monetary transactions that took place between you and the factory manager to pay the worker's wages?

"It does."

Herr Schaefer asked Kurt to explain to the court the names and figures in the ledger. When he was done, *Herr* Schaefer continued. "Major Rager, would you tell the court where you got the money to pay the wages for the laborers?"

"I used the money my mother-in-law gave me on a regular basis for the care of my children," Kurt replied.

I saw the prosecutor roll his eyes.

"And these children you are speaking of, they are really the children of your deceased wife and a man who was a Jew? They are of Jewish descent?"

The major hesitated a moment. "True."

"So, you both sheltered these Jewish children the entire length of the war, and you paid for their care from your own pocket while funneling the money from your mother-in-law to pay for the laborers?"

"That is correct."

"Your Honors," said the prosecutor, jumping to his feet once again. "It is his own business what he did with his money, but it has no bearing on the charges brought against him."

Herr Schaefer moved toward the table to his left and handed the ledger to the man next to the judges. "If it please the court, I am finished with the witness. At this time, your Honors, I would like to submit this ledger into evidence."

"Your Honors," said the prosecutor, "I object to the submittal of this ledger as a piece of evidence. Counsel for the defendant has failed to authenticate or collaborate any of the information found therein."

"Your Honors," returned *Herr* Schaefer, "if the prosecution has no more witnesses, then I am prepared to call a witness who will both authenticate and collaborate Major Rager's testimony."

All at once a sound of astonishment was heard in the courtroom. I looked around the room, unsure of whom *Herr* Schaefer intend to call next. The prosecutor told the judges he was finished with his case, complained that he had not been notified of any further witnesses, and sat back in his seat leaving *Herr* Schaefer at the lectern.

"Gentlemen of the court, I have located, with great difficulty, several of the men who are listed in Major Rager's ledger, at a displaced persons camp outside of Mannheim," *Herr* Schaefer said with renewed energy. "At this time, I would like to call *Herr* Ibraham Spuler to the stand."

The short, dark-haired man with a pointed beard who was sitting two seats from me, stood slowly to his feet. As he walked past me, I noticed the worn-out shoes on his feet, and I saw the tattered edges of the shirt he was wearing under an old, brown suit coat that was three sizes too large for his shoulders.

He held his hat in his hand as he moved toward the witness stand. His voice was soft and gentle as he took an oath and spelled his name for the record. Everyone in the courtroom was on the edge of his seat.

Herr Schaefer cleared his throat. "We have just heard Major Rager's explanation of the information contained in the ledger, and your name appears at the top of the list on the first page. Because time is short, *Herr* Spuler, would you please tell the court why you are here today?"

More than a few seconds passed as the man on the stand pulled out a handkerchief and wiped his eyes. "I am a Jew, and in 1942, I was listed for transport to a concentration camp where my family died and where I would have died. If it were not for Major Rager's courage and self sacrifice, neither I nor any of the men listed in that ledger would have lived to see the end of the war. He somehow successfully convinced the authorities that we had died, gave us new identities as workers in the factories, and made sure that we had shelter and food and a place to go during the air raids. I am here today, on behalf of all of the men, to say that we have suffered many things under the hands of German officers, and so we can tell you that while Major Rager wore their uniform, he was in no way one of them. This was well demonstrated by what he did for all of us."

A strange hush fell over the courtroom as Ibraham Spuler broke down into weeping. I let my own tears fall into my lap. A part of me can still not grasp what Kurt has done. I wondered how the judges could hear such a thing and not set my husband free.

The prosecuting attorney lowered his head and shook it slowly. The presiding judge pushed the microphone away from his face and whispered something into the ear of the judge next to him. Then the presiding judge pulled the microphone back toward him. "*Herr* Schaefer, do you have more evidence to share with the court?"

"I do, your Honor," replied *Herr* Schaefer.

"Of what nature?" asked the presiding judge.

"Of a similar nature."

"Your Honors," spoke the prosecutor again. "It is a gross waste of the court's time for defense counsel to parade all of the defendant's good deeds before the court as evidence that he did not commit the crimes for which he is to be charged. He does not dispute that he had a position that afforded him unprecedented power, and for that, he must held accountable."

"Is the court to prosecute every colonel, every major, every lieutenant, every sergeant, and every private who served his country by carrying out his duties for doing just that?" responded *Herr* Schaefer with fire in his voice. "You have been hearing in the current trial that is proceeding in this very room of the atrocities that were sanctioned and even ordered at the highest levels. Before you today is a mere major, who performed his duties as required, and beyond that, risked his own career and his life to do what he knew was not acceptable to his high command. Instead, he was humane. What kind of a precedent will you set if you throw his case in with the ones who gave commands to kill, to torture, and to maim?"

I watched each of the judges carefully as they pushed the mics away one-by-one and huddled with their personal interpreters behind the bench.

"What's happening?" I whispered to the reporter beside me.

"I have no idea," he responded.

After what seemed like a long time, the presiding judge motioned for the two attorneys to come forward, and they held a discussion with them that no one else could hear. *Herr* Schaefer turned away from the judges and went toward Kurt.

They exchanged a few words, and then I saw Kurt nod. *Herr* Schaefer returned to where the prosecutor was standing and nodded at the judges. The presiding judge reached for the microphone and waited for *Herr* Schaefer and the prosecutor to take their seats.

"It is the judgment of the court that the case of Major Kurt Rager, war production minister of Hessen, cannot proceed to trial as recommended by the prosecution. The charges of counts two and three: committing war crimes and crimes against humanity by participating in the enslavement of concentration camp inmates for use in slave labor and of profiting from the war are hereby dismissed upon evidence to the contrary. However, as the defendant has admitted to membership in the Nazi party, his case cannot be dismissed in entirety.

"As this hearing has been conducted under Rule thirty-four, the defendant must be sentenced or released. Therefore, by mutual agreement of counsel for both the prosecution and the defendant as well as the consensus of this tribunal, we will set a date for sentencing at a mutually agreeable time and date following the war crimes hearings that are now in session. Defendant is hereby released from subsequent class trials."

All of the sudden it was over. The judges got up and left. The military police came and took Kurt away, and *Herr* Schaefer shook the prosecuting attorney's hand and started packing his bag.

"What just happened?" I asked the reporter from Munich.

"They must have believed his story," replied the reporter with a shrug. "Excuse me. I've got to track down his family to get the whole story."

The reporter left in a rush and I searched the courtroom for Ibraham Spuler. When I could not find him, I pushed my way over to *Herr* Schaefer.

"Well, my dear. This is a step in the right direction."

I looked up at *Herr* Schaefer. *How was I ever going to thank him?*

He shook his head. "I can't tell you what will happen next, but I will contact you as soon as I have any further news."

I tried the best I could to thank him, but there really weren't enough words to tell him how I was feeling. I don't remember going back to *Frau* Theiss's apartment, but when I got there, I took little Hans in my arms and told him his father was going to be released soon.

I told *Frau* Theiss, the best I could, what had happened and thanked her for opening her home to me and for taking care of little Hans. Then we headed for the train station for the long ride home.

Frau Hoffmann met us at the door when we got home. After I put Hans down for his nap, I told her all about what had happened. When the children got home from school, I had to tell the story all over again. I didn't tell anyone but *Frau* Hoffmann about Kurt's beating.

I am exhausted from the hearings, from suffering from the affects of the war, from being without my husband for so long, but knowing that he will not be tried as a criminal, that he could be released soon, and that this nightmare might soon be over makes me think that I will be able to make it one more day.

....

April 24, 1946

Today is Wednesday. I am sitting out on the back porch enjoying a rather lovely day, while little Hans is taking his afternoon nap. There is still no news about Kurt's release, but we are all praying that it will be soon.

Yesterday, I got the first letter I have had from him since the hearing. Rather than trying to tell you what he said, I will just copy it down.

> My Dear Klara,
>
> You cannot know the relief I felt when I lifted my eyes in the courtroom and saw you there. At first, I thought it was only a dream. I didn't want you to see me in such a state, but do not be concerned. I am much better now. I probably shouldn't tell you, but I have been in lower

depths of despair than I thought a man could have until that hearing.

Now, instead of thinking of dying, my thoughts are consumed with the future. I want to start all over with you and the children. I have been giving it a lot of thought, and I am convinced that we cannot stay in Germany. I am hoping that we will be able to go to America to my parents. I want us to live where the Gestapo was not in charge, where the bombs did not fall, and where there is no reminder of the war.

For now, I think nothing but of seeing your beautiful face again and meeting my new son for the first time. Please give my love to Sepp, Annette, and *Frau* Hoffmann. I remain your loving husband.

Kurt Rager

Although I try not to think about it much, I do wonder what it will be like, once he is out and once we can go on with life. For me, it feels like time stopped the day the Americans came into Kassel, and everything since then has been one long, cloudy day.

September 1946

September 4, 1946

Dear Journal,

Last night, after I put Lenz and Sepp to bed, I heard them laughing in their room. I don't know what was so funny, but nothing is going to keep me from smiling. Kurt is coming home.

The day we have all been waiting for has finally arrived. This morning, I made sure all of the children had a bath, I combed their hair, and then dressed them in their best clothes. Sepp and Annette were beside themselves. Lenz and Liese seemed to be a little apprehensive at the change that they knew was about to come to our home. *Frau* Hoffmann was excited. She even spilled coffee all over the kitchen floor.

Just before noon, before we left the house, I changed little Hans's diaper. I didn't want him to be fussy, but it is so close to his nap time that I knew there was probably no way around it.

We arrived at the train station too early, but I didn't want to be late. Although they have begun to remove the rubble in the downtown area, there has been no rebuilding, so the train station is just as it was at the end of the war, mostly bombed-out. I found the station manager, and he told me the platform number.

It was a beautiful day for Kurt to come home although it was a bit windy. The children played on the platform to pass the time. *Frau* Hoffmann stood patiently by, reaching up frequently to secure her hat. I looked down at little Hans in my arms and smiled.

In his last letter to us, Kurt said that he would arrive on the one o'clock train from Frankfurt. He didn't ask for us to meet him, but I thought that we should. We were all there, except for Klaus, who had to go to work.

I reached down with my free arm and straightened my blue dress. It is getting a little worn, but I always wear it for special occasions, and this was definitely a special occasion.

As a gust of wind ran across the platform, I glanced over at the children. Then I looked down the platform toward the sun. Suddenly, I remembered. I remembered the day I had arrived in Kassel on that very platform. I remembered that Kurt had helped me down from the train.

For several minutes, I was lost, wandering through my memories of him. I thought about the day I met him in the park. I remembered the anxious moments as we sheltered in the basement during the bombings. And I thought about the effort Kurt had made to protect me and his children from harm. Right then and there, I bowed my head and thanked God for bringing us all safely through the war.

Little Hans squirmed in my arms, bringing me back to the present. I set him down on his wobbly feet. For the next few minutes, I held his hand as he tottled down the platform. We had waited all of this time. Certainly, we would survive a few minutes more.

Frau Hoffmann checked her watch and gave me an impatient look. By now, a hundred discouraging thoughts were gathering like storm clouds in my mind. I didn't want to face it, but we might have made the trip for nothing. Anything could have happened to prevent Kurt from coming home today. *Why wasn't the train coming?*

I looked down at little Hans. I wondered if he could sense how bound up I felt inside. The sun went behind some clouds and a cool breeze blew my hair into my eyes. I pulled my hair back behind my shoulders. When I looked up, my heart did a somersault. The train was coming!

I called the children over to where *Frau* Hoffmann was standing, and we lined up. A rush of air hit my face as the train pulled into the station. I searched the windows for any sight of my husband. *Frau* Hoffmann pulled little Hans from my arms when the train came to a stop and the doors began to open.

I stepped forward, and then I stepped back as people began to disembark from the train. I glanced down the platform. I cannot explain the relief that I felt in my heart when I finally saw him. He was helping someone off of the train, but in less than a minute, I was in his arms. As the tears were pouring down my cheeks, he held me tight.

I don't believe I have ever seen two children happier in all of my life than Sepp and Annette today. If you would stack all of the Christmas presents for twenty years together and put them in a room, they would have passed them right by and ran to their father. The tears started fresh again when I saw how they clung to him.

Before he could make his way to *Frau* Hoffmann, I took little Hans from her and turned to my husband. It has been a long time since I saw tears in his eyes, but as he reached for little Hans, I realized that even though I had felt so alone for so long, even though I had little Hans on my own and had cared for the children without him, I believe I have had the easier time of it.

"He's beautiful, Klara," said Kurt as he held his little hand, and then touched his cheek. I smiled proudly. Little Hans quickly buried his face in my shoulder. Even though I had hoped, I didn't expect him to go to his father, a perfect stranger, but I knew that time would change that. And now, we finally had time.

Kurt stepped back and greeted *Frau* Hoffmann, Lenz and Liese, and then he turned back to me. "Let's go home."

Although my husband is free, I can see that it is going to take a long time for him to find his place in this world. I try, but cannot seem to imagine how it must feel to have embraced a cause that eventually turned his whole world upside down. In the end, he was pitted against himself and everything he held dear.

Now he has paid the price, and I hope for all our sakes that we can put this nightmare behind us and go on. He once told me that he had made some terrible choices and that he was suffering for them. I think he has suffered enough, but I sensed at the train station and again this evening as I watched him interact with the children, that he is a broken man, and I do not know if there is any cure for that.

I am afraid that he will never be the same after all he has been through, but I know that I have got to be patient, and I am determined to love him and to care for him until he is firmly back on his feet.

October 1946

It is so hard to find the words to tell you what we are experiencing. While it has been such a relief to have Kurt here and free from prison and harm, our life together is not what I or even he has wished for. We are very happy to be together again, and he loves little Hans, but there is something dark in his countenance that only grows dimmer each day.

It did not take my husband long to realize that we have been living on one meal a day. If it were not for the extra food that Klaus has been bringing home from the American air base and the care packages from the States, we would have little, if any, food at all. Kassel is still a bombed-out mess. There are little plans or resources with which to start the rebuilding process.

I have not wanted to tell him, while he was imprisoned, of the dire straights we were in, but now, there is no hiding any of it from Kurt. He seems to see the situation as even more urgent than I do. What makes it worse is that there is really nothing we can do about it.

From the day he came home until today, he has been insisting that I take the children, Lenz, and Liese and go apply for immigration to the United States. I have always told him definitely that I was not going to leave him. We all know that it is unlikely that either he or Klaus will be granted permission to go to America because of their service in the German army.

So we have argued for weeks about the subject, until today, when Kurt finally told me that I must trust him—one last time. Oh, how the tears came flowing as I realized that he was right.

He has been like a trapped rat, walking around in our home at all hours of the day and night for the past month. There are no jobs for the men who are left, and there is no way for him to support us. We live in a ruined land. Kurt told me that he could not live another day with the thought that this is the legacy he is leaving to his children.

His words were like a lightning bolt to me. It was then that I began to realize that no matter how much I did not want to be separated from him again, if I did not take the children and try to start a new life for us in America, there would be nothing left of my husband. He is slowly slipping into despair. I am convinced now that it would be much harder on Kurt for us to stay and for him to have to look at us every day in this sorry state than for us to be far away.

Lenz, Liese, and I should be able to get permission easily to go to the States because we have been fugitives from the Nazi government. Sepp and Annette are Jewish, and they are mine now. That will make it easier for them. I can hardly bear the thought of it, but I know now what I must do, even if it breaks my heart.

January 1947

Today is Wednesday, and only a few days before Sepp and Annette's ninth birthday. When I look back only a few years, I can hardly believe how everything has changed.

Kurt came out of his study around noon and found me in the living room where Hans was playing with some wooden blocks. He had a look of hope on his face—a look that I have not seen for some time, and there was a letter in his right hand.

"Listen to this, Klara. I have been invited up to Berlin. *Herr* Schaefer has recommended me to the US Army task force that is in charge of rebuilding the Germany army, and I have been asked to join the advisory group."

I stood to my feet to look at the letter.

"This is a big honor," he added.

I looked up at my husband. "Does this mean that we can stay—that you will be employed?"

Kurt shook his head and lowered the letter to his side. "I will be in an advisory role. It is not a paid position, Klara."

I turned my eyes away, so that he would not see my disappointment.

"But this does mean that it will now be possible for me to get permission to come to the States. Don't you see, Klara? This means that I will be able to join you there."

Kurt actually had a smile on his face—that smile that always makes my heart melt. Oh, dear journal, I do love him so, and the thought that we may be able to begin a life together under better circumstances came over me like refreshing raindrops on a hot day. Can it be that the clouds of war are finally parting and we will feel the warmth of the sun again?

March 1947

March 22, 1947

Dear Journal,

Today is my last day in Kassel. I can hardly see to write this. My eyes are filled with tears. And I must hurry as we are to leave tomorrow morning on the train for Hamburg. The children and I are to sail the day after next for America. *Frau* Hoffmann helped me finish all of our packing, and we have set the luggage and my violin by the front door. I hugged her long and hard tonight before I wished her good night. I don't know what I will do without her.

I was surprised at how quickly we were approved to go to the States. I think the American government took pity on Lenz and Liese and me because of who father was. I can only hope now that once we are there, they will allow Kurt and Klaus to follow soon.

His parents wrote us a most gracious invitation, and they have done everything they could to arrange for our immigration, even sending us five third-class tickets on the ship that sails the day after tomorrow. Kurt's brother and his wife have kindly offered to take Lenz and Liese into their home, and they will take Klaus too when he can get permission to come. Sepp, Annette, Hans, and I will stay with Kurt's parents who live only three kilometers from Kurt's brother.

Yesterday afternoon, I came upstairs to get something, and through the crack in the door, I happened to see Kurt sitting on the bed holding Hans in his lap. He was speaking softly but seriously to his son. He told Hans how much he loved him. He told him that he needed to be a brave boy. He told him that he should look out for his big brother and sister. Then he paused a moment.

"You must take special care of your mother, Hans," he said softly. "She is the best part of me, and I could never do without her."

I was standing in the doorway listening to this private conversation. Kurt was sitting with his back to me, but little Hans looked up and saw me in the doorway. It was all I could do to keep from bursting into tears.

I can hardly believe we are going to be separated again, and I dread it. But I must say that I do understand deep inside that this is how it must be. Before I kissed him good night, I told Kurt that he should hurry over, because I want him to be there for the birth of his second child. And that is the hope that I will keep alive in my heart while we are separated.

I hope that we will not have to be apart too long, because every second I am away from him, my heart beats a little weaker, and every day without him is like being under the thin white cover in *Herr* Meissel's basement on a cold winter's night. I already miss him.

Now, after all of this, there is only half a page left in you, dear journal. I will have to get another journal when we get to America, because I won't be able to do without my constant companion.

As long as I live, I will never forget this place. The memories of Kassel will forever echo in my heart. Life is filled with such twists and turns. I didn't want to come to Kassel in the first place, and now I don't want to leave. But don't worry, dear journal, I remembered to pack Otti, and I won't forget to pack you.

Epilogue

My grandmother's journal, a priceless piece of our family history, was quite a revelation to us. In its pages, Aunt Annie and Uncle Joe learned the truth about their Jewish heritage. We will never know, but I would guess that grandfather never told them their true identity—out of a sense of protection and out of love.

Without it, I would never have known that the scrape above the eye of the special doll that Aunt Annie allowed me to play with at her house when I was a child was caused by a fall from the train the night they fled Kassel because of the bombings. Poor Otti.

Grandmother probably kept the Nazi award that my grandfather got because it reminded her that he was heroic and risked his life to save others. And she was brave. She was questioned by the Gestapo and played her violin for Nazi officers.

It wasn't until I was in college that I learned that *Bist du bei Mir* isn't a Christmas song. Grandmother always played the carols for us on Christmas day, and that was the last song she would play before she put her violin away. Grandfather would often ask her to play it again, and I remember how her eyes would light up with affection.

There is a picture in an old photo album of my grandfather holding a newborn, my father's younger brother, so I know that they were not separated for long, and they were never parted again.

Amid the darkness and fearful time of war, while she was hiding from the authorities and from the bombs, grandmother found God, or rather God found her. My father has her Bible, and I have seen the many passages she has underlined and the notes in the margins. She passed down her faith to her children and grandchildren by her quiet example and by well-placed words of wisdom. In difficult times, she would remind us all that God would see us through, something she knew by experience.

And in the ruins and treachery of war, she found love or rather, love found her. I remember well the secret language with which my grandparents would communicate with one another without saying a word. There was a strong bond between them as they shared life's road. Theirs was a happy marriage framed carefully with tenderness and respect.

Their generation is quietly marching into eternity. Although I can no longer sit at grandmother's kitchen table while she makes gingerbread cookies and hums quietly, I can still hear her voice in the journal. Through her writing, she has taken me back in time, and I feel as though I have been to Kassel. I have felt her joy and her sorrow, her fear and her relief. I have seen the dark clouds of war give way to the sunlight of a promising new beginning. And, like the melodious sound of a church bell in the distance, I have heard the echoes of Kassel.